Girlfriend
44
A Novel

Mark Barrowcliffe

ST. MARTIN'S GRIFFIN ☙ NEW YORK

GIRLFRIEND 44. Copyright © 2000 by Mark Barrowcliffe. All rights reserved. Printed in the United States of America. No part of this book may be used or reproduced in any manner whatsoever without written permission except in the case of brief quotations embodied in critical articles or reviews. For information, address St. Martin's Press, 175 Fifth Avenue, New York, N.Y. 10010.

www.stmartins.com

Library of Congress Cataloging-in-Publication Data

Barrowcliffe, Mark.
    Girlfriend 44 : a novel / Mark Barrowcliffe.—
1st St. Martin's Griffin ed.
        p. cm.
    ISBN 0-312-26166-7 (hc)
    ISBN 0-312-28768-2 (pbk)
    1. Triangles (Interpersonal relations)—Fiction.
2. Male friendship—Fiction. 3. Mate selection—
Fiction. 4. Young men—Fiction. I. Title:
Girlfriend forty-four. II. Title.

PR6052.A7263 G57 2002
823'.92—dc21   2001048600

First published in Great Britain by
Headline Book Publishing
A division of the Hodder Headline Group

10 9 8 7 6 5 4

Girlfriend
44

For Mum, Dad, Nan and Grandad

'Love then, and even later, was the whole concern of everyone's life. That is always the fate of leisured societies'
Napoleon Bonaparte

'Nemo repente fuit turpissimus'
No one ever suddenly became depraved
Juvenal, *Satires* No. 2

The legal details and police procedures in this novel are broadly true to life. However, I have taken liberties with them where I have felt like it. The law has never done right by me, so I don't see why I should do right by it.

Thanks to Wendy and Reg Bell, Marion Donaldson and all at Headline, Jeremy Handel and Fiona Hamilton, Danny Plunkett and Simon Rogers.

Special thanks go to Judith Murray at Greene and Heaton for encouraging me to write and for all her subsequent efforts. Thank you very much Judith, without you the only fiction I would have ever written would have been my news journalism.

Julie M. Gibson—was it something I said?
Get in touch if you're still alive. If you're not, please don't.

Dear Emily

I do not expect to emerge with any credit from what you are about to read.

This is goodbye. You always suspected that I couldn't love you and you were right. I respect you very much, and I care for you very much so, although you will find it painful, I have decided to tell you why we must part. You are not perfect.

I do not want to be unkind so let me reassure you that your shortcomings are largely physical.

If you were perfect, for me, you would have to be between 5'6" and 5'7" with hair that looks as if blonde and brunette had put their heads together and come up with a better colour. Your coif would be natural, about 12" long, neither curly nor straight but with an amazing wave to it that would come to life as you flicked it over your shoulder.

Your body should look like Bardot's but be capable of suggesting Hepburn's. Obviously your tits would be capable of looking either huge or tiny, as the dress demands.

Your skin should be blemish-free, apart from perhaps a charming beauty spot. It should have a texture to make alabaster look like a *quattro formaggio*, although you wouldn't give a damn for cosmetics – apart from when you wanted to dress like a tart, which would be often.

Your beauty should be idiosyncratic, within the above parameters.

Most of all you need kind, intelligent eyes. When I say most of all, I mean it's no good without the rest of the package too. Plenty of dogs (the sort that bark) have kind, intelligent eyes, but you take my meaning.

On this last point, I feel your eyes are intelligent but you naturally screw in your face when you talk, which holds them a bit close together. It means you always look as though you are calculating the price of something. This is unfortunate, because I know you are generous and free with the little money you have.

All the sugary sick things – the idiosyncratic way of flicking the hair, the lop-sided smile, the slightly theatrical way of smoking a cigarette – I'm afraid you'd be needing to do those too, if we were to have a chance.

There is a load of personality requirements which you score very well on. I very much admire your originality in thought and dress, for instance. I know that when I say things like that you always ask difficult questions such as: 'In what way?' It's hard to put into words, just take it from me that I do.

I am aware that this is a sorry way to end our relationship, and I didn't want the whole perfection thing to get in the way. I thought for years that I could get round it, that I could love women in all their diversity, that closeness was what it was all about.

I was wrong. You can't love someone if you think they've got a big nose, not properly. As a man, you might have kids with them, dogs, a cottage, etc. You might get caught in rain storms and drink wine in the sun, do all the romance bit, but when you look deep into her eyes it will be because you want to avoid looking at her nose. Don't worry, you haven't got a big nose – it was just an example.

Rest assured, there isn't just one model of perfection, this is just the one that appeals to my demographic, which, unfortunately, is also yours. There are probably five or six others, maybe more, across the range of men, but I can't see you as Miss Sexy Wellies, the ideal stockbroker shag, or the mini-skirt-at-minus-five-inner-city-dream-babe, really, can you?

Don't think me cruel, you just need to know where you stand so you can work your life around this, like living with diabetes. Most women are in the same boat, but they are with men who lack the self-confidence, or looks, or money to trade up from them. There are plenty of these about, men who grit their teeth as they look at their sagging wives and say, 'I'm no oil painting, she's the best I can get, I'll try to love her.' That's what the kind ones say anyway, and they go to their graves missing the girl with the smaller nose, the girl with the bigger tits, the girl who understands.

I used to think it was OK to be size ten, a great laugh, with a good figure and nice-ish face. It isn't. Size eight is the very fattest allowable, unless you're Marilyn Monroe, and we can't allow you an 'ish' or even a 'nice'. It's horrible, but it's true.

I know you will do well without me. You are a pretty girl, a wonderful girl, but just not pretty enough for me. All I want from a woman is perfection in body and mind. The rest – career, job, kids, money, success – she can look after while I go down the pub.

I am sorry for my sentiments. I had always tried to believe in the opposite – in love being blind, in working at relationships to overcome the little things. If you're wondering if it was another woman, it was. Is, I hope. I don't know. Whatever, she meets the criteria stipulated above, so I have to go for it. I know you'll understand.

I suppose it was Farley who made me realise all this, indirectly. Which brings me on to a bit of bad news – he's dead and I've inherited his flat. (The dead bit, clearly, is the bad news, although I know you didn't like him.) It's a bit complicated to go into by letter so I'll tell you all about it when you come back. Look forward to seeing you, and say hello to the penguins for me.

Cheers.

Your ex-boyfriend, Harry (Chesshyre)

1

Ineligible bachelors

My wife would normally have been in bed at 11 o'clock on a Saturday morning, but that Saturday emotional torment had propelled him upright long before his normal hour. Already, at 10, he was up and directing his bile at a piece of paper.

It was a year to the day since Gerrard's last girlfriend had finished with him and his anger, having subsided from the bare-fanged fury of the early months, was now at a level where he was calm enough to put pen to paper without perforating the Basildon Bond.

He had waited this long before communicating to her his observations on their separation because revenge, he had said, is a dish best served cold. From the way he was bent over the table, hackles high and emitting a low growl, however, it looked like he had just popped it into the microwave that morning.

I call Gerrard my wife because that is really what he is. We own a flat together, we buy furniture together, we share the bills. We used to be good friends but we have now learned to work around each other and have carefully honed the art of avoiding breaking the kitchen implements when we do come to blows.

Obviously, we don't sleep together – neither of us is homosexual – although we do pretend to be gay when convention demands. When we got the dog from the animal shelter, for instance, they wanted to know all sorts of stuff about us before they would hand him over. By presenting ourselves as lovers we appeared a more stable unit – and so a more fitting home for a former stray.

Some people can't believe that me and Gerrard have been together for so long – ten years as flatmates in various accommodation – without feeling some kind of attraction to each other. So let me, at some suspicious length, clear this up once and for all. As far as I am concerned the Christian Right should stop conjuring up the leering spectres of predatory homosexuals seeking to enslave children into a life of dark lusts and just put up a picture of Gerrard's wan gob. The slogan 'Men – do you want to wake up next to this?' would make the ideal advertisement for a wife and family.

I have to say that for me homosexuality is an attractive idea as I understand men far better than I do women, but it would be too heavy a responsibility. I already have too many identities to answer to. Being gay would be one restraint too many – one more thing to be, to explain at parties.

Homosexuality for Gerrard would be far too lofty an ambition; he is scarcely heterosexual, having only slept with three people in the last ten years. He tells me I meet the World Health Organisation definition of promiscuous. I tell him he meets the World Health Organisation definition of 'loser'.

I actually don't think I am promiscuous – although the WHO definition of two or more partners a year puts me in that fold. As I have pointed out to Gerrard, promiscuity is not defined by action, it is defined by intent.

If I tell you that in my life I have slept with over forty women then you'll probably have one of two reactions. If you're a man then some part of you will think, 'You roister toister, you sly old dog. Good on you, mate.' Some of you, of course, will think 'Why so few?' but those on the average eleven or so partners will feel mildly envious.

If you're a woman you may think of me as an emotional pauper with the morals of a cabinet minister. But there is a defence.

Given the fact that I'm running at nearly four times the national shag average, it is ironic, and a little sad, that ever since I went out

Mark Barrowcliffe

with my first girlfriend at sixteen (I started late) I have had one aim: to find my life partner, to make it to the big relationship – what we used to call marriage. I am gagging for it.

It's not like I used to be particularly fussy – all I wanted was someone who looked better out of a Hallowe'en mask than in one and who wasn't too demanding – and it's not like I'm ugly. In the course of my life up to that Saturday morning forty-three women had been attracted enough to me to allow me to suck their tits, put my penis in their mouths, dress up in a variety of clothing that I demur from describing, tie them up, spank them, have arguments with me about why I won't let them do that to me, have straight-forward sex with or without condoms, shag them in the bathroom, garden, pub toilets, tube train and other locations too unbelievable to record. At least three have, against my finer sensibilities, prevailed on me to sodomise them – one on her friend's bed. But a lifetime of gently exploring each other's personalities, reaping the rich reward of companionship as we approach our mellow years? No, thank you. They don't want that, these women, at least not from me, and that really is the only thing I ever wanted from them. How many women have I slept with? More than I would have chosen to, that's for sure.

I was reflecting on this as Gerrard, across the breakfast table from me, continued to thump at his letter with his pen, face rigid with anger and head weaving like a boxer's in a grudge fight. Women are all around me. To write his letter Gerrard had borrowed a pen given to me by an ex-girlfriend, I was wearing a shirt that an ex-girlfriend bought for me and sitting in a flat that my last girlfriend thought was bohemian but my present one thinks stinks. Even the location of the flat – Fulham with its pearl necklaces and gun dog shit – was influenced by a previous girlfriend who originally bought into it with me and Gerrard, an ex-girlfriend whose 'priorities have changed' and who now lives in Hoxton surrounded by installation artists.

Before me on the table were the faces of my most important girlfriends, all the putative Mrs Chesshyres, in a box containing my holiday photos for the last ten or so years, softly rattling as the table moved to the torment of Gerrard's pen.

I had this out for very good reason. My one proper female friend, Lydia, was visiting and I was trying to get myself into the mood to look upset that my girlfriend Emily had left that morning for a tent in Antarctica with fifty-six blokes with beards. She would be gone for a year, and though I was sad, a bit, I couldn't help feeling that a weight had been lifted from my shoulders. It wouldn't really do to let Lydia see that. You have to do the right thing with women – look like you're sad when you should be sad, delighted for friends' successes, remember birthdays, anniversaries, etc. etc. It takes a lot for men to do this; I can't help feeling it would be better if we all got given a book at adolescence on 'how to be human' in which we could mark the important dates.

So, as I said, I had taken out the box of holiday photos to get myself nostalgic about stuff. Lydia is very important to me and she would expect to see me miserable. It's important to cultivate your female friends, they are necessary to your self-esteem. It means there is something more to you than the beer, football and fags. Crucially, it hints at emotional depth and this is a powerful aphrodisiac to women in my cultural group. You can drop it into conversation when you meet them. 'I was saying this to my friend Lydia,' you can say or, 'that's interesting, a very close friend of mine, Lydia, feels the same way.'

I might also drop in the fact that Lydia is forty, to make me seem even more sensitive – gets on with older woman equals has great depth, being the prospective shag's equation. If you're after that kind of girl. I clearly don't mention the fact that I used to go out with her, that looks too much like obtaining a female friend by false pretences and gives the impression that I'm desperate enough to go out with someone eight years older. I am, in fact, that desperate but I just don't want to seem that way.

If this is making me sound calculating then let me reassure you that I was genuinely sad Emily had gone to the South Pole, but more at the form – lovers part for a year – than at the content – Emily and Harry part for a year. I was sad like you are sad at a film. It reminded me of the time I had seen two baboons making love at London Zoo. Unaccountably I had developed an erection. Did this mean I fancied baboons or was it just that the idea of sex had been suggested to me? Did I feel sad because Emily was going or was it just that the idea of sadness had been suggested to me? Was I upset? About as much as I fancy baboons.

I don't discount the convenience of the framework, of the formal side of relationships, having a girlfriend, of doing the right things, but I would one day like a little bit more. I would like the love bit.

It's not like we haven't tried, we've given the relationship thing a very good go, me and the women; we've had all the structure in place, we've just made a mess of the execution. I've met three sets of parents, four sets of brothers, shagged a sister and been punched by an uncle. I call that giving it a go.

We've done all the things that lovers are meant to do. Take my box of photos. Here's Kate, tense-faced outside the Louvre, then there's Kate tense-faced next to the gallery with the pipes outside. Here in the next packet is Sophie smiling womanfully in Wenceslas Square, despite the fact she wasn't speaking to me. Thumbing on we have Tabitha staring into space at the top of the Empire State Building. And look, on the bottom of the box a professional snap of an organ grinder with his monkey trying to cheer up Karen after I'd told her I didn't fancy her any more. He charged her £15 for the privilege.

I have one here of Wendy, smiling and happy in St Mark's Square, Venice. She was later sea sick on a gondola and I wasn't sympathetic enough. Great memories, photographs I can show to friends and say, 'Oh, look, here's us strangling each other. A magnificent backdrop, don't you think?'

In fact the only time I enjoyed myself on a holiday was when I went to Cornwall with mad Linda. We had a great time camping until she got off with a bloke in a pony tail, our surf instructor. At least they look happy in the picture.

Why had all these relationships failed, given so much effort on my part? My mother had asked a similar question when I'd finished with Wendy. 'What's wrong with this one?'

'I don't know, Mum,' I'd said, 'we were just incompatible.'

There was a brief pause.

'Your father and I are incompatible and we've been married for thirty-five years,' she'd said with a proud catch in her voice.

I couldn't explain to her how it never used to matter, this incompatibility, but it does now.

Gerrard had a big thing about incompatibility. I could have shown him every girl in my box of pictures and there would be something – usually physical, but sometimes he'd remember an unpleasant personality trait – he didn't like.

'What's wrong with her?' I'd say, showing him a picture of Caroline – anyone's idea of a good-looking girl, with a fantastic figure.

'Breasts the wrong shape,' Gerrard would say.

'They're breast-shaped, what shape should they be?'

'They don't point up at the ends,' he would give an 'I don't make the rules' sniff.

I would ask him how he knew, seeing as he had never had a look up her jumper.

'I just know,' he'd say.

There were a variety of things that would turn Gerrard off girls: wearing designer clothes, being too 'ballsy' in the American sense, having too much pubic hair, having an almost invisible line on the top lip, being too fat, being too thin, not having a kind face (I would say soppy), objecting to him farting, not agreeing with him, wearing Poison perfume (I was with him on that), going down the gym, looking unfit, liking to be dominated in sex, taking too much of a lead in sex, talking too much, being too quiet. The worst sin was being old, or rather going off the boil. He just did not find women of his own age, thirty-two, attractive. In fact, he didn't find the body of anyone over twenty-five attractive. 'There is,' he would say, as if delivering the law unto the Israelites, 'an appreciable difference between the body of a twenty-two-year-old and that of a twenty-seven-year-old.' It would cause him considerable anguish, thinking that if he ever found the right woman he was doomed to find her unattractive eventually. He had an image of himself forcing his way through sexual encounters with a drooping wife into his forties. I thought this showed a lack of self-knowledge. Gerrard would be much more likely to tell her she was getting old and unattractive and ask what she was going to do about it. There would be no forcing himself at all. Oh, plastic surgery, there was another of his dislikes.

Allied to this fear of ageing was the fact that he always went off having sex with any girlfriend after about the third time. As the novelty faded, he began to notice that the girl's nose was a funny shape, or that she was slightly overweight, or had skin blemishes, or something. But that's a common enough complaint. I drag it out past the three-shag mark by introducing props or fantasies but normally after about six months I'm pretty much going through the motions. It's not that I notice blemishes, just that I don't want the same fayre (I love spelling that word with a Y, it gives it the niff of warm sandwiches served by a bankrupt farmer in period dress) day after day. I wonder if women feel the same? Perhaps I'll ask one. I think my dissatisfaction is caused by boredom, Gerrard's by something else. He is capable of being nostalgic about events that haven't yet happened. The first kiss is for him the worst, as its freshness and perfection mock every kiss that follows.

I remember him saying to me once: 'That first moment, when you take off her bra. You're always chasing that, aren't you? You'll never get it back, the excitement of seeing a new lovely pair of breasts – providing they're nice breasts, of course.' I was reminded of a fairy-tale miser gloating over a hoard of jewels, or an addict describing the first hit, and felt in sudden need of a wash. I suppose I must have had my own hang-ups like Gerrard's because I had never really been smitten by anyone. Perhaps that's why I was still single.

Although my mother makes regular attacks on the marriage front, my dad only once had a go. 'If you'd been in my generation you'd have been married by now,' he'd said. The unspoken second half of the sentence was 'or still a virgin'. It's not like my dad to be jealous, but just in case he was I thought it as well to let him know how many women I'd slept with, adding ten for good luck. He went back to his paper smartish after that.

My dad, of course, was my role model as is the case for most boys who have a father on the premises. However, he has taught me as much about what not to be as what to be. Yes, he taught me to be kind, and to pick up litter and a few other things, but there are many ways of behaving that friends of mine seemed to adopt very naturally from their fathers that I just couldn't countenance. Consider the common male trait of taking control in a situation. Now I never do this, ever. You won't catch me offering to fix things or telling you what to do when driving. I think the reason for this goes back to one of my earliest memories of my father.

We had been going on holiday in our car. Our dog – a huge cross between a Great Dane and a Boxer – was notorious for his fountainous bouts of travel sickness. Luckily he used to make a fair bit of noise for the fifteen minutes preceding the first wet woof, giving us the chance to administer a travel pill. On hearing the first notes of canine discomfort my dad pulled the car to the side of the road. We stopped just in time for the animal to step from the car and disgorge the contents of his stomach into the soft verge. After a short pause to allow the dog to recover his dignity, my mum tried to feed him the pill. No easy task. Whatever delicious sweetmeat we concealed the medicine in, the dog would always consume the food and then lift his lip to spit the pill from the side of his mouth, like a cowboy expelling chewing tobacco.

After the sixth or seventh go my dad had seen enough. 'I'll fix this,' he said – words which to this day make my blood freeze. He went to the back of the car, opened the boot and produced a twelve-inch length of clear plastic tubing normally used for some occult mechanical purpose. My mum prised the dog's jaws apart and my dad, with a seaside magician's flourish, placed the tube a good way down the dog's throat. Putting the pill into the tube he blew hard, expecting it to be delivered with force to a point where the animal would have no choice but to swallow it. Unfortunately the irritant effect of my dad's breath, the pill and the tube caused the dog to cough. I have no idea what the velocity of a dog's cough is, but I do know it's a good deal faster than my dad can blow. The pill was returned at speed on a wave of dog breath down the length of the tube, hardly pausing as it passed my dad's tongue to a point where, as my father had rightly conjectured in the case of the dog, reflex action caused him to swallow it. The dog was delivered to an animal boarding kennels about two miles up the road, taking a large chunk out of our holiday spending money. That's why you'll never hear the words 'I'll fix this' or 'give that here' from me. You swallow your own pill.

This made me think how glad I was that I was free from the responsibilities of fatherhood; for the moment even free from the responsibilities of boyfriendhood. Looking through the photos added to my sense of relief that for a whole year, with Emily in Antarctica, I would not have to think about having a girlfriend. I would have all the kudos of having a girlfriend, I would be able to speak about her at parties, have a picture of her on my desk at work, but mercifully I wouldn't actually have to do anything beyond write the odd letter – especially considering she was on a survey out of all human contact for the best part of her time at the pole. All the social structure would be in place, I'd have time to look around and find someone I was genuinely interested in. Sex would be a problem, but then, when wasn't it in some way or other? I seemed to have reached a natural gap.

'What do you think of that?' Gerrard – I'd never worked out why we called him that instead of Gerry or Ger – had finished chiselling out his letter and was staring at me across the table, his jaw fixed and taut, stretching the skin over his emaciated face as if pickled, like Piltdown Man. I knew he was angry because he'd not fidgeted for a quarter of an hour. Fidgeting to Gerrard is what breathing is to the rest of us. Always, somewhere, there is an itch, though nowhere that a normal human being would want to be seen scratching – an itch in the armpit, an itch in the bottom, an itch, perhaps, up the nose.

Gerrard never held back on his scratching, no matter what the company. In his graduation photo he resembles a nineteenth-century general – one arm extended to take the degree, one invisible in the folds of his gown, servicing some unendurable vexation of the arse.

I was saved from having to express an opinion on his letter because Farley entered the kitchen. Even though I knew he was there, it was still a shock to see him; he had certainly never been to our flat before so early on a Saturday morning. If I am promiscuous by necessity, like an archaeologist gets dirty when searching for Roman coins, Farley is promiscuous like the sea is wet. It's an essential part of what he is – always and forever on the pull. In fact, he is beyond promiscuous, he is sexually incoherent. His sex life rambles and roves like a feral cat, without ever achieving a focus. True, he has slept with some beautiful women, but he is really not fussy. If he can't get a good-looking girl by the end of the evening, he'll just move on to an ugly one who'll be more grateful for his attentions and hence less resistant. He's tall and handsome with the gift of the gab and he goes about his work methodically, putting in the research hours. He reads *Cosmopolitan* in the same spirit that anglers read *Trout Monthly* and is not afraid of splashing out on some top clobber. He can afford to. When his dad, a bookmaker, died he'd left Farley enough money to ensure he didn't really have to work again if he was content to remain on a relatively modest salary for the rest of his life. As he had been on a fucking pittance as a reporter on *Grocery Insight*, a trade mag, he'd jumped at the chance to move up to relatively modest and had spent the last two years doing nothing, a career choice I very much envied.

Actually, I should point out here that Farley's first name is Mike, but I seem to know too many Mikes. We call him Farley so we know who we are talking about. I just want to make that clear because, with Gerrard being called Gerrard and Farley sounding like a first name, you might get the idea we were a bunch of posh public-school types. Just to be plain, we're all in that gone-to-average-university, got-media-job-that-sound-glamorous-to-your-mum-but-is-in-fact-incredibly-boring, clinging-to-well-off-working-class-roots-by-exaggerated-love-of-football and born-again-sexism set.

On the last point, Gerrard, being of a slightly different social profile from me and Farley, has not bought into the sexism bit. He is fleeing lower-middle-class roots by a kind of twisted New Manism. While we remind ourselves it's fashionable to say 'look at the tits on that', Gerrard is getting on with the serious sexism of expecting his women to share his every opinion and outlook.

You might argue that it's wrong to call this sexism in the true sense, because Gerrard expects everyone to share his opinions: man, woman, animal, mineral and vegetable. It's just that he expects it more from the women who become close to him. When we had the cat he became very angry with it because it killed a mouse and left it on the back door step. I think up to that point he had regarded it as a fellow traveller vegetarian, at least in sentiment, Kattomeat notwithstanding. The murder of the mouse (his words) made the cat a traitor to the ranks of animal kind and, worse, a traitor to Gerrard. It drove a considerable wedge between them.

'Morning,' said Farley.

Gerrard stiffened in distaste at the sight of Farley's cigarette. Smoking was a major bone of contention between us. He didn't so much want me to give up as want me to give up and sign a formal declaration that smoking was the preserve of total cretins, fundamentally and forever wrong. Furthermore he would have liked me to have put in writing that I only ever smoked out of wanting to look clever and for me to have admitted that I was generally bad while he was generally good. The thought of it made me light up.

'You haven't been fucking on our sofa, have you?' Gerrard asked

Farley with a violent emphasis on the 'fucking'.

Farley moved to the sink to pour water into the kettle. He carefully watched the little ball of the water gauge rise until it came to 'one cup' and turned off the tap.

It was a source of quiet wonder to me that Farley had stayed at our house. Saturday morning would normally have seen him trying to remember some office girl's name while she rustled him up a full English. Gerrard, who was generally and specifically opposed to change of any type happening to anyone at any time, was having to undergo his most shattering adjustment of world view since Paula, the target of his letter, tried a new lipstick colour. Then he'd been able to do what my mum would call 'play his face' (moan) until she changed it back. All the moaning in the world wouldn't alter the fact that Farley was here, and alone. 'You mean, you didn't score last night?' Gerrard's black brows quivered uncertainly above his sickly pan.

'No,' said Farley. 'Where are your tea bags?'

'In the cupboard.'

Farley found the packet, selected a bag and searched briefly for a clean cup in the other cupboards, before turning back to the sink to wash one.

'Quite a night then.' Gerrard was suppressing a smirk, as if in some way by not scoring, by *deliberately* not scoring, Farley was admitting there was something to be said for not sleeping with someone, thereby admitting that Gerrard's way of doing things was right.

'Not that unusual,' said Farley. 'I don't always go out looking to tug. I do have the odd night off.'

'When?' snorted Gerrard, like a hound nosing for a scent. 'Life-threatening illness, loved one in coma, funeral of mother?'

'More often than you'd think,' said Farley, lazily eyeing Gerrard's letter.

'You don't have to grip that so tightly, you know, I'm not going to take it off you. What is it?'

'It's a letter to my last girlfriend.'

'I didn't know you had one. I thought your last bird was Paula,' said Farley, looking impressed.

'It was,' said Gerrard, beginning to laugh. 'I'm afraid I don't have quite your hit rate.'

'Give us a look.'

'I was going to show it to Harry but I suppose you're a fairly good judge of women, from one perspective. I'll read it out to you, if you like?'

'Go ahead,' said Farley, in his down-the-nose Hertfordshire drone.

Gerrard read out the letter, controlling his voice at first, like a nervous policeman reading out a charge sheet at the trial of the century. But as the list of his wounds built – over fourteen pages of cramped script – I began to fear the vigour of his performance was posing a threat to the crockery.

Twice, he thumped the table and even Farley, who I was quite convinced could watch his family – if he had one – butchered in front of him without blinking, flinched. Once Gerrard thumped the wall, dislodging some flakes of paint. He panted and he heaved, he railed and he ranted. At one point I think I saw him flail. At least it looked like flailing, although it could have been somewhere between a flail and a thrash. As the climax approached his voice became dry with rancour, his words unclear, like an incantation through a desert wind, although I did catch 'traitorous', 'vermin' and 'gallivanting about without a care in the world' among them.

The storm spent, the letter finished, Gerrard sat down, hissing like a deflating tyre.

'What,' he croaked, 'do you think of that? Too strong, I suppose.'

'Oh, I don't know,' said Farley. 'Why not put something in about the genocide of the Marsh Arabs – I'm sure she can't have been entirely blameless.'

'Don't take the piss,' said Gerrard, 'I want an honest opinion.'

Farley sipped at his tea.

'Do you have to call her a thief and a slag?' he gently ventured.

'She is a thief and a slag, that is the chief plank of my argument, it's a central tenet,' said Gerrard, stirring his cold tea with unnecessary vim. 'She took our bookcase – a bookcase which I owned half of. That makes her a thief. And she slept with that hippie tosser in our bed – that makes her a slag. It's not an insult, it's a statement of fact. Anyway I don't call her a thief and a slag, I say that I suspect her to be one. That's different.'

'I'm sure she'll make the distinction,' said Farley, unconsciously picking up the newspaper. It was the review section, which I knew was a favourite of his, although I had never known him go to a film or play or read a book even. One of the things I always found mildly disturbing about Farley was his inability to be fully involved in any one activity. He was always doing something else, talking during a video for instance, reading a paper during a conversation, looking around the room when you were speaking to him. He didn't miss much, but I had the idea that he didn't quite get everything either. It was as if he was more interested in the review of life than life itself.

I'd noted in the past how he was drawn to extreme characters; one of his favourite descriptions of people he liked was that they were 'mad'. Perhaps that was it, he preferred people who were polite enough to present the highlights of their personalities in vivid colours, rather than the ill-bred deep and meaningful types who require you to wade through a lengthy introduction before getting into the action. I did sometimes wonder why he liked me, I was sure I wasn't one of these larger than life sad types, although he had caused me some nagging concern when I had discovered he routinely referred to me as 'Mad Harry'. Still, this was a step up from Gerrard's 'Fat Boy'.

Gerrard chooses to call me this, despite, in fact *because* he knows I am sensitive about my weight. I'm not that fat, I know I'm not – I'm only fourteen stone and I'm 6'1". But, to fit with my mental self-image, I should have the body of one of those Russian gymnast blokes who swings about on the hoops. So in fact I know I am fat, if you catch my drift.

This oscillating body image might be enough to paralyse a lesser man, yet I do take action to ensure that I always look in good shape. I have a very good way of standing in front of the mirror and holding my bicep across my chest to accentuate my muscles. If I hold my stomach in at the same time I can look quite fit. Unfortunately, there is only one angle from the infinite number available to me where this looks any good but I can unerringly find it. Just as an experienced potter instinctively knows where to place the thumbs to turn out the perfect vase, it would be difficult for me not to find it, it would feel weird. This is just how I stand in front of the mirror – much to the amusement of various girlfriends and my mother who have caught me in this position.

But the cover was recently blown when I bought one of those

cameras that you can set on a timer to take a photo of yourself. I decided to take a 'humorous' shot of myself stripped to the waist, to have a reminder of what I looked like in my prime. When I got the photos back I was drawn to one of two conclusions: either the developer had mixed in the shots I had taken of Emily bathing the dog with the 'before' shots from a Charles Atlas advertisement, or I was very fat. Anyway, I've now bought some fat-busting B complex pills which, combined with walking the dog, should have me stick thin in a week. I am of course also just about to join a gym, but there again I'm also just about to learn Spanish, get a pension sorted out, give up smoking and find out what I really want to do with my life.

'Well, what would you put, then?' said Gerrard. 'What's the politically correct term for slag?'

'Soiled dove?' I suggested. I'd been looking at the thesaurus where Gerrard had it open under 'prostitute'.

'It depends what your aims are,' said Farley, ignoring me. 'I'd say it's ancient history, gone. I'd just forget it. Next, please. If you want her back, that's a tricky one. I don't know, can't you give her some bullshit about how you accept the blame for driving her away and you'd like to meet to apologise?'

Apoplexy is a word rarely used today. Whenever it does get an outing it's generally taken to mean extreme rage. However there is an older meaning – that of a sudden loss of consciousness. It was in this sense that Gerrard was apoplectic, although perhaps just to protect himself from feeling apoplectic in the modern sense, if you see what I mean. He'd clearly blanked the apology sentence completely and concentrated solely on the 'forget it'.

'I can't forget it.' He shook his head. 'I don't think I should tell you this, but I will. She said something to me that's so terrible, I couldn't even mention it in the letter.'

I'd always wondered about these people who harbour grudges. How do they remember them all? Judging by the shifty way certain friends have treated me at certain times I must have been pretty well wronged over the years, but I've never known exactly how. I once received a bunch of flowers from a girlfriend labelled 'Sorry', with a small picture of a teddy bear crying. I didn't see what there was to apologise for, other than the teddy bear. I would carry grudges, plot revenge, the whole caboodle I'm sure if I could just notice or recall when people had done me down. If I have a motto it is 'I don't forgive, but I do forget.' I should be furious about the amount of books and records I have lent over the years, never to see again, but I don't know who borrowed them.

I have tried randomly accusing people but that didn't work. Lydia got quite angry when I suggested she'd kept my one copy of Thor's 1980s classic 'Let the Blood Run Red'. I didn't really like the record, but anyone who can blow up a hot water bottle to bursting point between the chorus and the guitar solo is my kind of musician. I'm surprised it's an idea the Beatles never adopted.

However, Gerrard had intrigued me, as I couldn't ever imagine Paula saying anything worse to him than what she'd said when she'd left him. She'd said he was a controlling, inflexible green Nazi whose belief in a perfect past made him resent anyone enjoying the present or having hopes for the future. By way of an afterthought she'd told him he had the spiritual depth of a fruit machine and that she'd received more sexual satisfaction from her last hernia operation than she'd had with him. It wasn't what she said that surprised me, far from it, I would have gone a little further myself, but the vehemence. Paula was normally the kind of woman who would be too polite to ask you to move if you parked on her foot. Like me, Farley was interested.

'Go on,' he said. He had put down the newspaper and was looking at a snap of me and Wendy crammed into the gondola, as natural as two feet in a single shoe.

'She said she loved me,' said Gerrard.

'So?' said Farley, for some reason looking at the same photo upside down.

'What do you mean, so? She said she loved me and then she left me.'

'Well, maybe she did love you, then maybe she changed.' He put the photo of me and Wendy back into the box and gave a theatrical shudder. He hadn't liked Wendy, but then he hadn't liked any of my girlfriends. He looked on them as a self-indulgent diversion from the serious business of my social life.

I'd once asked Farley why he only went for one night stands, to which he had indignantly replied that he didn't go for one night stands – he couldn't possibly be tied to that level of commitment. Although it was a joke, I had known him go home with a girl at around one in the morning and be back in the club by four. This, apparently, is standard behaviour in Mediterranean holiday resorts although I have rarely seen it attempted on a Tuesday night in central London.

Gerrard was approaching that dangerous ground where impassioned insistence gives way to ranting. 'She either loved me or she didn't. You don't fall out of love with someone – it just means you were never *in* love with them. So you either lied to yourself or you lied to your partner. Either way you're a liar.'

'Unvent your spleen, baby,' said Farley. 'It seems very possible to me that you can fall out of love. Maybe she changed, maybe you did.'

Gerrard paused, as if in deep regret for himself, or for the world. 'I don't change,' he said darkly. 'Ever.'

'Maybe you should,' said Farley. 'Are you perfect?' I enjoyed this question greatly, as it is almost impossible for a man to answer. Of course, we all want to just say yes, but we are so perfect that modesty forbids. Even our imperfections are proof of our perfection. Am I depressed? Then it is a mark of my sensitivity. Am I short-tempered? I am merely complex and artistic. Am I a drunk? Well, I'm certainly a *bon viveur*. Gerrard, however, seemed to have less difficulty than most in answering the question.

'No, I'm not perfect, but I am me. I'm constant and that makes me better than most.'

I couldn't let this pass.

'Go on then, in what ways are you not perfect?' I said. 'Make a list.'

Gerrard grinned.

'Well, I was wrong once.'

'When was that?' I asked. I knew the answer, but I wanted Farley to hear the line.

'In 1992. I thought I was wrong when in fact I was right.'

'You can't dodge out of this with humour,' said Farley

'I bloody well can,' said Gerrard. 'I've spent years preserving schoolboy wit, are you going to tell me all that effort was wasted?'

'Come on, how are you not perfect?' Farley was unusually serious.

'Well, that's ridiculous, how do I know? What am I meant to say? I wish I was kinder, I wish I was more pleasant, I wish I was more charming, I wish I had a bigger dick?'

'I'm surprised that's not on the list,' I observed. 'Paula used to say it was small.' I wasn't saying this to be cruel. Contrary to popular opinion I don't think most men care how big their penis is as long as it's big enough. No one wants a tiddler, but many of us are perfectly happy with a tench rather than a tuna. I was just saying it because that's what you say when someone says something like that. It's a burnt offering to the god of the conversation; once out and said we could proceed with a grin to the next point. At least we could have, had we not been dealing with Gerrard.

'She did not say it was small,' he said, precisely and with feeling, 'she said it was small-ish. Very different.'

'She did, actually,' I confirmed for Farley's benefit, in case he thought Gerrard was joking. I knew at this point we were moving from the marshy ground of serious conversation to the firmer sod of flippant exchanges.

Farley recoiled in mock astonishment. 'Small-ish is the same as small. Even big-ish is the same as small. It's arguable that even big means small. The only word that means big when it comes to dicks is "huge". Everything else means small.'

'Who cares anyway, I mean, have you ever had a complaint about the size of your penis?' I asked.

'No, but I've had complaints about the size of your penis,' said Farley.

Another burnt offering, but with the unpleasant odour of truth. Inevitably on a small social scene of twelve years' standing Farley and I had shared several girlfriends, though at different times, in the interests of good taste.

I smiled. 'What were we talking about?'

'Paula lying to me,' said Gerrard. 'She said she loved me and she didn't.'

'I don't think that's what we were talking about,' I said.

'Did you ever say you loved her?' asked Farley

'As soon as I realised that I did, yes.'

'When was that?'

'Well, it's embarrassing, but when she finished with me, I really did. The moment she said she was going, I knew she was the one for me.'

'So the only thing she could have done to make you love her

was to leave you,' stated Farley wearily, like a prosecution barrister with his mind on eighteen holes.

'No, I'm sure I was beginning to love her as she left. She must have seen that.'

The door went and the dog barked. It was Lydia who had, surprisingly, cycled over. I say surprisingly because her normal idea of exercise is rolling her own cigarettes. She had been good-looking years ago, in a too-much-make-up, pale-faced, dark-eyed-gothy sort of way, but when she had split up with her last boyfriend Kevin she had taken to drugs and buns. Surprising, really, because she had finished with him. Gerrard had said that her life had hit the crash barriers and it looked as though an air bag had gone off inside her face, which I thought was very unfair. He only said it to be funny though and that, as we know, excuses anything.

Lydia was pretty, which I suppose is a way of saying that she looked nice but wasn't my type, which I suppose is another way of agreeing with Gerrard. She had certainly put on a bit of weight, something she had failed to do when she and I split up, I was slightly disappointed to note. She'd always been bonny, but had slipped into what the personal ads call 'curvy' and cruel people 'fat'. The bike, I thought, was a good move. I hate to see a friend letting themselves go, even if I'm letting myself go at the time. She herself said that she was two pounds over her ideal weight so, by her own admission, she had bloated hugely.

She'd obviously cared for Kevin more than she had for me. I don't know why I was inclined to be annoyed by this because, although I had loved Lydia, I had always really wanted to go out with someone better looking – a desire that was fairly obvious to her, I think. I didn't want to feel that way, I just did. Sorry.

'Come in,' I said, remembering to look disconsolate.

'How are you? Did she get off all right?' Lydia pushed her over-large bike across the threshold, skilfully catching the dog's head between the wall and the front wheel in order to forestall a suicide dash for the road. She handed me a space-age brief case which, unaccountably, she had been carrying in one hand instead of strapped to the bike rack.

'Oh, fine, yes, very well. Excellent really. The plane took off and everything.'

'Wasn't delayed then?'

'Don't think so.' I closed the door with one hand and collared the dog with the other. 'Come back, Rex,' I said.

'Ben!' came a voice from the kitchen. When we had bought the dog from the home it had been called Ben, but every dog in the park was called Ben and I didn't like the look of their owners, too much of the Wellington boots and corduroys, so I had rechristened him Rex. It strikes me that the middle classes are ever more inclined to give their children names like dogs and their dogs names like children. The dogs are called Graham, Penelope and Ben; the children Talisker, Colour and Topher. The day can't be far off when someone has their daughter spayed by mistake.

So that's why the dog got his name change. Gerrard hated the name Rex, but then he hated the name Ben. I suppose it was the old antipathy to change again. He was lucky, I was going to call the dog Gerrard. I felt I had the right to change its name as I had paid for its release from the home. Besides Gerrard had a strange attitude towards the creature. You can always tell how he feels about it by his use of the possessive. 'Our dog has done an amusing trick.' 'Your dog has pissed on my bed.' 'Yes, he's wonderful, I've had him about a year' (normally to dog-loving woman), as opposed to 'I think your dog is ill, you'd better take him to the vet's.'

'Didn't you see her off?' Lydia was tickling the dog behind the ears. I realised she was speaking to me.

'No, they picked her up in a taxi and I would have had to get a tube back. Beside it's a lot of waiting around, isn't it?'

'Not if you love someone,' said Lydia to the dog.

'There's love and there's getting up at five in the morning. Come into the kitchen, Farley's here.'

Lydia came in and helloed everyone. Gerrard looked sheepish. Lydia riled him with her intelligence and her northern accent. It wasn't that she was a woman and clever that bothered him, it was that she was a Geordie and clever. In the neat compartments of his brain, Geordie equalled thick. He went by the old adage 'a Geordie is no more than a Scotsman with his brains kicked out.' Lydia, however, presented a challenge to this happy opinion. She was a Geordie and luminously bright. Anyone else would have conceded that they must be mistaken in a vicious stereotype of the North

East, but Gerrard was not so easily shaken. His conclusion was that Lydia put the accent on in order to be fashionable.

Another reason that Gerrard was suspicious of her was that he disapproved of her thirty-a-day roll up habit. The one piece of sexism he would admit to was disliking women who smoked roll ups. I knew for a fact that there were many more pieces of sexism within him, but that was his New Man or Sensitive New Age Guy sexism. It surprised me when I learned that these paragons of virtue allow any unpleasant side at all to show through, but it seems they all need a lapse or rather a LAPs – Life Affirming Piece of Sexism – to get by. Just like the normal fucked up bloke needs a female friend to show the world he's not all kebabs and curries, the committedly sensitive need an insensitive bit to show that they're a human being. Otherwise they become too suspiciously politically correct, over-polished like a dodgy second hand car. So at a party the chap who's been jawing about the theatre with the host's younger sister for an hour or more might glance appreciatively at her rear as she disappears for a comfort break, winking conspiratorially at the nearest man as she moves out of his cloud of opinions towards the cocaine/toilet queue. I'm not sure they know they do this but they do.

Lydia sat down and immediately began to roll a cigarette. In her mind, I'm sure, the roll up made her look like one of those sexy girls that idea-free photographers place in a man's suit with a cigar: Grubb's Tyre Lever Calendar Miss October, or even something from 1930s France. To Gerrard she looked like one of those school teachers who never found the right man and lived with a 'friend'. This was unfortunate, because I wanted him to think well of her, which he sort of did, in a threatened sort of way. All my friends, perhaps with the exception of Farley, felt a little transparent in front of Lydia, like earthlings in the gaze of an alien super mind. Farley wouldn't have felt inferior because he'd never valued intelligence too highly, as the genuinely clever do not.

Gerrard casually placed his steaming epistle down on the table. 'What's that?' asked Lydia.

'Oh, a letter to a friend,' he said, shrinking inside his collar.

'It's unlike you to write, Gerrard,' said Lydia, sitting down and removing her cycle clips from her suit trousers. As I watched her I came to the sick realisation that she must be on her way to work, on a Saturday. The weekend starts here? Not nowadays it doesn't.

'It's to Paula,' said Farley. He whisked a cigarette from my packet on the table.

'Got a new bike?' I said.

'No, I borrowed it, which rather neatly brings me to why I came round here. I've a bit of an announcement.'

'I'm holding out an olive branch,' said Gerrard, ignoring her.

To our mutual credit, neither Farley nor I raised an eyebrow. Farley simply took a long hard look at the appropriated Marlboro, as if studying it for a reaction to Gerrard's words.

Lydia looked slightly thrown, but seemed genuinely pleased for Gerrard. 'Good, it would be so nice to see you both together again. That's why I'm always reticent about setting up my friends together. When they split up you don't know who to invite round to dinner.'

'You haven't invited me round to dinner for a year,' he said.

'Seems she didn't have too much difficulty with where to send the invites then.' My two pen'orth chinked into the conversation.

Lydia smiled at my joke. 'Well, I haven't had many parties. I do hope you'll come soon, you could come with Paula.'

I silently noted the difference between 'many' and 'any', as attached to 'parties', and chipped in with a flippancy: 'I shouldn't splash out on extra cutlery just yet.'

'Not on the cards, then?' said Lydia.

'It's not impossible they'll get back together . . . I think they've got about the same chance as cat and dog,' said Farley, helpfully.

He went into a routine taken from a TV comedian – Harry Hill, I think – about how cat and dog used to live together and then dog borrowed cat's video card and didn't return the video. I was depressingly reminded of me and Gerrard.

'You've not made it pathetically insulting, have you?' I've always wondered how Lydia had this sixth sense for people's emotions.

'I've told the truth,' said Gerrard, raising his hands to push his ears flat to his skull as if anticipating a blow.

'Oh, dear,' said Lydia.

'Oh, dear indeed,' I said. 'Fancy a cup of tea?'

'Don't mind if I do,' said Farley, who had finished his first cup.

'I'd love one,' said Lydia.

'Have a look at the letter,' said Farley, 'we'd appreciate the female point of view.'

Gerrard passed over the letter at the fullest extension of his arm, as if feeding a caged beast. With his other hand he beat away the roll-up smoke. Lydia looked a little askance but knew there was no point in saying anything about Gerrard treating her as if she stank. The argument would start with her saying 'don't treat me like I stink', he would say that she did stink – of cigarette smoke, she would say he was very rude, he would ask how rude it was to come into someone's house and poison them. Someone should release a recording of this conversation that could be played every time anyone lights up in front of an evangelical non-smoker. Then we could all just talk about something else.

The letter taken, the smoke dispersed, he quickly put his hand to good use, attacking an itch that had sprung up in his trousers. The other hand he stored by placing his fingers into his mouth, ready for use when emergency threatened.

Lydia put on her glasses and read.

'As you read,' I cautioned her, 'remember, you'll have to look between the lines to understand just how caring and feeling he really is. Men have difficulty expressing emotion, we know that from books.'

'Oh, I don't know. He doesn't seem to have much problem with anger,' she said, finishing the first half sentence.

'That we can do,' I reassured her.

Lydia gave an uncertain 'Yeeees', and read on.

It occurred to me that, much as society encourages us to express our emotions, there are certain emotions we are very much encouraged to bottle. In fact there are some emotions that we very much should bottle. When I had met Emily's science chums for our only dinner party together I was, I am ashamed to say, feeling Media Disdain. This is the condition whereby the person working in the entertainment industry feels superior, by a degree, to anyone doing anything else. 'Oh, you're at the cutting edge of cancer research, are you? How splendid. I make documentaries that let us all gawp at other people's misfortune, don't you wish you were me?' She didn't thank me for expressing that emotion, and to be truthful I didn't thank myself.

Far from learning to be in touch with my inner feelings I

wouldn't mind passing a few of them the pearl-handled revolver, saying 'you know what to do' and seeing them take the one way walk into the snow. Take Celebrity Rage, which turns me into an armchair stalker. All I have to do is to see some young-ish successful man on the television, particularly if he is committing the worst sin in the lad's bible – trying to be funny – and I descend into fantasies about meeting him in a nightclub and attacking him, physically. I know it's sad, I don't want to feel it, but there's nothing I can do about it. If I was American I could get therapy, but being British that is out of the question.

I earnestly hope you are reading this long after the celebrity of the list I am about to furnish you with has faded, but I think you'll get the idea anyway. I have in recent weeks, in my head, punched the bloke from the Verve (substitute any currently successful coolster band full of thin blokes), kicked the poet bloke off the Late Show Discussion in the nuts, and thrashed Chris Evans with an electric cable. I have also, to my shame, planted one on Saint Bob Geldof on a chat show. A common feature of these fantasies involves me being famous in some very fashionable way.

I have tried to give up these sad dreams but they always come back. Perhaps I should try to do it in the way that smokers give up cigarettes – only allowing myself, for instance, other people's fantasies, heartily concurring when one of my mates wishes some sparkling nonentity would get run over, or only fantasising when I drink. I can't see it working though.

Lydia had ummed, ahhed and oohed her way through three pages before her next intelligible comment. 'Have you considered a dating agency?'

Gerrard looked hurt, but before he could reply Farley inter-jected, 'Oh, don't do that.' He was searching for a pen to do the crossword.

'Why not?' asked Lydia. 'It works for a lot of people, especially busy ones who don't have time to meet people.' I wondered if she'd tried it.

'Have you noticed these busy people always tend to be rather ugly? Perhaps having a high-pressure job makes you put on three stone and develop spots.' Farley had found the pen and was chewing the end while poring over the crossword.

'That's very cynical, Farley.'

'No, it's not. Dating agencies are wholly unnatural.'

'What do you mean?' said Gerrard, who I thought should steer clear of blind dates with anyone other than the actually blind and, for their sake, deaf. 'It's a bit forced, but wholly unnatural's putting it a bit strongly.'

'No,' said Farley firmly. 'They're anti-Darwinian. In the natural kingdom only the strongest get to breed, that's what natural selection is all about. Dating agencies select the weakest, the charmless, the stupid, the ugly and the fat. If we're not careful we'll breed a nation of super losers, we will reverse evolution, the place will end up being run by the kids who got picked on at school. We will have created a dystopia.'

I thought this line of conversation best stemmed, before Farley started *Ein Reich, Ein Volk, Ein Führer*-ing in the kitchen.

'How's the letter?' I asked Lydia

She seemed relieved to leave the dating subject.

'He says he loves her, that's good, and he recalls the time they went to the pictures together, that's nice. But I don't understand this bit about loose fish.'

'What?' said me and Farley.

'He calls her a loose fish. Are you sure she'll know what that means?'

'In the context, yes,' said Gerrard, industriously worrying at his behind.

'He didn't read that out. What is the context?' asked Farley.

'Debauchee, whore, trollop, harridan, woman of the town, demirep, hussy, drab, Jezebel, baggage, jade, quean, Messalina, Delilah, concubine, kept woman, tart, harlot, whore . . .' I realised, with regret, that Lydia was reading from the same sentence '. . . loose fish.'

'Why stop there?' said Farley.

'It's only a cheap thesaurus,' said Gerrard.

Lydia put down the letter and took off her glasses, adopting the very kind of 'let's talk about this' expression guaranteed to curdle the blood of all but the most doggedly sensitive man.

'You can't expect to find your emotions in a dictionary.' This made me wonder where we were meant to find them. I mean, our parents never gave us any. They'd probably have liked to have handed some over but were too afraid it might open us up to accusations of homosexuality. I'd made the effort to have some in adolescence, with the view that if I had emotions I could then repress them and hope for one of the mental illnesses, like depression, that were so fashionable in my youth. A bloke up our road had once written some poetry and got taken into a mental ward. He couldn't beat the women away afterwards, especially when he'd got his Joy Division-style raincoat. He, however, was thin so his mental illness was taken as the price an artist has to pay. Being bigger boned, people would just conclude that I was a sad fat nutter. The whole experience has had a bad effect on me. Whenever I see someone has suffered a nervous breakdown, or says they are 'sensitive', I always suspect they are just doing it to look clever. I felt moved to defend Gerrard, but largely from selfish motives.

'Hang on a minute, what's all this emotions stuff? It's not made it to the plural yet. One's difficult enough, give the man some credit.' Unrighteous anger on its own had used up half a notebook. If he ascended into self-pity I feared I'd be off to the shop for another couple of pads.

'Rip up that letter and concentrate on how she's feeling, not how you feel,' said Lydia.

'She's perfectly happy, isn't she?' said Gerrard, as if Paula was doing it to spite him. 'She's got a boyfriend she adores, a lovely flat, I bet, a great job. She's fucking fine.'

'She seems a little better than fine, Gerrard, at least when I saw her,' I said. One of the great things about being a man is that you are free from any responsibility to sympathise. This isn't as uncaring as it sounds. If I'd taken the 'tell me all about it' approach he would have concluded that he really was in a terrible predicament – I hadn't the heart to take the piss. I'm reminded of a time when he had his hair cut and I said it looked nice. He wore a hat for a month.

I think one of the reasons that Lydia and I are friends is that she has learned to live with these comments without openly disapproving of them or getting drawn into them herself. To me she's like the carer of an elderly invalid, spending her days in the reek of fart and decay, only noticing the smell when it registers on the faces of visitors. My problem, our problem, was that we couldn't not say these things any more than the old person could stop farting. We'd been at it too long.

'How do you think you're going to get her back then? She's been a year with a bloke she really likes, you treated her like shit, why should she come back?' asked Lydia. No further questions, M'lud, I thought.

'She should come back, she's in the wrong. She made the promises, she said she loved me. I never made a promise, I never broke anyone's heart.' It struck me that Gerrard was presenting his lack of commitment to the woman he was trumpeting as the love of his life as a good thing.

Lydia emptied an ashtray into the bin, or rather she balanced some cigarette ends and ash on top of a small Everest of rubbish that was coming out of the bin. I certainly wasn't going to change the bag as it wasn't my turn, Gerrard wasn't going to either because he was equally convinced it wasn't his. He, of course, was wrong. So for the last three weeks we'd been balancing bean cans on cereal boxes on top of tomatoes and banana skins, beer cans and tins of Sainsbury's Vegetarian Madras, to build a precarious sculpture of crap that I felt was a fairly good representation of our relationship.

Not only was it founded on stubbornness and bile, it reflected our tastes. Quorn sausages box – he. Chinese take away container – me. Eight to ten Safeway own-brand lager cans – me. One Radagast finest Czech lager bottle placed next to bin for recycling – he. Loads of bits of weird vegetables, some spilling on to floor – he. Rice Krispies box, most of cereal on floor – me.

Most impressive of all was the way it hung together, finely balanced in layers, like a hillside village that we had built side by side. As a team. If it was still there by the right date I was going to enter it for the Royal Academy show. I had suggested this to Gerrard and he thought it had a chance with a name like 'Opus IV Modern – Ultra, Maybe'. I thought that we should regard it as our first-born and call it Trevor or, this being wannabe West London, Spirulina.

This degree of squalor is not as bad as some people's. At least we are familiar with the concept of a bin even if the practical application leaves a little to be desired. There are tribes of men whose language contains no word for 'bin', the nearest approximation they have being 'floor'.

Lydia removed something sticky from the sole of her shoe. 'What do you think not telling her you loved her did to her?'

'At the time I didn't realise it.'

'No reason not to say it,' said Farley, from behind the paper. 'Really, I'm not being flippant. It's just polite after certain amount of time. It's like saying "thank you for having me".' He turned a page.

'To you, maybe. The trouble is – I've thought a lot about this – you can only give your heart once. I've realised, maybe too late, that she was my ideal, she was perfect for me. I've tried to let it go. I've done that for a whole year, and I can't. She was the one for me. Once you've had that there's no going on to any future relationships. They're all spoiled by the memory that you once had it right. I want that back, but I know I can't have it.' He scratched miserably at the back of his neck and looked around the room without meeting anyone's gaze.

'Gerrard, you look ill,' said Lydia. His pale features, which were already enhanced by the darkness of his hair, had taken on a candlewax complexion which I hadn't seen since we went on the waltzers at the fairground.

'Emotion sickness,' said Farley. 'It's caused by moving through pockets of turbulent feelings. It particularly affects those new to long-distance travel in these areas.'

'I'm fine. Eh, she just did, you know, understood me,' he said, answering a question no one had asked.

'And then she left you.' I felt it helpful to revisit the facts of the case.

'There's one thing worse for a man than a wife who doesn't understand him. One who does,' said Farley, who was now well into the sports section.

Lydia pressed on, despite the waves of puerility that threatened to overwhelm her.

'She understood your – what? Your fears? Your hopes?'

'I quite liked that,' said Farley.

'It sounds like something off the back of a matchbox,' I said.

Gerrard looked distinctly green about the gills. He had been batting on this particular sticky wicket for too long.

'Yes, she understood my fears. I'd say she did.'

Farley looked up from the Soccer Diary.

'What are your fears?'

'Eh, well, the usual really.'

'Like?'

'Loneliness.'

'Great line. "I want you back because I am lonely." Shall I clear her out a food cupboard now?' I said in earnest tone.

'If she understood you were lonely, surely she understood that she wasn't meeting your needs.' Lydia actually looked worried.

Gerrard's expression resembled that of a soldier who, having reached the end of a demanding run, is told it's once more around the blockhouse.

'Well, er, she understood that I'm dissatisfied with what I've got in terms of my job. That I hope for something more interesting.'

'She also understood you were going to do fuck all about it,' I said cheerily.

'And she understood that I loved her. That's what I don't get. I don't know how she can take my love and just throw it away for that vacuous long-haired twat.'

'Anyone want any toast?' asked Farley with an air of high ennui.

'Yes, please,' said Gerrard.

'It was a joke,' said Farley, 'but if you're making some . . .'

Gerrard moved to the bread bin, a life ring in a sea of questions.

'The letter,' said Lydia, 'is a problem. You can't expect the girl to take all that abuse and then think, "Oh, but he loves me." You've got it off your chest, now just throw it away. Write something simple, concentrate on the good things.'

Gerrard came back from the bread bin, took the letter from Lydia and dramatically folded it in half. He placed it precisely into an envelope and sealed it.

'This little missile,' he said, 'is hitting its target.'

'A target that seems located squarely up your own arse,' smiled Lydia.

'If it's love then it's worth fighting for, you've got to choose the weapons you're comfortable with,' said Farley, matter-of-factly, as if describing how to put up a shelf.

'A sentiment nobly adhered to by the Polish cavalry in World War Two as they charged the Panzer Tanks,' I observed.

Farley considered his position. 'If he apologises to her there's a chance it'll come over all false, but if he doesn't he's fucked anyway.' Falseness, as I have already opined, is not always a bad thing. If you don't like someone, for instance, and you tell them then that's good because it's honest but it's bad because it's brutal. You have to weigh up whether being brutal is worse than being false. I know this is startlingly obvious to most of us but, emerging late from adolescence, it had the flavour of a brand new discovery to me.

I was born with little nose for questions of sensitivity, so I have to do it by numbers. It is possible to make solid, reasonable choices, with a degree of work. I help myself by thinking of moral choices in terms of a game we used to play as kids. It's the one where you put your fist against your opponent's and then, on the count of three, make a shape with your hand: paper, water, fire, scissors, stone. If you get scissors against stone the scissors lose – they're blunted; scissors against paper, the scissors win; scissors against scissors – draw, try again. Amazingly this technique sometimes works when making choices, and allows you to explain things to people in neat polarities, as in, 'I slept with someone else (stone) because you do not show me enough attention (paper). Paper wraps up stone, therefore I'm OK.' This of course disguises the true opposition, which the five categories listed above can't quite encompass. 'I slept with someone else (stone) because I didn't think you would find out (window).'

Because of this technique my sensitivity is like a well-fitting wig – you only find out it's false if you go to bed with me. Only then will you discover that in my mind any inconvenience to myself is represented by fire; any inconvenience to you by paper. Still, it's a useful enough technique and good for judging others. In Gerrard's book, for instance, apology clearly got cut to ribbons by betrayal.

'I'm not apologising,' he said.

'Then write nothing,' Lydia said, tapping at the table.

'It's the best idea,' said Farley. Where did his sudden concern for the interests of others come from?

'Then I'd feel I was letting her get away with it. I've tried for a year, I've written nothing for a year. You're OK, Farley, you don't love anyone. You've never loved anyone. If you'd come across the perfect girl for you and then lost her, you'd feel different.'

'I have come across one. In fact, as we speak I am in love.'

The dog, who I'd say was doing a pretty good job as a barometer of the *esprit de corps* in the kitchen at that moment, stopped chewing at his vegetarian bone substitute (Gerrard's gift) and looked at Farley quizzically. I was waiting for the punchline, something like, 'I am indeed in love – with myself,' or some other weak joke. It never crossed my mind that he was serious. Farley in my kitchen on a Saturday morning was a shock, but Farley in love?

Gerrard was the first to react. He, evidently, had taken Farley seriously.

'Rubbish, you're in love until you meet the next shag, then you'll be in love with her.'

Farley exhaled the smoke of another of my Marlboros. He'd clearly taken more than one before I removed the packet.

'Have it your own way.'

'Who's the lucky lady, and has she had your blood tested?' Lydia said with slack face.

'She doesn't consider herself lucky. She's not interested, in fact. Bitch, innit?'

'She's a bitch or life is?' Like me, Lydia was never sure about the use of the slang 'innit'. In fact, I'm never sure of the use of any slang any more, which is a fairly good sign that you're heading into middle age. The other, of course, is Dadflesh, the puckered, older skin men get as they edge closer to forty. You only notice you've got it when you look at those photos of your eighteen year-old self and wonder where those gleaming cheeks went, to be replaced by this cellulite for the face. Gerrard had it in a minor way on both cheeks whereas I was relatively free of it, just some light looseness about the jowls. Kids bring it on quickly. The one friend of mine with a child has been sprouting it at an alarming rate. When I say the one friend with a child, you'll know I mean the one male friend who had a child and, through love or laziness, stayed with the mother. Farley, young by force of will, had no Dadflesh and no confusion about slang either.

'Life. She's not a bitch, she's dreamy.' The trouble with coming from Watford is that you say everything in a monotone more suitable for announcing train delays than making sweeping declarations of passion. 'The 5.45 to Wolverhampton has no buffet facility and your eyes set my soul ablaze. Ahhthanyou.'

However, Farley's duck's arse tones had never twisted themselves into the word 'dreamy' before. First he was in love, now she was dreamy. At any moment I expected a giant white rabbit to come in through the kitchen door, banging a drum and singing, 'Wake up, it's time to go work, have a banana.'

'Who is she?' I couldn't imagine what kind of girl Farley would go off the deep end for.

'None of you know her,' he said.

'Aren't you upset?' asked Lydia.

'Really bleeding.' There was no irony in his voice.

'You don't seem upset,' said Gerrard suspiciously. The dog moved to Gerrard's side, as he tended to do when in tacit agreement.

'What did you expect? Uncontrollable sobbing? You just get on with it, don't you? It's the only thing, you just get on with it. What's the alternative?'

'You could admit it to yourself,' said Gerrard.

'I could, I have, but I don't choose to make a career out of it. What do you gain by going in for the wounded act? Do you think you're going to get the mercy shags or someone's going to mother you? It doesn't work like that. Women want winners, winners who win in women's terms. Let them know you're hurt, that you're not going to take away their uncertainty and doubt, and they'll rip you to pieces like wolves. Give them the confidence, give them the vibe. Onwards and upwards, mate. This Paula thing – if you wanted her back it'd be a piece of piss, probably.'

Other, higher forms of life might have been interested enough in their friend to question Farley further on how love had entered and left his life. Gerrard, however, welcomed the invitation to return to talking about himself. I can't criticise him, I'd have done the same.

'How might I do that?'

'You've got to know yourself. Who you are, what you want and where you're going.'

I couldn't help feeling this was something of a tall order. I'd certainly never got round to it.

Gerrard looked puzzled.

'How do I do that?' Fair point, I thought.

'Look inside yourself, ask yourself what you see.'

Gerrard puckered his cheeks, like a slow-witted adolescent in a maths class. Is slow-witted adolescent a tautology? Mostly, I guess.

'You couldn't just give me a couple of pointers to get me going, could you? It's not particularly obvious, the two main questions, to me anyway. The where am I from and where am I going bits. They're a bit difficult, aren't they? It's back to the how do I become a better person bit. I don't see how that's done. You are what you are. How could I improve, emotionally?'

'You could always change sex,' said Lydia helpfully.

'You don't need to change sex, you just need to know where you're coming from. Then you can know what you want, then you can know how to act to get it.' Farley was unusually animated at this point.

'And how about you? Why don't you just get this girl if it's that easy?' Don't mistake this for concern. Gerrard wasn't at all interested in why Farley didn't use his knowledge to charm the girl of his dreams. Far from it. In fact 'why don't you just get this girl if it's that easy' actually translates as 'you're talking rubbish' which boils down, in bloke speak, to something like 'wanker'.

'It's not so easy with her.'

'Why not?'

'We were talking about you, weren't we?'

'All right, but how do you know what you want?'

'We really were talking about you, weren't we? Look, if you wanted to I could show you how to have her back within a month.'

'But what if she's happy with this bloke and doesn't fancy me any more?'

'Minor impediments,' said Farley, unbelievably smoking yet another of my Marlboros. 'If you know what you want and if you do as I say. Most people are very easy to influence.'

Lydia had clearly been quiet long enough.

'But this girl you're after, she's not easily influenced. Does that make Paula some kind of second-class citizen?'

Farley shrugged. 'I'm not interested in the morals of the case, I'm interested in the practicalities. It would be interesting to me to see if you could take a non-starter like Gerrard here and get him to win the race, that's all.'

'It's a better bet than sending her the Sermon from the Mount. Farley has a bit of a track record in this area,' I said.

'But it's disingenuous,' said Lydia.

'Hold on a minute,' said Gerrard. 'Ten minutes ago you were criticising my letter for being too ingenuous. You can't have it both ways. It's either deceit or it's true feeling, there's nothing in the middle.'

None of us argued with this. Farley because he could see he was winning, Lydia because she thought there was a chance he might tear the letter up, and me because I knew that having got Gerrard near to changing his mind once, we were unlikely to accomplish the feat twice.

'Come on,' I said, 'give Farley a go.'

Farley chipped in encouragement. 'You only live once, don't you?'

'I don't know,' said Gerrard, meaning exactly that. 'That's a depressing view of the universe. I was rather counting on the Buddhists being right. A clean slate appeals to me.'

He passed the letter quickly to Lydia, who confetti-ed it.

'Well done,' said Farley, 'you won't regret it. All you need is faith in yourself, and you can work on that. It's easy. You have as much hope as you'll allow yourself. All you have to do is go for it.'

'OK,' said Gerrard, 'I'll be counting on you. This could just about save my life.'

2

Each man kills the thing he loves

The news of Farley's suicide hit Gerrard particularly hard.

One evening, about a week before we learned of the death, I'd returned from work in remarkably good spleen to find Gerrard once more with his pen hovering like a dagger above the virgin flesh of a writing pad.

'I thought we'd agreed to ditch that,' I said, searching for the remote control so I could claim *Star Trek* before he pitched into some programme about global misery.

'It's not to Paula, it's to Farley,' said Gerrard, searing the first line of our address into the cool blue of the paper.

Gerrard always lays out his letters in classic business fashion, as we were taught at school. Even writing to his mum, he includes his address, her address and the date. It's all part of his respect for doing things the right way, for appearances, and I suppose only to be expected from a man who has always bought the same kind of shoes he wore at school from the same store in Brighton he had been to at school. Mind you, he's bought the same everything that he'd worn at school – leather jacket (despite vegetarianism), jeans and Breton shirt, charcoal grey socks – never black. He had been one of the trendiest people in his sixth form, so his older friends tell me, but never grasped the idea that fashion moves on.

Although he has for years resembled a sack of shit, and that of a kind manure merchants stopped using some time ago, he has a greater concern for appearances than your average spin doctor. There was one look for him – that of a sack of shit. He had found it, considered that it suited him, and now wasn't changing it for anyone. To Gerrard, clothes represented personality first and fashion last, via aesthetics and available budget.

I have found that it's much easier just to be fashionable without letting considerations of personal taste intrude – just look in the men's style mags and go out and spend a grand or so in the sales once a year. Buy nine or ten items – one of which should be a little bit risky or flamboyant – and never worry about it for a whole twelve months. I find it's better to take risks with the coat; you make an entrance and you can always take it off if you feel uncomfortable. If you feel OK you can keep it on. There are times when I have felt so OK that I've spent an entire evening casually sweating cobs for the sake of my appearance. Needless to say, flamboyance and risk taking were low on Gerrard's list of priorities, as he regarded certain shades of grey as altogether too gaudy.

His concern for his image was such that once he had gone out in a downpour, refusing to borrow the golfing umbrella I'd found on the tube. To him the umbrella said, 'I like golf and want to be seen to like golf. I fully support its values.' To everyone else, if they'd bothered to look, it would have said, 'I like being dry, I want to be seen to like being dry. I fully support the values of the dry.' It might have been just a hangover from the adolescence thing, though. You never know when that girl is going to emerge and say: 'What a nice looking bloke, but I couldn't go out with a golfer.'

I know that, in a lesser way, I'm guilty of this myself. I'd rather go naked than wear a rugby shirt. It's not that I don't like the game, it's a fine traditional English sport created by nineteenth-century public schools in order to encourage homosexuality and it's watchable if there's nothing else on TV, but a rugby shirt worn anywhere other than the rugby pitch doesn't say 'I like rugby', it says 'I am an ample-buttocked stockbroker'. At least to me it does.

I let Gerrard sweat over his writing as I thought he was justified in having a go at Farley. We hadn't seen him for weeks and Gerrard had already spent a couple of evenings grizzling about his non-appearance in the quest to retrieve the damsel Paula from the clutches of the twin dragons, Freedom and Self-Respect. There was also the advantage that Gerrard wouldn't be able to argue about the channel of the TV while writing.

I pointed the remote to the set, clicking past a child's distended belly, two channels of chefs being refreshingly light-hearted but passionate about the serious business of cookery, and someone I assumed was a concerned parent on a housing estate, although perhaps it was an unconcerned parent telling the presenter to piss off and leave her alone. I wondered if there was a body for unconcerned parents, who would write letters like: 'Sir, please reduce the age at which cigarettes and alcohol can be purchased to nought. I have sent my toddler to the shops for fags and whisky every day for the last week and twice he has been refused. If it gets much worse I will have to go myself. Yours, an unconcerned parent.' Probably not, but they'd be a better laugh than the other lobby. Someone once said that faith is the state of being ultimately concerned. I don't know where that leaves me, and I don't care to think about it.

I clicked once more and settled on the reassuring image of Spock's sharp-eared monolith of a face. I glanced at Gerrard but he was too steeped in choler to notice the Enterprise whirling above a cardboard planet. Gerrard's chief criticism of *Star Trek* was that it was 'unrealistic', which seemed to me to be missing the point.

Tricorder readings were taken, fazers set to stun and Captain Kirk made porcine advances to a sylph-like alien, before we returned to Scottie on the bridge. I took the opportunity to ask Gerrard why he was writing and not telephoning. 'Because I want to take great care over what I say,' he said with lips so pursed you could have been forgiven for thinking he was considering a second career as a ventriloquist.

'And what do you want to say?'

'Talk is cheap,' said Gerrard, although it could have been 'Got a gottle of gear?'

'That's why I always find it such an irresistible investment.' I blew out a smoke ring that wouldn't have disgraced a nuclear test.

Gerrard caterpillared his brows, mentally shredding the smoke ring and shoving it where I would prefer it not to be. He then noticed the TV. The sylph-like alien was telling the sumo-like captain, 'I will always remember you, Jim Kirk.'

'Turn this shit over,' he said, 'there's a programme on about complementary therapies.'

'What, miracle cure through shaving toads' toe nails?'

'No,' said Gerrard with a terseness that would make a Russian bureaucrat look like an over-eager graduate of a US customer care course, 'apparently a couple of acupuncturists have been using unsound techniques and paralysed half of Beverly Hills.'

'Good for them,' I said, 'or is it a comedy?'

'You're afraid of anything new, aren't you?' said Gerrard, which I thought was a bit rich.

'Not at all,' I said, 'I don't mind trying science – that hasn't been around for too long.'

Gerrard sat poised to resume writing. 'Is it faithfully or sincerely?' he asked.

'I think you're pretty sincere,' I said. He bored his signature into the paper, and, I later discovered, the cover of the *Oxford Dictionary of Quotations* which he was leaning on. If there are one or two more quotations in the rest of this book than you find strictly comfortable, I'm sorry. He left it on the coffee table and I've been reading it ever since. Gerrard sealed his envelope with a precise, neat swipe of the tongue. 'It's about time,' he said, 'that Farley saw himself as others see him.'

Against this background it's easy to understand why, when we discovered that Farley was dead, Gerrard was very upset. What does it say about the depth of your crisis when your friends kill themselves rather than face helping you? Of course, Gerrard knew on weight of evidence he had nothing to do with it, but you can't help taking these things personally. Especially when your own efforts to drag yourself out of the slough of despond have only succeeded in pushing you further into that very slough. And, to his credit, Gerrard had been trying hard to get out.

The weeks following Farley's speech on positive thinking had seen a refreshed, or rather less stale, Gerrard try a couple of hopeful night club trawls and visits to house parties. Once there he would spring into inaction, his back attracted by some magnetic force to the wall or the fridge. To his credit, he did cast a critical eye over his lack of success at these events and identified the 'gross inhibitor' in his attempts to meet girls: me. Apparently, whenever he approached a woman at a party, I would come in between them 'like Errol Flynn on Viagra'. I couldn't immediately remember eschewing the top-floor bell in favour of a rope at the window, or playing the piano with my 12" tadger, but I was flattered by the comparison.

Gerrard's problem was that I made it plain to a woman when I found her attractive, by eyeing her lasciviously – though in a silver-tongued, cavalier 'I say!' sort of way, not in a tongue-out, hot diggity dog manner – and by saying so, after some initial conversation.

I hadn't always done this, having spent most of the early-eighties wallflowering it with a floppy fringe while trying to project an air of intense artistic disquiet from the gloomier recesses of Tomangos night club. It was only when I noticed that my friends who behaved like Club 18–30 holiday reps got off with more girls than me that I dropped the stormy brows in favour of my Mr Positive, life's a riot approach. As Grandmaster Flash has so memorably observed, 'What you gonna do by standing on the wall? Get your backs up off the wall.' Actually I think it may have been the Gap Band that said this, as Gerrard very quickly pointed out when I reminded him of the quote. He also said I'd got the words wrong, but it doesn't really matter. Nothing like that does.

For women of a certain stamp, and those in Tomangos were of a certain stamp, it seems they'd rather you bared your arse than your soul. With my lofty self opinion at the time they'd probably have received more enlightenment that way.

Although the realisation that walking up to a girl and saying 'you look nice' was a better route to getting off with her than hanging about trying to look like Kafka upped my immediate hit rate, I did get some unpleasant reactions from a couple of girls who went out with me expecting me to flash the cash rather than the French existentialism. Unhappily, I was of the idea that misery equates to depth and depth to attractiveness – wrong in every part. So between Piña Coladas and beneath the shade of plastic palm trees, I would honk up the 'human life begins on the far side of despair' line. By the time the girls fled for the bus, they had received the clearest possible illustration of what I meant.

Gerrard, however, has never taken the Grandmaster's, or the bloke out of the Gap Band's, advice. He still believes Miss Right is out there and will recognise him when she sees him, as long as he wears the appropriate clothes and displays the appropriate opinions; as long as he is true to himself. So he will still sit on the wall at night clubs looking like a sex pest and hoping that the girl of his dreams is going to come up and say, 'Gosh, I admire you for clinging rigidly to the fashion of your late-teens. Marry me.' A brave stand on 'foam, froth and fun night.'

The sad thing is – all right, one of the sad things is – we both know that our approaches are wrong, or at least that at thirty-two it ill behoves us to have an approach at all, just as it ill behoves a man of thirty-two to have a favourite colour – you should select the shade for the occasion. The trouble is, Gerrard and I only have the one. It's like playing golf only using one club.

Farley, of course, was different from either of us when it came to women. When you are dumped by a woman, they smear you with some hormone or something that says 'Loser, steer clear', so you can't get shagged by anyone else for the next six months. The hormone makes you get inappropriately pissed and try to sleep with women with whom you've been good platonic friends for ten years. Farley, who had never, as far as I knew, had a relationship was the reverse of this. He exuded a natural insouciance, a hormone saying 'I don't care if I pull or not' that seemed to have women slavering at his ankles. It's an absolute fact that when you have a girlfriend you will get more offers from other women than you know what to do with. When you haven't you'll have all the pulling power of a Young Christian.

Farley, through being in a long-term relationship with himself, permanently had this 'sorted' air about him. Until, of course, he told me he was dead – at about 12 o'clock on an April Monday, when I picked up my voice mail.

It was a cloudy, close, thick blanket of a day combining heat and gloom in equal portions. The clinging air was made a good deal worse by the air conditioning. Not my office air conditioning, course – it didn't have any, like a lot of English offices – but it looked out on to the flat roof of a sandwich bar that certainly did. From the size of the fans I would have said it was staging a serious bid to become the first snack vendor to make a transatlantic flight. You had a choice: close the window and swelter or open the window and go deaf, while sweltering very slightly less. I opted for the second.

I always try to leave picking up my voice mail until later in the day because, on almost every occasion I have accessed it, it has been someone asking me to do something, and that is about as palatable to me as cold Alsatian sick (not that the warm variety very much appeals).

I don't know who it was who said that the best way of killing time is to work it to death, but they weren't far wrong. 'Time flies' says the clock on my office wall. If time flies for Harry Chesshyre, however, it is not as a sleek jet carving its way across clean horizons to bright lands of endless opportunity, but as a squat fat bluebottle against a window pane, repeatedly striving for a visible yet unattainable freedom.

In short, I don't like my work, and I suspect I don't like any work at all. I get bored at interviews. When employed I pick at my tasks like a child with food condemned to stay at the table until the last morsel has been finished. I feel resentful of the boss for expecting an honest day's work for an honest day's pay. I really can't think of any job that would sustain my interest for longer than a couple of days, Nipple Erector for *Penthouse* magazine, maybe, but even that must pall after a while. You've buffed one pair of supermodel tits, you've buffed the lot.

I suppose it's ungrateful to hate work so much when so many people find it difficult to come by, but that's the way the cookie crumbles, right behind some large bit of furniture where it's difficult to clean. My ideal role is that of house husband, although I'd want a nanny and au pair to help out, naturally.

Currently I am a researcher for a TV company. Researchers are the swabs on the vast ship of television, fetching and carrying the various bits of information required to run the programmes. I work on a show called *Your Rights, Their Wrongs* which is a consumer advice programme. My normal conversation with one of the people who will appear on the show goes, 'So the builders pulled up at your house on horses, hung their lassoes in the hallway, adjusted their Stetsons and six guns and demolished the place when they'd come to do the patio. If only there had been some clue they were cowboys.' I have to deal with many a sad sap who has been defrauded or treated shabbily and attempt to turn them into celebrity victims, dustbins where the nation can dump any leftover sympathy. It leaves me with a poor opinion of myself because I just cannot feel sorry for them. I'd love to, I really would, but I can't even though I've been ripped off badly myself once.

Gerrard got some people in to extend the back of the flat on the grounds they offered the cheapest quote. I pointed out to him, as we emptied our bank accounts, that experts in domestic affairs concur it is normally best to avoid choosing workmen with extensive facial tattoos and 'White Power' tee shirts, even if they do promise to convert your loft for a fiver. I also felt that part-time work with a travelling fairground was scant qualification for undertaking major structural repairs; a fact, I gently suggested, that could have been appreciated by the dimmer echelons of PE teacher. Admittedly Gerrard was justified in falling out with the bloke over his use of the 'W' and 'N' words for black people, but I did question the wisdom of placing a 'You don't have to be racist to work here but it helps' sign at the entrance to the kitchen. It just didn't seem conducive to a speedy, well-executed job.

Still, we only ended up being menaced out of the same sum that the builder from the Guild of Master Builders eventually charged after we'd got him in to fix the mess. But despite this experience, I still find myself thinking that some of the people I deal with deserve it. Gerrard and I deserved it. We deserved to pay more for our stupidity and greed, and the extra money was an inoculation against ever getting ripped off like that again. Researching for the show would be easier if one in every two complaints didn't come from someone who wears a baseball cap back to front. Is the inability to correctly orientate an item of American fashion wear genetically linked to the inability to spot a bogus trader?

My mother reminds me that not everyone is clever enough to stand up for themselves. She's right, but that only makes me less interested in them. Oh, well.

This last response, the 'Oh, well' bit, is the very thing Lydia normally counsels me against. I remember her once saying to me, 'I counsel you against identifying a flaw in yourself and then saying there's nothing you can do about it.' I took this rather badly, as I'd always thought my disarming honesty an endearing trait. 'People will think you're a moral coward,' she'd continued. I didn't bother to point out the advantage of having people concentrate on this single form of cowardice and missing the physical, intellectual and spiritual yellow streaks that have adorned the Chesshyre back for generations.

So, like I said, I was working my way through a pile of videos of terrible building work and teddy bears who had their eyes held in place by samurai swords instead of staples, getting a little wave of pleasure every time I saw someone who'd had a worse job than mine done, when the boss came into the office and pointed out my voice mail light was on. This meant I had to pick it up. But first a word about the surroundings.

Those of you who work in relatively affluent industries such as car manufacturing or pharmaceuticals will doubtless imagine a bright air-conditioned block full of handsome young men and women bent on having the time of their lives. This is what I had imagined when I opted for a career in TV – long lunches, glamour job, lots of available women, big corporation. Unfortunately it isn't like that. This is the world of the independent production companies, who live hand to mouth from one programme to the next, wondering where their next commission is coming from.

When I say 'the boss came into the office', I actually mean 'the boss came into his own front room', or 'the failed movie director fought his way past a twenty-year debris of broken dreams, piles of projects and pilot tapes that he could never bring himself to throw away, to gain access to the hovel'. Like many people whose formative influences were in the 1960s, Adrian, the boss, placed little value on cleaning or decorating. Farley had pointed out that the interior of the offices of Little Lemon Films, named after the first dog in space, most resembled a crack den, though lacking the *joie de vivre*.

I couldn't begin to guess what drove my boss Adrian on. It was as though he thought by winning refunds on defective washing machines and exposing small-time fraudsters he was making the world a better place. I suppose he was, but making the world a better place seems somehow to be missing the point of it all, like Gerrard with *Star Trek*. He didn't seem to be having much of a laugh along the way. Maybe his immoral level of hard work – sixteen hours a day on occasion – was meant to be some proof of virility, or of depth, but to whom and for what? A sixteen-hour day won't get you shagged by anyone other than the people you work with, and I was not about to shag Adrian.

I had considered trying to move on into the world of document-aries proper, the exposés of genocide and major fraud, but these didn't exactly ding my dong either. Take Adrian. His pride and joy was a documentary he'd done about how cigarette companies target children. By an incredible stroke of good fortune a thief who had stolen a cigarette company executive's briefcase off the tube was intelligent enough to realise that the information it contained was potential dynamite. A fan of *Your Rights, Their Wrongs* (for some reason), he'd brought it to Adrian, and in return for a promise of 'big bucks' handed it over. I think Adrian gave him £100.

When I watched the ensuing documentary I just thought, So what? Of course fag companies target the young, they'd be idiots not to. I would if I was in a cigarette company, wouldn't you? We don't need the evidence to prove it. Either ban smoking completely or let them get on with it. It's like when they show some maniac dictator burning and maiming enemies real and imagined. Of course he does, we don't need to know it. In fact, the world might be a nicer place if we didn't know it. I am familiar with the vicious ways of a host of despots across the planet. Am I going to do anything about it? Are you? The government presumably knew all about it in the first place and would have done something about it by now if they were going to. Just drop a bomb on the bastards and let me get on with watching re-runs of *Fawlty Towers*. So all the documentary does is import a little bit of Third World misery into our front rooms to distract us from the grinding tedium of our own existence. Documentary fever has got so bad that on Monday night you are almost constrained to entertain yourself as it's unrelenting gloom on every channel.

These were my thoughts as I clicked on my voice mail. There were a couple of messages from people asking if I'd seen their letters yet, one from a bloke who thought I was the complaints department at a store where he'd bought a defective Hoover, and then one that made me sit up and take notice. At first I assumed he was pissed and had just called my work number by mistake when he was trying to get me at home. Then what he was saying hit me as hard as it is possible for a realisation to hit, which is much harder than a dawning knowledge but not quite as hard as an unexpected threat to one's life. The voice was slow and heavy, as if speaking from a dream.

'Chesshyre, Chesshyre – Farley. I'm in Cornwall. Valiumed up, pretty pissed too. I want to mmevolve.' (I couldn't tell at this point whether it was dissolve, evolve or revolve, and frankly I couldn't imagine Farley doing any of them.) 'I'm going for the long swim. She won't have me, I've had enough. I'm going to do the job on myself, ... top myself.' He ran out of money here and the pips went. There was another call. 'I'm sticking a key in the post. No stamp, make sure you're in. I love you, man. You're in the will, you and Gerrard. Tell Gerrard I'm sorry. You're family, man, family.' The line, and presumably Farley with it, went dead.

The difficulty with being human is you don't always have the reactions you would choose. It surprised me that even at this moment of deep shock I still had it in me to get irritated that Farley was speaking like a hippie stoner. He had been talking in a funny way recently but the 'man' bit was difficult to stomach. I wondered who this girl was, who could drive him to 'dreamy', 'man' and suicide. What kind of girl would you kill yourself for? What kind of girl would you say 'man' for? It was a small consolation that he had died before he got on to 'dude'. Was this girl capable of pushing him that far? A friend of mine's dad had killed himself because of his wife, but she used to cut up his jumpers in winter and throw ice water at him as he went out to work in the morning. Farley had found it difficult enough to sacrifice a whole evening to one woman. Sacrificing his life seemed ridiculously out of character.

It's hard to know what to do in situations like these; it's even harder to know what to feel. No one prepares you for such messages, and although I could play the emotional violin, having watched experts, I wasn't ready for composing my own pieces just yet. I didn't want to confide in my boss. He was the sort of focused career type who probably respond, 'Never mind that, mate, we've got TV to make,' and buckle down to winning justice for someone who'd found a broken biscuit in a packet of Hob Nobs.

The only person I could think of asking what to do was Lydia, so I immediately got on the phone to her. She was, I was told, in a meeting.

Liberally dispensing the short shrift from the large sack I carry around with me, I insisted the receptionist get her out of the meeting, pointing out as an afterthought that ninety per cent of such gatherings are indistinguishable from a chat with your mates. The secretary ummed and ahhed, but then I played the death card and she went off, crying, to fetch Lydia. This I fail to understand in some people. I had informed her that someone she didn't know was dead and this was enough to turn on the waterworks. He was my mate and I wasn't crying, although I cry easily. The mere idea of there being pain in the world was enough to distress her. I'm not saying it's wrong, I'm just saying I don't understand it, although it probably accounts for why programmes raising money for children's charities do so well. I have to confess to unworthy thoughts when I see another X thousand pounds has been raised for Child Action or whatever. I think these charities should come with government warnings.

'Before you give, remember that children go on to become adults, the same adults that are murderers, thieves and day-time TV presenters. Ask yourself what you're saving. Then do the money yourself down the pub.'

I'd always been wary of sentimental types since I worked as a gardener for a very rich family when I was a sixth former. The mother of the household had an unbelievably large collection of stuffed toys and dressed always in pink. They owned a number of rental properties and she eventually did time for using rather too much of the heave ho when evicting tenants. Ever since then I have lived by the adage 'show me someone with a fondness for cuddly toys and I'll show you someone with a heart of stone'. The real attraction of these toys, like pets, is that they don't answer back.

Lydia came to the phone and said 'hello'. Although I had been expecting her to say this, for some reason it threw me and, for the first time since I caught Mad Linda riding the surf instructor's 'short board', I gaped. It's not often I gape, but when I do gape, I gape big.

Lydia said 'hello' again while I considered how exactly you break this kind of news to someone. If you tell them to sit down or something, it's the equivalent of saying 'something terrible has happened, but I'd like to increase the drama of the event'. You can't just drop it in after a few *bon mots* about the weather. It's difficult to present dramatic news undramatically; you get so used to hamming things up for the entertainment of your friends that when you have something that doesn't need hamming up, you don't know how to say it.

I weighed my options. Direct and unadorned (stone) vs breaking it gently (frilly paper doily). Doily wraps up stone but you can still see bits underneath, none the wiser. In fact, some the less wise.

On balance I felt it best to go for it like a particularly hungry dog at an uncommonly succulent rabbit; a mightily beefy bull at a gate that, in truth, has needed repairing for some time. 'Farley is dead,' I said. I then realised that I didn't actually know he was dead, had not wetted the illustrious corpse with my salty emissions so to speak and appended a prudent 'at least, I think so.'

The line went very quiet. Then, like the first notes of 'Mars, Bringer of War' – the sole classical piece I know, as the teachers thought it the only one with any hope of appealing to bellicose comprehensive schoolboys – her voice piped: 'What do you mean, you think so?' I had never heard anyone pipe before, without the aid of a pipe, and it had something of a chastening effect.

'He said he was,' I replied, deciding to adhere to the facts at hand, to forestall future piping.

'I don't want to pick holes in your logic at such a time, but if he said he was then surely he wasn't,' said Lydia, gaining a measure of control over her voice. 'This isn't some kind of stupid joke, is it?'

'I wish it was,' I said, sounding a bit too much like one of the more leaden TV detectives for my liking. 'He left a message on my voice mail last night saying he was about to commit suicide. He's in Cornwall, what do you think I should do?'

Lydia was quiet again. I guessed she was trying to outgape me on the other end of the line. I didn't really know why I was calling her. I suppose I just couldn't think straight and guessed she would have an idea of what to do, not that I expected her to have had much experience of having the most stable person she knew commit suicide miles away from his, and her, familiar surroundings.

'It doesn't sound very Farley. Do you believe he's dead? Have you tried contacting him? Have you tried calling the police?'

'No, I haven't. I thought I'd see what you thought first.'

'Well, I don't think, I haven't a clue. Have you tried calling the police?' The piping was returning but, despite it, I noted that Lydia is a woman not given to repeating herself without good reason. I realised that she was talking sense.

I was amazed that, even at times of high crisis, she had an instinctive feel for the correct course of action. 'The police, of course,' I said. 'Which police?'

'The British police, Harry, it'll be slower if you use the French.'

'Metropolitan or Cornish?' I asked weakly.

'Well, I don't know, do I? Start with the Metropolitan, they'll be able to tell you what to do.'

'What's the number?' I was sure 999 would be inappropriate. I'd say something ceases to be an emergency when the corpse has gone cold. However, I was aware I was being more than usually indecisive, so I quickly said I'd call directory enquiries. Lydia said something about us all being together that evening to offer mutual support. I didn't like this mutual idea one little bit. Farley hadn't even been her friend really. I didn't see why she needed support, she hadn't even liked him – she said he had a 'despicable attitude towards women', although Gerrard always thought it was because Lydia was the one person Farley wouldn't shag.

I'm not entirely without stain myself in this dept. That would have been my opinion too had I not known that Farley had in fact shagged Lydia, with great brio if she is to be believed, on several occasions. As she had said, it didn't improve her opinion of him but it did improve her sex life. When I had expressed surprise to Farley, he had said it was like having to start on the Pernod when there's not another decent drink in the house, so I could see that perhaps Lydia had a point on the despicable front. I still didn't see, however, how we would be offering 'mutual support'. I had fancied it would be a much more unidirectional affair, seeing as she had only slept with him. It's not like she was really his mate, in the non-zoological sense of the word.

I apologised to Lydia for upsetting her secretary but she told me not to worry. Apparently the girl got equally upset if anyone used the word 'famine', and could be seen to dab her eyes when she had to inform Lydia that job applicants were on the premises. The idea of anyone being rejected was too much for her.

I was surprised Lydia didn't seem more overtly upset. She didn't even seem that shocked, but she had been insistent there was no proof that he was yet dead.

I called directory enquiries for the local police's number. I am always a little bit apprehensive about tête-à-têtes with Plod. Like most people of my generation and class I had grown up regarding them as a kind of big-arsed, elasticated-trousered Gestapo. I firmly expected to go in to report a lost dog and emerge, twenty-five years later, a branded terrorist. People say that you know you're getting old when the police start to look young, but I think the true passage to maturity is marked when the sight of a policeman engenders relief rather than nervousness. I was still deep in the nervous territory.

As you would expect, I found the phone copper a good deal more composed than Lydia's secretary. She advised me to call Cornwall, but said she'd take my number. The woman asked me to get the Cornish police to phone her back to confirm I'd contacted her. I asked why they couldn't contact Cornwall themselves. 'Cost cutting,' said phone copper.

The Cornish police took an age to get me through to the right person but eventually a DC Arrowsmith came on the line and confirmed that a body had been found off the Newquay coast, and that they thought it was a man. I asked her what she meant by 'thought', as the criteria by which sex is judged seem fairly straightforward to me in humans.

'It's sometimes difficult to tell in cases of death at sea,' she said. 'If the genitalia are missing and various bits have been eaten or chewed up by boats, there's not a lot to go on to distinguish male from female. We can hardly find out if it likes the sound of its own voice.' She laughed heartily.

How wide the nation of women, I thought, remembering Lydia's secretary. I wondered what this copper looked like. I imagined her as slight and tough-looking, a face boiled hard by a poor upbringing and hearing too many sob stories. I had a very clear picture of her in my mind, but then I realised I was thinking of the woman out of that Scottish police series. I couldn't marry a policewoman anyway, too incompatible with my chosen forms of recreation.

'I haven't seen the body but it could be an unbelievable mess – face missing, the works. The trawlers get them. We had one that was only identifiable through the serial number on his colostomy bag. You wouldn't think you could lose your bollocks and keep your colostomy bag, but you can. Funny old world.' I reminded myself that policewomen had originally been employed to provide the 'gentle touch'. It made me speculate what the men must be like. I wondered if the apocryphal beatings suffered by my friends at the hands of the law in the eighties had simply been policemen trying to communicate. I feared that they were.

'Surely the fish can't get to him in under twelve hours?' I'd worked out that at the longest Farley could only have been in the water half a day. I later discovered that this assumption was wrong. He'd phoned on the Friday and I hadn't got the message till the Monday, but the normally razor-keen Chesshyre mental faculties aren't always at their silk scarf-slicing best at times like this. The policewoman repeated 'under twelve hours' in a rather sinister way and then ran through a fairly basic list of questions, from which it emerged that I was as near to next-of-kin as Farley had.

'He did say I was in his will,' I proffered.

DC Arrowsmith paused as if in thought at this point in a way that made me wish I had saved my proffering for another moment. She then asked me, in an unpleasantly relaxed and casual tone, for my address, Farley's address, and if I had a key. I explained that Farley had said on the answerphone message that he would send me one. The policewoman was very insistent that I should not touch it with my bare hands and that I should keep it safe until Cornish detectives contacted me.

She asked me for my answerphone number and code so she could hear Farley's message, and told me she'd phone it later. I told her when I would be in over the week and she said detectives would call me to arrange a meeting. And that was it. For the first time in my life I felt bad about having nothing to do. Nothing at all. Also, my innate suspicion of the police gave the spine a slight chill, especially when I considered Arrowsmith's telling pause over my information about the will. I nearly went back to looking through the complaint videos, but things weren't quite that bad.

3

A suitable period of mourning

I couldn't call Gerrard because he worked as a paramedic, a job he'd mysteriously ended up in after university, and was impossible to get hold of while he was at work, having a moral and physical antipathy to mobile phones. Gerrard had a resentment of anything that made life easier, from the spin dryer – wasteful of resources – to the car – don't get him, or it, started. His attitude to the mobile phone amazed me; he still looked on them as executive toys only used by poseurs. The practicality of being able to contact your friends on the move completely escaped him, as did the fact that every teenager in the country now possesses one. In Gerrard's book the mobile phone was still a fashion statement, and therefore bad. It would have to achieve the fashionless practicality of a postage stamp before he would be seen with one. Come to think of it, he didn't go much on 'showy designs' on postage stamps either. Using answer phones for screening out unwanted calls also drove him mad, as did car alarms, brand names of any kind, ties that were wider than a bootlace, and (I don't use the word lightly) a myriad of other things, but that's another story.

I did, however, leave a message at casualty telling Gerrard to call me whenever he got the chance.

The one advantage of having my kind of job is that no one need ever really know where you are. If I say I'm going to 'research with some complainants' Adrian will wave me off. If I wanted time off because my friend had died, that would be a different case all together. It is at times of great personal loss that the TV loser likes to show just how dedicated he is and Adrian would expect me to stay, probably longer than I would have done on a normal day. So saying something about a 'carpet that had fallen to bits inside a week', I headed for home.

'Kill 'em, tiger,' said Adrian.

As I ran for the lift in Covent Garden station, it did occur to me to wonder why I was rushing. There was nothing I could do. Also, I was heading for somewhere that mocked all haste with hot-breathed laughter that came from the bowels of the earth. When the trade in torture devices fell flat in England – around the middle of the nineteenth century – the makers of racks, thumbscrews and head crushers did not stay idle for long. They just got on with drawing up plans for its underground railway system: the tube. It is a truism, but also true, that the tube is a fine method of transport which is unrivalled in its ability to whisk you from one end of the city to another – provided you are in no particular hurry. If you are in a particular hurry, it would be better to walk – on your hands. If the Chinese had built the tube they would have quickly realised that it fell into the dominion of Monkey – God of Mischief and Frustrations, and a very good early 1980s TV series.

Londoners are largely inured to the tube. Being packed in like cattle and made to suffer death by a thousand cuts of minute delays is part of life for them. It's the visitors who really suffer. You see tourists on carriages, laughing at how ridiculously packed they are. And that is in mid-afternoon – before the rush hour starts. They don't realise that a tube train isn't really packed until your fingers go wrinkly like they do in the bath. One of the funnier thing is to hear a plaintive New World accent crying 'we can't get any more on' as a gaggle of fat bankers strong arm their way into the bulging carriage. An amusement of the damned, I suppose.

Anyway, as I was in no particular rush, the tube sped me to Fulham Broadway in a blink. It's not what you want that the railway frustrates, it's what you need.

When I arrived home the keys were waiting for me in the entrance to the hallway. Attached to them was a brightly printed label: 'Jay's Surf Gear, Bitchin' Price, £49.99'. Puzzlement didn't trouble my brow for long, however, as I picked it up and noticed the unprinted back of the label bore our address but no stamp. Next to the keys was a note on Royal Mail paper: 'Weren't in. Please leave £1.20 out tomorrow – Dave the postman'.

Dave the postman, I thought. Quite the village feel to it. I wasn't sure I liked it.

I automatically fed the dog, as I always did when I first got in – a good four hours early which meant that at least he was happy – and settled in to afternoon TV for half an hour before tackling the washing up. At 6 I was woken by Gerrard's return. Despite his slender frame, he is the only person I know who can slam a door open. He was mumbling something about 'fucking mess'.

It's sad but true that I was secretly pleased he was moaning on about untidiness because I held such a heavy trump in my hand. I knew this was an unworthy thought, but still I thought it.

He entered the front room, saying without pausing for hello, 'Can you take your dirty mugs out, please?' We had arrived at this agreed form of exchange because his preferred method of address – 'Have you any intention of clearing your fucking filth this fucking century?' – got up my nose. Gerrard had a problem with diplomacy. When we decided to do something about the amount of junk mail we get, flyers advertising pizzas and cab firms, all that sort of stuff, he had pinned a notice to our front door which read, 'Contrary to popular belief, this is not a waste paper recycling unit. Please deposit your shite elsewhere'. I think three lots of dog shit and five flattened drinks cans came through the door, along with all the junk mail, before he agreed to replace it with one saying, 'No flyers or circulars, please'.

Again I was faced with the how-to-present-a-sensitive-piece-of-news dilemma. I was mulling it over when I heard a voice not unlike my own say, 'I got a phone call from Farley today.' 'Oh, yes,' said Gerrard. 'What did he say?' 'Oh, this and that,' said the voice, which I now realised was coming from my mouth. 'Oh,' said Gerrard and went out into the kitchen. I used to get this problem at school when I was in any kind of trouble. I used to want to say 'sorry' but somehow smart remarks just seemed to come from nowhere. My nan used to have an expression: Before putting mouth into gear, check to see brain is engaged. I often forgot this and my words came kangarooing out without getting me anywhere in particular. Blake used to think the Archangel Gabriel dictated poetry to him through his kitchen window. I wondered if Gabriel had now run out of poetry and was concentrating on putting bollocks into my mouth.

I gingerly followed Gerrard into the kitchen, now in possession of most of my faculties. He was slicing carrots. One of the things I admire about Gerrard is his ability to come in from work and get straight on with various tasks. I need a good two-hour run up of tea drinking and TV watching before I get mobile.

'Gerrard, I really need to speak to you,' I said. This was one removed from the 'sit down' stamp of news breaking but my options were few.

'Speak,' said Gerrard.

'Farley's dead,' I said, once more in the school of bull vs gate.

'So what?' said Gerrard.

'No, I mean he is dead. He's killed himself.'

'Do I look stupid?'

I think my silence was what worried him. The question 'Do I look stupid?' is only one side of a coin. No one in normal circumstances can resist saying 'yes' or 'don't tempt me' or shrugging their shoulders or something, no matter how sophisticated they are. I tried to look sombre, even though Gerrard did look stupid.

'Are you serious?'

'I am.' My face bore a suitably downcast expression. I was downcast, after all.

'Christ,' said Gerrard. 'No wonder he didn't contact me.'

'It only happened yesterday,' I said.

'Oh,' said Gerrard, a little disappointed. 'Still, he must have been miserable for weeks. Christ.' He blew out heavily and sat down. We were silent for a minute or so. I was aware of the traffic outside, boxes of metal whirring on to unknown destinations.

'How did he kill himself? Not too much mess, I hope,' said Gerrard, the second being a professional paramedic's concern. 'Did he do it deliberately?' I think sometimes people want details of a particularly gruesome suicide as evidence of the depth of despair someone was feeling. Overdose? Cry for help gone wrong. Jumped in front of train? That's more like it, that's a real suicide. I can't say this line of thought is to my taste. If someone's disturbed enough to make a cry for help, it doesn't seem too great a leap to conclude that they need help. However, in Gerrard's defence, his job meant it probably took a lot to impress him in the goodbye-cruel-world stakes.

I told him about the phone call, the police, Lydia and the keys. The latter I had unwisely left on the kitchen table. Gerrard picked them up. He suspended them in front of him by their label, like an antiques expert examining a potentially rare find.

I offered him the note the postman had written. He placed the keys back on the table and read the note. Strangely he smiled, a proud little smile.

'They're marvellous the Royal Mail, aren't they?' said Gerrard, gazing at the note. 'Remarkable.'

I looked at him blankly. 'Yes, it's remarkable. Much more remarkable than our mate being dead, in fact.'

'Yeah, but delivering it with just that label ... it's incredible, isn't it?'

He moved over to Trevor the rubbish sculpture in the corner and emptied his top half into a black bin liner. He deftly twirled the bag to a close and tied it. Then he went out of the kitchen, through the front door and put the bag outside. I knew he was shocked. There was no way he would have taken the bin out when he thought it was my turn otherwise.

He sat down at the table. 'So what made him do it?'

'This girl, I suppose.'

'Christ,' said Gerrard, an avowed atheist with a passing respect for Buddhism, despite a conventional Jewish upbringing. 'I just don't see Farley killing himself over a woman. It's like he said – life goes on. You don't see him crying about it.' He scratched disconsolately at his arse. 'Mind you, you do see him committing suicide over it. Christ.'

'We don't know that he's dead, he could have just been pissed. For all we know he's forgotten all about it and just gone surfing.'

'Why would he send the keys?' asked Gerrard. 'And you said the police have found a body.'

I didn't answer his first question. 'True, but that's what policemen do, isn't it? They're always finding bodies – it's their job. It's like the dog coming back with a tennis ball.'

Mark Barrowcliffe

I knew I was on thin ice here. The chances looked good that Farley was dead.

'It shouldn't have sunk in yet,' said Gerrard, as I winced at his unhappy metaphor, 'but it has. I'm gutted. I'm outraged. I really thought Farley might be able to help me out. You know, tell me the secrets of the magic circle. If he's topped himself where does that leave the rest of us?'

I had to concede this was a good point, if a little selfish.

'What do you reckon this girl is like?' It was a thought that had been on both of our minds, I was sure.

'She must be pretty special. I mean, he's not what you'd call the romantic type. You can't see him going to pick people up on a motorbike.'

Gerrard hated the fact that I used to pick Emily up from her house in North London on my bike and bring her the eight miles over to Fulham. He didn't see why she couldn't get the tube, reasoning that I was wasting resources just to try to make myself more attractive to a girl. He overlooked important points – I liked driving my motorbike and I liked doing something nice for Emily. She had disliked the tube intensely and found it intimidating. Gerrard had become infuriated with her when he had pointed out that being on a tube was statistically less dangerous than walking down the street, and a lot less dangerous than being on a motor-bike, but she had still said she didn't like them. He thought he could confront her fears with numbers and they would just disappear. Gerrard couldn't see that my behaviour wasn't entirely cynical – just to make Emily dependent on me. I would admit it was slightly cynical. Nothing a man says or does for a woman he finds attractive is ever without the ulterior motive of getting her to like him more or making him feel good about himself. In fact, nothing nice a man ever does at all is ever free from the spectre of making himself more sexually attractive. But sometimes it is nice just to be nice. Honest.

'No, but he's not an android, he must have wanted love too.'

'I can't see it,' said Gerrard. 'Look at the way he behaved.'

'You can judge everything from a person's behaviour apart from their thoughts,' I said, quite pleased with myself for that.

'What's that supposed to mean?' said Gerrard. 'It doesn't mean anything, does it?'

'I don't know.' I was trying to think of examples to show how the aphorism fitted reality, but it wasn't really working.

'You can guess exactly what Farley thought from his actions. He went around on a permanent shagorama, met someone who wouldn't have him, ego took a huge knock – bingo. Suicide.' Gerrard thumped the kitchen table, endangering some flowers that Lydia had cut from the garden and placed in a vase. 'It seems obvious to me.' I didn't know we even had flowers in the garden.

I resisted the temptation to ask Gerrard if he had ever considered a career as a TV psychiatrist, one of the 'people suffering from paranoia may often read bad intentions into the innocent actions of others' brigade. I couldn't accept, though, that an ego dent would make Farley kill himself. I was constantly having to eat shit over poor jobs, unfancied girlfriends, unfulfilled expectations, yet I faced my weekends bouncy as a bunny. Suicide was far from my thoughts.

'I can't see it would just be ego. He must have loved her.'

'Farley didn't know the meaning of love,' said Gerrard.

'Do any of us?' I said, inwardly wishing I hadn't used such a question, which fell into the category of what car salesmen call 'pre-owned'.

'Have you ever considered a career as a shit screenwriter?' asked Gerrard. This was unnecessarily cruel, because he knew that I had. Not just a screenwriter, but a screenwriter of dross. I don't know why it appealed to me to see myself turning out wilful rubbish, but it did. It also made me marvel at the irresistibility of childish humour. Our friend was dead. If ever we should have found time for serious reflection this was it. But we kept coming back to the old patterns of speech, the chimp grooming rituals. I felt we should attempt to deal with it, to say something profound. As a matter of respect we should ponder emptiness or mortality or something. This should be a great bonding moment between me and Gerrard. I gave it a go.

'Makes you think though, doesn't it?' I said, realising that the line was hardly likely to be remembered as one of the great philosophical openings of our age. Gerrard looked at me with the horror of a man who had found his holiday was not matching the brochure.

'Makes me think what a load of bollocks life is,' he said sourly.

'It makes me think you can't trust anyone.' This, again, was hardly up there with the great moments of mourning in literature and cinema, but it was moving in the right direction. Worthy of a gritty inner-city TV drama, perhaps.

'What do you mean by trust?'

'No one is what they seem any more. No one puts in the window what they've got in the shop. When we had the gas man round the other day, you know what he told me? He'd just signed a record deal and was packing up to become a pop star. So we don't even get a gas man any more, we get a peak-capped ponce of a pop star. Nothing's what it seems any more, no one's true to themself.'

'Are you?' I asked. I didn't think this was much up from 'do any of us?' but there you go.

'I try to be,' said Gerrard, meaning, 'Yes, most certainly.'

'Why was Farley not true?'

'Because he was boasting about being Jack the Lad when all along he was just as much of a mess as the rest of us, though maybe in a different way. He was a sham.' I wasn't sure that Farley had ever boasted exactly, although I had boasted on his behalf, obtaining a kind of vicarious glory from stories about his life.

'You said it was the dent to his ego that made him kill himself. Perhaps it was something more – like someone who's always swum in the shallows suddenly finding himself in the open sea. Maybe that's what he did with this girl.' I was in shit metaphor territory myself there. Perhaps that's what death does to you.

'That's what I mean – he wasn't as big and brave as he said he was. He was a sham.' I feared Gerrard was going to start crying and that I would have to leave the room. Luckily for both of us, his eyes remained dry.

I couldn't really believe that Gerrard would get so upset by thinking he was wrong about the way Farley presented himself. It was obvious that Farley was a very complex character; such unusual commitment to a life of shallow pleasures showed that he was something out of the ordinary, if not in a wholly nice way. Gerrard seemed almost as let down as he had been by Paula's leaving him.

It made me think what we are doing when we mourn someone. You're mourning the fact you will never see them again, and that they will never taste life's pleasures again, but when the strong crumble and the sparkling lose their shine you're mourning something else as well. You're mourning the death of an idea – of an original way of living. You might not even like the person who's dead, but still you are upset. There is another reason too.

'Christ,' said Gerrard, 'that's the second mate of mine who's died. It all speeds up from now, doesn't it? They drop like ninepins until one day it's you. My gran said it all got faster after you were twenty-one. Christ . . . oh, Christ, Christ, Christ, Christ, Christ.'

Gerrard has a unique talent for making an already depressing situation truly desolate. I cracked open a lager, asking him if he wanted one. He said nothing but went to the fridge and got out one of his special Czech weird lagers that he'd carried back, heavy as a family curse, all the way from Prague. No wonder he got annoyed when I kept drinking them. Not only did it annoy him that I drank them, it annoyed him that I drank them lukewarm from their normal hiding place in his bedroom cupboard whenever I got in drunk. If I was going to thieve them, he reasoned, I may as well have the full benefit of them ice cold. Other people would have wished that I choked on the beer, but even when being robbed he was a perfectionist on the thief's behalf.

It was strange that I was having these thoughts, but I had no guide to what thoughts I was meant to have. Overwhelming grief, the sun never rising again, etc., seemed some way off. I couldn't tell how I felt. On the miserable side of things for sure, but I knew that I was only a beat away from laughing – not at Farley's death but because I'm only a beat away from laughing whatever the time and place. The only time I haven't been is when threatened with physical harm by bullies at school or once when I hurt a girl very badly, not physically obviously, but terror and shame are the only emotions that outscore levity. The others just wipe it away momentarily. I suppose laughter's the easier response, isn't it? I preferred to think that I wasn't laughing at Farley's death but with it, a kind of cosmic laughter. No, that's not true, is it? I was just being shallow, I suppose.

You can't really blame me, though. Unlike Gerrard, I have only known old people die before and, even though I cared for them, I felt nothing at their deaths. Or rather, the feelings I was meant to have had at that special time had difficulty overriding the feelings

I normally had day to day. I remember my Great Auntie Daisy, who I was very close to, having the misfortune to die on a Saturday night when I was twenty-eight. She was a remarkable figure, a pugilistic 4'10" who communicated with the neighbours via solicitor's letter. She once went to court for breaking the foot of a Mormon who had put it into her door way. While wondering that a woman of her size could slam a door hard enough to break anyone's foot, the magistrate concluded that the Mormon, all 6'5" of him, shouldn't have had it in the doorway in the first place. He'd also noted that the Mormon had been given a clear warning: 'Take your filthy foot out of my lovely hallway.' My auntie was found not guilty and had to be restrained from having another go at the Mormon on the way out of the court. When it came to fear, she was a giver rather than a receiver. She'd worked the same shifts as the men all through Hitler's bombs. It took a bit more than a giant God botherer to set her nerves jangling.

Daisy lived in a tiny two up, two down on the top of a hill and kept copies of its ground plan in a drawer. As soon as she considered me old enough to drink – about seven, I think – she would ply me with vast quantities of raw Scotch whisky. I soon got to realise that she filled the glass to the same mark whether you had your whisky straight or with ginger. I had mine straight. She'd pull out the plans to show me her grounds. 'If next door let their cat anywhere near my beautiful home,' she'd said, causing me to wonder even at that age and state of drunkenness how you let or do not let a cat do anything, 'I'll have them – bang!' She'd crash her own whisky tumbler down on the table and sweep her hand across the plans like an evil genius in a kids' cartoon. Later we'd go up to the back bedroom to jibe at the neighbours in their back yard through the window. The neighbour ran a dog-grooming business from home and my auntie did not approve.

'I'm watching you, my lady,' she'd shout. 'Look, Harry, she scrawps those dogs in the same sink as she does the cabbages.' Needless to say the public health officer had been called on several occasions and, to everyone else's surprise, he pretty much agreed with my auntie on the hygiene of the premises. 'He said it was filthy – and he's a darkie!' said my auntie, whose opinion of the cleanliness of anyone from the Indian sub-continent was not of the highest. He became, in her eyes, a great ally – an unenviable position. Luckily for him the nearest phone box to her house was a mile away up a steep hill. As her health declined and walking became very painful, she could only crawl up to telephone him a couple of times a week, although she kept a list so she didn't forget anything.

I visited her on the night of her death and found her with the window open, looking up at the bright cold stars. Her jackdaw's eyes had fear in them for the first time that I ever remember. The cancer had left her very thin, and she lay on her back, arms raised to greet me, so she looked like a scared little monkey reaching for its mother. I left before the end, not because I couldn't stand to watch her die but because my mates were waiting in the pub and I'd been out every Saturday night since I was fifteen. Besides, others were there to do the caring, my nan and my mum. Even as I went I wondered what it would take to make me stay in on a Saturday night, what crisis would be big enough to keep me away from the rituals of drink and jokes. Perhaps the grief and sadness do come, but only later and for a moment. They're coming now but I know by this evening, when the dog has been walked and friends telephoned and I'm on my way to wherever, they will be as distant as the stars that chilled my auntie with their call.

If the psychiatrists are to be believed, sadness sometimes comes in other forms, in rashes and hair loss. I have to say that my hair line is the same as it was when I was nine and my skin blemish-free. It's as if my brain has a defence mechanism against these feelings.

Also, I think situations have a weight to them. There are some friends with whom you always have that interesting conversation; others you're just with for whatever reason, humour or longevity of relationship or whatever. Particular exchanges, an interesting conversation or talk about sport, seem to happen every time you see that friend, you never have any other sort. Gerrard and I in the kitchen was always a situation of slightly confrontational banter, wannabe witticisms and cheap half cracks, or it was just arguing about the washing up. That was the form. If you introduced another element – sadness, grief, whatever – the form couldn't cope and kept trying to reassert itself through the conversation. It's not that we weren't upset for Farley, and for ourselves because we'd lost a mate, just that it's difficult to keep the grief in your head the whole time. It's like we just go back to what we know, pull the humour down about us like a duvet to shield us from the cold outside. Maybe this was what Gerrard was doing when he was commending the fine work of the Royal Mail, maybe it was a weak joke. Or perhaps Farley was just a cipher to us, representative of a whole way of life, enabling us to bask in his reflected cool. Perhaps we'd just go out and get another Farley like you get another video recorder when the old one breaks down. Was that why he didn't hit our grief buttons?

'Shall we go and get pissed?' I suggested.

'Of course,' said Gerrard.

If necessity is the mother of invention, drink is the brother of detention. I'm sure that if you took beer away half the ill-conceived, half-hearted, botched attempts at criminality or stupid schemes would evaporate overnight. I know this isn't exactly a revelation, but I'm looking for excuses for our subsequent behaviour. The chief theme of the evening provided the main reason for what was, on paper, the single worst idea available to us at that moment, short of self-immolation or taking out a time share.

The theme of the evening was: 'What was the girl Farley had killed himself over really like?'

We knew she must be pretty good-looking, that was certain. Farley would never fall big time for a dog. We could also guess that she must be pretty glam – in a movie-star sort of way. Farley didn't like homespun, girl-next-door types. He went for the Chanel No. 5, smelling like a cosmetics counter at ninety paces women if he could get them. We had no idea if she would be clever or not. The only time Farley had gone out with someone for more than a few days they had been fairly dim. I don't know if he liked to feel in control, but I doubted it. He was clever enough to stand on his own two feet without having to have a thick girlfriend to make him feel better.

He didn't need to be dominant. He didn't want other people to do what he wanted to do; he would just do what he wanted to do and sod everyone else. Girls either fell in with him or they left. Is that domination? In one way I suppose it is.

It's not like he didn't make the women feel special, ask about them or whatever. Farley was a curious blend of being interested in others and being totally self-seeking. Perhaps he just compiled information on people in order to be able to get his way more easily. Or perhaps it made him feel more human, studying people and thinking about them, he just wasn't human enough to act on it. Why did I like him? He was witty, which in Lad World excuses most sins up to war criminal status.

So would she be bright, this girl? Gerrard said no, and I kind of agreed with him. I'd always admired Farley's ability to score with dim girls. I only ever made it with clever, or at least intelligent, ones. I honestly had no idea what you say to the thick ones. This isn't snobbery – I'd be delighted if someone would come along and tell me. What do they want, these girls? Is it something more, less or different from what you offer the university classes? Maybe the answer is you can't score with them unless you can access the thick part of yourself. This is something I found difficult – I could be stupid or thoughtless or a prat, but thick was difficult for me. I'd built my whole personality from school on being bright, so if I was chatting up some girl and talking about – I'm improvising here – soap opera, I couldn't resist saying something a bit clever, no matter how wanky and obvious. 'Have you noticed there aren't any black people in *Coronation Street*?' I'd say, and the girl would look at me as if I'd proposed coprophilia there on the dance floor.

Farley had told me that what you actually do with thick girls is recount the story line of soaps in fine detail. Generally, he said, soaps were safe ground, but you have to know how to argue about them. Points of contention arise when you forget that it was Deidre, not Kate, who was sleeping with the factory owner. Kate had fancied him but had gone off him when he refused to help her father out financially. You can comment on the morals of the characters, 'He's a right bastard, him,' being a useful line. I hadn't really believed this but Farley had assured me that it worked. Shagging girls who were too thick to follow the plot of soaps was an entirely different technique, but tragically he had never told me how to do that. Saying something about how difficult it is getting someone to look after the baby during prison visits, I had guessed. But would Farley kill himself because he couldn't face a lifetime discussing the plot of *Emmerdale Farm*?

It had to be something more than that.

It was 9 o'clock. I'd bought my sixth pint and Gerrard's third – our normal drinking rate – before we both had the bad idea, almost simultaneously. The conclusion we reached had the inevitability of a mathematical equation. Since Farley had regularly scored with girls way out of our class, and that this one was something special even by his standards, she must be a rare looker. Since neither Gerrard nor I would have the courage to approach such a woman under normal circumstances but now we were presented with a gilt-edged opportunity to meet and 'console' her. Upset girl, shoulder to cry on, excuse for physical proximity . . . It all added up, to Gerrard and to me. I was no more proud of these thoughts than I could resist them. If you'd asked me in the cold light of day, would I want to seduce the newly dead Farley's girlfriend, I would have said no, but I wasn't in the cold light of day, I was in the warm light of beer. I knew the thoughts were wrong but . . . oh, well. Naturally I didn't bother to share these thoughts with Gerrard. I knew he was having them himself.

'I wonder if she knows he's dead?' said Gerrard.

'Unless he phoned her, the police didn't mention anything.'

'I don't suppose they would, but she should know.'

'Definitely.'

'How are we going to tell her?'

It was that moment that Lydia, on clouds of wrath, entered the pub. I remembered that she had been looking to console me, or to work towards mutual support, and would have gone round to the flat. I shuddered. Upset Chesshyre, shoulder to cry on, excuse for physical proximity. It's not that I found Lydia particularly physically objectionable, just that I find everyone physically objectionable who's not going out with me. It's like I allow one licence for people to touch me and that's only issued to the person I'm going out with. I don't even like shaking hands with blokes when I meet them.

I said something about being very sorry and about forgetting in all the confusion. Marginally mollified, she went to the bar.

'Does she look like she's lost weight to you?' I asked Gerrard.

'No, but then I never look at her.'

'What do you mean, you never look at her?'

'She makes me feel sick, so I never look at her.'

'I thought you liked her?'

'I do, sort of, but I just don't like to look at her.'

I could have criticised Gerrard's despicably sexist attitude, but then I realised you can't criticise someone for how they feel. You could no more criticise Gerrard for feeling sick when he looked at Lydia than you could criticise our old dog for being sick in the car. Unfortunately you couldn't put Gerrard into kennels until he got better. Well, you could, but eventually someone would notice. Even a greyhound isn't quite that thin a beast.

Lydia pull up a chair and I moved round, ostensibly to give her more space but really so no one would think I was going out with her. You might think this is weird, as I'd once considered her as a life partner, but then I consider everyone as a life partner – apart from Gerrard, of course. One day I will be rid of him.

'Any news?' asked Lydia.

'Not really, though they've found a body. Or a bit of one anyway.'

'Which bit?' said Gerrard.

'Didn't think to ask,' I said.

Lydia looked faintly ill, or iller.

'He said he'd done this over a girl?'

'Apparently.'

'Was this the girl he mentioned last time we were at your house?' Lydia tapped at the table. I wondered if anyone would ever commit suicide over Lydia, the flattering kind of suicide, I mean.

'Unless he'd fallen in love again since we met.'

'Not that unlikely,' said Gerrard.

Someone started playing the fruit machine next to us, which was the kind that says 'bad luck' in an American accent if you fail to win. Gerrard scowled in distaste and moved closer to Lydia to avoid the player's cigarette. Now it looked like *he* was going out with her. She began to roll a cigarette and I could see Gerrard cursing his luck for being caught in the crossfire. I knew he wouldn't move, he didn't want to risk upsetting the smoker who was practically blinding him with a B&H. I can't say I blamed him. The man looked the sort who could split walnuts with his eyelids.

'Do you think she knows what's happened?' Lydia was doing the concerned look again which, even at times of genuine concern, made me feel uneasy.

'I don't think so,' I said.

'Someone should tell her.'

'I don't mind,' said me and Gerrard, as a man.

Lydia looked at us like a school teacher who has just come in to find her pupils writing rude words on the blackboard.

'You're not going to try to get off with her, are you?'

'Bad luck,' said the fruit machine.

'I may as well have a look at her,' said Gerrard. 'I'm free at the moment and at least I won't have Harry spoiling it for me.'

'The next time you play you may win the jackpot,' said the fruit machine. Gerrard later confirmed you could detect a distinct note of sarcasm in its voice.

This competition thing has always been a large bone of contention between us. The problem when we go out together is that Gerrard thinks I deliberately try to spoil his chances of getting off with women, out of a malicious sense of fun.

'It's like when I try to chat up a girl at a party, you always butt in. You either get off with her or you ruin it for both of us with your elephantine intrusions. You can't just be happy for your friends if they're in with someone,' he'd protest.

He claims that other friends of his would help him chat up the girl by talking to her and telling her what a nice bloke he was.

I had several problems with this. Firstly, he was not a nice bloke. Interesting, witty, yes. Nice, no. I wouldn't have liked him if he'd been nice, some of my nastiest times have been with nice people – walking on eggshells in case you offend them by mentioning a serious subject in a light-hearted way or something. Secondly, when he said 'friends' he meant 'friend', and I knew the friend he was talking about. Far from being a selfless smoother of the way, I thought this friend was playing the 'He's a nice bloke, but think how much nicer I am for telling you that' card.

The 'friend' had also repeatedly stated his interest in a *ménage à trois* involving Gerrard, or anyone. In fact, the friend had said he was no longer interested in sex between only two people at all anymore. This gave his unctuous felicitations on Gerrard's behalf an unpleasant tang of self-interest. Thirdly, Gerrard's approach to a woman he finds attractive is so subtle as to be undetectable to the naked eye. It's the kind of UFO of an approach that is recorded only on blurry video images, related in tales by hicks from the back woods and that sceptics claim is a rumour spread by the credulous and mendacious. I'm sure an FBI investigation, given open-minded agents, could pick it up, but me on my own? No.

Of course Gerrard would argue that the mere fact that he was talking to the girl meant he was making an approach – single men do not talk to single women for long at parties unless they are interested in them sexually. If Gerrard was not interested in a girl sexually he would just talk to someone else. It's not like he was looking to make new friends or anything – he'd done that in freshers' week fourteen years ago and wasn't about to do it again. I knew he was right here, but, well, every man for himself.

It's not that I try to butt in on Gerrard, there's just an unfortunate clash of style. There are various methods with women and I favour the direct, the ABC as it's known – Always Be Closing. It's adapted from sales techniques and is often used by salesmen in their spare time. Demonstrate the goods, meet the client's objections, overcome them, close the deal. That way a quick rejection or acceptance is secured and everyone gets on with their lives.

ABC is by no means the only approach to women. Others include the Trout Tickler – normally coming from a touchy-feely kind of man with scant knowledge of the sexual harassment laws, who starts with an arm around the back of the chair sensing for any feedback, goes on to snake the arm around the back proper then, by degrees, on to the full tongue lunge, unless resistance is encountered. This is an adolescent staple that, surprisingly, works for some people into middle age.

Then there's the incredibly direct – the request for sex in the first few sentences. That's one best left to the devastatingly handsome, the famous and the mentally ill.

Despite what I've said about my dark days in Tomangos, Pale and Interesting can work well but you have to choose what you are interesting about and stick to using it in the kitchens at parties, talking to girls who are going to go to lots of galleries when they get round to it.

A few years ago politics would have done for a theme for the Pale and Interesting man. That, of course, is quite out of the question today. It has the same sex appeal as traction engines, with its odour of chips in late-night committee rooms and the sweat of men with beards. It is what earnest people who have never been in a night club do with their evenings. While the rest of us are enjoying ourselves, they are talking about the wants of 'ordinary men and women' – wants that can't be of any possible interest to civilised company and often involve parking and fitted kitchens. Besides, women today are no longer interested in politics. They are too busy trying to change the world.

For Mr Pale and Interesting, poetry might suffice – though again, most men choose to keep the slim volume more carefully hidden than the pornography nowadays, which they don't choose to keep hidden at all.

No, today is the era of popular culture, so you had better bone up on pop music, football and television if you want to make it. You could try opera, ballet and classical music too, as no one – at least at the parties I go to – knows anything at all about them any more. However, many people like the idea of knowing lots about them, so by offering a quick guide through your Margot Fonteins, or whoever, you might get someone to sleep with you out of gratitude that they didn't have to bother listening to her records themselves.

Talking of listening, a standard is the 'Mr Listener' approach, the kind of 'tell me all about yourself' line. This is meant to be the one which works best, but most of the blokes I know who use it extract a fairly hefty payback once they're actually going out with the girl, normally in asserting the right to express their own opinions through a loud hailer inches from the ear for a limited period of forty years or so. Its other major disadvantage is that it features in so many 'how to chat up the girl of your dreams' articles that she's bound to suspect something. It's not easy either. Most men haven't practised it since before adolescence, if at all. My Auntie Daisy used to contend that men had their ears blocked up when they came out of short trousers. My Uncle Jim would always say, 'Pardon?'

Other approaches include the 'chuckle her knickers off' bloke – he's normally tried and failed as a stand up comedian, or is thinking of becoming a stand up comedian. At one time every bloke you met had been in a band. Before long every bloke you meet will have been a stand up too. Still, there's something to be gained out of the 'I don't know how you've got the courage to do it' response from girls.

On top of this there is the straightforward 'tell her how much money you've got and what car you drive' – that goes down poorly with most of the artsy women in my demographic. If you want to play the wealth card with them you have to do it subtly, and I can't give any advice on how to do that as I have no wealth. Maybe you start collecting art, as I know a number of famous blokes on the tug do. It has the dual appeal of showing they're loaded and hinting at emotional depth, which we've already established is a key bird puller and self-esteem bolsterer, even if almost no men actually have any.

Finally, of course, there is the Search and Destroy – SAD to those in the know. This is the chap who approaches every woman in the room in turn until he either finds one mad enough to take him or they all hoof off in disgust. Generally this approach is best left to the truly desperate, which is why most of us find ourselves doing it from time to time, even though we know it is pretty much doomed. There is a sub-category of SAD who mentions his favourite names for children within seconds of collaring a girl, but good taste prevents me from going into detail here.

In fact, all of these approaches leave the mustard distinctly uncut with some women and all clearly contain the possibility of failure – she might not like the sense of humour, she might have nothing to say about herself or she just might hate you.

This is why Gerrard casts his bread on none of these waters. The chance of failure is too great. His approach could be termed 'ambient'. He finds it impossible to actually let the girl know he fancies her and expects her to pick up on it through a series of glances, although of course he immediately looks away if she should look directly at him.

He also employs a tiny hopping movement of the foot, which I must credit as an outlet for nerves. It's insupportable to think that he regards it as attractive. In his black and white world the girl either fancies him or she doesn't. So if he talks to her for long enough, or just stands near her for long enough, she'll give him the sort of green light he requires. This is not a subtle green light, as might be found twinkling invitingly on a Christmas tree. That wouldn't do at all. He wants a mighty laser searing its way into the night sky, etching the clouds with 'Gerrard, come and get me' in burning emerald. If she doesn't fancy him there's no point in him embarrassing himself by taking a punt at her, turning on the greasy charm. Or that is his philosophy. As he once said: 'She's not likely to change her mind, is she?' I pointed out that if he was right, bang goes the plot of most films ever to come out of

Bollywood. 'I hadn't thought of that,' he'd said, sawing at an itch in his armpit. He had a great respect for anything from the east.

So my point is that it's difficult not to get in there before Gerrard. I have normally introduced myself, made a series of ham-fisted attempts at humour and retired hurt before he has got off the starting blocks. The conversations normally begin with Gerrard talking about his insomnia – a subject on which he can be quite droll, for the first hour or so, then I pull up. I hover around, hearing snatches of 'warm milk and honey' and 'then a car alarm goes off'. Sometimes I wonder why he doesn't make a tape recording of this stuff and play it to himself whenever he wants to nod off. It works for me every time. Eventually he gets to a subject on which I can join in.

Gerrard is saying something like, 'Oh my God, I can't believe you know X from X, have you seen her recently?' He takes a little hop and gives the girl a glance that is over quicker than an Italian government.

The woman says, 'Oh, yes, I saw her last week.' Gerrard spies my flag on the horizon and quickly goes into defensive mode, back towards, body stance wide to take up as much space as possible, like a football defender shielding the ball.

'How [hop] is she [glance].'

'She's well,' says the girl.

I achieve eye contact with the girl and smile. I say, over his shoulder, 'Gerrard, you haven't introduced me.'

'No, I [glance at girl] haven't,' says Gerrard, also over his shoulder.

The woman says, 'My name is Y,' and extends her hand. At this point Gerrard is duty bound to move, which he does with the mannered good grace of an old English aristocrat surrendering his family pile to an oil millionaire.

I say, 'I'm Harry, pleased to meet you. Who do you know at the party?'

'We [hop] were [glance] just [hop, hop] talking about [hop, hop, hoppity] X,' says Gerrard through a ballroom dancer's grin.

'Oh, X, I was great friends with her. Does she still wear those amazing dresses?' I say.

'She does,' says the woman. 'She had on this incredible Versace number last time I saw her.' A description follows of folds, sequins, bits of crêpe, etc., which I make a fair fist of looking interested in. I say things like, 'Oh, I love that,' while Gerrard gazes blankly into space in the background, like a war film heroine who has just been told her husband's plane is missing.

After a while, during which I will have attempted to mention at least two former girlfriends to show her I'm not a loser, and Lydia to do the emotional depth bit, Gerrard will wake from his reverie, rejoining the conversation as was ten minutes previously.

'I [hop] like [glance] Versace,' says Gerrard – who is not quite sure if Versace is a dressmaker or a tennis player and who regards buying anything fancy as a waste of funds that could be going to the Third World.

'Oh, I don't,' I say. 'Whoever makes those dresses wants shooting.'

Gerrard at this point goes into a paroxysm of hops and glances that would lead fellow partygoers to believe he had come late but keen to Irish dancing. To the girl, however, he has spelled out in Morse code, 'Despite my earlier charm, I am a dangerous lunatic. Flee.' And if my luck goes to form, she's Versace's niece or something and heads off in tears. In fact, that's not true as I would never meet Versace's niece – I would meet a girl doing a PhD about camp fashion in the post-war period or making a programme on it. She'd still be upset, though.

'If anyone goes round to break the news to this poor woman it should be me,' Lydia asserts, 'she doesn't need either of you two making grabs at her. She's going to feel bad enough as it is – she'll feel so guilty he killed himself for her.'

'Well done,' said the fruit machine. I had had just about enough of its comments.

I didn't know if Lydia had ulterior motives, but I thought they were worth a passing examination

'I suppose you're not at all curious to see what this girl looks like yourself, are you?'

'Jackpot!' said Gerrard in a fruit-machine voice. Its tattooed operator gave him the beady eye, drew on his fag and inserted another coin.

'I can't believe,' said Lydia, 'Farley's dead and we're arguing like this.'

'You still haven't answered his question,' said Gerrard.

'I just want to save her from you two.'

'So it's OK to expose her to your curiosity, not OK to expose her to ours?'

On a surface level I knew Gerrard was talking a lot of sense here. We were ignoring, however, the question of lust. How you can feel lust for someone you haven't seen? Don't ask me, but I think both Gerrard and I were feeling lust simply for the idea of this girl. Some people who get marooned or stuck up a mountain or something are capable of enjoying the idea of a good meal or the idea of a good bottle of wine. Gerrard and I, stuck up a metaphorical mountain, just enjoyed the idea of this beautiful girl. I know it's not on to compare women to food – but, oh, well.

'You're missing a big practicality here,' said Lydia.

'Which is?'

'We don't know her name or where she's from.'

True enough. Farley had not bothered to tell us her name. I thought that, being a part of the past – or a non-possible future as one of Gerrard's more hippie mates had termed unattainable dreams – he had simply deleted her from his memory file. I hadn't thought he would delete himself.

'We have the keys to his flat,' said Gerrard.

'The police told me to stay away from the keys and not to touch them,' I told him.

'So where are they now?' Gerrard had the air of a gangster chief explaining the attractions of crime to a nervous first timer. 'You can run with the mooks or you can be a wise guy, Harry baby. What's it gonna be?' Obviously, he didn't actually say this.

'In my pocket.'

'We just go round to his house, pick out her number from his address book or whatever and call her,' said the real Gerrard.

'You're not on your fourth pint, are you, Gerrard?' Lydia was incredulous. 'How are you going to find her number? You'd never find her number out of all the thousands of girls' numbers Farley's got even if his address book's there. And I don't think the police would be very happy about you going round to his flat. They might want to investigate it.'

'The police aren't very happy about a lot of things we do, but still we do them,' said Gerrard, in ice cool mode. 'And I'll call every one of them if I have to.'

I had to hand it to him there, I was thinking small-time. Just the one girl. In fact Farley had banks of potential partners and we had the golden opportunity to contact them all.

'I bet you don't even know where he lives.' Lydia had guessed, correctly, that we had never been round to Farley's flat. Farley hardly ever went there, so why should we? There wasn't a bar in his flat, or any women. Well, not unless he'd been out to get one, if you see what I mean. However she had not guessed that, after his inheritance, he had sent me a 'change of address' card. I'd had it in my coat pocket ever since, along with a host of red bills, foreign coins from my last two holidays and some string. I hoiked it out.

'Christ,' said Gerrard, 'a change of address card.'

'Not exactly what you'd expect, is it, but here it is.'

The card, bizarrely, bore a picture of Puss-in-Boots with a spotted handkerchief on a stick across his shoulder heading off towards a castle in the hills. It was slightly mucky around the edges from being in my pocket for so long.

'Why did he choose one with Puss-in-Boots on it? Is it a joke?' asked Lydia.

'Something like that,' I said. I didn't bother to point out to her that sending a change of address card was miraculous enough. Not picking out the very first set that came to hand in the shop was above and beyond the call. Farley would have gone for the nearest. As long as I had lived, it was one of three cards I had ever received from a male friend. One of those was an air freshener wrapper with 'Happy Birthday, Bastard' written on it from my friend Brendan. Mind you, it had been my twenty-first. The card made me reassess Farley's character. He must have been quite excited when he bought his first home. It was difficult to imagine him being really excited about anything.

'I should keep this,' said Lydia, brandishing the card.

'Too late, 'said Gerrard. 'I've memorised the address. 22a Prince's Gardens, Brixton.'

'You shouldn't go round there,' said Lydia, placing the card back on the table.

'Actually it's 26a,' I said, reading the card.

'Oh, well,' said Gerrard. I've used the word 'insouciant' before in connection with Farley. Now Gerrard was insouciant. It always happened to him after about three beers, he magically became

James Bond. 'Come on, you only live once, old man,' he said, lightly tapping at his collar and pushing his chin into the air, as if he had noticed his dickie bow required a minute adjustment.

'I thought you said you didn't know about that?' I recalled our kitchen conversation.

'Yes,' said Gerrard, 'but either way you have to go for it. Either you live once and you need to grab the bull by the horns or you've got a few lives to burn so it doesn't matter if you fuck up in this one.'

'So questions of morals don't at all come into it,' said Lydia. 'Farley's not been dead more than a couple of days and all you two can think of is stealing his bird. It's pathetic. It's worse than that, it's horrible.'

'Hang on,' I said, 'we're not after stealing his bird. All we want to do is contact her and let her know what's happened. I can't say I'm not curious to know what she looks like, but that's it. I think we draw the line at jumping into his grave.' This was in 'all joking apart' tone.

'We do,' said Gerrard.

'Yeesss,' said Lydia, meaning, 'No'. 'You shouldn't do anything until after the police have contacted you anyway. It might look suspicious.'

'Good point,' I said. I thought it was time to draw the conversation to a close and act later.

'Why would it look suspicious?' Gerrard, when faced with a sleeping dog, was wont to go up and poke it with a sharp stick rather than allowing it to lie, as the animal would surely wish.

'Why wouldn't it?' said Lydia. 'Your friend dies and you start rooting round his house, what does that say?'

'You're right,' I said.

'It says we want to contact his girlfriend, which we do.' Gerrard had taken the recumbent mutt by the collar and was now giving it a damn good shake.

'I'd back off if I were you, Gerrard, I really would. Are you really saying you can't wait a few days? The police'll very likely contact you tomorrow.'

'You're an expert on police procedure now, are you?' Gerrard was fairly bellowing into the ear of the dormant canine.

'Look,' I said, 'I've got the keys and we're not going, that's it.'

'Glad to hear it. Whose round is it?' said Lydia.

'Yours,' we both said.

She took our orders, including a couple of packets of crisps, and went to the bar.

'What's the quickest way of getting to Brixton from here?' I asked Gerrard.

4

Golden girl

What does the name Brixton conjure up for you? To most whites living outside London it remains a powerful symbol of the strange and violent West Indian inner city, a no-go zone synonymous with riots and street crime. I have to say this has never been my experience of it. There are pubs, of course, where someone of my colour would not be welcome but, as with most of London, it is a relatively peaceful place. The WASP view of Brixton overlooks the fact that the West Indian population there has never been in anything like a majority and, compared to American inner cities, it is a model of racial integration. It is also, very rapidly, yuppifying. It defies its image as a ghetto. So much so that one of the friends from my home town, visiting to see a gig at the Academy, on nervously stepping from the mouth of the tube burst out, 'Fuck me, it's full of whites.'

I say this to show that Farley wasn't making a perverse choice to live as an alien in a riot-scarred shit hole, but was following a common trend to take advantage of decent bistros, a fantastic night life and brilliant connections for the centre of the city. The days of the petrol bombs and the riots might come back, but most of the residents fear them as much as the average householder fears subsidence – you only think about it when you see it happening.

If Brixton by night reminds me of anywhere, it isn't the West Indies but America. I have visited both places, but only on television, and it seems to me that the neon and the McDonalds, the crazies at the tube station, the Nation of Islam preaching on the streets, all recall New York rather than Trenchtown.

Farley's flat was at the top of a large old Victorian house about two minutes from the tube. I first wondered if we had the right place as the front door had the name 'Sharif' on a slip of paper near the bell. I checked the change of address card again and it was correct.

I pressed the key into the door and moved inside. Gerrard had the presence of mind to look through the letters, perched on the rack of a bicycle in the hallway, but there were none for Farley.

'What time is it?' I asked him.

He pulled from his pocket the remains of a digital watch he had won at a fair in 1984.

'Er, twenty past twelve, I think.' Like Gerrard the watch had long ago refused to be adjusted, and he wasn't very good at remembering if it was on British Summer Time or not.

I looked around the hallway. There's no point in doing this in most such places as they are usually very similar: chipped magnolia paint, dusty wood chip, a half-neglected rubber plant. Farley's hallway was no different. It even bore a fading embroidery inscribed 'God Bless This House'. I wondered if he had ever noticed it.

I took the lead as we ascended the stairs. Gerrard said something about how tidy the place was.

I turned the keys in the two locks of the door, having to do the bottom deadlock twice, as it had been unlocked in the first place. Feeling something like an archaeologist entering a Pharaoh's tomb, I stepped into the hallway. Directly before me was a coat rack, stuffed to bursting with Farley's coats, the quality of which would not have embarrassed a trend-setting rock star. Farley always picked the best labels – the ones no one has heard of. He was about my size too, but I put that thought out of my head. To the right was the kitchen and to my left a large living room lit by the city's friendly amber glow that permeated through the sky lights.

In the darkness, I could see the lights of the Radiogram, a large sideboard with record player and radio inside it, winking like a runway in the dark. No one else I knew had seen one since the late 1970s. Its presence in Farley's flat was an indication they were about to become trendy again. I wondered if he'd had it gutted and inserted some more advanced deck in it. Farley would never have bothered with a CD player, particularly as his favourite 'white label' sounds – those yet to be released beyond a few selected DJs and clubbers – never came out in that medium. It was one of the things that got on my tits about him, his elitism. Although on reflection he liked me, didn't he? Perhaps it was one of the reasons I'd kept him as a friend, it meant I too could be part of the elite.

'Shall we turn on the lights?' whispered Gerrard loudly, too close to my ear.

'There's no need to whisper, Gerrard,' I said, although I noticed that I was lowering my voice too.

I clicked on the light to reveal Farley's living space. Interior design naturally conforms to the principles of monarchy. One item, or one idea, sets the tone for the whole room. Farley, however, had taken a different view and organised his room democratically – each item, no matter how garish, was allowed its shout. Nothing in it matched exactly, although a few elements were clearly making an attempt to gang up on the rest of the room. The sofa, for instance, was in a kind of dark brown tight woollen fabric – expressing solidarity with the Radiogram and false bar with the rubber spear behind it. The lampshade was early nineties natural look, no more than four sheets of calico really. It was nervously siding with the coir carpet and unframed modern-artist-before-he-started-drawing-like-a-twat-type painting that was on the wall. The old chaise-longue had a tacit agreement with a Victorian roll top desk, pushed against the wall. They both made a nod to the original fireplace which was looking daggers at a mirrored door. The whole effect would have led you to believe an old lady, not a young man, lived in the room. I couldn't believe this mish-mash was going to look trendy to anyone, but I've been wrong about fashion before. Come to think of it, I don't think I've ever been right on that score. Which is why, with due respect for the dead, the coats were appealing to me.

'Hmm,' said Gerrard. 'Now we're here it doesn't seem like such a good idea. Maybe he did take his address book with him.'

'I'll get a beer,' I said. Luckily Farley actually had some beers in, cheap Heineken cold filters when I would have thought the clean lines of the Sapporo can were more up his street. Mind you, from the contents of the front room I wouldn't have been surprised to find a Watney's Red Barrel party seven, the 1970s flagship beer. His fridge was another contrast to the rest of the house. I would have bet that Farley had ninety per cent of his meals out, or from takeaways, but the cooler box was full of ingredients for salads and things, some of which I hadn't seen since the last time I went into a big supermarket years before. These things weren't even ready made up. They were raw ingredients which, presumably, he would have to cut up and wash and all sorts before he ate them.

There were organic tomatoes, mysterious close-cupped lettuces, orange peppers, a green crinkly thing and some radishes. I like radishes, and I hadn't tasted one for ages, so I had one. It was fairly fresh, a detail I supposed I'd have to tell the police after confessing I'd been there. I returned with the cold filters. Gerrard must have wanted his insouciance topping up because he took one despite his well-canvassed opinions on cheap beer.

'Where shall we start?' I said.

Gerrard said the desk seemed like a good place. The roll top was down. On it was a computer, along with dozens of scraps of paper: bills, restaurant cards from overseas and bank statements. Also there were computer disks, a bottle of wine, gratifyingly unopened, a candle stick, an umbrella cover, a full colour computer scanner – expensive by the look of it – a tube of cream of some sort, a toothbrush, a bottle opener, several used coffee cups, a copy of *Men are from Mars, Women are from Venus*, or whatever it's called, some camera film, two roll on anti-perspirants, a thesaurus, two travel guides to Mexico, some 7" singles, a watch and a UK road map. You couldn't see much desk. It had two drawers, similarly crammed with shit.

'This is obviously where he lets his hair down,' said Gerrard. He was right, the rest of the flat was spotless.

I made a stab at moving stuff about on the desk, dislodging things on to the floor. I couldn't see an address book.

'You're behaving like a burglar,' said Gerrard.

'No, I'm not, a burglar would just have nicked the computer.'

That gave me an idea.

'Actually, we should turn the computer on, see if there's anything worth reading.'

'It'll be password-protected,' said Gerrard.

'Best not try then,' I said, turning the machine on.

The computer sparked up, and sure enough asked for a password.

'See,' said Gerrard.

I hit Return and the machine began booting up. I had known Farley would never have been arsed with a password. Too geeky by half. What's the point of protecting your information if you've got nothing worth protecting? I tried to hide my smugness from Gerrard, allowing myself only a little 'told you so' under my breath.

I moused through Farley's files, or maybe cursed through them if that's what you do with a cursor, and after a bit of messing about I located two: one a spreadsheet file marked, conveniently, 'Girls' and one in a photo file marked, conveniently, 'Girls – pics'. Gerrard gave a little hop as I opened the spreadsheet file. It was a long list of women's names and numbers in alphabetical order. Next to each phone number was a box for estimated age and another for salient details. Finally there was a box for occupation – the great question of the century's turn, 'What do you do?' Typically, the list would say things like 'Carmen Mariner', estimated age '26', salient details 'Thinks she likes football. Met at Bar Italia after night in Club Lido. Friend involved next time?' Occupation: 'Didn't talk about it'.

'Christ,' said Gerrard. 'The fucker's got Paula's name on it.'

I gave a cold laugh before noticing that he had Emily's name on too. Neither had details next to their names – but even Farley wouldn't need reminding about the 'salient details' of his best friends' girlfriends.

'Probably not just ones he's slept with,' I said.

'Is there a boys' file?' asked Gerrard.

I had to confess I hadn't seen one. 'Both those names begin with B,' I said. 'They could be years old.'

I almost didn't want to do what I did next, nervously moving the mouse to the top of the screen and pressing 'Filter – sort by date'. The screen blinked and the women's names were rearranged into chronological order – most recent first. Paula's name was third on the list. Emily's was sixty-first. The dates next to them indicated that Farley had shagged Paula two days after he had offered to help Gerrard get her back. I couldn't remember exactly what I was doing six months ago, the date next to my girlfriend's name, but I knew I was going out with her. The evidence was difficult to ignore. Although I had only taken Emily on a 'best I can get at the moment, better than being on my own' basis, she had actually gone out and shagged someone before I had – pitching me a tent in Camp Loser.

Gerrard was agog, but far from displeased. 'Christ' he said. 'She's betrayed him as well. So he's not so fucking perfect, is he?' If it is possible to smirk with your mouth open, that was what Gerrard was doing.

'Which one do you think's the one he topped himself for?' I asked. I had concluded that my relationship with Emily was probably over and, having given proper time to grief and the healing process, it was now imperative I get off with someone new, ideally this girl of Farley's for revenge's sake – killing two birds with one stone. Preferably in the next five minutes. Most men don't display this kind of patience. The ideal is to get off with someone as your newly ex slams the door telling you she never wants to see you again and be shagging them when she returns five seconds later, having forgotten her coat. Come to think of it, actually getting off with someone as your girlfriend finishes with you is pretty much ideal, providing it isn't that that causes her to walk out.

Shallower men would say that it was important that the girl you get off with as your ex walks out on you should be very good-looking indeed, but my fantasies are more modest. I would just like her to be better looking than my immediate ex in a very annoying way. For instance, if my immediate ex was always worried about having a fat arse, the girl I would like to get off with would have a very shapely behind. If my girlfriend was worried about the size of her tits, I would like to get off with one of those girls who can't run because it hurts. It's all I ask. It's not revenge, it's just a race between you and the girl who dumped you to the point of maximum self-esteem. A race I had already lost.

'I don't know,' said Gerrard, 'but we'd better find out. I wonder how Paula's going to feel when she finds out her latest lover boy really wanted to settle down with someone else?'

It would have taken too long to explain to Gerrard that a woman of Paula's intelligence would hardly have shagged Farley under the illusion he was going to march her up the aisle in the next ten minutes. That she would feel sorry he was dead, not sad that she was left alone.

We looked down the list of women. I knew Farley had been seeing the death girl for probably around six weeks or so. He averaged, it seemed, about three girls a week. I was touched he bothered to keep their phone numbers – some might say it was sexist to catalogue and file women in this way, but to me it showed a genuine old-fashioned courtesy. Any girl who phoned him would be made to feel like he remembered her, like she hadn't been the latest on the conveyor belt – even if she had been. But eight weeks previously the numbers slowed down. There was Paula, who we knew about, and a girl called Estara d'Beaufort – I could have guessed her occupation as actress even before I saw it next to her name. The salient details bit read 'Works in Brown's restaurant'. Farley was fond of sleeping with actresses, but I couldn't see him going ga-ga for one – their twin obsessions with themselves would have repelled each other like two North poles on magnets. I remembered meeting an actress with him in a Soho bar a couple of years ago. He had suddenly lunged at her and given her a full-tongued kiss of youth club duration and intensity. He must have been snogging her for a good hour – prompting the barman to ask them to 'take it home with you'. When I'd asked him what had prompted such action he'd said that he'd done it for me. He wanted to shag the girl but had known I wouldn't want to leave the bar at that point. Planting his tongue in her mouth was the only way he could think of getting her to shut up. I don't condone such behaviour, I simply record it.

The only other girl on the list for the last eight weeks was Alice MacNeice – with no details at all next to her name. No phone number, no occupation, nothing salient, nothing. She was top of the list.

More interestingly she was also number four on the list, the eight-week anchor point. This time her occupation read 'TV –

money'. There was a phone number, but again the salient details were blank.

'I think that's the one,' I said, tapping the screen.

'Not necessarily,' said Gerrard.

I had forgotten, in my excitement, that the only way to get him to agree with your conclusions was to make him believe he had arrived at them himself. One day he would make someone a wonderful husband.

'Which one do you think it is then?'

Gerrard scanned the list for a minute or two.

'Could be any of them,' he said.

'Well, in that case, we may as well go for the one I think it is.'

After a bit of 'what iffing?' Gerrard agreed that Alice was a good place to start.

I was about to phone when he reminded me of the picture file. We closed down the spreadsheet and brought up the picture directory. There were about seventy pictures on the hard disk. All of them were labelled 'Alice': 'Alice on Dartmoor', 'Alice + Horse', 'Alice outside National Theatre'. In fact Alice in a whole heap of un-Farley like activities. For the second time that evening, inappropriate smugness threatened to overwhelm me. 'Actually,' I said to Gerrard, 'I don't think it is her, shall we try another one?'

He furrowed his forehead. 'Just open one up,' he said, in the tone that others reserve for 'I must insist you leave the club now, sir'.

I clicked on 'Alice in rain'. The screen filled with colour and I was in love. 'Woof, fucking, woof!' I heard myself saying in faux-begouted-major's accent. 'I could pleasure that in m'top boots.' The picture was a mid close up of a girl of about twenty-four, umbrella in hand, laughing. The background was green, a park or a wood or something. Her long straight-ish mousy hair was disordered and she was wearing an oversized rain jacket – probably Farley's – and carrying a copy of *Time* magazine. She was beautiful – more than beautiful. Not like a cover girl or a model or an actress, but like the strong, bright and wonderful women that actresses play. There was no glossy sheen to her beauty, but an intense inner shine. She sparkled with a light in the soul, and you could see she was careless of her looks, with her wind-blown hair and lack of make up.

Mark Barrowcliffe

She had a kind face with huge green eyes with something slightly Russian in her look, or oriental or something. Just strange and exotic. You could guess that she drove an old Italian sports car and discarded her cigarettes with more care than she would discard a man's soul. I'm sorry, but you could.

When I was at college it was very popular to have stills from films as posters. There was one from a Czech film that I'd seen in a girl's room of a man kneeling on a platform as this beautiful girl got on to a train. This girl was the one that most resembled Alice. The film's producers thought it entirely plausible that the man on his knees would spontaneously propose as she set off for a new life, or went to the shops, or wherever she was going, and they were right. The actor was meant to be projecting pure romantic love. I now knew what he was thinking for real: Shag me, take me, marry me. In whatever order you choose. I suppose that *is* romantic love. Mind you, he was probably gay and incapable of feeling it for her.

In a sense, there isn't much point in this description at all. True beauty is an art form in itself and words are only an interpretation of it, like a photograph of a great painting, a film of a book, or, worse, a book of a film. Still, I suppose it gives you an idea.

Years ago poets would have said her lips were like red coral or her skin like alabaster – and there was some truth in that, she had a beautiful pallor to her, but you could imagine she would easily absorb a sun tan. But to me Alice, the image of Alice, seemed like a repository for dreams – where fantasy is made flesh She had at once an air of incredible sophistication and of vulnerability. She seemed capable of bearing every paradox men ask of women. She had an incredibly dirty look to her – sluttish, an admiring adjective one of my less PC friends used to use – but it was magnified a thousand times by her air of innocence.

Another of my friends had once said to a girl that the voice of her eyes seemed deeper than any rose. She'd asked him if he'd thought of that himself, and he'd said of course he had. 'That's funny,' she'd said, 'so did e.e. cummings.' But, whatever, that was how Alice appeared. I looked into her eyes and saw the end of the quest, the end of trudging reluctantly to parties, clubs and bars. I saw the days by the sea, the nights by the fire, the car breaking down next to a beautiful château – all the glorious clichés of romance. Here was a girl to grow old with. I wasn't sure I was entirely ready for children yet, but for her I would try.

Our future together was clear. I would propose to her at a station, like in the photograph, prove myself to her tyrannical father by some wild act of bravery, be separated from her for years by war and return to find her holding my picture and looking five to seven years younger than she did when I left. She would contract a terrible disease and doctors would tell me – sorry, us – to fear the worst, but I would travel to America to find some controversial treatment that a brilliant young physician would assure me was our only hope: 'A 30 per center at best.' She would be cured and we would celebrate by becoming incapably drunk on a sunny day on the river. I would be hit by a car on the way back and she would spend the next six months nursing me back to health, our love growing ever stronger. There would be a charming scene where she was helping me to take my first steps. Then, on my third week back at work, I would be falsely accused of embezzling funds – hang on a minute, if this is a fantasy I wouldn't be at work but never mind – and she would fight to clear my name, discovering the one piece of evidence that would incriminate my scheming boss. The compensation would be huge and we would live the rest of our lives in luxury.

We would travel to Paris and be rude to the French before they could be rude to us, so we'd have to be quick. We would be pissed in Prague, coked up in California, blitzed in Berlin. We would go to Sainsbury's together only to laugh over the organic vegetables, have minor disagreements over the tastiness of borscht, otherwise food would just magically appear. Our lives would be enchanted, immaculate – like the bit when they're going around on bikes in *Butch Cassidy and the Sundance Kid* – and completely lacking in administrative tasks; there are no tax returns in Arcadia.

I know it's a lot to get from a photo, and perhaps jumping the gun a bit, but really this girl was top fig. All the more remarkable was that this photo was taken by Farley, who I knew regarded it as an achievement not to cut the tops off people's heads when using a camera.

I was about to say something about it to Gerrard when he got in there before me. He and I have reference points, five or six stories that always come up whenever we meet old friends. Years ago we had been in a pub in Wales and the landlord, commenting on a very pretty girl who was with us, had used an expression not heard regularly for one hundred years.

'Christ,' he'd said, 'she'd draw spunk from a lodging-house candle.'

Both of us had found the phrase very amusing, for its colour and for what I can only describe as its violence. It was because we'd found it mildly shocking that we felt compelled to repeat it. A third party, particularly a woman, would not have all the background and would conclude that we approved of talking about women like that – which we did, but not in a straightforward way. So I was glad it was Gerrard who said it this time, in an ersatz Welsh accent, aping the barman's pelvic thrust.

Two things were remarkable about this. The first was that he and I agreed on a woman. Normally Gerrard's ideal woman looked like a fourteen-year-old boy with smallish breasts 'that peak up at the end, though not too much' (I am quoting). Her hair should be dark and cut in a short bob, he maintained. She should wear ruby red lipstick, but otherwise not too much make up. She should not be at all assertive, but not a doormat either. On reflection, Gerrard's ideal woman in many ways *was* a fourteen-year-old boy – given that he admired girls who thought it funny when he farted and held their heads under the duvet.

The second remarkable thing was the smell of cigarette smoke that had entered the room. Neither Gerrard nor I was smoking.

I would like to record that the first thing I noticed about her when I saw her in the flesh was her way of smiling, or her dress sense, or her conversation. I noticed all these things at a later date, but right then they passed me by.

I hadn't noticed the size of her tits on the photo. We might have looked directly at her tits anyway, at least I might, in a half-eyed surreptitious sweep of their general area. Gerrard would have found them far too fascinating to look at them in anything other than a nanosecond leer. As we were both seated, I on a swivel office chair, Gerrard on a dining chair, a swift about face brought me directly into line with them, too close for comfort, less than two feet away. I really had no choice but to look at them, that's the only way I knew they were there so I could look away. It's like girlfriends who insist that their men don't look at other women.

How can you know you're not supposed to be looking unless you look in the first place? You can't just guess that a good-looking girl is going to walk across your eye line. Anyway, I did feel a little self-eonscious staring at her tits, close to me, so I looked away, which was easier said than done. I ended up turning my head to the far left, like a child straining to avoid unpleasant medicine.

I saw out of my peripheral vision that She was wearing a black, velvety all in one cat suit with a zip down the front and a small elliptical hole at the neck that revealed her cleavage. You see, I tried to look away but my eyes just went back there. Her tits looked enormous – but I later realised that was only because the rest of her was so slim. Not thin but slim. She had the body of a woman who had been thrown out of the Royal Ballet because they couldn't afford to keep her in sports bras.

Her general appearance was that of a girl spy from a sixties film. All she would have needed to complete the outfit was a gun with a silencer on the end to replace the cigarette she held in 'ready to shoot' mode, right hand on left elbow, left hand ready to reintroduce cigarette to mouth. I wondered why she had dressed up like that to meet us. Perhaps she *was* a sixties spy and that was her karate outfit. You could see every curve, although her body gave the impression of being one curve, one perfect disturbance of space – I'm sure a skilled artist could capture her shape with a single line and you would be able to recognise it as hers. Just looking at her, I knew she would have a hard time getting on with other women. The only equivalent I could think of in a man was Farley, who was so good-looking and well dressed that he got most blokes' backs up before he even opened his mouth. In fact, I normally hate good-looking men myself, because of the way they . . . er, because I'm jealous. There is nothing so annoying as perfection in others, no matter how hard they try to disguise it. Not that I'm ugly myself, I'm just not super league, which is where I want to be.

'What's a lodging-house candle?' she said in a voice of uncertain provincial origin, although I feared, in light of Gerrard's hip-thrusting pantomime 'boyo' impression, that it might have been Welsh. She came closer, staring short-sightedly into the screen.

There are certain questions everyone asks upon a surprise meeting – who are you, how did you get in, what are you doing here? At the very least, when exploring your dead friend's flat and confronted by the most beautiful woman you had ever seen, not two feet from her tits that sweep as wildebeest majestically to the shore, it behoves you to fly backwards in astonishment or something. It's just the done thing. On the other hand you can just gawp – which was the course of action preferred by me and Gerrard. In retrospect I am reminded of the gaze of two dogs, transfixed by a single bone.

'Well, are you going to sit there gawping like goldfish or are you going to tell me who you are?' she said. I still couldn't place her accent. There was something incredibly confident about her, the way she held her ground under our gaze, but also something theatrical in her poise, how she posed with her cigarette, something.

'We're friends of Farley's,' said Gerrard.

'So I gathered from your conversation. You're lucky I didn't run you through with the bread knife. I thought you were burglars.'

'I'm Harry and this is Ger.' I always use Gerrard's shortened form when I don't want to sound posh. Shouting 'Gerrard!' across a pub is never a recipe for a quiet night, and I think of it as a turn off for girls. I still haven't accepted the idea that middle-class men can be attractive to women. I always equate a middle-class accent with a ringing declaration of homosexuality, despite ample evidence to the contrary. 'We're not burglars,' I said, against my mounting nervousness. Good-looking girls – really good-looking girls – always make me very nervous. I can talk to them if I'm introduced to them but I always feel like a teenager, or like Gerrard. I suppose I become shy. I assume that the obviousness of my desire is like a spiritual halitosis, that the girl knows how good-looking she is and any expression of attraction towards her is a cliché. Trying to chat her up, trying to speak to her, is the equivalent of going up to Frank Sinatra and saying, 'Hey, Frank, you did it your way.' It's not like he hasn't heard it before.

'No, I think there are some quite sophisticated burglars now-adays, they don't all sit around swearing and bickering. Burglars have the decency to keep quiet, so as not to wake people.'

'We weren't bickering,' said Gerrard, who was now on his feet and limbering into a bit of a hopping routine.

'Yes, we were,' I said, for comic effect. I was very conscious of the need not to get hostile, as I often do to the beautiful. This is not from some deep-seated misogyny – at least I hope it's not – it's because I find beautiful women so attractive and so desirable that I have to go out of my way to show them I don't find them beautiful or desirable, to show I'm competing on their level. It's a kind of 'you're not getting one over on me' gawky adolescent, pig-tail-pulling thing. I do this whenever I meet pop stars – which in London media circles is more often than you'd think. I always end up saying something rude when I want to say something nice.

Alice's reaction cut through all of that. She just smiled and my soul flipped.

She looked past me to the computer screen, where her photo was still displayed.

'Oh, that's Farley's funny camera thing you're looking at, isn't it?' she said.

Curiously, she didn't ask what we were doing looking at her holiday snaps. Neither had she asked us why we were there.

'Well, I'm not standing here talking to you in my pyjamas, I'm going to get changed,' she said.

'You sleep in that?' I said, in a voice straying into the 'only audible to dogs' pitch. In fact I don't think I said it at all, I think I piped it. In the course of a day I had gone from hearing someone pipe for the first time ever to piping myself.

'Yes, what's wrong with it?'

Neither Gerrard nor I said 'Christ', though both of us wanted to. But Christ wasn't going to help us get what we wanted now. In fact, even with my scant knowledge of religion, I knew that Christ specifically frowned on it, as he had made crystal clear through a host of apostles and prophets.

'Nothing at all. I mean, isn't it rather warm?'

'I'm always cold at night, no matter what the temperature,' she said, with the air of a French actress declaring she could never love again. 'Fetch me a beer, would you?' And she disappeared in a *pas de deux* through a door in Farley's mirrored wall, gracefully knocking over one of his tall 1960s airport ashtrays on the way. Of course, she didn't stop to pick it up. Insouciance – it's what it's all about.

A previous generation of men, or men of a different class, might have approached the fridge in the style of a schoolyard scramble, limbs flailing in a cartoonish bid to be first back with the beer. Gerrard and I however stayed rooted. Neither of us wanted to appear over keen; knowing Gerrard he didn't even want to appear keen at all in case it put her off. I reminded myself who I was and went to get the beer.

When I returned he hissed, 'I see you're getting off the mark.'

I placed the beer down on an occasional table. 'She need never know it was me, Gerrard.'

'Look,' he said with the air of a dad saying, 'This is the last time I'm warning you, laddie,' for the fourth time, 'it was my idea to come here, right – she's mine. I have first go. All right?' He fairly rasped the last two syllables, like a crocodile calling for her young. I didn't bother to pick him up on 'having a go'. After all, this was a woman we were dealing with here, not a fairground hoopla stall. Anyway, if anyone was having first go, it was going to be me.

'Saying "all right" in an aggressive way isn't any more likely to make me agree,' I whispered, aggressively.

'Keep off,' said Gerrard, rasping once more.

'Why?'

'Because you go out with all sorts of girls. There's only a narrow band I find attractive and she's right in it. Her hair ... it's incredible. It's like blonde and brunette had put their heads together and come up with a better colour. She's the one in a million I can like. You can make do with all sorts.'

'Oh, thankee, sir,' I said, doffing an imaginary cap. As I've already explained, Gerrard wasn't so much afraid I'd get off with the girl myself as just ruin his chances, although he was flattering me in order to bend me to his will.

'Please, Harry, just this once.' His dark features seemed to be contracting inwards under the terrible gravity of his desire, his brows coming down to meet his five o'clock shadow.

'Please, Harry ... Fuck off, no!' I said. 'She's beautiful and she looks a right dirty cow. My son, you ask for the one thing I cannot give.' I put my hands together in prayer.

'Awwwww,' said Gerrard like a toddler who has been told he must share his chocolate with his brother, or like Daffy Duck in a fit of pique, his face condensing to a black dot. I didn't know why he didn't just make a play for her like anyone else. In some way my presence seemed to inhibit him, luckily. 'No, seriously,' he said, laughing slightly in a 'we're all mates who understand each other' kind of way, 'let me have a go.'

'No, seriously,' I said, aping his laugh. 'No.'

'I can't fucking believe you!' He was suddenly angry. 'Farley was a real mate of yours. He's hardly cold in the water and you're thinking of fucking his girlfriend.' He was pecking at the air with his index finger, like a battery hen pecks at a seed dispenser, no matter that it's empty.

'I'm not thinking of fucking her. At least, I'm not thinking only of fucking her. And he was a mate of yours as well, have you forgotten that?' We were both standing now.

'I knew him, that's all,' said Gerrard. 'You're going to fuck her. In fact, you're going to rub my face right in it by going out with her and shagging her repeatedly and noisily in the room next to mine. Christ!'

Although Gerrard had brought this happy image to my mind, and although I thought he seemed to think my getting off with Alice was a formality – 'Just sign here, sir, and you can take her into the bedroom now' – I still felt an answer was necessary.

'You were shattered by his death. You should still be shattered.'

'Life moves on,' said Gerrard, in a signal departure from his normal philosophical position. 'I can't believe how selfish . . .' he was beginning to continue.

'In my surprise and abject fear I forgot to ask you why you're here,' said Alice, emerging from behind Farley's mirrored door like the moon breaking over water.

Gerrard went silent. I remained silent. In some regrettable lapse of concentration we had forgotten to tell her that her boyfriend had committed suicide, mad with love for her. I was aware Gerrard was looking at me, although I was looking at Alice, now wearing a pair of slightly over-sized men's brown trousers and a T-shirt with *New York Times* written on it, in the masthead typeface. She looked gorgeous, world weary but fresh, careless and scruffy in a way it would take others hours to simulate. I'd like to record some fault or flaw here, to prick your sympathy. But, reader, I must record there was none. I know you won't be liking her very much at the moment but she's all right, believe me.

For the third time in twenty-four hours I was faced with the problem of how to break the death news. It was the worst I'd had to face. The not telling her straight away charge was going to be a tricky one to beat. No bull-at-a-gating here, I thought.

'Farley's dead,' said Gerrard, horns reducing the five bar to a pile of matchwood.

'What?' said Alice. 'Are you joking?'

'He killed himself,' I said. I didn't want Gerrard to be the sole focus of her attention.

Alice sat down on the sofa. 'Hang on a minute ... Farley, the owner of this flat, has killed himself? I don't believe it. Why?' A man, I thought, would have asked how; an easier question to answer.

'We're not sure,' I said, in the role of TV policeman again.

I half expected Gerrard to chip in with 'yes we are, it was because of you', given his penchant for sledgehammer honesty, but he contented himself with looking quizzically at me.

'Why do you look like that?' Alice asked him.

'Like what?'

'Like you do know why he killed himself.'

'No reason,' said Gerrard. He must fancy her, I thought, he's lying. He wouldn't do that for just anyone.

'He may have been upset about your relationship,' I said, carefully substituting the word 'relationship' for the word 'you'.

'What makes you say that?'

'He left a message.'

'What did it say?' Her bottom lip began to tremble.

'He said he was going to kill himself because the relationship had split up.' She put her head into her hands and started to cry, and for the first time I too felt like crying. I could feel my eyes fill up and had that top-of-the-roller-coaster feeling you get when you are about to start bleating. I cry quite easily at the best of times – I cry when I'm happy, even, pathetically, when I remember great sporting feats. It's strange that I can cry with fear, or with joy, or when I've been dumped, or at *Animal Hospital* on the television, or the Muhammed Ali life story, but that I don't seem to cry at the death of a friend. This lachrymose tendency as a boy at school marked me out for the wrong kind of attention from my peers. If your eyes start to water when someone starts picking on you then it only serves to egg the bullies on. They brand you a softie. I suppose you are a softie.

This has caused me a fair bit of mental strife over the years. When I was fifteen I asked the doctor if there was any way I could have my tear ducts burned out. He was a tough sinewy Scot who had formerly been in the army and treated me to some military-style stress counselling – he told me to pull myself together. In other words, you have to burn your own tear ducts out, using the fire of your manly character, no one's going to do it for you. But although I have since sought to toughen up, it's still the tears that give me away. I'm not sure it's a sign of any great depth of emotion, maybe it's just a cross between sentimentality and cowardice. I felt a tear on my face and I felt like going up to Alice and putting my arms around her. But I couldn't. It would have felt like I was betraying her, cashing in on her grief. It would also have got Gerrard's back up, not that I would mind about that.

'Do you want anything?' he asked maddeningly sitting down on the sofa next to her. He had his legs crossed away from her, which psychologists tell us indicates dislike, though in this case you would have to say the psychologists were wrong. Gerrard was being polite, giving her space because, like me, he didn't want to be seen to be diving in.

'We didn't have a relationship,' she said, a little bit more composed. 'He was just kind to me. My boyfriend and I had split up and Farley said I should come away with him on holiday to take my mind off it. He said I could stay here while he went surfing for a few weeks. I mean, something might have happened between us but I wasn't ready. I liked him, you know, a bit, and I knew how he felt. You could see it the way he moved even, but I wasn't ready. I wasn't. And I hardly knew him. Now he's dead. It wouldn't have seemed right, jumping into bed with another bloke just a couple of days after you've broken up a serious relationship. You just don't do it, do you?'

'Oh, no,' I said, hoping Gerrard would bite his tongue. 'It wasn't your fault. He must have been unstable. Normal people don't kill themselves over a girl they haven't even slept with – or gone out with rather.'

'What time is it?' asked Alice.

Gerrard reached into the musty depths of his pocket again for his Palaeolithic digital. 'Half-past one,' he said. 'I think.'

Alice smiled through her tears, like sunshine after rain, I thought, which is most unlike me.

'That's an amazing watch, let me see.' Her arm flickered towards Gerrard, in a movement like a trick of the light, and he took the opportunity to turn his legs towards her with a neat buttock twist as he gave it to her. Rain after sunshine, I thought, which is like me. 'Gosh,' said Alice. 'That's brilliant. I hate those people who walk round in all this designer bollocks – that's all you need, isn't it? Very green too, keeping it for so long.'

'It's all I need,' said Gerrard, smiling in what I guess he thought was a winning way but which in fact made him look like Harpo Marx. I could see the green bit had gone down well with him. 'Although maybe a Rolex would be a better idea, or one of those atomic watches that's accurate to millionth of a second, like a proper bloke.'

'You'd look like a man of style,' said Alice, for irony, but without showing it in her voice, which I liked.

'And I'd know exactly how late the bus was. It's annoying having to approximate it only to seconds.'

Alice laughed. Presumably she thought he was joking to show up the pointlessness of an expensive watch, which he was, sort of. However, Gerrard often boarded a late-running bus with words to the driver like, 'Ten minutes, twenty-eight seconds late. I hope it was a good game of cards.'

'We shouldn't be laughing like this. I still can't believe he's dead,' she said. Her smile had gone again.

'It's hard, isn't it?' I said in sympathetic tone. I'm not very good at sympathy. My first instinct on hearing of the misfortune of close friends is to turn it into a joke. I learned that in the playground. Sympathy doesn't suit me, I always end up sounding like a fat agony aunt, studiously sincere like a professional carer or one of those people who says 'How does that make you feel?' on late-night TV.

'You know what I feel like doing?' said Gerrard. 'Getting really pissed. There's no point in being miserable, is there? It's not what Farley would have wanted.'

I wasn't quite sure about this. I would have thought Farley would have wanted public mourning on the Princess Di scale. But the get pissed idea had twin appeal for me. I would be able to spend longer with Alice, and we would be moving out of Gerrard's territory into mine. In fact, I was surprised he had suggested it. Gerrard was a notoriously poor drinker who would be pie-eyed after four pints. I don't know if he really got drunker than me, but he liked to stay in control and so would feel the need to rein back. I don't see the point in that. Surely the point of consuming a mind-altering substance is to alter your mind. Stopping at the two-pint mark is like walking out of a thriller when the suspense gets too much. Losing control never seems like a problem to me although I wish I could get drunk more easily, it would save me a fortune.

However, at the back of my mind that evening was the suspicion that Gerrard might switch to coffee and put in a Wilde-at-the-height-of-his-powers-style performance while I Jabberwockied myself with drink.

Alice looked uncertain. 'Is that in the best taste?' She looked a bit glassy-eyed. I wasn't sure if she was reeling from the shock of Farley dying or if she was just unsure about getting pissed with two strangers.

'Sure,' I said, 'is there much in the fridge?'

She shrugged her shoulders. 'I bought some tequila from duty free last week. I haven't opened it yet.'

'You like tequila?'

'I love tequila.'

'*Arrrrrriiiiiba!*' I shouted, forgetting that Farley was dead.

Gerrard looked at me as if I had asked her if I could light a couple of her farts. Alice, however, seemed a little cheered up by the joke. She laughed and went into the bedroom humming the tune from 'Low Rider', in a slightly down way, if it's possible to hum 'do da do da do da do, do do do da da' in a down way. Gerrard followed her with his eyes in disbelief, as if she had actually sparked up a fart and was trailing it, *à la* aerobatic display, as she receded into Farley's room. He made more head-shaking gestures and 'keep back' signs to me, while I theatrically pretended to read a magazine. She re-emerged with a massive bottle of yellowy spirit. 'This is the genuine Mexican stuff, it'll knock your *cojones* off,' she said. 'Gerrard, be a dear and get the lemon and salt from the kitchen would you?' I liked the 'be a dear' bit. Very sophisticated, very fifties, very Margot – Margaret – I can never remember which it is – Rutherford.

'I wonder what he was thinking when he died?' said Gerrard, projecting heavy thoughtfulness. I knew he regarded his sensitivity card as a good one to play against my Jack-the-Ladism. It's not that he was particularly sensitive, to anyone other than himself, but he could project the signs more easily than I could. He had learned to look like he was listening. He was very skinny as well, which is always equated with emotional depth. So by cutting the levity, making us feel sorry for our inappropriate level of good humour, he brought the fight on to his own territory. Even if he failed, he would still be in the conversation, he would still be there, like a tennis player hanging on in a demanding rally, biding his time to regain the centre of the court.

There's nothing as bad as that feeling when you're talking to a girl you fancy and your friend's on good form. You try to telepathically project 'it's me you should like, me, not him. I'm much more your type', as she gurgles with laughter above the party's babble at his sparkling wit and accepts a smooth olive from his proffered bowl. 'No, thanks,' she says, as you push forward the desolate remains of the tortillas. But while you are present there's always a chance. If you're still there at the end of the fight you may just land the knockout blow, no matter that you've been outpointed over twelve rounds. Sorry about the mixed metaphors.

We both ignored Gerrard's question about what Farley was thinking when he died – a feeble attempt to remain on the sofa – although I guessed it wasn't 'hey, nonny nonny, a pint of the usual in m'special tankard, George'. 'How long did you know him?' I asked. Gerrard, slunk off to get the lemon and salt.

'A couple of months. We went down to Dartmoor together, had a lovely time, but really I hardly knew him at all. I suppose I should feel more upset. I mean, I do feel upset, I'm crying, I do but I don't know. It's one thing after another . . . I'm feeling a bit numb to it, I wonder when . . .'

'There's only limes!' Gerrard informed the Greater London area from the kitchen.

'That'll do!' Alice bawled back, and laughed again. 'He seems quite a character.'

This was one avenue of discussion best left unexplored. 'If you like that sort of thing. You wonder when what?'

'I wonder when it's all . . .'

'Where's the salt?' Another blast from Gerrard, audible I was sure to Channel shipping.

'In the cupboard on the right-hand side of the cooker!' replied Alice, also giving it an extra decibel for luck.

'When it's all going to end?' I hate completing people's sentences for them, but like a rabbit in a trap, someone had to finish this one off.

'I can't find it!' I felt Gerrard was physically wrestling back the initiative from me. He had clearly decided to fight me at my own game. If he wasn't going to be in the conversation, neither was I.

'Have you had a lot to deal with recently?'

'Is this it, in the orange container?' I was sure I saw the paper on Farley's desk lift under Gerrard's foghorning.

'The one marked Salt?' shouted Alice, giving it full lung. It occurred to me that the neighbours must have thought some sort of bizarre row was taking place.

'Yes!' Gerrard hollered at a level normally reserved for moments of major scientific breakthrough or ruination on the horses.

'That's it,' Alice croaked from the strain of the volume.

'Were you very. . .?'

'Here we are then,' said Gerrard, slightly hoarse, coming back in with some sliced limes on a plate, three glasses and a tub of salt.

'Harry was just asking me if I was very close to my last boyfriend,' said Alice, which was funny because I hadn't been asking her that at all, although I was going to. If you are going to stand a chance with a girl you need to assume a certain level of intimacy, without being intrusive. I would normally have reserved that kind of question for later in the evening, but Farley's death gave me special licence.

'Oh, yes?' said Gerrard, putting the plate on the floor.

'I felt close to him sometimes, you know, but I don't know. He never seemed to want to grow up,' she said, throwing her hair over one shoulder. I inwardly shuddered at this point, and resolved to appear more mature. I pictured myself smoking a pipe. 'I liked him being funny and everything, but emotionally – arrested development. At the age of twenty-eight you'd have thought he would have seen something more to life than getting pissed with his mates every weekend.'

'Who does that sound like?' said Gerrard. ' "You'd have thought he would have seen something more than getting pissed with his mates every weekend". That could be your epitaph, Harry. Apart from it's not just the weekend with you, is it?'

I'd had him way off the court, somewhere near where the umpire comes in, with the unexpected success of '*Arrrriiiiba!*' but here he was working his way to the net. A series of distractions followed by some hard-hitting wit and I was rocking. I came back with a lame, 'And what's your epitaph going to be, Gerrard? Just "you'd thought he would have seen something".' Gerrard grinned like a mastiff who'd just eaten a plate of sausages. He poured salt on to Alice's hand and offered her the plate.

'It's always the tough one, isn't it? What makes us click, what makes us stay together. Do you know what you want in a woman?' I wondered if Alice was conducting a conversation on her own, without our input.

Gerrard poured her a small bath of tequila. She sucked the lime, drank the tequila and licked the salt. I could see his face flicker with irritation, suppressing a terrific urge to tell her she was doing it the wrong way round.

'Go on, Gerrard, say what you have to say.' I knew he would have to comment on the lime/salt arrangement and so appear like a pedantic tosser.

Alice glanced between me and Gerrard. 'Oh, I'm doing the lime thing the wrong way round, am I? I always do that. Left brain, right brain. Oh, dear.' She poured herself another tequila and did the thing in the right order. 'There you are.' She smiled. 'That's better.'

I couldn't tell if she was irritated with me or if she was amused.

'The order doesn't really matter. It's important to enjoy it,' said Gerrard having vast fun at my expense. I was losing it here. I had to get him back on to shakier ground.

'What was it you wanted from a woman, Gerrard?' I said, praying for some insights to come like mouldering socks from the dark laundry basket of his brain.

'Oh, I can go on, now we're all sucking and licking in the right order, can I?'

'It's important to do that.' Alice laughed again. This was turning into a fully paid up, card-carrying nightmare. Gerrard went on, 'Love, really. I want someone who's capable of giving their love wholly and completely to me. I don't want half measures. The rest, the looks and everything, are immaterial. Obviously they've got to be intelligent, though. University standard, even if they haven't been,' he said. I wondered where he had learned his new love of lying.

'How about a new university, would that do?' I asked, hoping to spark him into a round of prejudice against former polytechnics. I failed.

'You don't think looks are important?' said Alice.

Gerrard, who had ostentatiously licked the salt, drunk his tequila and sucked the lime, coughed slightly as the spirit went down the wrong hole.

'Looks are important, but there are so many different sorts of women, you know. I could be in love with almost anyone. It's personality that counts. With looks it's more a matter of what you don't want than what you do.' Like tits – sorry, 'breasts' – that don't conform to the formula $DxDy40(XY)$ to the power of whatever I remember from my differential calculus, I thought. Looks to Gerrard were intensely important. According to the quotations dictionary, George Bernard Shaw said, 'Beauty is all very well at first sight, but who ever looks at it when it has been in the house three days?' Gerrard was more of the school who couldn't take their horrified eyes off ugliness if it had been in the house three seconds.

'What don't you want?' asked Alice.

I enjoyed that question, though if Gerrard answered it in full the leaves would be turning brown and we would be feeling the nip of frost on our noses by the time we got out of the flat.

'Just little things, really. You know, make up and stuff. Eyes, lips, nose, ears – no one likes big ears.'

He was trying to reduce his list of dislikes into the non-pathological range, but there was no way he could leave out big ears.

I remembered when he had got off with a girl at a fairground we once went to – I'm not making this up, we went to a fairground aged thirty and with no kids – he'd kissed her and put his hand beneath her hair only to discover she'd got big ears. He'd recoiled

Mark Barrowcliffe

as if he'd been bitten by an asp. Just as well really, she only looked about fifteen and I'm sure I heard her say she hadn't decided what GCSEs she would be taking yet.

'Ears?' said Alice. 'I don't think looks are important at all. Everyone looks the same at seventy. It's a matter of getting on with the person, isn't it? You don't have to agree on everything but you need a large measure of agreement.'

'A very large measure,' said Gerrard, lowering his tone towards the end of the sentence. 'I mean, there wouldn't be any point going out with someone who was into mobile phones and expensive restaurants or killing animals for fun, if you didn't like that sort of thing.' I wondered if the 'if you didn't like that sort of thing' would allow him to reveal a hitherto unsuspected love of hare coursing, should that be her bag.

'Oh, God, don't you just hate mobile phones?' said Alice. 'I think they undermine the quality of your life. No one has any private time any more.'

I could see Gerrard mentally rubbing his hands, steeping deep in oily glee. 'And expensive restaurants?' I said, hoping she was a regular at Michelin three-star joints.

'Well, sometimes,' said Alice. 'But I prefer a home cooked veggie stir fry.'

Gerrard listened in pleasure, like a demanding old music master hearing an exceptional pupil go through a difficult exercise.

Given that she was a metropolitan woman, and seemed to be vegetarian, it was too pale a hope that she enjoyed dressing up in a red coat and hot footing about the countryside seeing dogs eat other dogs in defence of chickens. A bizarre mental image of fox hunting as the English Civil War floated through my mind. Those dogs that stand with the chicken on one side, those against on the other. I put it out of my mind in the interests of sanity and decided it was time for a change of tactics. Argue with her, I thought, see if she likes a row. And throw in a couple of compliments.

'It's easy for you to say looks don't matter. You're very beautiful. Looks do matter and none more so than one's own.' I detected a mild wilting in Gerrard's posture, like a lettuce whose day had passed, as I uttered the 'you're very beautiful' bit. ABC – Always Be Closing.

Alice looked straight at me. 'Well, neither of you are exactly ugly.' That knocked the wind out of my argument tactic's sails.

Gerrard sipped at his tequila – he hadn't downed it all in the first place. I knew what was coming next. He believed a good way to charm girls was to ask them incredibly personal questions. This surprised many of his acquaintances when they heard it for the first time, as they thought of Gerrard as shy. I couldn't quite square it myself. The only thing I could equate it to is those people – normally men – who have very long hair for years. Then when they decide to get it cut they don't go for a normal style, they go for a skinhead. It's like in breaking through a personal barrier they have to go as far as they can the other way. Mind you, I admire Gerrard for this – it's a good ploy – although the girl can end up finding him about as sexy as a nuisance caller. It does, however, have the effect of putting her on the back foot, getting her to remember him as unusual – all the boy tricks.

'Which one of us is best looking?' asked Gerrard in an 'I'm obviously being cheeky' tone, leaning forward to Niagara more tequila into Alice's glass. Was he trying to get her paralytic? I've never seen the point in this really. If one person or the other is unconscious drunk, sex lacks something of the two-way exchange which makes it so much fun. When sex is on the cards a gentlemen never goes beyond wildly inebriated. To vomit once in an evening shows an understanding of the spirit of excess; to vomit twice shows too gauche an enthusiasm and is the preserve of schoolboys and those new to Ouzo.

'Him,' said Alice, pointing at me.

'No,' said Gerrard, 'you're wrong there.' I had to give him marks for brio, even though I knew he'd been fazed.

'Ask questions like that, you're never going to get the answer you want, are you, my dear?' I loved the way she said 'my dear', in a camp way, like a nineteenth-century aristocrat. She was a little camp, Alice, if girls can be camp. What I didn't love was that she was very near to flirting with him.

'So he's not better looking, then?' said Gerrard. Sod me, I thought, now he's flirting with her, using my good looks, or lack of them, as the means of his flirtation. Brilliant but evil. I would have to play a modesty card and, as Gerrard well knew, I didn't have too many of those.

'I'm not really in the mood for considering boys' good looks, one way or the other,' she said, suddenly deflated. Thank fuck for that, I thought. Alice lit another cigarette with a match from a book and blew on it daintily as a child might blow on a dandelion. She had a kind of ancient beauty, I thought. There was a piece of DNA that had only been tweaking itself since it was driving the poets potty in the Renaissance, or launching ships and things in Antique Greece. No need for major alterations in the double helix there.

'I'm sorry,' said Gerrard, 'I was just trying to cheer you up.'

'I know, and it was very sweet of you. We should be cheerful, for Farley's sake, shouldn't we?' She put her hand on Gerrard's knee. Things were not going the way that I wanted. I wondered if I should introduce a graphic description of Farley's dismemberment in the hope of removing that hand from Gerrard's knee and up to her eyes or something through grief or revulsion. Best not, I thought, don't want to be the bearer of bad tidings. Better to come over as reverential guardian of Farley's memory, particularly as she'd said there was a chance she was going to get off with him.

'Yes,' I said. 'What do you think he would have wanted us to talk about?' There is no way in a month of Sundays I would normally talk like this but I had to break Gerrard's vice-like grip on the conversation.

'Him,' said Alice.

'What shall we say about him?' Gerrard began.

'What were his best qualities?' I said, fearing we were in for a protracted head scratching session on this one.

'He was kind,' said Alice.

Neither Gerrard nor I coughed tequila up our noses. A testament, I thought, to our breeding.

'He was,' I agreed. 'What else?'

Alice banged down her latest bucketload of tequila.

'He was ornamental.'

'I'm sorry?' Gerrard spoke for us both.

'He was ornamental. It's a man's only responsibility nowadays. He was decorative.'

I could see she was a little drunk and wondered if she was being wilfully provocative. If so, fine, it's just a different form of teasing.

'Don't we have a responsibility to do things as well?' asked Gerrard, sluicing more tequila into her glass.

'No, not any more. You have no barriers left. Men have gone through them all, or all the ones worth going through anyway. The world is how you want it, there's nothing to change. You have to grub about for goals in the undergrowth, you have to become one of these shabby little toilers who break speed records or sail around the world or something. The breakthroughs of tomorrow belong to us. The women. We still have our world to shape. For a woman to be on the board of directors is an achievement; for a man it's a disaster. One shows a triumph against all the odds, the other a collapse of the imagination.'

She was slurring a bit here so I decided to think she was drunk although I suspected she'd said this before, which in itself is a good sign. If a woman gives you a prepared speech she is clearly trying to impress. In previous generations she would have laid out the best china.

'How about medicine? Men and women are making worthwhile breakthroughs there.' Gerrard tended to view medicine as the sole repository of virtue in the world.

'Medical breakthroughs are environmentally unsound,' said Alice. In fact, declaimed Alice.

'Well, they do use some dodgy materials and they're very nasty to rats,' wavered Gerrard.

'Quite,' said Alice. 'And they save people. The advances of medicine are the retreats of civilised living. Doctors should pack up and go home for fifty years. Every time I hear about some new cure, another thousand saved, I wonder how many more bastards are going to be alive to try to knock me off my bike in their cars. How many more flocking to the superstore, pumping their pollution up my nose and chucking their condoms into the sea? That's male fucking medicine for you.'

Gerrard dipped his head to the side, like a connoisseur tasting a new wine of uncertain palate. I wondered how she'd feel if someone near to her was very ill, but decided to let it go as she was fixing me with her deep green eyes. Moral outrage, as I've already recorded, isn't my strong point and, anyway, she was probably right about men. What was my job if not a decoration, a pass to say 'I work in the media, it's OK to sleep with me'. I often wished someone would come and relieve me of the responsibility to work, but I couldn't see that happening unless I won the lottery, and that was unlikely to happen. I like to cultivate an air of recklessness, so I don't do the lottery.

Gerrard, I noticed, was out on his feet and Alice had withdrawn into pensive mode. I couldn't have faced another tequila so I fetched myself a beer. I cracked the can and then we all sat as if waiting for the dawn.

The end of the conversation had a sobering effect on Alice. She sat rocking on the sofa, thinking to herself, I suppose. After half an hour or so of saying nothing she spoke again, quietly and slurring slightly.

'Farley was a genius in a way. He had a brilliance to him and it was effortless, which is the only sort worth having. Effortless brilliance, brilliant. There's nothing more trying than a tryer, especially in a man.' She laughed into the remains of her drink. 'He was like a brilliantly positioned lamp, which is the way a man should be. I've been out with enough saws and hammers, trying to shape the world into what it already is.'

She smiled and blew out smoke. I wondered if she was quoting this bit from some play.

Original or not, her words were jarring a bit with the 'I hardly knew him' line of earlier. The sick realisation that the brilliantly positioned lamp had probably shagged Alice in a variety of positions too hideous to contemplate crept up on me. Still, you're going to like me if that's your attitude, I thought. I imagined myself lying in a hammock overlooking our palatial Mediterranean villa. 'Must you bring your work on holiday with you, darling?' I'd be saying, as I saw her with a laptop. 'I've nearly finished reading this book and I need someone to talk to. Come, tell me what gifts you are going to buy for me.'

Some people are turned into animals by drink, some to bores or children, but Alice just projected a greater intimacy, a soul warmth. My tiredness and drunkenness made me want to go to sleep in her arms, as long as I could get Gerrard off the sofa. I felt spaced out, a survivor in the dawning light. I noticed, with satisfaction, that Gerrard was asleep. Tiredness was always going to be my greatest ally against him. Typically for an insomniac, he spent most of the time he wanted to be awake propping his eyelids open and most of his time in bed alert as a stoat. As he usually did when sleeping, Gerrard looked like a mental patient who has been given the chemical cosh to avert harm to himself and the community. His eyes were demented slits, a hand attached ape-like to his hair and his tongue filled his lower lip. In this condition he looked like that face children make when mocking the mentally ill and shouting, 'Mong!'

'Ah,' said Alice gently. 'Doesn't he look sweet?'

'No,' I said.

I tried to get more on to her wavelength by imagining myself as a piece of interior design, but I couldn't do it. Images of lava lamps, mirrors and candlesticks went through my head. Each had its appeal, but none seemed to work. A better idea, was to think of Gerrard, my immediate competitor, in that way. I saw him as a cheese plant in a doctor's waiting room, rapidly filling up with chewing gum and discarded fags.

I was very strongly aware of how much I wanted her. At the butt end of the drinking session my mind was fogged with images of women saying goodbye for the last time, my tears and theirs, my anger and theirs. In the morning gloom, with a half drunk head and an ashtray for a soul, I understand the idea of melancholy, when every bad thing that has happened to me feels connected to every bad thing that has happened ever.

'We should go,' I said.

She nodded. Even through the tequila and the tiredness I felt the knife in my stomach, but I had to say it, and before Gerrard woke. I wanted to kiss her, and let her take the rawness of the dawn away, but I knew a tongue lunge would be counter-productive.

I could hardly get the words out, but I did because I had to and because it's the form.

'I'd like to see you again.'

I felt the empty spaces of the dawn stretching cold beyond me, damp light shrinking my body inside my clothes.

'Sure,' she said. 'Give me a call. I'm here for a while, I suppose. Maybe I'll see you at the funeral.'

I moved to the sofa and kissed her on the cheek, pulling back in case I just collapsed into her warmth. She smiled and looked into my eyes. Her expression said, 'We're going to get through this together,' which was mighty big of someone I'd just met. Gently, and reluctantly, because I didn't really want to leave, I shook

Gerrard awake. He sat up straight and stared into the distance, still half in some nightmare. 'Alice,' he said, 'I want you to sleep with me.'

'Not at the moment,' she said, shaking his knee to bring him round. 'But play your cards right and you never know.'

'I'll call a cab,' I said.

5

Reluctant stereotypes

The interview with the police did not go well.

As I've already recorded, I have an innate distrust of the boys in blue. This rests on two planks, or tenets as Gerrard would have it. The first is that it is, and always has been, fashionable for young people to distrust the police, and I think of myself as a young person. The second is that they have, in my experience, proved themselves untrustworthy.

For instance, when I was about seventeen, I had a friend, Reg, who did deliveries for an abattoir. He had an alarmingly earnest friend called Paul who was press spokesman for the local Animal Liberation Front eco-terrorists. When Reg's abattoir suffered a minor spat of vandalism the police, who had been watching Paul, concluded that Reg was the inside man – a suspicion all but confirmed by the fact that he had long hair. Crime enough, one might have thought.

Accordingly, they hauled him in at five in the morning for a grilling. It wasn't the assumptions the police made that bothered me, it was their lack of basic procedure. After two hours of police time and tax payers' money, during which Reg received only light physical intimidation, one of the brighter plods thought to ask him if he had any previous convictions.

'Oh, yes,' he said.

'What for?' asked the sleuth, doubtless envisaging affrays at fox hunts and bomb attacks on animal research centres.

'Poaching,' replied Reg.

Needless to say, he was free to resume his round within minutes. This is just one of a whole shed load of incidents that have led me to expect a combination of malevolence and incompetence in any dealings I have with coppers. The lard arses who visited us over Farley's death did nothing to change my opinion; they were a couple of thugs in elasticated-waist leather jackets who I could see gave themselves a pretty free hand with the subsidised pies and chips in the police canteen. To their credit, however, they were on a level of organisation beyond that I had previously encountered in the police. They had phoned first to make an appointment to come and see us.

It was an unseasonably hot late-April day when they turned up: fine if you were seated in the cool shade of our kitchen, but too warm for walking around in an 80 per cent viscose suit and cheap shoes. Ladies may glow, gentlemen perspire and horses sweat, these policemen oozed, appearing on our doorstep like very serious contenders in a wet beergut competition.

Despite my admitted prejudice, I always find it better to try to be civil when dealing with the law. It's a safety measure, like respecting the changeable nature of the weather when walking in the Lake District by taking the right clothes, or nipping back from the bus stop to make sure you unplugged the iron. It's probably unnecessary, but sod's law says that the one time you don't do it is the one time you'll regret it.

There's also the fact that being interviewed by the police makes you feel a bit special, one of those few times in life when you feel part of a drama, like your opinion matters.

So, even though I was sad to see that the potentially fanciable DC Arrowsmith had not come with them, I invited them in and asked them to sit, which they did with surprising grace, like circus elephants upon podiums. I enquired if they wanted tea or toast, which they did, by the bucketload, and with Gerrard's help answered questions about whereabouts, ours and Farley's.

Gerrard had been working late Saturday and afternoon Sunday, giving him very little time to nip west and butcher anyone. I had been out Saturday with my friend John, which had turned into a bit of a large one and I hadn't woken up until five on the Sunday when I'd gone to see my friend Pete, who needed consoling now that his girlfriend was pregnant. The plods wanted details of times and conversations. I couldn't remember anything we'd said on the Saturday night, but then I never remember anything anyone says when I'm out. Luckily, I recalled the clubs we'd been into – The Cross for a passé kind of dance evening and then on to Start in Wandsworth, which is open until eight in the morning, from I don't know what time. I pointed out that both clubs had video surveillance if they wanted film of me going in.

I was more able to remember the conversation with Pete as I was proud of a joke I'd made when he'd told me he was to be a father. I'd told him to look on the bright side – at least he'd get to shag the baby sitter. Plod Two laughed in a 'you wanker' kind of way, but Plod One just said, 'A bit early for him to be lining up baby sitters, isn't it?' The police can be very literal.

I remembered that I'd been a bit jealous of Pete, not so much for having the baby as for moving to the next stage, for getting on with it, so we'd had a conversation about a new motorbike I was thinking of buying with the kind of money he'd now be putting into cribs and things. He'd said something about 'I wouldn't be so sure if I were you', by which I took it that he wasn't too happy about the prospect of impending domestic bliss and was thinking of hitting the ejector button. I'd left Pete's at about one in the morning. 'And was in work at 10.35 sharp,' I said, my smile fading as I noticed a snarl on Plod Two's lip. Plod One made a mark on his pad.

Reading upside down I could see NEITHER MARRIED (32!!!!). NEITHER DIVORCED. OWN FLAT TOGETHER!!!!!! on Plod One's pad. Also he had written the word BATS? with Gerrard Ross under it and BOWLS? with mine in the same position accompanied by a reasonably skilful line drawing of people playing cricket, although I think the batting and bowling were intended in their usual sense of referring to sexual activity.

I had already observed with regret that the policemen were deeply into the 'Is he a poof territory?' that so many people find themselves in with Gerrard; his thinness, his arm-flapping, his campness sparking the doubts. Anyone who knows him well never has these thoughts, as his terrible misunderstanding of women and appalling fashion sense mark him as highly unlikely to be homosexual. I realised with mild concern that the plods were concluding by association (which is the way that policemen's minds have to work if they are to do their jobs properly) that I was gay too.

On the positive side, they seemed to like the dog. I had flea shampooed him earlier in the day, leaving his fur with a mysterious yet alluring scent of lemon. Plod One ruffled the animal's ears and remarked that it smelled like his wife. We all laughed, apart from Gerrard who tutted, and Rex, who snuffled as he retreated, literally, from the hands of the law. He was a discerning beast who had doubtless noted, given his keen canine snout, that Plod One was a stranger to anti-perspirant.

I sometimes find it hard to believe that I have a dog, something to care for, to come home and feed. But here I am, a two walks a day man, a fixture in the park, known to the woman in the pet shop. I feel quite proud in one way, but unpleasantly fixed in another. The round the world trip, the job where I can't take him into work, are now out of the question. Some days, if Gerrard's going straight out from work, I can't even go for a spontaneous drink any more, I have to come home to put him out and feed him. Farley used to point out that the advantage of kids over dogs is that you've got a woman to do all the boring bits, while you can do the fun stuff like taking him to football matches or showing off to him at sport. He was joking, sort of.

Our alibis were, as far as we were concerned, established, our noses clean, copy books mercifully free from blots and, as there was a pause while we watched the dog scratch his neck, all seemed to be well with the world. I handed over Farley's keys, omitting to mention our trip to see Alice, and assumed that that was that. It was then that I casually remarked, in a spirit of civility and light chat, that Plod One did not have a Cornish accent. This was a mistake.

'No, sir,' he replied stuffing his thumbs into an already over-stuffed waistband. 'I moved from the South East. Too much traffic, too many folk in a rush,' he said as if I went out every morning with the express purpose of hurrying people along. He looked directly at me and then up to the noticeboard near where he was sitting. At his eye level was a picture of Gerrard mincing down some road in his Breton shirt on a Greek holiday we'd been on. I had drawn a moustache on him and written 'I am what I am' on a card underneath the picture. I got the feeling the subtleties of this kind of joke were lost on Plod One.

'I've often thought it must be nice to live in some country backwater.' I was trying to build bridges.

'Penzance is not a backwater, it's a lively modern town,' said Plod One, his Cornish accent thickening down the length of the sentence. 'Not that we're based in Penzance central, but we get to go in a fair bit.'

'I'm sure,' I said. 'No, I'm sure it's much nicer than here. I mean, you can't go out without getting mugged or burgled. Sometimes simultaneously.'

'Let me tell you, we see our fair share of serious crime in Cornwall, whatever you lot think,' said Plod Two.

'I'm sure it's rife,' said Gerrard a little too flippantly and camply for the plods' liking, I guessed.

There was a brief hiatus while the police composed themselves and the dog moved towards the kitchen door. I've already noted that he is a particularly sensitive animal, and I can only guess that he felt the questioning was going to get tougher and wanted to be in a position to make good his escape.

'You feature in Mr Farley's will, sir,' said Plod One who had now developed a Cornish burr you could have snagged your coat on.

'Do I?'

'Yes, sir, he mentioned it in your voice mail message that we accessed.'

'So he did.' My voice had become unaccountably posher, effete even. I sounded like Anthony Hancock doing Noël Coward. Stop it, I thought, you went to Highlands Comprehensive, not bloody Eton.

'And yet you forgot that, sir,' Plod Two chimed in, clearly eyeing me for a potential 'fall down the stairs'. I reckoned he had seen the cut of my jib and concluded that it needed readjusting, preferably through some no-nonsense treatment in the cells. He had a funny way of looking at me. It made me think that, in his terms, he understood me more completely than anyone I had ever met. He understood the flounce to my character, the half-arsed ideas, the things said for effect. And though doubtless he would say things for effect, they were different things and for a different effect; he understood that I wasn't in his sense a proper man, and that he didn't like me a whole heap.

I got the idea that he hoped I was homosexual because it would be less of a challenge to him. The idea of me going out with a woman, least of all a good-looking one, would have been an anathema to him. It made me want Alice to walk in right there and then so I could say, 'See, you fat macho bastard, see what I'm shagging (I substitute the 'what' for the 'who' to sound more tough). Have you, with your darts and your beer, with your blue plastic belt, ever, ever been out with a woman that resembles her? You have not.' I omitted from the fantasy that I had not, ever, ever, been out with a woman who resembled Alice, but I had asked her for a date and sort of got one, which was more than he had ever done.

The policemen were clearly expecting some sort of answer as to why I'd said nothing about Farley mentioning me in the will. They were looking at me with the 'we've got all day' expression that normally means someone wants to be in the pub in the next five minutes.

'Yes, well, it has been a bit of a strain.' 'Strraaiiin,' I said, like one of those deliberately camp voices they use to advertise gay chatlines.

'Indeed, sir. Are you aware Mr Farley changed his will only two weeks ago? In your favour.'

I said that I wasn't and he leaned forward to me. Now I have a thing about body space at the best of times. If I'm going to get intimate with anyone I prefer a high-bosomed nymphet, not a high-smelling policeman. I would normally have recoiled, but I felt recoiling might have been taken by this hefty Peeler for a total and complete admission of guilt, so I recoiled slowly, if such a thing is possible.

'This is the very kind of thing that gives the professional policeman cause for concern, sir. What, sir, do you think a jury would make of that, sir?' said Plod One in an accent that would have made Long John Silver sound like an over-educated metropolitan fop. Each 'sir' was pronounced 'zurrr' in a way only heard today in tourist board advertisements for the county. It is also worth noting here that there are only so many 'sirs' a sentence can bear before 'sir' begins to take on its opposite meaning, namely 'arsehole'.

'He was a generous and thoughtful friend?' I was trying to help, I really was. I could see he was sounding me out as a potential murderer, but instead of being scared I felt curiously flattered. It's so rare nowadays that someone genuinely takes an interest in you. Also, many of the murderers you see on films and TV cut quite a dash, and here I was, almost elevated to their ranks. I saw myself on the front page of the Sunday tabloids: 'Washed Up – Evil Schemer Who Drowned Friend'. 'Handsome and brilliant socialite says, "I did it because he began to bore me".' For a second I got a glimpse of what it must feel like to have achieved something, to be able to stand out from the crowd. I guessed I wouldn't have felt that way had I actually killed him.

'I don't like being lied to, sir,' said Plod One, attempting to shiver my timbers with a verbal cannonball. I always think quiet menace is the most effective sort, but Plod One had opted for the loud variety. I was glad I was not wearing a wig, or I would have feared it was about to be blown into the waste disposal unit.

'We don't like being lied to.' Plod Two obviously felt the point needed underscoring.

'You're in the wrong job then really, aren't you?' said Gerrard. His love of the truth, as I have said before, sometimes places quite a burden on our relationship. He obviously thought this was very funny. He told Lydia about it four or five times afterwards.

I allowed myself a cheeky little smirk. When I smirk I try to suppress it with the result that I look rather simple. I swear I saw both policemen finger imaginary truncheons.

Plod One drew back. 'When you spoke to DC Arrowsmith you said that Mr Farley had been in the water for less than twelve hours. How did you know that?'

'I don't know, I just assumed he'd killed himself the night before.'

'Why?'

'Well, he'd hardly be likely to kill himself before the weekend, would he?' interrupted Gerrard.

'Why not?' The plods were both stumped here.

'He'd miss his Saturday night out.'

I would normally have observed that a Saturday evening at the Golden Sands caravan park in Padstow or wherever he'd been, would be likely to speed most people to their appointment with the eternal, but I kept it to myself.

The Plods looked at each other.

'What makes you think he was planning a Saturday night out?' asked Plod Two.

'What do you mean by planning?' asked Gerrard, reasonably, I thought.

'Planning, sir. Preparing for, readying himself.'

'Well, he wouldn't have been planning, would he?'

The two policemen looked baffled.

'Why wouldn't he be planning?'

I thought it would be helpful for me to interject at this point.

'We ... he ... don't really plan in that sense. He'd just wait to see who called.'

The policemen clearly took a dim view of this laissez-faire attitude to social arrangements.

Plod One tried again, with the reluctant patience of an old-fashioned schoolmaster forced to teach by liberal methods.

'You know he was going to go out though. How?'

'Because it was Saturday night,' said Gerrard and I, as a man.

'So you're telling me that at the age of thirty two this bloke goes out every Saturday night?'

'Yes,' said Gerrard.

'Where?' asked Plod One.

'Wherever,' said Gerrard. 'To parties mainly and clubs – discotheques.' He stressed the last word in the manner that one imagines white settlers used to explain the 'Iron Horse' to the oppressed masses formerly known as Red Indians. I wondered about Gerrard's hostile attitude to the police; not so much its origins, which were pretty much the same as mine, only with a lot of grudges about industrial disputes that had nothing to do with him thrown in, but its wisdom – more than that, its sheer bravery. Gerrard's normal idea of taking a risk was buying two pints of milk instead of one and praying that we used the lot before it went off. Still, I reasoned that as a paramedic he would be more used to dealing with the police – whom he still occasionally termed the 'repressive state apparatus' – than me.

Plod One's jaw stiffened, while Plod Two looked wistfully at the teapot.

'Oldest swinger in town character, eh?' said Plod One in a 'Thinks he's smart, does he?' tone, clearly threatened by the lifestyle of the former Farley, the present corpse.

It was only then that I really looked at the policemen. I'm trying to be kind in my description. Both, as I've already recorded, were fat but in a vigorous, sweaty, muscular way. You certainly wouldn't have wanted to tangle with either of them. This was the fat of food taken on the run, long kebab-fuelled nights on the case, of cooling balm of beer poured on fraying nerves. It was functional fat, fat to pin down a criminal with or block a doorway as a means of escape. They looked so unpleasant to me that I wondered how they ever did the nice cop, nasty cop routine. Maybe they contented themselves with nasty cop and incredibly nasty cop, though I wouldn't have taken a guess at who was who.

Plod One was bald, his hair the classic nightmare bog seat shape – still sprouting viciously at the sides but almost entirely absent in the middle. As if attempting to compensate for the shame of his naked dome, he had taken full advantage of the functioning follicles on his top lip and grown an exuberant blond 'tache. Some are born to baldness – it's in their genes; some achieve baldness – through stress and poor hair care, and some have baldness thrust upon them – particularly after tedious stag nights and rugby club annual dinners. Plod One looked as if he was bald by choice, because it suited his internal mood, one of damp afternoons in overspill towns and DIY superstores.

One of the main things people such as Plod One dislike about people like me is that they think we are looking down our noses at them. Did I look down my nose at him? Did I think I was better than him? Yep, and I'd be willing to take tests to prove it.

He had run to the country for whatever reason: peace and quiet, or lack of traffic so he could drive his car more easily, or something. Avoiding people like me wasn't on his list, although he certainly would want to avoid people like me if he regularly came into contact with them.

I had run from the provinces specifically to get away from people like him and the things they do, the places they visit. I don't want to go anywhere near the ordinary, hardworking men and women who are the backbone of this country. I grew up with them, I did my stint in Garden Gnome-land and that's me finished. I want to stay here in London, getting off my tits with a bunch of over-opinionated media twats who wouldn't know a day's work if it came up and bit them on their pampered arses. I don't want the dignity of labour and a job well done, I want a laugh. Each to his own, you know.

Staring into the policeman's face, I tried to look for kindness or wit or sincerity, but instead an awful realisation swept over me. Plod One was about my age, or perhaps younger. I instinctively felt for my hair, which to my relief was still there, a little too thick and luxuriant if anything.

More than ever these days age seems like a choice, and Plod One had chosen to be middle-aged. What I had chosen to be, I don't know. He noticed I was staring at him.

'Can I ask you a question, sir?'

I resisted the temptation to reply 'you just have' because it would have been out of place and also because it's not funny. 'Yes.'

'Were either of you having a homosexual relationship with Mr Farley?' I took my stare away from Plod One with all speed.

'No, we're not gay. Neither was he.'

Both Plods pushed their chins into the commodious folds of their neck pouches, simultaneously raising their eyebrows in pantomime surprise.

'Really, sir?'

'No,' said Gerrard, flapping his wrists, camp as a row of chiffon tents. He enjoyed camping it up as it made him more attractive to women, though I couldn't see what the point of it was here.

'Are you sure?' said Plod One in a clotted cream voice more suited to saying, 'Berries on the branch before Michaelmas, no good'll come of it, I tell'ee.'

'Why would we lie?'

Plod One shrugged as if it was obvious. 'Because you might find it embarrassing.'

'We wouldn't find it embarrassing. We're not gay but we don't think there's anything wrong with anyone who is. I expect you do?' said Gerrard, curling a surly lip like the King in *Jailhouse Rock*.

'No, sir,' said Plod Two, deadpan. 'Both DC Atkins and I have very confused sexualities, and we've both opted to be quite open about it with our colleagues in the force.'

'Right,' I said, completely unsure if he was joking or not. It made me like him a lot more.

'Just cut the crap, John, and get on with it,' said Plod One, DC Atkins.

'I will indeed cut the crap,' said Plod Two with a cold edge of steel to his voice, the kind of cold edge of steel that I surmised was ideally suited to cutting crap. He opened up a grey moulded plastic briefcase and produced a neatly opened envelope in a clear plastic bag.

'This letter, sir, we recovered from a pile at Mr Farley's flat. Would you look at it without opening the bag?'

He passed it to Gerrard who studied the envelope, thrusting his tongue into his lower lip in Mong mode. He put his hand inside his jeans and scratched thoughtfully at his balls. He rocked back and forth, like a Mogadonned Rabbi at the Wailing Wall.

'It's my letter,' he said, and shrugged the nonchalant shrug of a deeply guilty man.

Plod Two produced another sheet of paper from his briefcase.

'Would you care to read this photocopy of your letter and tell us what interpretation a reasonable person might put on it?' I thought that was a tough one for Gerrard, to whom unreasonableness was a way of life.

' "I want to kill you, you fucker. You've let me down for the last time. Watch yourself in future. 'Hatred springs freshest from friendship's bed'. PS, I want my Verve album back",' said Gerrard, trying desperately to make his words sound pleasant, even complimentary.

'Would you mind telling me what interpretation we might put on that, sir?' Plod One was beefing up to Plod Two's theme.

'I was angry with him. He was going to help me out with a girl then he didn't. It's hardly the work of a master criminal, is it? Writing a threatening letter before you kill him.'

'And are you a master criminal, sir?'

'No,' said Gerrard petulantly, looking down his nose at Plod Two.

'Therefore it's not impossible that you did write that letter, is it, sir, and then kill him? Being a London ponce and not a criminal genius it's not impossible you made something of a blunder, is it, sir? That's what I'm thinking. That and life imprisonment.'

The last two words of Plod Two's sentence knocked the stuffing out of Gerrard's arrogance and he took on the sickly look I had last seen on the dog when we fed him some off-message chicken.

'I didn't kill him, I was at work,' said Gerrard, suddenly wispy in voice and gesture. 'And I'm not gay.'

'Although you are a male nurse,' said Plod One, as if presenting a conclusive piece of evidence.

'Paramedic,' insisted Gerrard.

'Oh,' said Plod One, slightly crestfallen. He crossed something out on his pad and went back to the letter.

' "Hatred springs strongest from friendship's bed"? Exactly what did that mean? Why bed, sir? Why the mention of bed?'

'It's a quote.'

'From where? We like to have the full facts,' said Plod One with the confidential manner of an auntie reassuring guests she only uses the finest jam.

'That's nice to know,' I said

'No one likes a smart arse, sir,' said Plod Two through gritted teeth.

I knew this wasn't true. I love smart arses. In fact one of the qualities I most admire in the arses that I know is their smartness, but once more I thought it best to demur from confrontation.

'It's a quote from a poem,' said Gerrard.

'Written by?' said Plod Two.

'Me,' said Gerrard, quietly. The dog, who had re-entered, gave him the wide-eyed look of alarm he normally reserves for when you tell him to get away from the table while you are eating.

'Recently?' said Plod Two.

'When I was at school,' said Gerrard, looking a very sorry bunny indeed.

'So it's hardly a fucking quote then, is it?' I burst in.

'Leave the questioning to us, sir,' said Plod Two.

'Sorry.'

Plod One seemed unable to stay off the gay theme for very long. In fact, he seemed more intent on getting us to confess that we were gay than he did on finding out how Farley died.

'You do realise, gentlemen, that the lifestyle you've been

describing entirely fits that of a gay man? Our briefing documents clearly state that the gay man goes to DISCOTHEQUES very regularly, enjoys just the sort of music you have here on your wall,' he tapped a flyer on the noticeboard – something about 'banging tunes' that I'd put up because I thought it would depress Gerrard, who couldn't accept that anyone produced music without guitars, 'is often affluent through lack of children (the evidence was skimpy here, for the affluence, I mean) and, though promiscuous, is in a relationship, often cohabiting with a *de facto* spouse.' He made a hand movement, indicating me and Gerrard.

If you had asked Gerrard to spray tea all over the dog via the orifices of his nose, in normal circumstances he would have been unable, and morally unwilling, to do it. On this occasion, however, he wasted no time in immersing the animal in a fairy mist of nasally delivered Ty-phoo. The dog sniffed and licked at the cloud that was engulfing it.

'Steady fucking on!' I shouted. 'I don't mind being branded a poof, but if I was I'd have better taste than that.'

'Fucking likewise,' said Gerrard, macho as John Wayne ordering you down from your horse. I'd noticed we'd both started swearing. Throughout our interview with the policemen we'd unconsciously or consciously camped it up, fairly poorly I thought, so that at times we sounded like we were auditioning for the lead roles in a prison version of *Brideshead Revisited*. The suggestion that we were lovers, however had us both into 'Bare knuckle boxing? Game for girls,' territory, a territory that was reasonably alien to both of us.

There was a strange hissing and spitting noise, which at first made me wonder if the dog had been in the bin and got a bone stuck in his throat again, but it was Gerrard, sounding like a tiger that had bitten on a bar of soap.

'We'll take that as a denial then,' said Plod Two, obviously impressed.

'You can,' said Gerrard, pawing at his mouth. 'Look, we both have cast iron alibis for the time Farley died, we both liked him, although I had fallen out with him temporarily, and we're both sorry he's dead.'

'Alibi,' said Plod One. 'Interesting choice of word.'

I decided at this point to use the tactic that mothers, who know little of the internal drives of the teenage psychopath, recommend against bullies. Ignore them and they'll go away.

'Check them out,' said Gerrard.

'Oh, don't you worry,' said Plod One, 'we will. Don't you two boys be running off anywhere now. Make sure you stay where we can find you.' He was back in the 'we don't get many strangers round 'ere' accent and I wondered if he ever listened to the Cornish people talking around him or whether he preferred to found his new identity on films about eighteenth-century smugglers.

'Actually,' I said, stroking the dog's wet ears and attempting to change the subject, 'he does smell nice. It's like Calvin Klein, CK One.'

'Unisex, is that?' said Plod Two with a glance between me and Gerrard. I was surprised he knew what I was talking about, but then I reminded myself of the fetish that the lower orders have for designer labels. 'We'll contact you when we need you to identify the body,' said Plod Two. He turned to his colleague.

'Come on, George. We're wasting our time with this pair of tarts. Neither of these two could find their arse with both hands, let alone organise a murder.' He stuffed the letter and photocopy back into his briefcase and closed it. I was surprised to find myself quite hurt by his scorn. Why did this bloke's opinion matter to me?

'Is it easy to get tickets for *Starlight Express*?' asked Plod One.

'I've really no idea,' I said, honestly. Gerrard shrugged, wondering if the good cop/bad cop interview technique had been replaced by, bad cop/surreal cop.

'I didn't think you would have, you pair of poofs,' said Plod One, smiling, as I and the dog corralled him to the door. I failed to see how my lack of knowledge of a musical on roller skates qualified me as a homosexual, but there again I am not a policeman.

'We'll be calling again after we've conducted a proper search of his flat,' said Plod Two.

'Right ho,' I said, wondering if they had met Alice and what she had told them about our visit.

6

Those are pearls that were his eyes

I had been nervous about seeing Alice again since the minute I left her but as the morning of our meeting approached, the morning of Farley's funeral, the feeling, already like waiting for exam results on the day of your driving test, grew more intense. This was not all bad.

Work became strangely interesting, a break from thinking about her, and I was bizarrely able to concentrate for periods of up to an hour. I managed to wrap up four episodes-worth of complaint celebrities, misery stars, within a week. Exploding fondue sets and time-bomb Teasmades became, if not interesting, capable of consideration without having to suppress the urge to run off. I even set up a deal with the Federation of Master Builders to expose dodgy workmen – in particular the very dodgy workman who had presented the business end of a screwdriver to me and Gerrard. One night – in front of the boss, obviously – I even stayed late. Anything to get Alice out of my mind.

I knew the funeral would be make or break, the big one for me. I had to at least set up a date with Alice there, though you could hardly think of a worse time or place to do it. I was willing to explore every avenue, and even tried some motivational techniques from a management video Adrian was reluctantly shooting for a bunch of businessmen he termed 'suits'. I presumed by this he meant 'people who wash'. I spent five or ten minutes every hour staring into the bathroom mirror saying, 'You don't ask, you don't get,' and, more aggressively, 'When exactly did you decide you wanted to finish second?' My reflection looked challenged and replied, 'Second? That's a bit ambitious, isn't it?'

When I got home, I read men's style magazines, scanning the pages for the ideal funereal get up. There was nothing specifically on the topic, but over the course of a week or so I got a good feel for what people were wearing in dark colours. I even phoned GQ and was told 'wit is in' for funeral gear and that they might consider a feature on it – in three or four months, which was no good to me. At least I think I got through to GQ, but I was convinced I could hear laughter in the background while the journalist was talking to me. I wasn't exactly sure what 'wit' meant, and the images that came into my head didn't seem in the best taste, least of all the wreath playing the tune from *That Sinking Feeling*.

I had thought of calling Alice, to see if she was OK, or rather to show her that I was phoning to see if she was OK; but having secured a meeting with her – albeit at the funeral – I didn't want to give her the chance to back out. I knew that Gerrard wouldn't call her, mainly because he would have to ask me for Farley's phone number but also because he wouldn't have known what to say. I did want to find out if the police had talked to her, but I thought that in their dank, suspicious brains this might come over as collusion, or whatever shorter word they would choose.

We had difficulty getting someone who had the time to cart Farley's body up from Cornwall, so I had nearly a month to brood on my choice of clothes, or rather not to brood but to part with a good amount of cash at store where I trusted the assistant's taste.

What I am about to describe may now sound disgusting to you. It'll probably sound disgusting to me now, but believe me, at the point I am describing it, it is the height of fashion. I know because in addition to checking it out in the men's magazines I also called a couple of model agencies, pretending to be a journalist from GQ and asking them what their style tips were for suits. I was doubly sure to ask about what looked good on the beefier (fatter) models, so it would suit me.

I chose a slate-coloured single-breasted three-piece by Spencer – high-buttoned waistcoat available exclusively, I think, from Made-on-Earth on the King's Road, a black silk shirt and black silk tie – same place – and a pair of black Chelsea boots. The whole outfit cost less than £800, but I felt pretty good in it. On my finger I had a silver ring with a star on it for the sake of seventies kitsch, which has been fashionable for some time now. I was going to go for a small French bloke-style bag to complement the get up, which was certainly what the magazine had advised, but I was still rattled by the way the coppers, those fat bulges in the thin blue line, had been convinced I was gay, and the laughter in the background at the office, so I didn't bother. It's funny that this should have concerned me, but I suppose being brought up to think of gay people as lower than vermin (a rat doesn't choose to be a rat, a poof could get some treatment, almost any one of my relations could have said) leaves some residual homophobia, even if I'd rather be rid of it. I still can't bear to see men kissing or holding hands in public, but there again I don't much like it in heterosexual couples either. On balance I'd rather be homosexual – no, bisexual if I had the choice. It would improve my chances of scoring no end, but I can't even summon the will to try. It's like my school teachers said, I haven't got any backbone.

Getting away from this theme – I'm not gay, right, we'll just leave it at that – and back on the clothes, a part of me had considered taking out a bank loan and buying some Armani or some such rich-bitch designer, but I thought Alice would think that was tacky, which is different from kitsch. Good taste is represented by the Emperor's new clothes when everyone is admiring them; tacky is the Emperor when people realise he's not wearing any. Kitsch is when we all decide it's quite a laugh to go around naked anyway.

It's a rule that to be truly treasured, loved as opposed to venerated, fashion must spend some time as the apogee of bad taste, at least in Britain. To me Armani is, and has been for a while, tacky just because of the people who wear it, or him. It's not that I would never wear his stuff, but I'd wait for it to make the move to being kitsch.

One thing that I find amazing about the truly rich – who I do see occasionally in my marches through Chelsea – is their uniformity. Some of them are obviously creative and interesting people, but they all choose to spend their money on the same gear: Armani, Land Rover, Harley Davidson, Chanel – and most of it looks terrible. Blue blazers for the men, jumper over the shoulders for the women, boating shoes for casual wear, Church's or Jimmy Choo for smart. It's remarkable that people to whom money grants freedom undreamed of in history opt to live under such restrictions.

The rich have money, the rest of us have to make do with style. There is a little of the elitist in me, hungover from my days as a punk rocker – the elitist that says if you've heard of it, it's already unfashionable. As I've already said, this is definitely the case with the club scene where this week's hot potato is next week's cold chips. The point of clothes is to express individuality up to a point, but more importantly to show you're a member of a clique, a discerning clique, not one any stockbroker with a Saturday afternoon to spare can buy his way into. Having said this, most of the time I look like a sack of shit and have regularly attended social events in the soup kitchen chic I spend most of my working life wearing.

We hadn't actually known where to bury Farley. For someone so rootless nowhere seemed appropriate, short of having his ashes snorted up the punters' noses in the women's toilets at Gossips night club. There was no football penalty spot to cover for him, no allotment to fertilise, no beloved home vista for him to look out on in his final repose. We had no idea where his parents were buried and, although we knew he came from Hertfordshire, it seemed like unnecessary effort to find out. He'd never really mentioned his parents in life, why should we conclude he'd want to be with them in death? It's a puzzle to me, people who get buried in family plots – eternity must be like one long Christmas Day, trying to get on so as not to upset Grandma, arguing over the celestial remote control, wondering how much of your life, if that's the right word, you can reveal to your relations without worrying or disgusting them.

Cornwall seemed a good bet, since that's where he had drowned and we wouldn't have to transport the body back, but I wasn't going to sentence Farley to eternity in some bucolic hell hole surrounded by plastic piskies and ghoulish suburbanites on holiday with four generations of family including toddlers with earrings.

So we opted for Brixton. Since that's where he chose to live, we reasoned he must have liked it.

The police had reluctantly closed their enquiry on Farley after a few days of sniffing around and one of following us. Plod Two had phoned two days after his first interview to ask why Gerrard had avoided him by jumping on a bus that morning. Gerrard told him he was catching it to the tube station on his way to work like he always does when it's too wet to cycle. Plod Two had grunted – or I can't imagine that he didn't – and asked a couple more questions before enquiring where he could see *The Mousetrap*. I heard Gerrard saying, 'Look in *Time Out* magazine', 'my pleasure' and 'the policeman did it', before putting down the phone.

Gerrard said Plod Two wanted one of us to go down to Cornwall to identify the body, which I wasn't very keen to do. I reasoned that Gerrard, to whom horrid death was bread and butter, would be better psychologically suited to the grisly business than myself. He muttered something about introducing me to a few realities of the world, but I didn't really see how gore and dismemberment were any more real or instructive than anything else. This is one of the problems I find with films and books about serial killers, or people doing unpleasant things to others. As a social phenomenon, murderers are no more revealing than teenybopper pop stars, though slightly less repulsive and possessing greater moral fibre. I have no wish to be informed of the doings of either.

'Truth,' an acquaintance of my youth who liked dressing as a vampire, and who could sit through Jim Morrison's poetry without so much as a smirk, had once told me, 'is revealed at society's extremes'. Well, yes, but it's also revealed at its centre, and anywhere else you care to look if you're willing to give it close attention. We don't need to peer into the dark side of life. When I have fantasies about good-looking women, I don't need to be reminded that they go to the toilet just like the ugly ones, and I would be worried about myself if I did.

These things were in my mind as I told Gerrard, 'I don't want to see the body.'

'You're scared, aren't you?'

'Of course.'

A grin spread over his face akin to that I had seen the only time I had played him at chess. He had narrowly beaten me and had refused to play me ever again, meaning that he was, empirically, better than me – a 'fact' he was fond of repeating. As we had played alone, I simply claimed I had beaten him whenever it came up. Now I've lied about it so much I can occasionally convince myself it is true.

'This being something that most people encounter and deal with at some time in their lives, what does that make you?' he asked, although I sensed he would gladly provide the answer.

'A coward?' I ventured.

'Coward,' he repeated, rolling the word around his mouth like a toffee.

'I'll come with you if you like,' I said.

'You're not scared of the train then?'

'Not if I can sit in the middle and travel backwards, before nightfall,' I said.

I was surprised at this line of thinking from Gerrard. I thought we both took it for granted we were cowards; on every level of our being an instinct for safety and repose conquering all thoughts of selflessness or adventure. I thought we were both pretty proud of the fact. Cowardice to us was a mark of intelligence. Appealing to my bravery was going to get him nowhere. We had discussed the subject while watching a programme about some American politician who'd decided the Vietnam war was a good time for a long holiday in Canada. Would we have fought in wars like that or would we have run away to some neutral country? We would have fought, we concluded, we would have been too afraid of the consequences of absconding and have lacked the resourcefulness to move. Neither Gerrard nor I would have had the courage to dodge the draft.

In the end we didn't go on the train to Cornwall, we hired a car. Gerrard didn't like this idea on the grounds of environmental damage, etc., but we hoiked in Lydia to come with us and brought the dog as well, so it was cheaper than taking the train. This for Gerrard was the clincher, particularly when it turned out I could get it for free.

We set off in the early morning a day after we'd got the call to come and identify the body. I hired the car on the firm as, quite genuinely, I had been investigating something about a bloke who had sold off a whole stock of faulty bungee-jumping rope in Totnes or somewhere. I didn't bother telling Adrian that I had cleared up the whole case on the phone, but never mind. I figured that a ten-minute visit for tea, and whatever they eat in Devon, to my doyens of disaster should be enough to convince him that I'd been working. Apparently the rope in question degenerated after ten or so goes to give an inconsistent bounce, hardly stretching at all, snapping the jumper's ankles or not stopping them in time from burying their heads violently into the crash mats. No one had been killed yet, largely due to the use of big crash mats, although an MP from the yellow party had been knocked cold opening a fair somewhere. I make no comment other than to say that I was deliberately stalling my exposé to allow the bungee operators a clear go at the pop festival season.

We were lucky that Lydia had come at all. She'd stayed at our flat the night before we went to Cornwall in order to ensure a quick getaway. She'd brought round a video of *Casablanca*, which I agreed to watch because it's one of those films you should be able to say you have seen, even if you don't really want to watch it. Besides, most girls have seen it, so it's obviously another string in the deep and interesting bow. I have a bit of a prejudice against black and white films as my parents would never watch them after 1976 when they bought the colour telly. My dad said it wasn't value for money to invest in colour and still watch black and white. I think he had a point.

Naturally the film had to be paused at certain points: once to allow me to go out for more beer, having polished off my first six in record time; twice for Gerrard to receive phone calls, the first for twenty minutes, the second for nearly an hour.

As if this wasn't enough, Lydia's patience had been further tried because Gerrard and I were doing impressions of the Cornish policemen over the top of the film, saying, 'Of all the bars in all the world you had to walk into this one, moi loverzzz!' at the top of our voices. I thought I'd do her a favour by turning the conversation to the film itself.

'Not many people know that Humphrey Bogart had an affair with Ava Gardner,' I said, as if daring them to contradict me.

'Who later married Sinatra,' said Gerrard, which surprised me. I would have thought he would have hated Frank Sinatra because he wore a suit and didn't sing about 'real issues', like workers' rights (ha-ha).

'Who later married?' I asked, wondering if we could get all the way to André Previn from Sinatra, maybe even as far as the Morecambe and Wise show and so back to Angela Rippon, *Come Dancing*, Terry Wogan, and on to a whole list of people who want shooting.

The plane was starting up on the runway and tears streamed down Lydia's face. 'Quiet,' she said, 'television is not an interactive medium.'

'Write in and tell them that,' said Gerrard.

I chuckled at his joke

'Shut up, please, shut up!' said Lydia, her eyes fixed on the screen.

'Television *is* fully interactive in many parts of the world. They've got these new set top boxes that give you full Internet access – everything,' insisted Gerrard.

'Don't forget Ceefax, that's been around for ages,' I helpfully reminded him.

' "You'll regret this, maybe not today, maybe not tomorrow, but some day," ' said Humphrey, me and Gerrard at the same time.

'Quiet!' howled Lydia.

I had a strange glimpse into how psychopaths must feel. Her begging only egged me on.

'Will there ever be a star to match Bogart's celebrity?' I asked.

Lydia snatched for the remote control and turned off the television.

'We were watching that,' said Gerrard.

'No, you weren't, you were talking above it.'

'Well, it's not a god,' said Gerrard. 'It's not, "pray silence for m'lord the TV".'

'You're either watching it or you're not,' said Lydia, giving it to him in a language he could understand.

'We were only joking,' I said.

'You were joking for the whole length of the film. We had Gerrard and the policemen at the start, then half an hour on Long John Copper vacuums his Sierra half way through, and, as a final straw, will there ever be a star to match Bogart's fucking celebrity?'

'Perhaps De Niro?' I ventured.

'Raaabish,' said Gerrard.

Lydia turned her face to the wall in disgust.

'Remember, Lydia, the more often a joke is repeated, the funnier it gets,' said Gerrard, like Obi Wan Kenobi letting Luke Skywalker in on some Jedi adage.

I was reminding him of this the next day as we sped West at roughly 120 m.p.h. down the M4. 'How often do you think I've done this?' I said.

'Please slow down,' Gerrard was saying, curled into the foetal position on the back seat. I knew he was curled up because as part of the joke I was looking at him. Lydia, who was raised on the modern gothic, was laughing and steering from the passenger seat.

'How many times have I done this?' I asked, hands retaking the wheel.

'Too many times, too many times!' shrieked Gerrard, his arse chewing buttons off the seat.

'And what happens to a joke the more often it's repeated?' I asked.

Lydia cackled hysterically, while the dog, I could hear, was munching into something Gerrard had in a packet. Part of the delay we had suffered that morning was him going to the shop to buy in provisions for the trip because 'you can't find anything nutritious on the motorway', which I thought was part of the fun. Normally he would have bought enough to last the whole two days but he'd realised stuff was going to be cheaper in Cornwall, so he should buy something there. Lucky for him, really, because he was too scared to emerge from the crash position to stop the dog eating his food.

'Stop it,' he said, although I'm not sure to whom. The dog gave a low grumble of disapproval, though the rustling didn't cease.

'Look, my hands are back on the wheel, this is a reasonable speed,' I said, stamping the accelerator the remaining quarter of an inch into the floor before moving into the middle lane and braking violently to allow some red-faced bloke in a Jaguar to overtake us, shaking his fist.

The unmistakable smell of vegetable Scotch egg was filling the air, along with grunts of pleasure from the dog and more pleading from Gerrard. I wondered if the Scotch eggs were going to inflict the same kind of anal catastrophe on the dog as they did on Gerrard. I mentally prayed for dry weather on the way back, as I was certain we were coming home with the windows open.

As we continued we had to slow, coming off the motorway and passing Stonehenge. I pointed out the barrows to Lydia, explaining how the ancient people had buried their dead and mentioning Beaker People and massive rocks that came from miles away in a mish-mash that I thought sounded convincing. It's amazing to me that if you talk without pausing people believe you, and it's also amazing to me that I have the need to do this. Why do I present myself as an authority on subjects of which I have no knowledge?

I think this is a complaint that affects a lot of men. It certainly affected one of my uncles, Dave, and indirectly his wife Audrey. She worked at a large rep theatre in the wardrobe department, and was occasionally invited to cast parties. She could never go, however, because my Uncle Dave would always ruin it by regaling various actors with his experiences acting in the works review. 'First night nerves? Don't talk to me about that, you're doing it in front of a bunch of strangers, I've got to show meself up in front of me mates,' he would tell the politely withdrawing RADA types. Whatever the subject, Dave knew best. Here was a man who, on having Einstein's discovery of the flexible nature of time explained to him, described it as 'obvious if you think about it'. 'Yes,' I'd said, 'but only if you think about it in the right way, which is rather the difficult bit for most people.' 'Oh, ah, yes, I'd agree with that,' he said. I'm sad to relate that it was me who had been doing the explaining. Such scientific insight, I guess, is the benefit of an English degree.

I rattled on to Lydia about the halcyon days when Stonehenge had a huge festival every summer, a free innocent celebration where impish traveller kids, no more than seven or eight, would sell you phoney acid and drive about in stolen cars. Lydia said I had told her before, which was likely because I only have so many stories.

The speed having calmed, Gerrard was shaking the dog and saying, 'You're a very bad boy indeed,' in a tone guaranteed to make him think he was a very good boy indeed.

We travelled down through Devon and over Dartmoor, where

we stopped to let the dog worry some sheep (not really, farmers) and walk off what Jeffrey Archer would call the veritable feast that he'd had at Gerrard's expense – one pack of veg Scotch eggs, one wholemeal pasty of some sort, half a French stick and a container of hummous. The food at the National Trust centre was gladdeningly exorbitant and unhealthy, as Gerrard can, at no price, proceed with an empty stomach.

We finally arrived at a campsite outside Penzance at about six o'clock and pitched our tents. One of the penalties of taking a dog is that there are few bed and breakfasts where you can house them, and those that there are run by fat women who call dogs 'doggie woggies' and children 'kiddiewinkles', an attitude that no civilised type can bear. This is why we opted to camp. The worst that can happen to you on a camp site is that you camp next to some bunch of underprivileged teenagers with a ghettoblaster or, worse, overprivileged teenagers with a guitar.

We got cans in that night instead of going to the pub and sat around a fire on the beach talking to some ugly Israeli hippies. One, a tall bloke in a 'Bad Boy' T-shirt, disappeared with Lydia just before the end of the evening and didn't come back. I considered having a go at his sister but didn't want to give Gerrard any ammunition to use with Alice. Even though he went to bed relatively early, he has a radar for this sort of thing.

One interesting fact, however, did emerge. It seemed that Lydia had a new boyfriend called Eric. The hippie girl told me it was one of the first things Lydia had said to her when they met at the off licence. She expressed surprise that Lydia was going to sleep with her brother but I pointed out the English tradition of relationships not counting when on holiday, which she said seemed quite civilised. I felt quite insulted that Lydia had not chosen to tell me, her best male friend, something she'd relate over a couple of cans of Carling Black Label to a soap dodger.

We were scarcely out of our tents before I told Gerrard that Bad Boy had porked Lydia. I didn't want to tell him about Eric because I thought that was up to her. Gerrard ruminated like a ruminant as we drove out of the campsite before he enquired, 'So was that your first taste of a roundhead lance?'

'I'm sorry?' said Lydia

'Your first drive with the roof down?' said Gerrard.

'I don't know what you're talking about,' said Lydia.

'Shagging without a foreskin, what's it like?'

What gave Gerrard the right to ask these questions? Nothing and everything. In my group of friends, having any privacy at all is regarded as rather bad form. Like a hangover from school, nothing is taboo as long as it can be treated as a subject for ridicule.

'I should have thought you of all people would have known,' replied Lydia.

'But only from the doer's end, not from that of the doee,' he said, horribly emphasising 'doee'.

'What are you on about, Gerrard?'

'You shagging that bloke, that's what. You couldn't have ridden a streamlined model too many times before,' he was giggling.

'Just because I went back to his tent doesn't mean I shagged him.' Lydia's dismay made me wonder if my assumptions had been correct. 'Why would you want to know from me anyway, couldn't you ask one of your girlfriends?'

'I always do,' he said. 'But it's an ongoing survey. I'm trying to build up a representative sample of the population.'

'Might be a long wait if you take part in all the experiments yourself,' said Lydia.

'Precisely,' said Gerrard.

'I didn't shag him. And what makes you think I've never done it with a circumcised bloke before?'

Gerrard frowned. Because he considered Lydia ugly, and because he'd never sleep with anyone he didn't fancy even if he was really drunk and there was no one else about, he couldn't see that anyone else would want to sleep with her. Few men in Britain are circumcised. He'd often spoken about being the only Jewish kid in his class at school, and having to suffer taunts of 'Gas!' as he took a shower after games, so Gerrard reasoned that Lydia was unlikely to have come across one before. The idea that she had slept with other circumcised men meant that either he was wrong about her attractiveness (impossible, he would have thought) or there were more circumcised men about than he had thought. This last idea was terrible to him, as he had been made to feel like he alone was missing out at school when actually there were plenty of others like him, he had just been unlucky there had been no one in his class. Gerrard often used the words 'missed out' or 'mourning' to describe his attitude to his lost foreskin, although I never quite saw what he was missing out on. Surely if you never had something you can't miss it? But Gerrard could. I just thought his grief over the loss was an affectation, designed to give him emotional depth when chatting up girls.

This chat up ploy, termed the foreskin withdrawal strategy by Lydia, was a high-risk one, but I think Gerrard gambled on it showing him as curiously open, honest and funny, able to take a joke against himself. He ran the risk of coming over as a victim of a strange and fierce madness, but few women forgot him. He didn't use it all of the time, of course. As I've already mentioned, insomnia was the staple line.

'You did sleep with him, I heard you,' said Gerrard. I thought this would be difficult as chez Bad Boy was a good two hundred yards from our tents.

'You heard wrong then,' said Lydia. 'I slept in his tent and that was it.'

'Who's this Eric then?' I was ready for a change of subject.

'How did you hear about him?' asked Lydia, with what I thought was a tinge of anger in her voice.

'I just heard you had a new boyfriend and that his name was Eric.'

'Since you ask, Eric's my . . .' said Lydia.

'Don't change the subject. If you didn't sleep with him what were those noises then?' asked Gerrard.

'That was me sleeping with his sister,' I said. Although this was a total lie, it fitted the flow of the conversation, as a surprising and arresting thing to say, and it made Gerrard jealous of me – not jealous that I had slept with her, he didn't fancy her I was sure, but that I had slept with anyone. That fate had granted me a woman I was willing to sleep with when it had not granted the same to him. This would have been a satisfactory outcome for all under normal conditions, but I had forgotten Alice.

I didn't so much see Gerrard smile – owing to all round political correctness he was in the back seat of the car, Lydia in the front – as feel the smile on the back of my neck. 'Very interesting,' he said.

'Only joking,' I insisted, slowing down to avoid one of those fluffy manifestations of farm life that I think they make into jumpers.

'Eric's my . . .' repeated Lydia.

'Oh, yeah,' said Gerrard. 'Enjoy yourself, did you?'

'Eric's my . . .' said Lydia again. Although I couldn't see her eyes I had the impression, from the tone of her voice, that they were glazing over.

'I didn't sleep with her.'

'You weren't in the tent last night.'

'Eric's my . . .'

'I slept with the dog in the car.' I did actually. Gerrard farts too much.

He made a politically unacceptable pun on the word 'dog' and continued, 'What was it like? I'm conducting an ongoing survey.'

'How's the new boyfriend then? Let's hear all about him,' I said to Lydia.

'Don't wriggle out of it. You shagged her and you know you shagged her,' said Gerrard.

I pulled over to allow some ramblers past the other way. For some reason they said 'good morning' although I was sure I had never seen any of them before in my life. Gerrard said 'good morning' back but Lydia just mouthed something about Eric and I mumbled a bit. The dog gave them a token bark.

'You shagged her,' said Gerrard, who I could see in the mirror was folding his arms.

'Eric's my fiancé, he proposed last week,' said Lydia.

There are few things in the world that have the power to stop me and Gerrard arguing once we have started. This revelation was not one of them. It made us pause, but it could not make us stop completely.

'Gosh, Lydia, you never said,' I said, dying to have a go at Gerrard.

'Congratulations,' said Gerrard, poking me in the back and mouthing 'you shagged her' at me in the mirror.

'What's he like? And no, Gerrard, I did *not* shag her.'

'Not like either of you two,' said Lydia.

'Penzance is down that way,' said Gerrard.

'Thank you, Gerrard. The way that the large sign saying "Penzance" is pointing?' I said. 'Is it OK if I bring someone to the wedding?'

I heard Gerrard adjusting his position.

He launched in: 'You never bring anyone to weddings, you always leave your girlfriend behind so you can have a go at the available talent. You'd ask your bride to miss the reception at your own wedding on the off chance you'd pull. Who are you going to bring, you bastard?'

'Alice,' I said.

'We'll see about that.'

'Is there any chance we could talk about my life-changing event?' said Lydia.

'Sorry,' I said. 'What should we ask you?'

'I'm in hell,' said Lydia. 'I really am in hell.'

'You're not taking Alice,' said Gerrard as I pulled into a large car park overlooking the sea. I'd done what I'd set out to do and made him forget my gaffe about the hippie girl at least.

The viewing of Farley was remarkably brief. I didn't bother to look and neither did Lydia, despite her embarrassing eighties period when she'd listened to a lot of Goth music and talked about the fascination of death. On reflection, I'm surprised our friendship survived this particularly boring interlude and I sometimes thought it was out of gratitude she put up with us now.

We checked in at reception and the morgue bloke came out, a spotty chap with fuzzy hair and a clipboard.

'We're here for Mr Farley,' said Gerrard.

'Oh, yes,' said Fuzzy Bloke. 'Farley, drowning. "Full fathom five thy Farley lies", if I remember my Shakespeare.'

'What?' said Gerrard.

'Sorry,' said Fuzz, 'but it's not often you get a chance to use jokes like that.'

'Famously quoted in?' I said.

'Sorry?' said Fuzzo.

'Just show us the corpse, will you?' said Gerrard

I couldn't resist trying to trump Fuzzy Bloke on literary knowledge.

'T. S. Eliot's "Love Song of Alfred J. Prufrock",' I said, wondering if it was in fact another of his poems and if I'd got the J and the Alfred the right way round. Eliot had never much appealed to me; he was so opaque I suspected that there had originally been crossword grids attached to his major works. Four down, Mid-winter spring is its own season. (8,3). Five down, Sempiternal though sodden towards sundown, (4,6). First correct answers win two free tickets for *Cats!*

'I got it from amateur dramatics, I don't watch much TV,' confessed Fuzzo.

'Is it through there?' said Gerrard, gesturing to a door with 'Authorized Staff Only' written on it.

'Yes,' said Fuzzo, well bested on the culture front, 'follow me.'

Gerrard did the business with the corpse, with the air of a sarcastic parent reassuring a child that there really was no monster under the bed. Although the head was bloated and cut – Farley had been discovered when a jet ski hit him – Gerrard said it was easy enough to identify him through his designer clothes and blond hair.

There was a high level of drugs in the blood – Prozac, however, not the Valium Farley had talked about in his message – and lots of alcohol. The bloke at the morgue said that Farley had signed his death warrant as soon as he had swum fifty yards; even if he had changed his mind, he would have been unable to swim back. The area that he had chosen had a rip tide that would shoot you a mile out before you knew it. At that time of night, drunk and cold, swimming in against the prevailing current would have been impossible.

'You have to swim across rip tides, not against them,' I said, demonstrating knowledge picked up from a surfing lesson.

'I know that,' said Fuzzo.

'I'd be surprised if you didn't,' I said.

It had been discovered that Farley had checked in at a local campsite, and his tent had been found abandoned. Apparently, this would normally have been an inconclusive piece of evidence because people are always forgetting tents and at £50 a piece it's cheaper to buy a new one than to go back for them. The Farley tent, however, was typically expensive – around £400 according to the morgue bloke – and he reasoned that Farley would definitely have come back for that. Also, there was a copy of the collected works of Sartre, which is never a sign of good mental health in anyone over the age of twenty-one. The police had searched for his car, but I could have told them he didn't have one. Farley had spent most of his time since the age of eighteen in Greater London, so there hadn't been any point in his learning to drive.

The identification, along with the combined circumstantial evidence, was enough for a formal acknowledgement of Farley's death, said the morgue bloke. He thought the coroner might call us to give evidence but it was unlikely. The body would be free in a week, he guessed, and we would have to arrange delivery with a firm of undertakers – a fee that he guessed would take up the best part of whatever inheritance he had left.

I think I spoke for Gerrard too when I wondered aloud how much that would be.

7

Other worlds

The morning of the funeral saw Gerrard and me waiting for Lydia outside the pizzeria a hundred yards left from Brixton tube.

No one in their right mind meets anyone outside the tube itself. Well, twice anyway. Despite what I have said about Brixton's exciting multiculturalism and rising affluence, the entrance to the tube is like a vision of what might happen to the rougher parts of the Bronx, should they allow standards to slip. Brixton tube is where you go if you've been thrown out of being homeless, and meeting someone there is like waiting on a maximum security psychiatric ward without the maximum security. When you are at your lowest ebb, when you are like unto the ram with his horns beset in a bush, when you feel you cannot go on, ask yourself the question, 'Do I live in Brixton tube station?' If the answer is no, then there is some way back.

Not that the inhabitants of the tube station are hopeless, far from it. Theirs is not the whining, pleading, mewling desperation of the mainstream dispossessed. The Brixton beggar does not sit, head bowed, with a sign saying 'Hungry and Homeless, please help'. No, this is what businessmen would call 'proactive' begging, of the sort that used to be so dear to those blokes with eye patches who hung about on the Spanish Main a few years ago.

The Brixton beggar demands money with the delicacy of the ghost of Blackbeard shaking doubloons at midnight from a whey-faced merchantman. Often covered in blood, breath like a cutlass blow, buzzing with filth, carrying some noxious intoxicant – lager or glue, who can be sure? – and shouting 'Money!' this beggar has the unique ability to go through your pockets and be sick on you at the same time.

But don't go thinking he's alone, this chap. Oh, no. In fact, if Michael Jackson had fancied saving a few quid on making his *Thriller* video he would have found a very convincing cast of ghouls in Brixton tube, willing to lurch about behind him for the price of a can of Kestrel. Better still, if he just danced about with a fiver sticking out of his back pocket, I'm sure he could have achieved a very professional-looking undead-style dance routine with zombies lurching at his every turn.

In the absence of the king of pop's choreography, the Brixton regulars, at least five or six of them, circulate like expiring goldfish in movement and memory, making the same demands on the same people again and again. It's not unusual to find yourself subjected to three or four assaults by the same person, should your date be late.

A key rule for those who do find themselves here is not to smoke. For one it's against Underground rules, but more importantly it attracts the beggars like so many Captain Kidds to a stricken galleon. Make the mistake of exposing your fag packet to their fingers and it won't be so much emptied as sacked.

Farley used to occasionally play a horrible trick on these people. He would ask whether the soiled supplicant wanted a pound or a cigarette. When they made up their mind, after a period of trying to take both, Farley would turn triumphantly to the tube station and shout, 'You see, beggars can be choosers!' I had considered putting that into my funeral speech, but decided against it.

On top of the hard-core werewolves there will be about twenty or so B-grade nutters, courtiers of the pirate kings, still with some life outside the tube but through glue, crack or alcohol, working on promotion to the ranks of the Brixton fixture. These are not terrifying, but they can be a little worrisome and annoying, particularly as some of them have really irritating lines to catch your attention, like 'Can you lend me £4 million pounds? Oh, well, just one will do then,' or they just stand next to you, repeatedly tapping your arm while saying 'son' regardless of your sex.

The depressing thing is that this is roughly equivalent to some blokes' chat up techniques. Maybe that's what I was doing at parties and clubs, begging – for sex and companionship. If I had been a tramp my style for getting money would have been more of the, 'Hi, I'm Harry, I'm a tramp, would you like to come back to my cardboard box for coffee?' It's a lot more low-key, an altogether more upmarket approach to begging.

At the top of the steps are the religious and political fanatics. On any day you might encounter any combination of lazy students selling papers about workers, lost-eyed preachers offering ways to find yourself, old women who smell of state aid declaiming humanity and praising God or vice versa, all manner of yammerers and hammerers screaming above the traffic at the indifferent procession of faces to and from the tube. The least worrisome of these, for me, are the two red bow-tied brick shithouses from the Nation of Islam, who declaim 'the white man has had his compassion bleached out,' and 'by all means necessary'. I figure they might see an opportunity to have a crack at their oppressors by joining in if someone did mug me, but at least they're clean and are not going to try to convert me.

So like I said we were waiting for Lydia at the pizzeria, me, Gerrard and the dog, who wore a black scarf fastened by a black paper carnation which Lydia had made. I wasn't saying much as I was preparing myself to meet Alice whom Lydia – after argument between me and Gerrard – had contacted by phone. Alice had e-mailed her a list of Farley's friends and we had had some fun picking the real ones from the casual shags. We'd gone just on the ones we'd heard him mention and got to around ten or so.

I leaned against the window of the pizzeria, smoking, while Gerrard had got caught about twenty yards away by a stray political type with a placard who had escaped the orbit of the station and had something to say about animal rights. I wished Alice was there so I could use my line about 'we've heard a lot about animal rights, but never enough about their responsibilities', which I thought mildly funny. I asked the dog exactly what he had done for me that day, but he didn't reply.

I looked at Gerrard. From the way he was dressed you could

almost believe he was one of the political or religious nutters himself. To understand his dress sense, however, you first need to understand the philosophy behind it.

He starts from the premise that to think about clothes at all, to try to project any impression of yourself, is inherently false and therefore undesirable. You should buy solely stuff that you like, no matter if it causes dogs to bark at you and small children to throw stones in the street.

When it comes to suits, he has never got beyond the idea that he should buy them with some room to grow into. Combined with the fact that he is unaccustomed ever to looking smart – a good suit is equated with lack of compassion in the Health Service, even at a job interview – he comes to the art of suit wearing like a boy on the way to his barmitzvah. He would never buy a suit by choice, but accepts that they are unavoidable in certain situations. In short, he looks like he has been forced into smart clothes at gunpoint, and he scratches, tugs, removes and replaces the jacket, loosens and tightens the tie constantly to make sure the world knows this is the case.

A final salient fact is that Gerrard's suit is the one he graduated in over a decade before, the cheapest one he could afford with his parents' money – he'd used the left over for inter-railing around Europe. You can see why I felt at a considerable advantage.

The combined effect of clothes and demeanour made Gerrard look like the sort of rattish schoolboy who lurks outside news-agents asking you to go in and score ten B&H for him. Except that Gerrard would never have smoked at school, he was far too rebellious for that.

Given my description of our modes of dress, you might have thought that he was less keen to impress Alice than me. This is about as far from the truth as it is possible to be. Gerrard was desperate to impress Alice, so desperate that he was unwilling to disturb his familiar patterns of dress even a smidgen. In his mind, any attempt to try something new or fashionable would be spotted a mile off by her as falseness – the ultimate sin. He had already moved a grievous distance in wearing a suit at all; wasting money on a new one was beyond him.

On top of all this, Gerrard's natural antipathy to change ruled out a new suit entirely. He had found the look he wanted, why should he change it unless it wore out beyond all possible redemption – which in Gerrard's case was a bloody long way off. I sometimes thought he would have been happier if he'd had fur: always the same, always regenerating, and essentially part of him. There's no falseness in fur, not your own anyway.

Earlier that morning, swallowed by the folds of his suit, literally immersed in the fashion of the mid-eighties, he emerged from the flat looking slightly cowed, as if his mother had given him a scrubbing behind the ears and told him to stop being so cheeky. As always he was carrying his favourite accessory – a plastic supermarket bag of a certain age.

'What's in there?' I asked, knowing that the answer could conceivably stretch the credulity of a flat earther.

'Waterproofs,' he'd said, tapping his nose like a fisherman revealing the recipe of his secret bait. I pointed out that it wasn't even cloudy, being a beautiful, comfortably hot May morning, but Gerrard had just mumbled something about being prepared if it turned nasty and rushed back to the flat for an apple in case he got hungry.

I wondered if I would find something to say to Alice. Weirdly, I couldn't clearly remember what she looked like and didn't know if I would recognise her. I often have an unclear image of people I know quite well, I can't fix their faces in my mind very firmly.

I pressed my back into the cool of the window. The city smog stuck my shirt to my skin, although I knew I still looked pretty good. I couldn't hear what Gerrard was saying above the traffic but later found out that the bloke with the placard had accused him of being an extremist.

I ran through our forthcoming encounter in my head, although I knew the real key was not to rehearse dialogue but to relax. I told myself to relax, which is about as useful as asking someone who has lost something where they last saw it. Being told to relax is stressful in itself. I remember my dad, when teaching my mum to drive, would put his face about an inch from her ear and, veins bursting at the side of his head, scream, 'Relax, relax – before you kill us all!' This when scarcely out of the back entry. In hindsight I don't think it was conducive to her learning to take the whole family, catcalling at every missed gear, with her every time she went out in the car, but I'm no driving expert.

'Hi, how are you?'

'Well, and you?'

That should do it, an easy start. I had to make sure I didn't
wade in with wisecracks or anything straight away. I had to let her
set the mood. I sang a little rhyme to myself, to the vague tune of
'Onward Christian Soldiers':

Let her direct conversation, ask her about her mood,
Do not talk like an idiot, close your mouth when chewing food.
Avoid loud biological functions, in word or in deed,
Be reserved and sophisticated, deeby deeby beed . . .

I got a bit carried away with this and made up nine or ten verses,
involving not getting too drunk and pretending to be nice to
Gerrard. It was obvious that any unpleasantness directed towards
him, any continuation of the husband and wife act, could be very
counterproductive. Irresistible as it was to us, other tended to find
it very boring; so much so that Lydia had sworn, after our Cornish
trip, never to spend any longer than she had to in our company
again. Individually we were OK but together – no, thanks.

I finished another verse under my breath about demonstrating
kindness to animals before crouching to stroke the dog, saying, 'I
took you out of that dogs' home and I can put you back there, my
lad. Now on with your piano lessons.' He slobbered fondly on the
arm of my suit.

'You look happy,' said a voice at my side 'Oh, doesn't he look
sweet? Fancy meeting you here.'

It was Alice. She had a way of gliding up unnoticed; she'd done
it to me and Gerrard at Farley's flat and now she'd done it to me in
the street. I hadn't thought she needed to come past the tube to get
to the cemetery or I would have been looking out for her. She
looked gorgeous in a black crushed velvet dress that recalled
Fenella Fielding from *Carry On Screaming*, my first sexual fantasy.
Disconcertingly, I could see straight down the front of it as she
bent to fuss the dog, though mercifully for the lie of my seams she
was wearing a bra. She carried in one arm an extravagant bunch of
gladioli, which reminded me that I hadn't got any flowers myself.
Normally, I know, these things get sent to funerals but I knew
none of Farley's mates would be organised enough to send them

in advance so I'd told Alice to get people to bring them with them. She'd asked if Farley wouldn't have preferred a donation to a charity. I had to laugh.

Anyone else wearing that dress would have looked like some manky hippie or Goth, but Alice shone out of it like a Technicolor bride of Dracula awaiting Christopher Lee's Count. I was struck by her amazing skin tone, a light golden tan that in that dress somehow made her seem paler, more diaphanous. Her delicacy, her fragility, made me feel lumpen and inadequate, like I might break her by mistake if I moved too quickly. She had a small beauty spot on her left cheek that I didn't recall seeing before. I stood up but she remained crouching by the dog.

'Just singing a hymn,' I said, advancing one leg in front of the other like a long-distance runner waiting for the starting gun, to hide what a romantic novelist would term 'the proof of my passion'. 'I'm getting in practice.'

'Is he having hymns?' she asked, (her head disconcertingly level with my crotch.)

'Don't know,' I said, 'we just asked for the standard package.'

'He wasn't religious, I don't think.' Alice stood up, adjusting her dress with one hand. Her eyes hardly moved but, like a great screen actress, she conveyed a weighty concern through a slight gesture, just putting the tip of her tongue between her teeth.

'Well, it hardly matters now he's dead, does it?'

The corners of her mouth turned down. 'Surely if it matters at any time it matters when he's dead?' She really had an incredibly expressive mouth, and I made a mental note not to tell her.

There would be no way of conveying that information without invoking every romantic cliché, stage, screen or book, that's ever been written. It almost made my skin crawl to think it. Perhaps when we were married, in some dispassionate conversation, perhaps in an argument, I could say it. 'If you wanted me to buy more spaghetti why didn't you write it on the list? If it's not on the list it doesn't get bought, it's a fact, indisputable – like your having a very expressive mouth.' That would be OK.

'Suppose so.' I was contemplating taking her down to the cemetery, which was quite a walk, immediately and leaving Gerrard to pick up Lydia, but thought that wouldn't go down to well.

'Who are you waiting for?' said that expressive, almost dextrous mouth. I invoked the image of the potential misery star MP I'd spoken to in Cornwall, or Devon or whatever it's called, in order to enable me to walk properly. Like all MPs, he had bad breath that would melt your glasses, the memory of which now fought with the sight of Alice's mouth and tits. I would not normally give politicians air time, but he was quite keen to appear on the programme, so that was at least two minutes of transmission I didn't have to worry about, and as a bonus there was a very amusing video of him knocking himself out. After we'd got the serious business of tracking down the rogue bungee bloke out of the way we could sell it on to some home video comedy programme.

I found I had a problem with Alice that I had often encountered with other beautiful women. I couldn't look at her, but I couldn't not look at her either. I wanted to give her the normal eye contact that a normal man gives a normal woman, but I was so in thrall to her, so disabled by her beauty, that I couldn't remember what that was.

I would meet her eyes, then become conscious of staring, so I'd tear myself away to look at the traffic. Then I'd look at the traffic for too long, so it would seem that my attention was always elsewhere, like a yuppie at a party that could be rather good for his career. Then I'd realise that to look normal I'd have to look at her properly, so I'd catch her eye again and as quickly look away. Unfortunately, the best way to mark yourself out as a lunatic is to try to appear normal. I ended up with the shifty deportment of a man reading a car magazine in a newsagent's but finding his eyes flicking towards the pornography, or a dog who knows better eyeing a pie on a table.

'Lydia and Gerrard,' I said. 'We could all walk down together.' I gained some freedom from the tightness of my trousers by imagining creatures with skilful mouths, like camels and tapirs.

'Sure,' said Alice, as if putting her lips over a lollipop, 'I'm keen to meet Lydia. Will anyone be saying anything about Farley at the funeral?'

'I've got a few words I've put together. Well, an Oscar Wilde quote really.'

Actually what I had was some words Oscar Wilde had written

on the death of the painter Aubrey Beardsley, which I'd adapted to fit Farley. I knew I could allude to some massive knowledge of Wilde with Alice and Farley's mates afterwards, but actually I'd read the quote in the style section of one of the newspapers we kept in the toilet. The temptation to pass the words off as my own was certainly there, but the gang of club thugs that Farley knew would be more impressed by the label 'Wilde' than they would by the words themselves, if they were impressed by literature at all.

Alice gave a little gasp of delight and surprise, as I imagined she might when first engaged coitally. 'Which one?'

I pulled a piece of paper from inside my jacket and read: ' "Superbly premature as the flowering of his genius was, still he had immense development, and had not sounded his last stop. There were great possibilities always in the cavern of his soul, and there is something macabre and tragic in the fact that one who added another terror to life should have died at the age of a flower." '

'That's lovely,' smiled Alice 'really lovely,' as I imagined she might post-coitally, 'but what's that about adding another terror to life?' She put her tongue between her lips again and I was forced to think of a ruminant chewing on a fig, or Gerrard ruminating, which had more of the desired affect.

'I set it in context,' I said.

'Hellooooo,' said Gerrard, with a little hop and a glance at me, 'how are you?' I noticed the animal rights bloke had gone, leaving his placard behind.

'Great,' said Alice. This was just the sort of start I had hoped for, rather than twisting about worrying that lust was spoiling the line of my suit.

'You look terrific,' said Gerrard, extending his arms as if holding up a painting, and I knew he meant it because he would never say this to a girl just to be nice. He just couldn't bring out of him what wasn't there.

'Thank you,' said Alice, 'you don't look bad yourself. Still want to sleep with me?' Suddenly, my trousers were as loose as a hairdresser's tongue and I was free to go.

'We've got ten minutes before Lydia gets here,' laughed Gerrard with rising glee, actually rubbing his hands together. I forced myself to laugh along. He was hopping, but not enough for my liking, which meant he was relatively calm and relaxed.

'Or you could sleep with *me*?' I slid in.

'Yes. Both of you if we've got a whole ten minutes.' Alice smiled with her eyes which were incredibly kind and intelligent. That got a hop out of Gerrard as he and I hooted hysterically, although I think we both felt sick at the suggestion.

'Glad to see we're all in deep mourning,' said Lydia, who had just arrived. She too was tanned, or had less of a glare to her, and held a bunch of flowers, white roses, and was wearing something black, I think. 'Shit,' said Gerrard, 'I haven't thought to get any flowers.' Lydia ran her eyes over Alice more closely than I thought strictly polite.

'There'll probably be a flower stall near the cemetery,' said Alice. 'I'm Alice, you must be Lydia?' She extended a hand, and again I was reminded of an Egyptian princess by her pose although her hair was a nicer colour. Lydia pressed the flesh and said she had heard a lot about Alice, Alice said not too bad she hoped, and Lydia said quite the contrary. Gerrard and I both apologised for not introducing them.

I noticed Lydia was fingering Alice's sleeve with fascinated attention. 'Lovely material' she said, like a Romany promising fecundity for the price of some heather. Gerrard extended a paw to fondle the cloth of the same sleeve, saying, 'Really lovely.' I wasn't going to be left out so I grabbed hold of the other sleeve. 'Fantastic,' I said. I was reminded of one of those old pictures of the Blessed Virgin meeting some humble types, or of a Queen curing the poor by touch. To the passer-by, however, we probably looked like we were trying to pull her in two or tear her dress off her – by no means an uncommon sight in South London.

'It's an old thing of my mother's,' said Alice. Gosh, I thought, she even knows how to take a compliment.

'Hmm,' said Lydia, clearly meaning, 'It would be, wouldn't it? You couldn't just buy it at a shop and pay heaps for it like a normal human being. It had to be free, didn't it, you lucky, conceited cow.'

'Just threw it on,' said Alice, sparkling from the garment like a diamond from a crown.

'Hmm,' said Lydia, meaning, 'Die, conceited cow.'

'It's quite tatty really, if you look closely.'

'Hmm,' said Lydia again, twitching her free hand as if she wanted to close it around Alice's throat.

'Shall we go?' said Gerrard who seemed, like me, to fear the next 'Hmm' might see Alice pitched into the traffic

'Hmm,' said Lydia.

'Do you mind letting go of my sleeves?' said Alice.

'Sorry,' we all said.

The throng assembled, we made our way down Effra Road towards the cemetery. When I said we had decided to bury, or whatever, Farley in Brixton, I hadn't realised there wasn't actually a cemetery in Brixton, which meant we had to bury him as near as we could get to it – West Norwood. Let me tell those non-Londoners among you this doesn't have quite the same glamour, but never mind, he had to go somewhere.

It's a long walk from Brixton tube to the cemetery and, as none of us knew the buses too well, we didn't want to risk public transport. Alice strode off in the lead, strode being the operative word here because, as a sports commentator might observe, the girl had pace. So much pace, in fact, that the rest of us were having some difficulty keeping up.

This exacerbated an already fraught situation. Both Gerrard and I wanted Alice's exclusive attention on the walk, but it was important to arrive at her side accidentally. Jostling for position, off-the-ball challenges or shirt pulling were not in the spirit of this game; they would single out the jostler, the late challenger, the shirt puller, as a tryer, as a wanter. As I have already noted, you don't want to be caught wanting by the woman you want, because no one wants a wanter. Unfortunately we were both forced to practically sprint to keep up with her, vying for her attention at full hoof like pressmen after a no-comment politician. Lydia, shorter by far than Alice, Gerrard or me, was left puffing along in the background like the assistant of the Three Musketeers, as played by Roy Kinnear.

By the time we had got past the Ritzy Cinema, less than fifty yards, there was already an identifiable *peloton* leaving Lydia behind, with Alice clear favourite for the *maillot jaune*.

'So did the police call on you?' I was breaking sweat as we motored past that big church that's been converted into a bar.

'Yes,' said Alice, 'they were a bit odd.'

'I'll say,' panted Gerrard.

'They asked me to go and see *Starlight Express* with them,' said Alice, crossing a road without pausing to look left or right.

'Did you go?' asked Gerrard, briefly nosing in front as Alice, the dog and I paused for a post box.

'Can you lot hang on?' I thought I heard Lydia call, but her voice was lost in the traffic noise.

'I didn't bother,' said Alice, effortlessly gazelling into the lead as I tore after her.

'Did they ask you about us?' I asked.

'No,' said Alice, scarcely into the walk and already threatening to develop red shift, 'just a lot about my private life.'

'That figures,' said Gerrard, tongue lolling with lust or exhaustion.

'And a lot about *Starlight Express*,' she said, hovering at that uneasy speed where Newtonian physics can bear no more and Einstein is forced to step in.

'Are you sure you're not wearing roller skates yourself?' I muttered, as much as it's possible to mutter when approaching the limits of your aerobic capacity. (Even the dog appeared to be labouring a little.)

'I always walk this quickly,' said Alice, who had heard me and, if anything, was speeding up.

Gerrard pumped away furiously at her side, carrier bag pistoning back and forth in his hand to propel him to greater speed, his bony frame moving inside his over-large suit, face eager as a child about to win the sack race.

'I love this part of town,' he gasped, making small talk at 180 heartbeats a minute.

'Yes, it's nice,' said Alice, inspecting her nails at warp four.

I noticed my shoelace was undone, but that wasn't going to stop me. Kids half my age flew planes home on one wing in the last war. I pictured myself holding hands with her on some boulevard, being dragged along like a rodeo cowboy behind a mustang. I glanced over my shoulder and couldn't see Lydia. 'Hold on a minute, I can't see Lydia,' I begged.

Alice stopped, with a change of direction that wouldn't have disgraced Maradona, allowing me and Gerrard to regain our breath.

'Why do you walk that quickly?' I asked.

'It's a habit. If you walk slowly blokes assume you want to have sex with them.'

'What?' I said.

'They get time to come up and approach you. If I walk at this speed the worst I get is sad bastards tooting their horn at me.' I feared immobility again as she wrapped her mouth around the word 'horn'.

'How disgusting,' said Gerrard. He had little truck with those who could convey the full range of their desires via an automotive safety device. One honk for 'Wahey', two for 'Wahoo!', three for 'Shall I compare thee to a summer's day? No, get your kit off.'

Lydia steamed into view. 'Will you lot fucking slow up, or they'll be burying me as well.'

'Sorry,' said Alice, 'my fault.'

'Hmm,' said Lydia. Her attempt to smile only made her scowl seem more severe. The horror of having to make a play for Alice while my ex-girlfriend looked on welled up inside of me as Gerrard and I looked at our shoes. Lydia would assume that I would be making all sorts of unfavourable comparisons between her and Alice, and looking at the pair of them, I could see why. Lydia was forty or so – ten years past her prime and fifteen or more past the age that is strictly desirable in a woman. Alice was around her mid-twenties, which I consider ideal for a man of my age, although she looked younger, which I also consider ideal. She had an effortless beauty while Lydia every ten minutes adjusted her make up in her pocket mirror, like an artist grimly pushing colours around a palette without ever getting the blend right. I know this sounds nasty, but what do you want me to say? That I didn't think it? I'm afraid I did, as I thought it every second of the time I went out with her. Unluckily my low self-esteem and her low standards (together with high charm) had combined to keep us together for a long time. I'd thought companionship was more important than physical attraction. Yes, I know, I can see it now, but at the time it seemed viable. Mind you, we should be grateful, some people get caught like that for forty years.

Lydia was a wonderful, brilliant, funny woman and I didn't even know Alice properly. She could turn out to be as mad as a balloon, but it was a risk I was more than willing to take.

The situation left me with a problem. I had to talk to Lydia, out of friendship and common human regard for her emotions. I couldn't spend all day drooling over Alice. If I didn't talk to her she would see that I was going for Alice, which as Lydia was engaged I had every moral right to do, and which she knew I was doing anyway. We all knew, however, that I had no actual right, had received no feminine certificate of liberty, only a provisional licence to go out with other girls as long as she wasn't about. It was one thing telling her about Alice, it was another rubbing her face in the truth: that I was showing more enthusiasm in five seconds in Alice's presence than I had in two worthy, dutiful years with her. I also knew if I did talk to her I would be losing out on Alice time while Gerrard worked his oil. In the short term, the dilemma was solved for me.

'Here,' said Alice, and linked arms with Lydia.

'Sorry, Lydia,' I said, linking her other arm.

'Hmm,' said Lydia. The number and frequency of 'hmms' was causing me to think that we could record her conversation and release it as a spirited stab at 'Flight of the Bumblebee'.

This chain of arms, of course, excluded Gerrard who hopped a little jig, zig-zagging from side to side like a man in a hurry waiting to negotiate a busy road. There was, however, no way in, so he had to content himself with walking behind us, talking into Alice's ear in what I assumed must have been a very irritating manner. We proceeded at an appropriately funereal pace, Alice and Lydia talking about Eric, who is some sort of designer, Lydia hmming less frequently. I concentrated on showing my skills as a good listener while Gerrard bobbed and weaved behind us interjecting gratifyingly irrelevant comments, such as, 'Design, I like design.'

We finally made it to the cemetery and waited outside a large 1950s chapel building, built in metal and concrete, permanent but with the appearance of being prefabricated. It reminded me a bit of my old school, or of the factories near where I'd grown up.

At the gate I bought an expensive wreath and Gerrard bought some big orange flowers. He expressed regret that there were no daffodils available. I asked him if they weren't a bit cheap for a funeral, but he said he liked them. Gerrard is a man of inexpensive tastes. I say this although it had been my idea not to bother with a support car for the hearse so as to cut down on costs. Farley wasn't going to mind, seeing as he was dead.

None of Farley's other friends had arrived yet so we waited for the coffin to turn up. Me and Gerrard had designated ourselves to act as pall bearers, along with help from the undertakers.

Some funeral bloke in overalls was directing a man in a florist's van to put some flowers against a spot on a memorial wall at the back of the chapel. We asked him where to put Gerrard's flowers and he directed us to plot seven. We tramped the gravel round to the wall and located the appropriate spot. There were two other bunches for Farley, one just left by the van man. That read, 'Farley, man, sorry I couldn't make it. *So* busy at work. Later – Jools', and the other, from a bloke called Tony, had a poem on it about falling leaves and the sky shedding tears which was too execrable to relate. Despite his lyricism, Tony too had failed to turn up. I read the dedication on Lydia's flowers.

I went to her bunch first, even thought I was bursting to look at Alice's, because I was forcing myself to act with restraint. 'Farley, you stupid bastard,' it read, 'we'll miss you.' Which was something I would have expected from a Special Forces colonel rather than a media girl. Alice's dedication read, 'When the gods wish to punish us they answer our prayers. Sorry I answered yours.' This struck me as a bit morbid, and very egotistical, but I recognised the quote. 'That's Wilde, isn't it?' I said. 'Like mine.'

'Yes,' said Alice. 'I hope it wasn't me that made him do it, but if it was I thought I'd say sorry.'

'Are you a big fan of Wilde?' I was hoping I could remember more from what I'd done about him for my degree.

'Isn't everyone?'

'Quite,' I said, as I imagined Oscar might have said it.

'I like Wilde,' said Gerrard, 'very funny, I think. Yes, very funny.' I wondered if he could turn all the way round inside his suit without changing the direction it was facing.

'What's your favourite work?' I asked.

Gerrard stiffened slightly. As someone who had done psychology at college, he was clearly at a bit of a loss when it came to culture. 'Who could name a favourite?' he said. 'They're so complex and layered.'

'That's so true,' agreed Alice.

I was about to ask Gerrard to name a work, any work, by Wilde but remembered what I had promised myself about not having a go in front of Alice. So I just said, 'Great answer, Gerrard,' through teeth so gritted they could have been a motorway in winter, and ushered the mourners to the front of the building.

Gerrard took one last glance at the flowers. 'Not much fun out of those for a tenner,' he said. 'Don't we get any more use out of them?'

'The shorter and more expensive a pleasure, the more delicious,' I said. I was still trying to be Wildean, but failing

'Hmmph,' said Gerrard, who was more one for long, cheap pleasures. 'Hmm,' said Lydia, who, I remembered, felt roughly the same.

The funeral was at 11, another twenty minutes, and I tried to ease myself into a suitably sombre mood. I looked for something poignant or mystical, like a lone raven flapping across a snow-covered landscape, but I saw only the rather pleasant May day. The cemetery smelled of cut grass, Alice looked lovely and, give or take, I was holding my own with her. As an added bonus, I had my back to Lydia and Gerrard; all was well with the world. Another bunch of mourners exited the chapel, but they looked to be having a laugh if anything. Looking past Alice's shoulder I could see a girl among them who I quite fancied.

Last out, lighting a cigarette, was Farley's mate Andy in combat trousers and T-shirt. He was wearing sunglasses and a Walkman and nodding his head to what I guessed was Speed Garage or whatever was fashionable at that minute, imitating the cymbal crashes with his fingers.

'Harry,' he said, nodding but making no move to take off his Walkman.

'Andy, almost didn't see you there,' I said, although he didn't understand that it was a joke about his camouflage gear.

'Just catching the last service. Old geezer. Died in a nursing home.' He looked round at Gerrard, Lydia and Alice and then back to me. He was too cool to speak to any of them without an introduction, and probably too cool to speak to any of them with an introduction. I didn't want to risk unleashing him on Alice so I just nodded, I hoped coolly.

Not all the mourners had taken the death of the last chap so lightly as I could hear an old woman's voice crying, 'Oh, Jim, Jim!'

I looked across and saw the woman being led into a waiting funeral car. She could hardly stand from grief. I thought of me. Would I ever know what it was like to be loved totally, to have the devotion of a lifetime and to have lost it utterly on a warm day in early summer? I filed that away as a useful thought to bring up with Alice later, to show depth, although I would have to make it sound less self-centred.

'There are worse feelings,' said Alice, who was watching at my side and had seemed to guess my thoughts. 'Imagine what it's like to lose someone you didn't care about who you were with for forty years and then they're gone. Imagine what a terrible feeling it would be to feel released by your partner's death, and to wonder why you hadn't released yourself years earlier. You'd be more like a functionary at the funeral, there because it's what you expect of yourself.'

'A funeral where you realised you had lost yourself?' I said. She nodded and pursed her lips.

'It helps to have belief, I think,' said Alice. 'You know, if you're convinced of the sanctity of marriage vows, or believe in the family and think you've given support to your kids or something, it would be a luxury.'

'Serious beliefs have lost their charm, no one finds them remotely amusing anymore,' I said. This was only the third time I ever had said this, but I was pleased to have got it in so early in knowing Alice. The problem now, of course, would be remembering not to say it again. Gratifyingly she laughed and said, 'Especially Salman Rushdie.' I was glad she'd got this first time. There's nothing worse than saying one of these *bon mots* and the girl not hearing them properly. Then you don't know whether to repeat them, when to repeat them . . . oh my God, it's a right old mess.

Mind you, I knew I would repeat it, I repeat everything I'm pleased with. The more I looked at her, the more she did remind me of the picture I'd seen of Katherine Hepburn or maybe Audrey, I can never remember the difference, but more sensual, with bigger tits.

I had experienced grief of a sort as detectable to the naked eye as atomic decay. One of my ex-girlfriends had died apparently, years after I'd last seen her. Gerrard had met someone who knew her and said that she had died. He didn't ask how, though, which was unfortunate because I would have liked to have known. We hadn't been that close, but still I would have liked to have sent a card or something. If I lived to hundred, would I hear forty-three times that someone I had been out with was dead? Or maybe forty-four, though I wasn't going out with Alice and didn't want her to die. If I had forty-three girlfriends, and say three or four major ones, did that mean I was going to go to four funerals in roughly the same position as the grieving woman?

Where did that leave me? I'd been out with one girlfriend, years ago, on or off for nearly five years, making that relationship longer than many marriages. If she married and then died, where would I be at her funeral? Husband and family to the left, former long-term lovers, passionate trysts and one night stands to the right? Would I be hearing a speech by someone else, who I thought just didn't know her despite rings placed on fingers and canapés consumed? And if, to have children or out of boredom or desire for kudos or companionship, she had compromised on her choice of husband, how strange to be mourned into the ground by someone you regarded as the third most dear love of your life.

Alice's position was peculiar, I thought. Farley couldn't muster a partner in the modern sense, only a fling. A passionate fling, but a fling, or maybe just a crush. Still, it was nice of her to come, even though it was probably she who pushed him over whatever edge he was standing on.

Alice spoke. 'I don't suppose grief has to be wholly pure. Even bad relationships have some function. They give you a structure. Death would take that away and leave you not knowing which way to go. You'd have to cope with not making a dinner, or not ironing a shirt for a man you hated, in a weird way.'

'You don't iron shirts, do you?' asked the crumpled Gerrard, appalled but slightly fascinated. I hadn't noticed him earwigging.

'Only my own,' said Alice, smiling sadly as the car took the woman and some others away.

'Right,' shouted a red-faced man, 'who's coming down the pub?' There was a chorus of 'right you ares' and the rest of the mourners made for their cars.

I tried to restart the poignant conversation with Alice, hoping for more bonding miserable reflection.

'My old next-door neighbour,' I began, about to embroider an already truly heart-rending recollection of bad choices and men who die young.

'Who's the chick?' I heard Andy ask Gerrard, and I swear I heard him say 'drag queen' in reply. Andy looked surprised but impressed.

'Here's the hearse,' said Lydia.

The hearse, which I took to be ours, whispered up the drive and pulled to a halt in front of us. I took out the Co-op business card and held it up. The first undertaker we'd been to had been so keen to stress the benefits of a family firm and personal service that I'd twigged he was nearly twice as expensive as the Co-op – which runs a funeral service as well as a chain of worker-owned supermarkets. The Co-op also had the advantage of having depots in Cornwall and London, so we didn't have to pay the Penzance hearse to wait all night.

The undertaker saw me waving my card and came over. 'Mr Chesshyre?' He spoke in a quiet, restrained voice which made me question if we could have got it cheaper if we'd had one who farted and made rude jokes. It must be a strain, I thought, being totally professional all day. You couldn't even have a laugh in the car on the way back, although I suppose they do.

At the same time I saw the vicar come out. He had asked me for a few words about Farley and I'd typed them out at work. Alice was talking to Gerrard, which I didn't like. The girl I'd fancied drove past in a Mini with a tall hairy bloke. I spoke to the undertaker and gave the vicar the sheet of paper and he told us to hang on a minute before we brought the coffin in. Alice was trying not to laugh at something Gerrard had said, as was everyone. Even I caught a fit of the giggles, although strangely my eyes were filling with tears.

After a couple of minutes the vicar re-emerged to lead us back inside. Gerrard and I shouldered the coffin, along with the undertakers, Lydia took the dog and we went in. I was surprised at how light Farley was, in death he was insubstantial, but Gerrard said that was because of weight distribution. 'Corpsed up and ready for funeral action,' said Andy.

Once inside, we put the coffin down on a conveyor belt leading to the oven and took our seats. Unfortunately Alice had sat between Andy and Lydia, so there was no point rushing to gain the best position.

There was only me, Gerrard, Lydia, Alice and Andy in the place, no one else had turned up, and I guessed none of us really wanted to hear the service but out of politeness, to Farley or to the vicar or maybe to ourselves, we were staying. These things are meant to close chapters, to provide a framework, an ending, but we were unused to these things, these marking points, and didn't really like them. I even found weddings slightly depressing, apart from the number of available and emotional women, for their time-marking qualities. In any large event there are the echoes of other large events: the first day at college, the last day at college, a twenty-first birthday party, the day you finished with your first girlfriend or boyfriend. You look back and say, 'Was it that long ago? Am I that old?' In a way, Farley's funeral was bigger than all these things and, selfishly, I didn't want to feel older when I remembered it every May. It wasn't just that, I obviously felt sorry for Farley, but shared emotional events are somehow terrible to me; to look back and say, 'Are we still in contact with those feelings or with each other? Are we so different now?'

The vicar got us to sing a hymn, which Andy somehow managed in very good voice without removing his Walkman. He made me wish for an older church that would have burned him at the stake, or at least given him a severe warming, for such behaviour. Gerrard, an avowed atheist, obviously did not sing. Lydia kept nudging him and rolling her eyes towards the vicar, but not one note was forthcoming. I didn't really blame him. He'd have first had to accept religion and then convert from Judaism to go along with it, which is rather a long journey to make on a warm afternoon. It wasn't that the rest of us were any more godly than Gerrard, it's just that to us belief deferred to manners.

The vicar said something from my sheet about Farley, which he made sound quite convincing for someone who had never met the bloke. More sensitive souls than we might have wondered at our hypocrisy, putting the irreligious Farley through a Christian burial, although I don't think he would have cared one way or the other. The vicar did stall over the 'slept with enough women to make Errol Flynn look like Francis of Assisi', but I had been forced to put that in to make sure Alice put Farley firmly behind her. Naturally, it was better coming from a man of the cloth than from me; it made it seem more impartial.

The vicar, who was really rather good, even said something about the possibility of redemption for everyone, God's incredible forgiveness, how you basically don't have to bother leading a decent life if I read him right. I did have a suspicion that by stressing the 'mysterious' depths of God's love, the love that 'passeth understanding' and the 'frankly baffling' (I'm sure that's what he said) decisions that may be made on the final day, he was having a sly dig at Farley, but there you go.

It was then my turn to speak, so I got up on my hind legs and went through a bit about Farley being one of the most interesting people I've ever met (true), what an incredibly generous person he was (false – don't know why I said it but I suppose the occasion got to me, maybe I was just trying to please the vicar), and how much we'd all liked him (true-ish). I then read the bit out of Wilde and noticed that Alice had suffered an attack of the waterworks. This, as a vicar might have said, was pleasing in my sight.

I sat down and the vicar moved back towards the lectern. Gerrard, however, who had been showing some signs of discomfort throughout the speeches, face contorting like a man with a pip under the plate of his false teeth, had seen and heard enough. Before the vicar could resume his place he nipped in front of him with a deft hop and had gained command of the lectern as easy as getting served before a girl at a bar. Gerrard held up one hand in a 'halt' sign to the vicar, then turned and grasped the lectern with both hands.

'Look,' he said, in a tone that made me fear we were in for some plain speaking, 'as I see it – sorry, Vicar – this is all a load of rubbish. Farley was a self-centred roué, amusing in small doses but morally bankrupt. There is no forgiveness for him, one, because he doesn't deserve it, and two, perhaps more importantly,' he leaned forward over the lectern and enunciated his words one by one, 'because there is no God.' The vicar shrugged and made a 'maybe yes, maybe no' sign with his hand.

'The best we can hope for, and this is indisputable scientific fact,' the very words put ice into my spine, 'is reincarnation.' Gerrard's audience looked on in polite, if surprised, attention. 'If you think about it, in the expanse of time, which we all accept goes on forever, any combination of atoms will repeat itself eventually after billions and billions of years. So the combination of atoms that was Farley will happen again. He will live again. Those atoms will also, in the vastness of time, be configured as a mouse with an ear on its back, genetically modified fruit flies and all manner of hellish mutations, probably more than pleasant ones, but it is not my place to dwell on those here. So, to sum up, we live in an amoral, Godless universe that contains a greater scope for hideousness and torture by far than it does for beauty and happiness. May Farley rest in whatever peace that universe will grant him. He didn't have much in life. Thank you.'

Gerrard returned to his seat at a determined march.

I looked at Alice, who was sitting in what I was pleased to take as rapt horror. Lydia was shaking her head in disbelief, Andy was changing the new magnetic micro-casette thing on his Walkman.

Only the vicar seemed impressed. 'Thank you for that heartfelt speech,' he said. 'May I say how unusual and pleasing it is to hear a young person who has thought so deeply on issues of theology, even if I do not completely concur with what he has to say.' I reflected on the distance the church had travelled since the more bullish stance towards heretics it exhibited in its first 1700 or so years.

We all, apart from Gerrard, knelt to pray and then the vicar sparked up the last hymn. Farley's coffin disappeared behind the curtains to be cremated. I think it's impossible to see those curtains close over a coffin without thinking of the possibility of an encore, and it seems strange they should put something so comic into a place of grief, but there you are, that was the end of Farley.

The vicar shook hands with us all on the way out, like you do to the opposition after a particularly tough game of football, pressing some leaflet about confirmation classes on to Gerrard.

We went outside into the sunlight and flowers to see another group of mourners coming in behind us. This lot, dressed in typical consumer-programme complainant gear, looked a lot more upset than the majority of the previous party. There was an enormously fat young woman in stretch leggings weeping uncontrollably. She was comforted by a stone-faced bloke in a very cheap suit. Behind them, and surrounded by a posse of foot-shuffling towerblock teens in track suits, was a hearse with the small white coffin of a child inside. In white flowers on the coffin's side it said 'Paris', which I assumed was the name of the kid. I lit a cigarette, my first for what seemed like hours.

'There are other worlds,' said Alice, to no one in particular.

'Shall we get out of here?' said Lydia.

'Yeah, that's enough grief – Ed,' I said.

'Christ,' said Gerrard, looking at the weeping relatives, 'it only needs a little crippled boy playing an accordion to make the scene complete.'

As we left the vicar was trying to intercede in a scuffle that had broken out among the child's mourners. Someone was shouting about someone else coming there to gloat. I couldn't imagine anyone doing that but, like Alice said, there are other worlds.

8

How the lady gets
sawn in half

We walked back into trendy Brixton, away from the shabby
suburbia of West Norwood. Alice and Gerrard were talking. I heard
'very honest' from her and 'indubitable fact' from him. We decided
to go to Bar Humbug, below the old church. Somehow the sight of
the child's coffin had affected us more deeply than our own funeral
and the rest of us didn't talk much on the way back. We knew
nothing about the kid in the box, and would have certainly disliked
the family mourning it. We probably would have disliked the kid
too, but you're just programmed that way. You could call it the
universality of the human experience or you could call it mawkish
bollocks. I didn't have the energy to decide.

Andy had to go, 'Places to be, people to see,' and headed for the
tube. I watched his be-Walkmaned head disappearing into the
bright traffic. I will never see you again, I thought. Under normal
circumstances that would have been a source of some comfort, but
right then I don't think I was in the mood for any more loss, no
matter how insignificant. And at least he'd turned up.

Inside the neo-Gothic crypt of the bar I decided to get pissed,
however unwise in view of the presence of Alice and the fact that
I was in charge of an animal. I ordered pints of lager all round, but
they had stopped serving draft a while ago and I had to make do

with bottles. Farley would have approved, as pints are unfashionable in some quarters. There was no one else in the bar that early, the restaurant part had not yet opened and everyone else had gone for lunchtime drinks to places where they could sit outside.

'It's a bit dead in here, isn't it?' said Gerrard, lowering himself mantis-like into a silk-draped chair.

I made no comment but sat down facing him on a sofa. Amazingly, brilliantly, Alice sat next to me. Lydia pulled round an adjoining chair.

The depressing effect of the funeral had made Gerrard and me forget about vying for Alice, and the dice had fallen my way.

'Did you see that little child's coffin?' she said. Her face was puffed up from crying, and I imagined putting my arms around her, making everything all right.

A brief flash of a recurrent fantasy I'd been having entered my head where Alice is being attacked by a couple of disadvantaged youths, who looked alarmingly like the teen snotters at the funeral, and I leap in and Kung Fu the pair of them, taunting them with Mohammed Ali-type lines before delivering a couple of bone-splintering strikes and leading her off to the altar to the sound of agonised 'innits' from the bloodied heaps of designer sportswear that once were her assailants.

I'm thirty-two,' I thought, thirty-two and thinking like this, even now, at such a time. I taunt my dad for twitching his lip when the underdog bites back in cowboy films, particularly that one where Clint Eastwood asks 'Are you laughing at my mule?' but here I am, doing it myself.

'Terrible,' said Lydia.

'Are you OK?' said Alice to me. 'You look awful.' I had been shaking my head and turning down my mouth, like a student confronted with an unanswerable exam paper, as I'd mentally crescent-kicked a gun out of the hands of a drooling psychopath. 'Let's see how you fight on even terms,' I'd been saying, while sheltering Alice behind me. Why me? I thought. Wittgenstein got to speculate on the nature of meaning, I'm stuck with superhero fantasies.

'Just the day, you know,' I said. 'Farley and that kid, terrible.'

'I thought your speech was really moving,' she said, extending the sylph-like around my shoulders so I could feel her breast against my arm. 'Farley would be proud his friends felt so much for him. And your speech, Gerrard, very moving.'

Denied the ability to hop, he was seated, Gerrard had to be content with sitting up in his chair and crossing his legs first one way and then the other.

'It's, er . . .' he writhed inside the tent of his suit, gesturing in the air with his hand, as if to pluck Alice's arm from my shoulder '. . . true. It's true.'

'Yes,' said Lydia, 'I found it particularly moving when you said that bit about him being morally bankrupt.'

'He meant it in a nice way,' I said, wondering how much I smelled after running around in a suit in 80 degrees. I remembered the coppers, glittering in their slime. My words had a bad effect, as the sylph-like was withdrawn from my shoulders and placed on Gerrard's knee.

'I thought he sounded like he cared, and at least his speech was honest and from the heart,' she said. Three figures, all in black, confronted us in Farley's flat. Two carried razor-sharp samurai-swords, one touch and you could lose an arm, the third a wicked long flail. Jaw stiff but limbs loose, I took up my fighting stance, armed only with a cushion.

'It was very brave.' I realised Alice was talking to Gerrard, which was a bit unjust considering the way I'd just ducked, causing the flail ninja to all but decapitate one of his own swordsmen.

Gerrard, already sitting as tall as a buck rabbit in the wheat, sat taller.

'I just couldn't stand that vicar pretending to know him when he didn't.' Gerrard shook his head like a pensioner surveying a graffitied bus stop. She still hadn't taken her hand off his knee.

The second swordsman advanced. I dodged twice, pushed the cushion into his face to blind him, and delivered a backwards spinning punch to the side of his head snapping his neck with the force of the blow. 'Looks like it's just you and me,' I said to the flail man.

'That's what he's paid for,' I said, throwing myself to the floor and just avoiding tasting the flail. 'I think it was nice of him to put so much feeling into it. He could have just read it out like a shopping list.' Backflipping upright, I delivered a tight drumroll of punches to the ninja's face. He collapsed to the floor, semi-conscious.

'It's insincere,' said Gerrard. Alice still hadn't taken her hand off his knee. I pulled off the mask of her third ninja attacker to reveal Gerrard's face. 'Well, who's the pretender now?' I said, holding his own flail to his neck.

'Well, it was insincere of us to hire him then. We should have just said we'd do our own service.'

Gerrard was led away by the police and Alice collapsed into my arms.

'I didn't ask for him,' said Gerrard, as Alice finally removed her hand from his leg. Lydia came back from the bar with seven bottles of overpriced lager on a tray. The bottles had proved too small to last very long so we'd all gone double trouble, apart from Gerrard who was still on his first drink.

'You wanted the standard package, that's the standard package,' I said.

'You're bleeding,' said Alice. One of the swordsmen had caught me on the chest, cutting me lightly and ripping my shirt in a very sexy way. 'Don't worry about me, doll, how are you?' I said, kissing her softly as her night dress fell from her shoulders.

'Boys,' said Lydia, 'this does get a bit boring.'

'Sorry,' we both said as I scanned the headlines detailing my epic struggle and Gerrard's lifetime incarceration.

'Most people in this country aren't Christian, the standard package should not be Christian,' Gerrard pedanted.

'Well, thank God they're not all Nihilists like you,' Lydia told him.

'At least Nihilism's something to believe in,' said Alice, before I could. She was trying, I think, to lighten the tone, but I could only think she had pinched a joke I always use without me ever telling it to her. Unless I had said it and forgotten that night in Farley's flat. That was reasonably likely. Or perhaps it had come off the telly. That was likely too.

'I always say that,' I said.

'Must make it very difficult to order a drink,' said Alice.

'Oh, do you want a drink?' I said.

'Liar,' said Alice.

'Sorry?' As Wooster would have it, while far from being nonplussed here, I wasn't exactly plussed either.

'You said you always say at least Nihilism's something to believe in, then you said something else, making you a liar.'

'Come on, catch up,' said Lydia, beckoning with her hands as if encouraging me to jump on to a cart.

'Oh, a joke,' I said, 'I'm not very good at humour.'

'Don't worry your ugly large head about it, dear,' said Alice, archly – which is a way people haven't commonly said things since the late 1800s – 'boys generally aren't, although lots of them are funny.' I couldn't work out if she was being generally teasing, or whether she was having a go at me in particular, so I just gave a standard, 'Miaow, saucer of milk for the girl in the corner,' in a camp voice. I hoped she was joking about me having an ugly large head. Gerrard took orders for round three and went to the bar. I wanted to ask Alice to come out with me again but I couldn't because Lydia was there. I reminded myself to ask more about her fiancé. Did I have the brass balls, the front, to ask Alice out in front of Lydia? I didn't.

Alice laughed at my saucer of milk statement, which was a relief. I was a bit wary at this point, as the natural reaction to being told most blokes aren't funny is to try to prove you are a spectacular exception. If Gerrard got in on the act too we could be in trouble – there's nothing so dull as two blokes trying to outdo each other with humour. However, where my humour was quite loud and strident, Gerrard's was altogether more reflective, so it was easy for me to crowd him out. I calculated that I could probably reduce him to silence, but I knew that might not do me any favours.

There were, of course, risks for both of us as we both relied heavily on self-deprecation, but we also both relied heavily on others not believing it. I remember telling one girl that I had an incredibly small penis. This, by no means the pinnacle of humorous statements, was meant to show how unconventional and iconoclastic I was, but she'd believed it and as a result had nearly not slept with me. Gerrard returned and sat down.

'Lu men du pu the ho per in fnee,' he said, hopping from buttock to buttock and proving that where there's a will, there's a way.

'What?' said Alice, leaning towards him.

I'd heard Gerrard use this trick on a number of occasions, or rather not heard him use it. When talking to a woman he fancies he will often lower his voice in the manner of a cancer doctor imparting an unfavourable diagnosis. This has the dual impact of making him, he thinks, sound nicer and softer, and making the woman lean towards him to be heard. It's probably nothing so conscious as a technique, only idiots knowingly use techniques. These are the kind of people that come up to women and say 'I think I'm in love with you' or 'Get your coat, you've pulled' (used to be funny, isn't anymore). Gerrard's library-level voice comes from his incredibly sexist view of women, which makes him believe they look for softness in a man. My incredibly sexist view says softness is largely a female trait, so why would a heterosexual woman look for that – not that they look for harshness, if you see what I mean. There's a wider point here. When women talk about sexism, they tend to mention it as if it's only one monolithic thing. Sexism comes in many shades, some of which clash with each other, and some of which aren't even amusing or enjoyable to the sexists perpetrating them.

'Lots of men do put their whole personalities into being funny,' said Gerrard slightly louder – like a man being forced to repeat an embarrassing statement in court – and meaning me.

'It's the classic bore,' said Lydia, 'the man who thinks he's there to entertain people and won't let anyone else have a word in edgeways.'

'You have to sing for your supper a bit, don't you?' I said, bridling at the tacit assassination of my character.

'On limited occasions,' said Gerrard, as grave as a judge in a fifties film.

'I read that women value humour in a man,' said Alice, clearly, or rather obscurely, in some way joking herself.

'But it says in my *Cosmopolitan* that they also value the ability to listen,' said Lydia.

'Well, you can't have both,' I said, without thinking.

Both Lydia and Alice laughed like drains, as did I when I realised what I had said. I meant it though.

Gerrard snorted, though softly like a nan having difficulty with an over-strong mint. 'I actually once knew a bloke who used to try to get off with women by telling them jokes. You know – a man goes into a pub . . .'

'And what does he do, this man?' asked Alice.

'What?' said Gerrard, in the manner of, 'Darling child, light of my life?'

'Does he have a parrot on his shoulder or what?' Thankfully she was getting drunk. Approaching my fifth microscopic beer I was bordering on tipsy, but a good way away yet.

'No, he told jokes, thinking women would find them funny,' said Gerrard who was also getting left behind in the humour.

'Tell us some of the good ones?' said Alice.

'I've got one,' I said.

'Women don't find jokes funny,' Gerrard insisted.

'I went into a club the other day and asked the barman for an unusual cocktail. The barman said, "Why don't you try a Kurt Cobain?" I said, "What's that?" '

Gerrard saw his chance. 'It'll blow your brains out?' he suggested, hoping to deflate the punchline.

'No,' I said, although that had been part of the joke. 'I asked the barman what was in the Kurt Cobain, he told me I could have anything I wanted in it. I said, "What, twenty-three pints of Guinness?" He said, "Yes, if you want." I asked how much it was. He said, "It's free." I said, "Free?" He said, "Free." I said, "I can have twenty-three pints of Guinness, call it a Kurt Cobain and it's free? What's the catch?" He said, "You just have to sleep with Courtney Love." I said, "I'll have half a pint of shandy and I'll bloody well pay for it." '

There were some groans and head holding.

'See,' said Gerrard. 'Women don't like jokes.'

'We don't like *that* joke,' said Alice, laughing. 'That doesn't mean we don't like all of them.'

'Do you know a joke then?' said Gerrard, clearly in a state of some bewilderment.

'Yes,' said Alice. 'How many couples does it take to change a lightbulb?'

'I'll tell you another,' I said.

'Let Alice finish,' Lydia, told me.

'Sorry,' I said, desperate to make up for the failure of my previous effort.

'Don't know,' said Lydia. 'How many couples does it take to change a lightbulb?

'One. The man to change the lightbulb and the woman to bring up the kids, do a job, cook the meals, wash and iron the clothes, throw the lightbulb packet away, tell the man he's good at changing lightbulbs and be really thankful he's handy around the house.' She said the second half of the sentence with exaggerated sincerity.

'Feminist tommyrot,' I said like an old brigadier and we all laughed, I thought at my riposte rather than the joke itself.

'Where did you hear that?' asked Lydia.

'I made it up,' I said.

'No, Alice,' said Lydia.

'I made it up,' she said.

Gerrard laughed again.

'Do you know what I'm looking for in a partner?' said Alice. This halted my move towards the bar.

'No,' said Gerrard.

'I'd like to go out with a horse.'

Gerrard physically grasped his groin, as I did, mentally.

'Why's that?' asked Lydia.

'I'm looking for a stable relationship!'

'Are you?' I said, pleased, although Gerrard and Lydia laughed.

'You don't want to get saddled with one of those!' shrieked Lydia.

'I bridle at that suggestion,' said Alice, laughing hysterically, and clearly pissed. It wasn't that funny. I thought I'd help them out.

'Hay, hay,' I said.

'What?' asked Alice.

'Hay, *hay*,' I added with emphasis.

'Oh, that's not funny, Harry. Now hoof it to the bar,' said Gerrard. I didn't quite like this. Although I really like witty girls, I do like to be cracking a fair few funnies myself. I was clearly having difficulty getting in on the game here.

'I'll be back in a bit,' I said, and both girls creased up laughing. I gave a wink that said 'Don't mess around with the wizard of wit', although it wasn't until I was at the bar that I realised they'd been laughing at an unintentional pun.

While I was at the bar I was trying to think of some funnier jokes so I could be the centre of attention again. Nothing sprang to mind.

We stayed in the bar until about 9 o'clock, helped by a bit of speed Gerrard had with him. It was at 7, suitably drunk, that I got my chance. Gerrard went to the toilet, Lydia to the bar, which was now more packed, and I was left with Alice. There are only so many ways to say 'Will you go out with me?' and at the age of thirty-two, I should have worked a few more of them out.

'Alice,' I said, fixing her with a drink-glazed eye, 'I've had such a wonderful day,' this perhaps wasn't the best start since we'd buried our friend and watched a grief-in-the-seven-ages-of-man display on our way in and out, 'I'd really like to see you again.' I didn't know where to go from here. As a rule I like to start casual, so it's easy for the girl to reject without shooting me down too badly. I usually say something like, 'I was thinking of seeing that new film by whoever,' so she can just say that she doesn't like his films if she doesn't want to come.

Luckily, she was just as drunk as me, which was very drunk indeed. This meant that sophistry didn't really matter. At a certain point of inebriation, all you need to do is to communicate the desire. The yes or the no won't depend on how you wrap it up.

'Yeah, I'd like to,' she said, fixing me with her limpid pools. I wasn't sure if I should try a tongue lunge. In normal circumstances I would have gone for it, on an 'if you don't ask, you don't get' basis. But with Lydia and Gerrard poised at the bar and in the toilet like the avenging hordes of the Israelite, I didn't feel like risking it. Then she kissed me on the lips.

Whoever wrote 'a kiss is still a kiss' was oversimplifying things massively. How many different types of kiss are there? There's the 'take me home and ravish me now, you mad beast' kiss. This wasn't one of those. There's the 'stop bothering me and go to sleep' kiss. This wasn't one of those.

There's the defensive 'keep off, you've been eating onion' kiss. There's the 'give your auntie a kiss' kiss. There's the perfunctory 'wait till I get you home, you bastard' kiss, so beloved of people who have been waiting an hour for their partner to turn up at a party. And of course there's the 'watch out, I've just put this lipstick on' kiss. None of these fitted the bill.

This was a tentative 'promise of more to come yet not quite sure we should be doing this and I am very drunk' kiss. It had a more hesitant finish than a 'promise of more to come, I am very drunk but I want you madly' kiss, but a firmer attack than a 'not quite sure we should be doing this but I do find you alluring though you will have to wait' kiss. At least, this was my reading of it. I hoped I wasn't putting a hopeful interpretation on a 'I'm so unbelievably drunk I don't know what I'm doing and will be seriously reconsidering my position when I'm sober' kiss. It lingered slightly longer than a bounce on the lips but not so that you could call it a snog.

The whole affair was over in under half a second but, I regret to say, it felt, well, like fire. I know these similes are normally reserved for the less reflective feather of soft rock ballad singer, but there you are. It burned. I felt a delicious electricity in my throat, like I'd eaten something strange and sharp. She smiled, drawing me in to her ocean-deep beauty. I had a feeling of immense planetary change in and around me, as if on a spring dawn or an autumn dusk.

Something was spinning. I had a glimpse of us with children, all of them strong and smart, though not as strong or smart as me. One of them would be very musical because I'm not musical myself and so I can't feel threatened in that area as I know I can't compete. Another would receive some medal for lifetime services to football, saying, 'This basically belongs to my dad. He gave me so much help.' I saw Alice aged sixty, still beautiful, still smiling ocean deep, encouraging me to take younger girlfriends, saying, 'Variety is the spice of life.' This was going to be perfect.

When I was about sixteen I used to have girlfriends back to my room. My mum always asked me what I did up there and I would always say that I was reading poetry, an excuse that neither of us believed. What I was really doing was spending four hours trying to get some girl's bra off, and usually failing. However, my mum takes her parenting responsibilities very seriously indeed – particularly the surveillance role. So, armed with a tray of light refreshments, she would launch half-hourly commando raids on the room, bursting in shouting, 'Tea, anyone?' like New York cops shout, 'Freeze, wise guy!' I remember her actually rolling in, head over heels like they do in the movies, but that can't be right.

Anyway, my speed of withdrawal from clinches with women has been fairly finely honed by this early training. So when I saw Lydia, my ex-girlfriend, out of the corner of my eye, I flew back as if confronted by the foulness that should not be named.

Alice was a little bit surprised, but seemed to get the picture when she noticed Lydia. I was pleased to see that, for her too, physical contact in public was a no no.

'Next Thursday then?' I said.

'Yes,' said Alice. 'Give me a call to arrange it.'

'Right,' I said, expressionless as a Vegas cardsman surveying a winning hand.

Gerrard returned and I went to the loo myself. Once inside I jumped up and down in front of the mirror and shouted 'Yes!' a couple of times. I then looped around the room with my arms out like a Spitfire doing victory rolls over the earthbound corpse of a 109 and shouting 'naganaganaga' in imitation of a machine gun.

'You seem happy,' said a voice. A bloke had come in behind me.

'Oh, football,' I said. 'Just football.'

Back in the bar Gerrard had taken my place on the sofa. I was actually pleased about this because it cleared up the problem of what level of physical intimacy I was going to be on with Alice for the rest of the evening. If I'd been sitting next to her I would have worried if I should put my hand on her leg, if I should not put my hand on her leg, would an arm around the back of the sofa be OK, would it be appropriate for that arm to touch her? As it was I was in the chair and those questions didn't come up. There was still the problem of the goodbye kiss, cheek or lip, polite or passionate, but that was a way off. I was light-headed, from the kiss and from the beer. The problem with the bottled stuff is that it gets you drunk, which isn't exactly the point of drinking. Drunkenness is a journey on which it is better to travel than to arrive. This is why I always go for the weaker varieties.

Gerrard was speaking, I assumed about reincarnation. 'It's obviously the case, if you think about it for just a second,' he said.

'Though not so if you give it any more lengthy consideration,' I put in.

'What are we talking about then?' he asked. His knee was touching Alice's. When I had beaten Gerrard at chess, he had been a knight and a queen up and gloatingly certain of victory. I'd seen the possible checkmate only a move before I achieved it. It was that feeling I had now, a masterspy captured by an evil genius but knowing that the bombs he has set are about to go off. Touch her knee, I thought, go on. For tonight, my friend, you lose.

'Don't know, I just thought it sounded good.'

'The story of your life, Harry,' said Gerrard. Pathetically, he was smiling, really enjoying himself. I was raising the cup of victory, its taste already sweet on my lips, and he was asking me if I'd like any more sugar.

Lydia mumbled something incoherent. She had an amazing ability to go from completely sober to very drunk in the space of a couple of drinks. The bar was now quite full and people were pressing up against the backs of the seats, the usual Brixton mix of shady types and affluent slummers, straight-acting gay boys and gay-acting straight boys, gangs of proudly sophisticated media girls and proudly loutish media boys along with lots of people I couldn't see having dinner, although I guessed there would be at least one older failed film bloke dressed like a bohemian but smoking a cigar. There always was.

Alice looked very drunk, but her kiss and the amphetamine made me feel sharp and alive.

'I think I need to go home,' she said.

'Gosh,' I said, fixing her with what I hoped was my sparkling gaze, 'I could go on all night.'

'You usually do,' said Gerrard, still grinning like a baby gazing at a bauble. It occurred to me that he had asked her out but I knew he wouldn't have had the courage, and even if he had, she had already said she was going out with me.

Lydia again mumbled something incoherent. Alice said she thought she should get a cab with her. She refused our offer to walk them to the cab as the bar was on an island in the middle of two main roads and she would only have to wait for a minute

I was going to get up to kiss her goodbye but didn't want to seem too keen. As it was she came to both me and Gerrard, giving us both perfunctory cheek kisses. I was going to squeeze her arm and whisper, 'See you Thursday,' as she kissed me, but I was scared that I might sound like a loser. I was glad Lydia didn't attempt a kiss as she looked like she might barf at any second. Actually, the pallid, pre-hurl glaze quite suited her. It made her look bizarrely glamorous. Mind you, a lot of people look glamorous to me after I've spent a solid day's drinking.

I watched Alice go, black dress floating through the crypt door, once more the Technicolor vampire I'd met earlier in the day. Then Lydia stepped across the line of my vision and was gone too. I thought of how many times in the future we might be together, how many times I might leave with Alice.

I hoped I could sell my share of the flat to Gerrard, as I was tired of living there. Otherwise we'd just have to put it on the market when Farley's will came through. By that time we might both be rich, or at least our idea of rich, which I've explained does not extend to yachts and jets but does mean that life would be one long holiday in a decent package resort for me, or on a mountain trek for Gerrard.

'Well, that's my Saturday sorted out.' I realised he was speaking to me, rubbing his hands briskly enough to constitute a fire risk.

'What?' A big Rasta bloke was asking if the girls' seats were free.

'I'm seeing Alice on a Saturday night.' He stressed the 'Saturday night' with a meaningful peck of his brows. It was then that I realised I had my chess memory the wrong way round. It had been Gerrard who had won and gloated over me. I felt my gills go green and thought I was going to be sick. If you ask to go out with a girl and she suggests midweek it almost certainly means she has no intention of sleeping with you. OK, she might end up sleeping with you, but there's no immediate intention there. Saturday night, however, means no work in the morning so anything is possible. It's not quite a statement of physical desire, but it's not far off. I had willingly put myself into a no sleeping berth, as I'd thought I'd take it easy. Here was Gerrard up in first class.

'Free, free as the wind,' he said, on the verge of rapture. The Rasta bloke looked at him like he thought he was contemptible, but sat down anyway.

'You're seeing Alice?' I said.

'I'm picking her up at her flat at eight and we're going for an Indian.'

'How romantic.' Then a bad thought struck me. 'Is she still at Farley's flat?'

'No,' said Gerrard, 'she's moved into her own. Got the address in here.' He tapped his jeans pocket and then his nose.

'Game over, I think,' he said, sarcastically pleasant.

'Well,' I said, picturing him dead, 'best of luck.'

9

First blood

I'm not the sort of bloke who habitually goes around crushing sleeping pills into his friends' food. However, shagging Alice was now a priority; I had to get in there before Gerrard.

If he slept with her before I did, the situation would not be entirely lost, but I'd be odds against and facing dire consequences, win or lose.

The address was in the condom pocket of his jeans – he wouldn't have dared transfer it to his address book out of superstition. If God saw he had written it in before he'd even been out with the girl, he would be sure to give him reason to cross it out.

Gerrard would not have changed his jeans for weeks because washing powder damages the environment, water is wasted, etc., and he was still of that frame of mind that sees no other reason to refresh your trousers other than that they are what my mum used to call 'wringing in filth'. Changing to go out in the evening was too much like putting on a front for Gerrard.

So the only way I was going to get the address was by sneaking into his room when he was asleep. He is an insomniac, so this would prove a bit difficult.

Any excuse I attempted to obtain the address, 'need to tell her about XXXX', would have been completely transparent and would only have allowed him to bask in the warm glow of my misery. I wasn't going to come clean and demand the address, tell him I was seeing her first, because I didn't want him prepared. So really my only choice was to knock him senseless.

Was I worried about the morality of this? No. In fact, I thought I might be doing him a favour by helping him to a decent night's sleep.

One of the reasons Gerrard suffers from insomnia is because he spurns real drugs in favour of herbal sleeping pills. I thought of crushing a few more of these into his dinner but we all accept that, in medicine, the word 'herbal' is pretty much a euphemism for 'useless', so on the Monday I nipped into my GP's and told him I hadn't slept in a month. Dr Stamp was one of the older breed of doctors who had entered general practice when it was a medical school mediocrities' dustbin, not one of the new lot who actually attempt to practise medicine. I had tried his partner once, a boy of around twenty-eight. Obviously I didn't like having a doctor who was younger than me – it reminded me of my age – but he also didn't seem to have Dr Stamp's willingness to do as he was told. The final straw came when he was explaining how my normal soap might cause the skin rash I had at the time to get worse. 'Some perfumes in soaps may exacerba—' He paused halfway through the word and checked my four-day growth, dog-smeared coat and haystack hair. 'Exacerbate' was obviously not a word I would understand. 'Cause it to go mega,' he'd continued in the tone of a 1940s radio announcer. That was the end of me and him.

Dr Stamp, happily, didn't know any long words to avoid in the first place, although I suspected he used to make a few up in order to sound clever. 'You're suffering from acute parasitic nervousness,' he'd say, 'you need antibiotics.' Or, 'I see you have the ague. You need antibiotics.'

He welcomed me in and, with perfect bedside manner, relaxed me with a half-amusing anecdote about his previous patient, an Asian woman who works in the shop down my road. Apparently she has some gynaecological condition that medics find hilarious. Naturally he handed out the sleeping pills, full, proper, chemical, put-you-to-sleep sleeping pills, without any obtrusive questions about my state of mind. As I left, I made some joke about only four of them killing you. 'No,' he doddered, 'it would take sixteen to kill even a baby. Forty's my recommended exit dose. There's only thirty in the prescription, would you like more?' There, I thought, is a doctor who's responsive to his patients' needs.

On the Wednesday night I offered to cook food, in repayment for Gerrard cooking me dinner a few months before. Actually, I offered to buy in an Indian because cooking isn't one of my accomplishments. In fact I haven't got any accomplishments, not in that sense. Cooking is a male accomplishment. We do it in the same way that nineteenth-century ladies learned needlework: not because we want to but because it is an accoutrement we believe will make us more attractive to the opposite sex. Car mechanics, you might think, would fall into this arena but it doesn't. Fixing the car of the modern woman just makes her feel dependent on you – a feeling she generally doesn't like.

Cooking, which by any sane measure is really her job, shows that you have a little something about you, a sensitivity, a liking for the tastes and sensations of life – nay, a budding mastery over them – hints at sexual experience and, most importantly, puts her in the driving seat. There is the obvious attraction of role reversal to the modern woman, but also you are dependent on her – will she like it, has the soufflé risen enough, does the choice of wine show taste, does she think there is too much salad cream in the béarnaise sauce, have you left it in the microwave for too long? Of course, she's hardly likely to spit it out screaming, 'What is this filth?' so she's kind of duty bound to be grateful, without feeling she is. It's almost flawless, really. OK, it's a bit tacky, because where those men who decide they have an artistic temperament used to write poetry, now they cook. It's the same attempt at self-aggrandisement without such a risk of appearing pretentious. If you take it to a high enough level you can even use your talent as an excuse to bully and boss people around, to make yourself look good at the expense of others the way real artists do. It's a cheap ticket to the culture club.

With mechanics, a woman has to be grateful if you just get the car moving, and she doesn't like the feeling of obligation. It's useful but it's not sexy. No one ever said, 'Get out of my garage, philistine, you don't appreciate the way I've set up those tappets.'

Cooking also makes the man feel good: sophisticated,

uninhibited by social norms, but manly. Because the great chefs are male even though it's a woman's world, you can enter without anyone questioning your sexuality. Unlike making your own clothes, for instance. Actually, as a man, if you make your own clothes the main person questioning your sexuality is normally you.

I have no accomplishments like this, mainly because I'm too lazy to learn, but also because I'm confident enough to make a play on my own merits such as they are. That's give or take the odd searing bout of self-pity. Normally I would feel that I would never have a chance with a girl like Alice no matter what I did, so there would be no point in investing the time in learning a musical instrument, or how to Salsa, or Feng Shui or something.

I was speculating on this on the way back from the Light of Tandoor curry house. I always claim that Gerrard has curries too hot, that you can't taste anything in a vindaloo, but he insists that you can. Whatever, strong curry makes a great mask for heavy-duty pharmaceuticals. I had already ground the fifteen pills to a fine powder in the kitchen earlier so it was an easy job to mix it into the curry on the way home, one of those strange automatic loos providing the cover.

Gerrard gobbled it down without a word, watching some documentary about how bad people hurt good people. He commented afterwards that he thought the food was unusually sweet for that curry house, but said he quite liked it. Then, as the late-night cop hour began, he fell asleep, annoyingly in his jeans. I'd hoped he would pyjama up before crashing out, but you can't have it all. I shook him a couple of times, said, 'Wake up, you miserable fucker,' and then slapped him. On he slumbered in happy oblivion. I then put my finger into his condom pocket and fished out, surprisingly, a condom and also the note. With typical thoroughness he had written down her address and work and home phone numbers. In the interests of good taste, and a desire not to say hello to my last meal again, I hoped he hadn't drawn hearts on the back of it. He had.

I copied the numbers out and was about to replace the note when it occurred to me to rub a couple of crucial numbers off, but I thought that would be unworthy and immoral and, more to the point, detectable. I replaced the note in his pocket, along with the condom. I took a quick glance around his room which revealed an *Evening Standard* advert for weekend breaks in Venice, torn out of the paper and left on his desk. I took that, returned downstairs and sat back to watch the cop show.

After an hour or so Gerrard, surprisingly, woke up, groggily announced he was going to bed and staggered out of the room. This rather shook my faith in scientific medicine. So much for fifteen being nearly enough to kill a baby, it hadn't kept Gerrard under for any more than sixty minutes. I made a mental note to try complementary therapies next time I wanted to drug and rob one of my friends.

My best way forward now was to sleep with Alice on the Thursday night before Gerrard took her out on the Saturday. I was fairly sure Alice wasn't the sort to go out with both of us, a nightmare so horrid it didn't bear thinking about. If I couldn't get her into bed, then my only other route was to stop her seeing Gerrard on the Saturday. I resolved to attempt both, without delay.

I rang Alice on the Thursday to confirm our meeting. I was at first told that she only took calls in her lunch hour and to speak to her PA for a time to call her. I couldn't believe anyone of twenty-four or whatever had a PA. When I was twenty-four I didn't even have a job, never had had a job and didn't bloody well want one. I didn't know what a PA was when I was twenty-four, other than something used to amplify bands. Mind you, I didn't know she was twenty-four, she could have been five years either side. Anyway, I finally got through, ha ha-ing about how drunk we'd been. I was pawing the *Evening Standard* ad as I spoke to her, involuntarily tapping at my penis and contemplating on taking on a large gamble.

I had never been in credit with my bank for as long as I'd been at work, so spur-of-the-moment extravagances were normally out of the question. However this was an exception. No woman I had known had starred in that many sexual fantasies in one week before and, considering I was expecting a fat wedge from Farley, I thought it was justified.

Obviously I couldn't ask her on the phone, before we'd been out together, before we'd actually swapped saliva or more meaningful juices, so I had to leap in and book it anyway. I really couldn't think how I was going to bring it up. 'Hi, I have two tickets for a weekend in Venice, like I always do in my high-powered job in non-entity TV research.'

'What kind of food do you like?' I said, remote controlling off the tape of the latest programme, where some lowlife twat in a cheap earring and bad tattoos had been saying, 'It's wrecked my life, really it has.'

'I hope so,' I said.

'What?' said Alice.

'Nothing,' I said. 'Where would you like to go.'

I didn't wish to seem ostentatious so I thought one of the cheaper three-star joints would do, depending on my bank loan. However, I knew Gerrard would be taking her to some curry house, he always did, and thought a good course of action might be to take her to a really expensive curry place. She wouldn't want it two nights running and Gerrard would be forced to spend money on food he didn't like, which would put him in a bad mood. If she did agree to go for curry he would take her to some horribly authentic vegetarian gaffe in a muggers' paradise part of London where you can eat as much as you can stomach for £4.99. She might find this charming, but not as charming as a chance to don the glad rags and wash down a palatable meal with a couple of bottles of Bollinger and brandies at £20 a throw.

As I've said before, Gerrard isn't exactly mean, it's just that he has a heightened sense of value for money. Eating out is not value for money, because you could cook it yourself inside. Paying for decor and ambience is just an abomination. People in the Third World are starving, after all.

'Do you like curry?' I asked.

'Not really,' she said, a tinge of disappointment in her voice. Good stuff, I thought.

'Thank God,' I said. 'I hate women with inexpensive tastes. How about The Ivy? Would you like to go there?'

She laughed and said she had never been there, but I knew that it was exactly the sort of media tart establishment that would impress her. It had impressed me on the only time I'd been there, when Adrian had got me to sign up for *Your Rights, Their Wrongs*. I didn't realise at the time that the reason he could afford such expensive meals was that he paid such bad salaries.

'It's the kind of place where you have to dress up a bit, if you don't mind?' I ventured, knowing that 99 per cent of women will rip your arm off at such an offer and you don't want to go out with the other one per cent anyway, even if you think you do.

'No, great,' said Alice, with enough enthusiasm to sever the member at the shoulder.

We arranged to meet at The Artemis. I didn't know if I was laying it on a bit thick. Hooking up at an ultra-modern champagne bar on your first date is not far off asking her what kind of condoms you should bring, but I wanted somewhere she wouldn't feel out of place in her best clothes. I thought its plastic, chrome and rubber interior, the architectural equivalent of power dressing, would allow me to make a few snide comments at its expense and then we could go somewhere we actually liked.

I also wanted to make it clear, by my choice of an expensive venue, that my interests weren't platonic. I'm not one of those men who thinks that because he has spent a month's salary on a night out with a girl he has a right to sleep with her. No, I realise that this merely provides the setting, the rest needs to be supplied by the right degree of unctuousness – unct, or whatever the word is – wit, pleasantness, etc. But I definitely wanted it to be obvious that I was making a bid to impress.

Not all men are possessed of such liberated sensibilities. One of my ex-girlfriends reported that she had been out with a work colleague, whom she liked, and allowed him to pay in a restaurant. 'Right,' he said as he signed the cheque, 'I've laid out a good amount of money on you tonight, so later on you're going to be wearing your ankles for earrings.' There are times and places at which a gentleman may make direct equations between money and sexual favours, a useful test of the ripe situation being 'Am I having this conversation through the window of my car?' Otherwise, some things are best left unsaid. And unthought.

Selecting expensive bars and restaurants also made me feel that I was giving this the proper degree of effort. I didn't want to mess it up by cutting corners, taking her to a dodgy pub, even though I hoped she liked dodgy pubs. The Artemis made my skin crawl, with its self-satisfied got-it-alls-but-wanting-mores and office workers treating it like some kind of wealthy theme park, but I learned years ago that first dates must be chosen with the girl in mind. I used to think it was best to take them to one of my favourite or habitual boozers so they could get a good idea of what I was like, until I realised that was the problem. You don't want a girl to see what you are like until you have shown her you can be something else, at least not if you're me. She's not going to put up with the excessive drinking, terrible untidiness and self-obsession if you ram that down her throat from the off. Would Alice like Artemis? I hoped not, it would have been a nightmare to me to go out with a woman who expected to go to places like that every week, but I hoped she would like, well, what my dad would call being treated like a lady.

It was in this spirit that I dialled the travel agent's handling the weekend in Venice. I went for the mid-priced one, my credit card groaning beneath the burden. If she didn't want to come, I thought I could always take Lydia – or I might ask one of her workmates whom I quite fancied. Asking a girl I hadn't even bought a drink for to come to the home of romance with me might smack of stalkerism, however.

It took me some time to think of an excuse for having pre-booked the holiday in Venice, but I finally got it. I would say I'd won it in a competition and that I could use it any time.

I had been slightly worried about Gerrard since I had poisoned him. I hadn't seen him for three days, though there was nothing unusual in that – I'd been out on Thursday and so, probably, had he, and I hadn't wanted to risk waking him to check he was OK when I got in. I was a bit concerned in case he'd had a dodgy reaction to the pills. More than this, the Saturday night thing disquieted me. For a start, I couldn't believe my own stupidity in going for Thursday, and for a second, wondered if Gerrard had suggested Saturday, or if it had been her.

Alice wasn't the type to play us off against each other so I couldn't work out what was going on. I couldn't believe she wanted us both as friends. Why go out separately?

On the Wednesday night before I met Alice I had a nightmare. My nightmares are not the far-off Delphic coded affairs so beloved of biblical Pharaohs and the Sunday tabloids, they are literal, down-the-line jobs. Here I was at a wedding. Alice and Gerrard stood smiling at the altar. Next to me was my girlfriend with her back to me. I couldn't see her face as she was wearing a headscarf. As I watched Alice and Gerrard exchange kisses, I felt a tongue in my ear. I turned round to see my girlfriend was our dog in a dress. There was then a tap on my arm. It was my mother. 'Cut your cloth to your measure,' she said, glancing meaningfully towards the dog.

That had been her perpetual advice since I'd been young. The desperate thing was that I'd always cut my cloth to my measure. My only stipulation about going out with a girl was that she should be willing to go out with me and be unable to play one of Macbeth's witches without heavy make up. I'd never held out for the perfect one, sticking with the Emilys of the world rather than waiting for the golden girl. Now for the first time in my life she was within reach. I would write to Emily and dump her. Then only my flatmate stood in my way.

10

If and iffy

I spent Thursday in a sweat of anticipation. Adrian my boss was even less visible than usual, as we'd been nominated for best consumer programme in some award so he was out 'leveraging other projects', whatever that meant. I had plenty of free time to browse the shops for some clothes. I had the bank loan for a couple of grand, so I headed down to High Street Kensington to buy some stuff. Throughout the day I had various fits of the horrors: Alice not turning up, Alice thinking I was trying too hard, Alice meeting someone other than me or Gerrard, and worse, far worse, Gerrard getting off with her.

By the time I got to The Artemis I was decked out in a cream PVC jacket, safari-style, brown shirt, also safari-style, cream trousers and brown Chelsea boots, all from the Hype clothes market. Believe me it looked OK, even if our office cleaner did say I looked like a *tiramisù*. That had taken me back a bit, I didn't even know what a cappuccino was until I was twenty-three and here was a working-class person fully up to speed on *tiramisù*.

I'd planned to be there a good quarter of an hour before I was meant to be, to give me a chance to settle down with a drink, and also to be surprised reading. I think it's good to be caught reading on your first date. The girl walks in and, even though you've been threatening to bore through the windows with your eyes looking for her, you pretend not to notice her. When she gets within ten feet you look up and say, 'Oh, hi.' This has the combined effect of appearing much more cool than if you were sitting at the edge of your seat simultaneously chewing your fingernails and chain-smoking, which is what you want to be doing, and it allows you to show her what you are reading. This is important as it offers a glimpse into the person you would like her to think you are, rather than the real you. With practice, the real you can be concealed until at least the tenth year of marriage, by which time weight gain and stretch marks will make it impossible for her to get anyone else. I, unfortunately, have not reached such peaks of deception and only normally manage to stop the farting, heavy drinking and incredibly depressing view of life and humanity for about half a year.

Back to my decisions on the literature front – a Jane Austen novel is always a good one for women in my demographic, or maybe an autobiography – Noel Coward or an artist rather than some footballer even though all women seem to support Manchester United nowadays, or the idea of sleeping with their better looking players, anyway.

I always go for *Private Eye*, the satirical magazine. It shows you have a knowledge of, but a disdain for, the world of politics and business and it shows you have a sense of humour, which we all know is so important to women. If I was a woman I would beware of a man reading anything by Jack Kerouac, or anything that's about a young man feeling too deeply, as it shows his literary tastes haven't developed since he was seventeen. There are also a number of obvious no-nos: car magazines, pornography of any sort (hard to tell the difference), or any sporting stuff among them.

Unfortunately the newsagent's I went to was out of *Private Eye*. I was going to buy the *Economist*, but then I thought I would come over as the kind of man who knew the name of his local councillor and was concerned in some way about Europe. I settled for a copy of the *Times Literary Supplement*, which I'd never read before but always intended to.

If all this sounds like subterfuge it's not really, it's just the male equivalent of putting on cosmetics, enhancing an already present characteristic. There can be no more cause for complaint at finding out that your new boyfriend is not quite as emotionally literate as he displays himself to be than there can be at discovering your new girlfriend's foundation covers a little more than you would like. I suppose you could argue that the girl is going to have the courtesy to keep wearing the make up whereas men rarely readjust their masks once they slip, but there you have it.

I had expected Alice to be late but I still couldn't read the paper. I was slightly concerned that the The Artemis I remembered was nothing like the one I was now in. My recollection was of a modern piano bar, but this place was decked out like the lobby of a hotel that had ambitions to move out of the budget sector. In place of the olive-green rubber floor I'd remembered was a beige carpet, scored with burns where its better class of customer had stubbed out their better class of cigarettes. No-talent modern art hung on the walls and it was lit by tasselled lamps that wouldn't have looked out of place in a banker's bedroom. I could accept that Alice would think I had bad taste, of a self-consciously modern, airport lounge sort, but not this cosy rubbish.

The clientele was, however, unchanged – the normal bunch of media tarts talking about their concerns in loud voices, of 'projects' and things that were 'wonderful'; how good their own work was and how bad everyone else's. I dislike posh people even more than I dislike inner city scum, though it's a close-run thing.

I distracted myself by eating an entire plate of olives that were left on the bar and looking at some office girls who'd obviously decided to come in for a bit of class. It struck me that if this was my idea of class too, perhaps I should not have such a high opinion of myself.

The barman shot me a dark look, as if to tell me to leave some olives for someone else, but perhaps I was imagining it. I was amazed that I didn't feel self-conscious here. At one time, when I first came to London, I would have seen the complimentary snacks in a posh-ish bar and had to say, 'Are these for the darts team or can we all have some?' I would have had to emphasise the fact I didn't belong there. Now I blended in, more or less, and I didn't seem to mind.

At eight o'clock, our appointed time of meeting, the thought that there might be two Artemises first entered my head. One rubber, chrome and swish, the other this one, like the foyer of a travel lodge. At five past, ordering my third glass of champagne, I asked the barman if this was the only one. He said it was. Had it always been like that? A far as he could remember. At ten past, I allowed myself a little look outside and lost my seat at the bar. I decided I might look better leaning up it anyway. It's hard to look really cool on a bar stool. At quarter past I had to go to the loo, desperately. At seventeen minutes past, on my way back in, I saw her there, at the bar, talking to some squat bloke, like a dryad talking to a dwarf.

At one time it was easy to be beautiful. Poor nutrition and dentistry meant that most people had never seen someone well fed and possessing a decent set of teeth. Today beauty is common-place: on TV and in newspapers, in advertising and film. In the global village you have to go out of your way to avoid it. This is why it's so difficult to truly stand out, why it's so difficult to be like Alice. She was just the best-looking woman I had ever seen, anywhere, ever. I had already promised myself that if I got to go out with her I was never doing the lottery again, not that I did it anyway, or being scared on an aeroplane, or avoiding open spaces in thunderstorms. I would have had one negligible chance come up in my life, it was too much to believe there could be another.

I stood moonstruck, outside myself and distanced, englamoured and dumb. She had a beauty to burn the air. It was probably the champagne but, to me, her image seemed to shimmer, as if the common medium of light was struggling to transmit such a rarefied presence.

Alice wore a short, smart floral dress and sandals, leaving her legs bare. In one hand, held high like a wand, she twirled a champagne flute. A thousand women could have worn those clothes, but not one would look like she did. You could imagine the designers begging her to wear their stuff, to exalt it with her body.

I felt totally, incredibly, out of my depth, heavy and lumbering, wanting to run. I couldn't. Time was car-crash slow. God, I want to sleep with you, I thought, at the same time as picturing my mother with a tape measure and some cloth.

Alice saw me at about ten feet away and stepped through the dazzled air to kiss me on the cheek. I thought I was going to faint, but I managed, 'Alice, sorry I missed you, I was just down the hall,' in a broad Birmingham accent for some reason. It seemed as if I moved under a great weight of water. My head was ready to collapse

The man who was with her, in toff standard issue blue blazer, light trousers, blue checked shirt and red face, hovered uncertainly in the background. I'd clocked him earlier getting blown out by a couple of secretaries. I didn't know how he'd got the gall. She hadn't been in the bar two minutes and already he was in. Someone opened the pressure valve and we began to move as normal again.

'On the loo?' said Alice, unnervingly.

'Well, around it,' I said.

The wait, competitiveness, feeling threatened, being surrounded by people I didn't like, the drink, it all came together, snapping my personality outside my body, allowing it to run around the room on its own, free from any control.

'Where are you from?' I heard myself say.

'Sorry?' said Alice. I asked her again.

'Anglesey, the island.'

'You don't sound Welsh.'

'Why did you ask that?'

'I'm from the Midlands, although I sound more like a northerner, I'm told.' What was going on with my mouth?

I was looking past Alice to the toff. He had a flattened face and skewiff eyes like someone had given him a good biff with a frying pan. My own eyes narrowed, like those of a policemen confronted by a sex pest, a fighter pilot seeing the Red Baron float into the cross hairs. How dare you approach this girl? I thought, though looking at it later I had to admire him. Face like a child's drawing, banker's personality (I was guessing, but I knew I was correct), wearing City camouflage, still he piles in to the best-looking woman in London, possibly in the world. And they say public school isn't worth the money. It had imbued him with a confidence wildly disproportionate to his charms. I hated him, because of what he was, because I was nervous and because his presence was making me act like a wanker.

'Stone me,' I said, still in the Birmingham accent, 'Charles.'

'Yes,' he said, like another posh bloke might say, 'How dare you?'

'You used to be in the army but now you're in the City?'

'Have we met?'

'No,' I said, 'just a lucky guess.' I smiled and turned to Alice for approval of my cleverness and bravery. Surprisingly, I got it. She chuckled and said, 'Charles just bought me a champagne.'

'Great, saves me the expense,' I said, still in the Birmingham accent but a little too aggressively. Disdain spread across the banker's face, although he didn't speak. He knew he only had to let me keep talking and I'd hang myself. The more nervous I became, the more of an idiot I would act; the more of an idiot, the more nervous. I wanted to take Charles in my stride, suave and laid back, a *mot juste* here, a 'must be going' there, but if it continued in this vein the bouncers were going to have to separate us. If Charles had looked down his nose any further his head would have rolled off backwards.

'Actually,' said Alice, 'I don't much like it here, shall we go somewhere else?'

'Yes,' I said. ''Bye, Charles.' I spoke with exaggerated pleasantness.

'Actually,' he said, with cold eyes, 'the name's Algernon.'

He held up his hand and waved a little wave to Alice, as you might wave to a toddler, if you were that sort of person. I resisted the temptation to mouth 'She's mine' at him as we left, because it didn't matter any more. I didn't have to compete with him, in wit, style or money, because I had taken the girl and that was a hurt deeper than any insult. It would have been kinder to shoot him.

Once outside I apologised for my behaviour. Amazingly, brilliantly, she didn't mind.

'I thought you were very funny. I hate people like that, they're all such clones. He should be looking for a girl in a scarf with pearls.'

'He'd look even uglier in that,' I said. 'Why did you take his champagne, though?'

'Oh, I'll talk to anyone,' laughed Alice. I pictured the trail of slavering distraughts that she must have left over the years.

'His name wasn't Algernon, was it?' I had to check.

'No,' said Alice, 'it was Charles.'

We set off into Soho, down the bright and gay Old Compton Street, while I told her how much The Artemis had changed. She said it must have been before her time as she hadn't known it any different. Once again I doubted my memory. Outside a shop featuring mannequins of heavily muscled men in leather she held my hand. Some girls just do this, but I was sure it had meaning and I felt the top-of-the-rollercoaster feeling again. We walked on, hand in hand, me as self-consciously proud as an adolescent with a cigarette, until we reached a pub, the name of which I don't remember.

We went inside and I decided the best time to let go of her hand, which I didn't want to do, was as we went through the door. This I did, and it seemed to go down without complaint. I wanted to put my arm around her as we went to the bar, but I thought this was too much of an old-bloke, bird-is-mine move.

The pub hadn't been refitted for a good twenty-years, a miracle in Soho. It was underlit with a sleaze to its tobacco-ed dark wood and gleaming brass that made you feel you had entered a club where, if you passed ancient tests, you might be permitted to remain forever. Unlike the bright new bars of pine and shine this was a place for people who wanted to stay, rather than to go, somewhere.

It even had a proper jukebox, stacked with crap records no one other than the landlord wanted to listen to unless they were a teenager in the 1950s and their heart was still breaking, and a sign reading 'Anyone caught smoking over the pool table will be thrown out'. Not asked to leave, I noted. Thrown out. I knew I would like whoever ran this place, particularly as there was no pool table in sight. Perhaps they had just left the sign for its ambience. Best of all it was a city pub and proud of it – no tradition-u-like horse-brasses or fixed-to-the-ceiling pots and pans – just theatre posters from when places like this were popular with forty-a-day actors, before they all went down the gym. When I was a kid I used to really like these pubs, although I go to them less frequently now. Not enough girls.

I had a pretty much permanent erection by this stage, which I can laugh at in retrospect but it was seriously hampering my movement and I was willing it to go down. I thought of Gerrard on the toilet and gained enough respite to carry the drinks back to our seats without obvious embarrassment. I did hope he was all right. To have one friend die in mysterious circumstances may be regarded as a misfortune, two begins to look like a court case. In retrospect I wasn't sure I trusted my GP to tell me the right doses of sleeping pills but, as a judge would doubtless observe, I should have thought of that at the time. Would Alice visit me in prison? I wondered.

She sat opposite me and the awful reality of having to find something to talk about for the three or four hours before I could conceivably suggest coffee at her place dawned on me. It's not that we didn't have anything in common, I was sure we did, it's just that I was nervous. It's like parking a car. On your own, stereo on, fag in one hand, you fairly wink at the difficulty of backing it into the tightest spot between a Rolls and a hard place. On holiday with a girl however – arguing over routes, dog sick in the back, still having to explain that you saw the boy on the bike miles before she screamed and attempted to grasp the steering wheel, angry that she keeps pressing her foot on an imaginary brake every thirty seconds – you're bound to shave the paint on something in the campsite car park.

I also wanted the evening to be over quickly so I could stake my claim to her. Once I'd got my fingerprints on her tits she was effectively safe from Gerrard.

A couple of loud gays gave squawk next to us, so I decided to try one of my favourite lines.

'The love that will not shut its mouth,' I said, gesturing towards them.

Alice smiled, faintly. Oh, God, I thought, now she thinks I'm homophobic.

Actually, I rather like overly camp gays, it's just that I'd thought of the reverse to Alfred Lord Douglas's quote and couldn't, at any price, allow the opportunity to use it escape me, no matter how offensive it was. I find camp gays' loudness, their theatrically projected opinions, their flapping and clucking, touching. They think someone is listening, they think someone cares, but unfortunately no one does any more, apart from in the provinces and who gives a shit about them?

I certainly wasn't going to give them any more attention than I'd give to traffic noise, I was only interested in Alice. Or should I say myself in relationship to Alice?

The Zen master swordsman, the Japanese contend, is so practised that even the most elaborate moves are performed without thought. He does them as unconsciously as breathing, changing to accommodate his opponent's thrusts as naturally as the sea breaks against a coastline. I was in the reverse of this camp, more Nez than Zen, painfully aware of my entire being from my over-sweaty PVC jacket (why PVC, in June?) to the fact that the button on my boxer shorts had come undone and that the resulting pant twist was threatening to neuter me. I also itched, everywhere, but particularly up my nose, the very place where it is least possible to scratch in polite company (at least the cheeks of the arse can be clenched and buttocks agitated against a seat without causing too much consternation). I was also very conscious of my voice, which suddenly sounded very flat and boyish, like it does whenever I hear it on tape. Of course I had the usual new girlfriend feeling – a pain brought on by the combination of suffering a painful erection and struggling to restrain a fart like a fist from breaking into the room. But that was par for the course, I could handle that.

I had drawn up a small list of topics as a precaution against a tongue-tied fit descending on me and reducing me to the eloquence of an eight year old when his auntie asks him if he has a girlfriend. I knew if I could get to the three or four-pint mark without making an idiot of myself I would be sufficiently relaxed to stop worrying, so I had taken the precaution of thinking through the conversation in advance – like using a pair of psychic stabilisers before gaining your balance on the bike of your mind. It's like playing pool in a pub – a few jars and you're relaxed, playing your best form. At a certain point it all goes pear-shaped, normally about the sixth, but by then you're too drunk to care. There was the tactic of allowing her to choose the topic of conversation, but I didn't want her to ask anything about me because that would have meant I would risk going off on one, not letting her get a word in edgeways. So out of politeness I set the agenda on her. Topic one was her new flat and how she was settling in.

'Fine,' she said, 'I was going to call you, I couldn't remember giving you my number.'

'Oh, you did,' I said. 'So what's it like then, inside?'

Conversation about a girl's flat must always be initiated at the start of the evening. If it's brought up anywhere near the end it's too obvious an injunction for her to show it to you. However, if you express curiosity about it early doors, it's legitimate to return to the subject nearer cab time.

On the other hand, what's wrong with being obvious? Why do you always have to ask if someone wants to come in for coffee? Why should it put someone off if you just say, 'Do you want to come in for some sex?'

The idea, I suppose, is that women would think it too crude, although they don't think it's too crude to actually have sex, just to say they're going to. And why is coffee the chosen euphemism? Why not tea, or brandy, or biscuits, or cheese? Forget the cheese.

'Very basic, you know, but it'll be fun decorating it.' Alice sipped at her pint. No lady-like halves for her. I was glad to see this, the ideal girlfriend being a lad in knickers. Not literally, mind. Actually, this isn't true. The ideal girlfriend drinks like a lad, wants to stay out as late as a lad, has a lad's sense of humour and dislike of shopping, but doesn't try actually to be a lad. It's a very embarrassing sort of woman indeed who tells dirty jokes and sings rugby songs. Having said that, it's a very embarrassing sort of man who tells dirty jokes and sings rugby songs. None of my mates do that.

In fact, I suppose I don't want women to be like men at all, only to have their emotional needs, their confidence, if you like, their lack of questions about their appearance. The answer to the question 'Does my bum look big in this?' is the same as the answer to 'Am I an alcoholic?' If you have to ask, then the answer is 'yes'. If you take the equivalent in a man, say 'Am I too short?', they don't go around making a song and dance about it, they just honestly and openly take it out on everyone else while it quietly eats them up inside. A woman's response to her inadequacies is self-blame, a man's is dictatorship. If Hitler had been female he wouldn't have needed the subjugation of continents to prove himself, he would have been too busy trying to catch his reflection in shop windows to see if his 'tache was straight. I'm aware that I've just argued that I want women to be more like Hitler, which isn't true at all, just more confident in a healthy way, or at least not to ask me questions I can't answer.

From over the pub some bloke was listening to his girlfriend talk but looking at Alice. Even the gays seemed to have been ruffled by her presence and were clearly talking about her.

'I'm not actually clear what you do for a job?' I said, going to topic two.

'I'm in licensing TV rights – I sell stuff for programme makers all over the globe.'

'Who do you work for?'

'At the moment the BBC, but I'm thinking of going out on my own. There's so much potential around the world at the moment, and I think I've found a niche I can exploit. It's very exciting actually, especially as I really believe in the product.'

I'd switched off and had to pull my eyes away from her tits. The glass collector had no such scruples, however, and had to be fended off by a stern glance from Alice.

'It's like, in China at the moment there are more people learning English than there are citizens of the US, it's a totally unexplored frontier and . . .' She said something more about rising affluence in the new economic zones leading to a growth in TV advertising opportunities.

'Do you speak Chinese?' I asked.

'How tseei neeeae Mandarin,' she said, or something similar. 'I did it at college. I think it'll make me a millionaire through licensing by the time I'm thirty-five.'

'Is it true that the Chinese for "I'd like six eggs, please" is only marginally tonally different from the words for "I'd like six small boys' penises, please?" ' I had heard this was an easy mistake to make in a Hong Kong market, if you tried hard enough.

'I've never heard that one.' She smiled and put her tongue between her lips, which didn't do much for the trim of my boxer shorts. 'No, I don't think so, not in Mandarin.'

'What is the Mandarin for "I'd like six penises," just in case I'm ever in a market?' I said.

She made some noises that sounded like someone sharpening a dog. I gave a couple of goes at repeating it which weren't successful, but seemed to amuse her enough. I was glad she was lightening up. I have no idea how to get off with serious girls, how you create the mood for romance while talking about some irrelevance like the economy. Nowhere in the albums of Mr Barry White will you find a reference to the needs of British industry or the plight of people in a plight. Christ knows how anyone managed to reproduce in the Calvinist era.

'I will be a millionaire by the time I'm thirty-five. You don't believe me, do you?'

Mark Barrowcliffe

'I do,' I said. 'It's a long way off yet, though, isn't it?'

A young bloke in off-the-peg instant clubber gear at the next table leaned across. 'Ooh, Chinese,' he said. 'You couldn't teach me to say, "You have offended the honour of my family and you have offended the honour of the Shaolin temple," could you?' He had American-teen crazy-coloured red hair and a goatee beard to complement his 'Cool Cat' T-shirt and indoor sunglasses. There were probably 100,000 of his type in London at any one time, although you were normally safe from them in pubs. The predictability of his clothing, however, had no dampening effect on his spleen. It did not cause him to reflect on himself and say, 'Hold on, standard clubber, that girl is with another.'

One of the problems with a trophy girlfriend, as a mate of mine once observed, is that you have to keep a trophy in a cabinet. I was beginning to see what he meant. I was at a loss to defend her because I had never been in this territory before. No one really hits on B/C grade girls if they're with a man. With an A+ girl on my arm it seemed I was invisible. This heightened my already high paranoia. At any minute I expected her to turn to me and say, 'Look, I'm really sorry but I'm only going out with you for a bet,' and walk off with some pop star or someone.

'What's your name?' said Alice.

'Zak,' said the clubber, extending his hand.

'Well, fuck off then, Zak,' said Alice, smiling broadly. She had clearly handled creatures of his stripe before. I tried to look tough in case he started something. This isn't usually much good. Although I had spent many an hour at school practising the thug's vacant-eyed stare, Emily, my South Pole girlfriend, said it gave me the look of an old spaniel beholding its beloved master. Unlikely to send potential assailants quailing from the room, then.

'Touchy!' said the bloke, returning to his alcopop, presumably to quench the fires threatening to crisp his ego.

'Do you get that a lot?' I said. I told her I'd heard that really beautiful girls don't often get approached by men because most are too scared of rejection. See how I seamlessly slipped the compliment in.

'I get it more in the street than in the pub, I think it's because they can't run off in here,' she said, tapping her cigarette on the edge of the ashtray.

[196]

'Logically, it should be the other way round. It's much more embarrassing to get rejected by an ugly girl. If they're desperate and still don't want you, you know you're in trouble.'

'You sound like you speak from experience,' said Alice, fluting her mouth to blow out a smoke ring. 'But thanks for the compliment.'

'I am never seen with ugly women,' I said, like a politician avowing a deeply held principle, 'I always keep my hood up when I go out with them.' As I was saying the words, I realised that Alice might be one of those girls who think it's offensive to say anyone's ugly – even someone conspicuously very ugly indeed.

'How many women have you been out with?' She blew another big smoke ring. I took a gulp on my beer, finishing the first pint.

No man in his right mind yields this kind of information to a woman without the application of hot tongs. There's no way of getting it right. You don't want the girl to think you're a virgin and you certainly don't want her to think you're a slag, particularly if you are a virgin or a slag. So what do you say?

'Never really thought about it,' I said. 'Do you want another beer?'

'I'll have a half.' She had only skimmed the top off her first pint. 'You must have some idea?'

'Oh, I don't know, ten. Fewer probably. How about you?'

'About fifty,' she said.

That bit in the cowboy films, where the hero comes into the saloon bar full of villains and they all turn to look at him, that deep, bursting silence, that was what I felt now.

'What? Full, full, full, er, boyfriends?' I said. If she was twenty-four, that wasn't bad going.

'No, one night stands, snogs, all that.'

'You can't include snogs in the figure. Snogs are snogs, not partnerships. I snogged you, am I your boyfriend?'

'You didn't snog me, that was a peck. It doesn't get added to the list.' She hadn't answered my boyfriend question. If this had been pint six or seven I would have said, 'Any chance of getting added?' and gone for the tongue lunge. As it was I just gave what was meant to be a cheeky shrug.

On the boyfriend point, I knew that Gerrard would consider a girl his girlfriend if he had just held her hand, which I suppose is nice in a weird, potential stalker kind of way.

I desperately wanted to get another pint in but if I walked off it would appear I was going because I was shocked, which I was. I wasn't appalled at the prospect of a woman sleeping with fifty people, twenty-five if half of them had just been snogs. I had been out with a girl who had slept with fifty people in one summer at college, until Seasonally Affected Depression had stopped her tricks halfway through September. I'd found her sexual enthusiasm fascinating. It was just the idea of her shagging fifty people, my Alice, my soiled dove. I knew I hadn't a leg to stand on, I myself had shagged forty-three people and would have shagged more given better looks and a favourable wind. I didn't want it to make a difference, and I knew that after a couple of minutes' reflection it wouldn't, but at that moment I understood what the Catholic father of one of my first girlfriends had been on about when he'd found she was on the pill. 'No decent man will have you,' he'd said. At the time I'd reflected that, even if this were so, she still had an enormous field to choose from but here I was, sixteen years later, turning into him, a man I'd despised. I was shocked, and I was shocked that I was shocked.

'Are you shocked?' said Alice.

'Oh, no,' I said. 'It's not that many, is it?'

'I don't know. I regret it sometimes. I wouldn't like the man I settle down with to have seen half so many people.'

'*Mas o Menos*,' I said, picking out an expression I'd heard in Spain. I still didn't know what it meant. 'It shouldn't matter to anyone if you'd slept with four hundred. Now is now, the past is the past. How many of them were just snogs then?'

'A few,' said Alice. It seemed she was testing me in some way, and I wondered if she was making the figure up. If she was twenty-four, and had probably started sleeping with people when she was fifteen, then it was only around five a year, which isn't that many, especially including snogs. There was the fact that she said she was breaking up from a long relationship when she met Farley, though. That would have taken it up at least two years, so we would have been talking nine minus two, seven. Sevens into fifty go seven. So an average of seven a year – one every seven or eight weeks. However, she might have been unfaithful to her boyfriend so that might reduce the average to five, one every ten or eleven weeks . . .

'Were any of them at the same time – not literally, but were you ever, er, unfaithful?' I said, not sure of the answer I wanted, and knowing I had no right to ask the question.

Alice took on the shocked expression of a golf club captain who had just seen a lady playing before twelve on a Saturday. Then she laughed, somewhere between amusement and disbelief. 'Talking of fidelity, how's Emily?' she said.

There was a smell like burning. It could have been the plastic of a fag packet in an ashtray but it wasn't. It was the unmistakably bitter odour of sabotage. I began to wish I'd put more sleeping pills into Gerrard's curry. When had that bastard talked to her? I really did need a pint.

'Emily who?' I said, turning my head like a dog confronted by his owner with a large turd on the sofa.

'Emily, your girlfriend in the Arctic.' She had dropped the expression of surprise. I could tell she wasn't outraged but teasing me, which was OK because we all know where that leads.

'I haven't got a girlfriend in the Arctic,' I said. Technically this was true. Emily was in the Antarctic.

'I heard you had. Some scientist, some hopper about in dungarees,' she said. I thought, marvellously, that I could detect jealousy in her voice. Perhaps Gerrard's plan would backfire.

'Emily's an ex of mine, she's on an Antarctic expedition and we've finished with each other. She's met someone else while she was out there, I heard last week.'

'You don't look very upset about it,' said Alice, as if being casual about Emily was being casual about her.

'Well, you know, it's over. She's become very cold since she started working with penguins,' I said. Luckily she thought the pun was funny, probably the only human being in the world who would. Is that love? Someone who finds your bad jokes funny?

'Tell me about her,' said Alice, leaning forward and arching a brow. 'What attracted you to her?'

This was a tough one. The real answer was 'she was there and she'd have me'. She was the girlfriend to complete me, so I could be the whole man. I was reminded of my Uncle Dave, who'd told me I should get married so I'd have time for other things. When

I'd asked what he'd meant, he said, 'Working on cars,' which was his passion, 'or whatever you choose.' He seemed to imply that once you had the ring on the girl's finger you could stop all that going out, the restaurants, cinemas and pubs, and get on with what you were really interested in – draining the sump on a 1968 Sunbeam Rapier. To be down the garage, a single man on his own, would have made him a sad bastard. To be down the garage with a wife watching soaps in the house, that was normal, he had passed the test and could get on with his life.

I couldn't portray Emily as what she really was – a stop-gap girlfriend, a totem to ward off the spirits of loneliness, somewhere to go when my mates stayed in with their girlfriends. It's not the sort of stuff a girl expects to hear. If you're the sort of bloke that will go out with a stop-gap girlfriend, the girl you're trying to get off with reasons she might be a stop gap too. On the other hand I couldn't lay it on too thickly because there was the danger Alice would think I was still pining for Emily, and page one, line one of the female book of rules says: Don't go out with a bloke on the rebound.

'Oh, she was great fun when we started going out, but it was almost over by the time she left. She's a lovely girl but I don't miss her.' I think I'd covered the bases there – showing myself to be the kind of bloke who goes out with lovely girls but has enough emotional strength to recognise when it doesn't work out and put it into the past.

'That's not what I heard,' she said in a manner so accusatory I half expected her to call for Exhibit A. She really did have amazing skin tone.

'Might I enquire what you heard and, as I think will prove more revealing, who you heard this from?' I said, standing to go to the bar. If ever a question was rhetorical, this was it.

'Oh, a little bird told me.' She was altogether more playful and coy with this statement. I didn't know if I was coming or going, but I took the chance to shift the conversation away from the dark skies of interrogation and into the warm benison of humour.

'Was this little bird wearing an over-large suit and scratching its arse at the time?' I asked.

'Might have been,' said Alice, shrugging beautifully. So he'd poured this poison in her ear at the funeral.

'I thought so,' I said. 'Remind me to buy a large cat for that little bird on the way home.'

I went to the bar and ordered the drinks. So Gerrard had got there first, ladling on the concern for me – 'He has been dreadfully upset about his GIRLFRIEND going away, he does miss his GIRLFRIEND so much, I feel so sorry for him, Farley dead and most beloved GIRLFRIEND away at the pole' – to get the necessary information into Alice's head.

It was a good ploy. Even if I did sleep with Alice now she would, on some level, think of me as the kind of bloke who would be unfaithful to women. I accept that every bloke would be unfaithful to his girlfriend if he got the chance, but we have to proceed under the illusion that this isn't so in order to guarantee the mental stability of our partners. I'm not saying that no bloke ever is faithful to his girlfriend, fear of discovery, laziness, ugliness and limited social circle all mean that many are, but I've never met a man who wouldn't be unfaithful if he thought he could get away with it. Perhaps that's just the people I know.

In the noble interests of preserving the myth, if not for myself but for mankind as a whole, it was a stroke of genius that I'd said we had broken up and turned a situation of dire peril into one of clear advantage. 'I am free, your fears are allayed,' I was implying. Gerrard hadn't counted on *that*.

I returned with the drinks. I'd got myself a double whisky chaser too, under a hail of daggerish looks from three blokes at the bar who had probably been labouring under the happy illusion that Alice was alone.

'Why would Gerrard tell me that you were going out with Emily still if he knew you weren't?' I found it difficult to believe she needed it spelling out to her, even though I hadn't in fact told Gerrard that Emily and I had split up – principally because we hadn't. I made a mental note to write to Emily and hope that she got off with some rock-climbing scientist with a beard and an Internet tan before she got back.

'Did he tell you anything else about me?' I knew that once Gerrard got on a roll he wouldn't have been able to stop.

Alice bit her lip. 'He said a few things.'

'Like what?' I imagined he would at least have told her that I had some terrible venereal disease and was probably gay.

'Er, he said you had difficulty forming relationships with women.'

I thought this was rich from a man who had difficulty forming relationships with anyone. I even suspected the dog found him a little wearing. 'What evidence did he give?'

'He said you were a porn addict.'

'And?' I knew it couldn't have ended with such a light accusation. Gerrard says I am a porn addict because I have bought three dirty magazines in my life. What he does not say is that he borrows them regularly and would have some of his own if only he could pluck up the courage to buy them. In his defence, Gerrard is not a great fan of masturbation, he says it's all over too quickly, precisely the reason most of us like it. To him it feels hollow. I did suggest that he take his right hand out to dinner, or buy it a nice glove if he was looking for something more meaningful. I don't know if he followed my advice.

'He said Emily had taken the job in the South Pole to give you time to recover from your impotence.'

'Impotent *and* a pornography addict, an interesting combination,' I said. 'Anything else?'

'He said, er, a few other things.'

'Go on, I may as well have the lot.'

'Untidy, selfish, lazy, unambitious, mean, probably gay. Oh, and that you'd got herpes.' She delivered the list deadpan, like a supervisor assigning duties to a crew of cleaners.

'He showed remarkable restraint,' I said. 'Did it occur to you that there may have been a spark of self-interest in what he was saying?'

'Yes,' she said, pouring the half into her pint glass, 'but even if it were true it's not much different from most blokes I've been out with. It sounds a bit like my dad.' Again, I couldn't tell if she was joking or not, which is my favourite sort of humour.

'It's not true,' I said, 'any of it. Especially the herpes.'

Alice put her elbows on the table and rolled back her hair with her fingertips, her palms massaging her temples and giving her eyes an oriental curve. If anything she looked more beautiful.

'Surely the pornography bit is? I thought porn addict was just another term for "man",' she said, lighting a cigarette and then sliding nearer to me on the seat.

'Can we change the subject?' I said, leaning into her. It's a common male strategy to try to turn the conversation a bit saucy, to get the girl in the mood, but talking about my taste in jazz mags was saucy like it's saucy to use ketchup for massage oil.

'Why does Gerrard try to run you down?' said Alice. 'It's like he's not confident about himself unless he's beating you.'

'He's a sad loser,' I said. Understatement has always been a gift of mine.

'I think he's very attractive on the whole,' she said, touching my knee. 'He has a kind of feline grace to him, reminds me of a matinee star.' She took her hand off my knee and put it on my shoulder, immersing me in her perfume and cigarette smoke. I had mixed emotions: the heady intoxication of Alice's aroma (stone) vs Gerrard's feline grace (pneumatic drill wielded by tattooed road digger). It's generally a bad idea to try to grease your way into a girl's affections by discussing your flatmate's similarity to a fifties swoon merchant.

I desperately wanted to ask her whether she intended to go out with Gerrard; her physical proximity to me suggested that she didn't but her words suggested she did. I tried to continue the gently teasing exchange, having read, in a novel one of my girlfriends got free with *Cosmopolitan*, that this is the sort of thing women like.

'And what about me, do I resemble a movie star?' I said, theatrically brushing back my hair.

'Oh, yes,' said Alice, 'my favourite. Very well-groomed.'

'Which one's that?'

'Lassie.'

'Funny,' I said, 'most women who know me well enough say I'm more like Black Beauty.'

'Gerrard said you had a small one,' said Alice, enjoying the conversational joust.

'Surely he said I had a small-ish one?' Although the adjective had been meant to insult Gerrard, he had actually found it very funny and I couldn't see him missing the chance to make a comic distinction in front of Alice.

She looked as stunned as a rabbit that was no longer in the headlights but well on the way to the engine block, via the radiator.

'That is exactly what he said, exactly, small-ish. How did you know that?'

I relayed the comments of the unhappy Paula, lacing in details from her farewell speech for good measure and taking care to give Alice details of the way the retributive letter had to be prised from Gerrard's unwilling fingers, Farley's offer of help – the whole gamut, the full montoire – finishing with, 'I'm willing to submit myself to any test you deem necessary to prove myself,' in the over-sincere manner of an American general.

'That won't be necessary,' said Alice, rather disappointingly.

'It's no inconvenience,' I said.

'Gosh,' said Alice, acknowledging my line with an eyebrow and lighting her umpteenth cigarette, 'he's a bit of a weirdo, isn't he?'

I told her that I also understood grass to be green and the sky, on the whole, to be blue.

'Do you know, we got one of those murder mystery games to play once, the sort where you have to pretend to be Baron Whoever or Lady Thing and play a part for an evening. Gerrard wouldn't do it because he said acting wasn't being true to himself.'

'What's Emily like?' she said. Alice had a great propensity to jump subject, especially away from ones I was comfortable with, such as Gerrard's searing inadequacies. I remembered that he had said her hair had an incredible natural wave to it, a life of its own. She flicked it carelessly over her shoulder, as if its beauty were an irritation to her.

'He doesn't mind dressing up in women's clothes at the drop of a hat. Any fancy dress party excuse and he's there with the skirt, dipping into the Max Factor . . .'

'What's Emily like?' said Alice, returning to the unhappy subject.

'She's very bookish – you know.' I wanted to curtail this one as soon as possible. Ex-girlfriends are no fit subject to be discussing with intended girlfriends.

'Did you love her?' I didn't see what this had to do with anything, although it was a tricky one. Of course I didn't love her. As Lydia had memorably observed, I wouldn't know love if it came up and bit me on the arse. I pictured Alice biting me on the arse. It might be nice, I'm an open-minded kind of bloke.

'I loved her but I wasn't *in* love with her . . .'

Alice burst out laughing. 'I hope you didn't tell her that?'

I was at a loss to know why. I had said this to every girl I'd dumped since I'd been fifteen – which was only three. I'd always gone for the preferred male route of acting in such an unpleasant way that they had dumped me, saving me the emotional difficulty of the finishing speech. I'd been brought up to believe it wasn't polite to make girls cry, but no one had said anything about driving them into a fit of outraged indignation with late cancellations of dinners for two in favour of going out with the lads, forgotten birthdays, non-existent sexual performance, talking to the dog more than I did to them, running them through Ali's greatest victories at least twice-nightly and, of course, incredibly heavy drinking. Bizarrely, some girls seem to like, or at least not mind, this sort of performance so the only thing to do then is to make a pass at one of her best friends. That normally does it.

'What's wrong with saying "I love you but I'm not in love with you"?'

Club Boy, who had been bending his ear in our direction, caught half of this and dropped his jaw in disbelief. I think he thought I was finishing with her.

'It's a cliché. It's like saying, "I'm not ready for a relationship yet." It's a polite way of saying sod off.'

'That's what you said to Farley.'

'I didn't want to go out with Farley.'

This was music to my ears. I'd guessed from her lack of total devastation that she wasn't that close to him, but I was unclear as to exactly what their relationship had been.

'Why did you go to his funeral then?'

'I was staying in his flat, for one, I thought I owed him one, and I was interested in you, for two,' she said. I think I actually blushed as she returned her hand to my knee. Although did she say 'you, for two' or did she say 'you two?' I thought it best not to enquire.

I wanted to kiss her and to say how glad I was to have met her, but that seemed inappropriate. The timing was OK but I can't stand people who neck in pubs and I felt it was time to get her out of the bar and into the restaurant. 'What sort of blokes have you been out with, apart from Farley?'

'My last boyfriend was a diplomat at the French Embassy,' she said, as if everyone's was.

'Are you serious?' I asked. I hadn't thought anyone actually knew diplomats or classical musicians or international jewel thieves. I'd kind of thought they were joke ciphers for sophistication, wheeled on whenever TV ad writers want us to see their product is used by the top people. The idea of Alice going out with one, especially a French one, seemed ridiculous. Or rather her going out with him and then going out with me seemed ridiculous. I'd thought I would live my whole life without coming into contact with that world, even remotely, and I'd have been very happy that way. Obviously I had met some rich kids at college, but they were either public school boys with a two-dimensional idea of cool – heroin, sunglasses, toff rebellion band the Rolling Stones – or they were girls with foreign names and a passion for architecture and bad old films. There was no one I'd liked or wanted to be near.

'Yes, he was the First Secretary, he was quite a bit older than me.' Funny, she'd said he was twenty-eight. That's not what I call quite a bit. Maybe she'd lied about his age when she mentioned it in Farley's flat, so as not to seem like a weirdo.

That was cliché number two, the ambassador with the beautiful young girlfriend.

'And now you've moved up into all this,' I said, gesturing somewhere in the direction of the pie warmer. I took it as our cue to leave for the restaurant.

The Ivy had been full up so I'd decided to take her to a trendier place, Detroit, a sort of underground restaurant posing as a night club. It had cave-like sandstone walls and was dimly lit by 1960s-style sci-fi lamps which resembled tin, wall-mounted flying saucers. The menu was thankfully sparse, just five or six items, so you didn't have to wade through a culinary *War and Peace* before making your decision. I like a chef who has the courtesy to choose your food for you; after all, he's the expert. I don't want some ill-bred democrat who wants to provide something for everybody.

I assumed she was vegetarian, as all women are, so mentally pencilled in the salmon as a low-offence option. I was amazed when she went for the steak, so I had that as well. That would be sure to give Gerrard pause for thought when he ran her through the doors of the Bel Swami curry house, or whatever flock wallpapered hell he decided to subject her to.

We ordered the wine, and I narrowly resisted the urge to ask for house as I always do. The one we chose was red and cost £27.90 a bottle – about the best I have ever bought for myself.

I received a few gratifyingly jealous looks from a very trendy, good-looking bloke at a table to our left who was with a beautiful dark-skinned girl whom he had obviously just realised wasn't quite a top-of-the-range model.

'How did you meet him?' I had decided to return to the diplomat. I was pretty sure I had never even seen one, and practically certain I had never slept with one.

'A Buckingham Palace garden party. A friend of my boss's got invited and he asked me if I wanted to come as the plus one.'

I bet he did, I thought. A Buckingham Palace garden party? Now that I would have gone to. Free beer. However, I didn't like the sound of this boss's friend. I wondered if he was one of the favoured fifty.

'Do you often get invited to things like that?' I wondered if beauty was enough of a passport.

'Quite often. You know, I'm quite outgoing so I meet all sorts of interesting people.'

'I bet you do,' I said, and meant it. 'These interesting people aren't mainly men, are they?'

'Yeeees,' said Alice, thumping me affectionately in the ribs. More horseplay, excellent.

'What do you reckon about architecture, then?' I said, feeling I had to show some level of competition with this last bloke, but also to devalue his world at the same time. I don't know why, she had finished with him, but I felt jealous. I hoped it didn't get on to opera because then I really wouldn't have a clue. For years I'd thought the ENO meant David Bowie's mate Brian. (It's an opera place, for those of you who don't know, not far from the old Marquee, where the Sex Pistols used to play.)

'It's very useful,' said Alice. 'Where would we be without it?' She was clearly being foolish, which I liked.

'What's your favourite bit of architecture?'

'I suppose my flat, the one that keeps me warm and dry,' she said, staring fixedly at me. I was intensely aware of the distance between us, an indecent twelve inches.

'Function over form for you then?' I said, looking at her form and thinking about its function.

'Not really, it's just personal things are more interesting than public ones. You get a say in choosing them and shaping them. I do like some buildings, though, I love the Pompidou Centre.'

'Oh,' I said, knowledgeably, 'the one with the pipes outside?' This is a common ploy of mine. If I don't know anything about a subject I'll say something deliberately stupid, deprecating my own knowledge and, very neatly, indicating I am actually a bit of an expert. Why I can't bear to admit I'm a total ignoramus who only ever reads the sports pages of the paper, I don't know.

'Yes, that's the one. Do you mind? You've got something on your eye.' She wet her finger and wiped something off my face. I resisted the urge to stab at her tonsils with my tongue.

'What else do you like, how about older stuff? Abroad.' I was willing pictures of St Mark's Square and gondolas into her mind.

'Prague is very lovely, I've heard,' she said, tickling her cigarette ash into the ashtray.

'Anywhere else?'

'I've never been to Rome.'

'Ah, Italy. They say Rome isn't its fairest jewel.' I tried to psyche a picture of the Lion of Venice through her forehead and into her mind. People in masks floated through my consciousness, a carnival, a revel, the Campanile, over-priced drinks, tourists in horrible jesters' hats. Say Venice, I thought.

'Florence,' she said. 'Firenze.' She pronounced the Italian version of the name with the relish of a Serie A football commentator celebrating a winner from the Azuri. 'It's meant to be wonderful.'

'What's the Italian word for Venice?' I asked, deciding to take the hedge trimmers of directness to the maze of this conversation.

'Venezia. I've been there actually. Twice.'

'Oh,' I said. 'Did you like it?'

'Wouldn't go again. Too many tourists. It's over-run.'

This part of the evening seemed to be running like a well-gritted machine and with a heavy heart I pictured me and Lydia boarding the plane together as Gerrard took Alice out on the town in a whirl of lights, dancing and contraceptive purchase.

She saw the expression on my face. 'It's not like I don't think I'm a tourist, I'm not one of these who think of themselves as a traveller and everyone else as a tourist.'

I saw the opportunity to reel off a few pat lines. I'd always hated the distinction between tourists and travellers myself and had got a bit of a routine on it that normally made girls laugh.

'I used to think of myself as a tourist,' I said.

'And now you're above that?' Alice offered me a Silk Cut. I lit it, carefully positioning my fingers over the holes near the filter to make sure none of the goodness got out.

'Well, I went through a stage of thinking I was. I used to think I was a holidaymaker, but now I realise I'm not up to that. I don't want to make my holiday, I want it all on a plate.'

'So where does that leave you?' said Alice. I think she enjoyed the deliberate perversity of the argument.

'I'm a sun seeker, really. Sun, sand and carnal vices beginning with S, that's what I'm after.' I drew heavily on the Silk Cut, burning it quickly to the end. Silk Cut aren't the right fags for pulling hard on. They're the Fiat Cinquecento of the fag world: useful for day to day around town, but don't go looking for performance.

'You appear to be forgetting one thing.' Alice was very earnest. I asked what, fearing some moral Gerrard-style point about the impact of tourism on developing countries which were only developing because of the tourism.

'Beer,' she said sharply, like a sales boss reminding a trainee of some rudimentary point.

'I am terribly, terribly, sorry,' I said. 'I will *never* forget that again.'

The food was delivered. Luckily we had both finished our cigarettes. There is a level of addiction to fags that makes you view food as an unpleasant interruption to your smoking.

'Are you going to be able to make it all the way to France for Lydia's wedding?' said Alice, as naturally as someone enquiring if I liked my steak.

'I'm sorry?' I said.

'Are you going to France?' Alice delicately shovelled in some chips.

'For what?'

She looked at me like a parade ground sergeant who has just detected a fleck of dust on a squaddie's tunic. 'For her wedding. Pay attention, Bond.'

She hadn't told me she was going to get married in France, why had she told Alice?

'How did you find out she was getting married in France?' I said. I had guessed it was probably that Lydia never got a word in edgeways with us. Ever since Farley's death Gerrard and I had been pretty self-obsessed, or Alice-obsessed. Still, I thought, she would have had a second to talk about it.

'I asked her,' said Alice.

'Simple but brilliant,' I said. I hadn't even mastered listening to other people. Here was someone who could listen and ask questions back.

'I hope I haven't spoiled anything for her.'

'No, I doubt it.'

'The bloke's name's Eric, he's a designer, he's half French.'

'Good,' I said. 'That's very good.' I thought Lydia had told me that, although I wasn't sure.

'Lydia's great, isn't she?' said Alice. 'I think we need more women like her. She's a great role model for younger women.'

'Not for you, I hope,' I said, nervously eyeing the bowl which had contained the chips and wondering if Alice was a Death-by-Chocolate girl.

'Well, yes, she's a successful career woman, she's funny, she's sorted. Why not?'

'She's fat.' I didn't say that, thankfully. I wasn't quite that pissed just then. 'No, no reason, you're right.'

'Who are your role models?' she said, looking like a drama student who had been asked to portray 'fascination'. I was glad to get away from the subject of Lydia, although this was just the sort of licence to bore I didn't need. In my state of mild squiffiness it was almost irresistible.

'I thought only black people and single mothers had to have role models?' I said. I knew I was going off on a risky one here but I was getting reasonably drunk, so I thought, Sod it.

'I beg your pardon?' said Alice, suspecting unfashionable and, nearly as importantly, unacceptable racism.

'You only ever hear about the need for black role models, you never hear that white middle-class men need them too. I thought we'd got away without having to have them.'

There had been a lot on telly about this. I had been surprised to hear one of my dad's mates saying young black people needed role models. At least that's what I think he meant when he said we should make an example of a few of them, but I could be wrong. The working-class Midlands would not be your first port-of-call if you were seeking examples of racial tolerance.

'You have more than anyone else.' Alice crossed her arms – which everyone knows is not a good sign.

'Like who?' I was genuinely mystified.

'The Prime Minister, captains of industry, almost everyone in power . . .'

'They're not my role models, I don't want to be like the Prime Minister.' I knew that I couldn't be that nice to people for so long, even if I would have had MI5 and Special Forces at my hest.

'But it shows what's possible for someone like you, if you want to do it.'

'Shows it's possible to be a twat.' I knew from my first swear word of the evening that I was getting drunk. It's not that I don't swear, I just don't swear when trying to present the best part of myself, whereas I am incapable of uttering two words without an expletive when I go to football.

'You must have some heroes?'

'Heroes and role models are different things. My two heroes when I was a kid were Muhammed Ali and David Bowie, but I didn't want to be the first heavyweight champion to combine political radicalism with awesome make up and heroic cocaine abuse,' I expounded. No, really I did. People very rarely expound nowadays, but I was expounding all right.

I had tried boxing and being in a band when I was a kid, sometimes simultaneously. It had taken me ten years to realise I hadn't the musical talent to become the next David Bowie, or even the next David Drago (don't look for him, he never made it). Luckily, boxing has a way of making you very aware of your shortcomings much more quickly. I floated like a brick and stung like an aromatherapy product for soothing chafed skin. Still, the black eyes gave me street cred at school. I've never worked out why bruises and scars are the sign of being tough. Surely it's the person who put them there who's tough? Funny, lads don't see it that way.

As my nan had observed, on numerous occasions and normally after ten forlorn attempts to ask me what I wanted for dinner, it was a pity there was no world championship for mouthing off. I'd have been top of the heap, as I was about to prove. All lads like to air their opinions and to have them listened to, but with me it is something of a disease. A wave of drunkenness hit me and I felt my mouth start. I'd pointed out earlier that no woman in her right mind is interested in politics – which is just another word for men talking loudly – but there I was, seduced by the limelight of her attention.

Unfortunately the last proper political discussion I'd had was in the mid-1980s, when politics was trendy, so I was a little off the pace in terms of small issues like the death of Socialism, and the near-fatal illness of Capitalism. I had moved on a little, but not much. Back then I wouldn't have understood how someone could find a men's group funny, or have wanted a car. Well, I might have, but I would have kept pretty quiet about it.

'Role models are just something you want other people to have, if you don't like the way they behave. It's another form of racism, really. I mean, do you need a role model, do you want someone to set you an example?'

'No,' said Alice, 'but . . .' I was going into one, so I interrupted her.

'Exactly. Black youth doesn't need role models, it needs fair economic opportunities. Why do some white people think it's possible to become Prime Minister? Because it is. Why don't I? Because it isn't. Why don't blacks think it's possible to become lawyers or captains of industry? Because, a couple of flukes aside, it isn't. You won't get your role models until you have equal opportunities, and by then you won't need them. Furthermore . . .'

'But . . .' said Alice.

'Furthermore,' I said, warming to the sound of my own voice, 'the whites who present themselves as role models are entirely inadequate. I mean, do you look up to God-bothering, family-centred career politicians who can't even perform a basic task like visiting a prostitute without making a mess of it? I don't know anyone who lives in a family, other than a few provincial freaks. They can't have any idea how most people live their lives.' I knew I was ranting appallingly, in girl-repulsion mode, but there was no way of stopping now. I would have found it easier to keep in a mouthful of bees than to restrain the flow of words. There comes a point in every man's drunkenness where nothing is so fascinating as his own opinions. Some, myself high among them, need no beer to start them. Beer is simply an excuse, one among many, such as someone saying hello to you, or standing near you at a bus stop.

The best excuse of all, the one that means you will redouble your arguments, is being asked to shut up. It adds the fuel of righteous indignation to the heat of your debate. If someone tells him to be quiet, a man does not see himself as a pub bore who would do well to let his meat stop his mouth. In his own mind he is Malcolm X fighting FBI attempts to gag him, a lone voice of reason crying in the wilderness, the man who saw it all *before* it was too late, a searing flame of truth in the damp mizzle of polite indifference. He isn't ruining a meal and drowning your enquiries about your friend's new job, he's offering a vision of new England. I was that man.

'These are the people who tell us drugs are dangerous but wars aren't, that we have to spend money on posh minority arts tastes, like ballet and opera, but who, for the best part of a century, said that if we were allowed to use our money to buy a drink after 11 o'clock at night we may very well go stark raving mad. These are the people . . .'

'But what are you going to do about it?' asked Alice, her face like someone searching for the image in one of those three-dimensional pictures.

'Do?' I said. 'I'm not going to do anything. What do we pay the politicians for?'

I slammed down my glass defiantly on the table and the couple next to us studiously looked the other way. I had some sympathy. I wouldn't have wanted to sit next to me either. Alice had a look of longing in her eyes, as if she could almost taste the paint on the cab that would take her home. She leaned forward, and I half expected her to head butt me.

'You're so funny,' she said, tapping me with the back of her hand on the chest, a radiant, sexy smile on her face.

Christ, I thought, this really is the one for me.

11

Stage six

The next morning on my answer phone was a message from myself reminding me to ask Lydia about her engagement. There was another, also from me, in a much more drunken voice, reminding myself to ring up about Farley's will. We'd handed it over to the solicitors six weeks before and it struck me they were dragging their heels, though no doubt the lazy sods would say they were moving as quickly as they could.

The journey back from Alice's flat had been difficult. The day was overcast and the tube terribly hot, the subterranean London air solidifying like chip fat against my skin. Through every possible obstacle – delays, drunks, overperfumed women and underperfumed men – I made it home. I think I would have been all right if it hadn't been for the Malibu I'd drunk when we got back to Alice's house. As it was every desiccated sense was filtered through a glaze of coconut. The taste was like a party guest who, still present at breakfast, did not quite know if it should stay or go. Every lurch and start of the train threatened to force a decision upon it and see it burst through the nearest opening.

By the time I got in I was desperate to rid myself of my glad rags and get into the shower

After listening to the messages – which included one from Lydia asking me to call back – I went quickly to the bathroom to run the inappropriately named power shower, which produced not so much a stream of water as accelerated condensation in the bathroom. You weren't sure if you were getting wet or just sweating more. Nevertheless it did the job of peeling off my crust of stale cigarette smoke, beer and grime. Away it came, Gerrard's fresh lemon soap changing that flea-ridden feeling to a delicious electricity; lime conditioner that Lydia had left round our house softening my hair and soothing my soul.

In a way I almost didn't want the hangover to go. I felt ennobled by it, as if weary from passing some great test. The headache, the torn coat, the gone-off lager smell, the stained shirt, all were trophies of a great night out, welts in my armour to show I'd faced down the dragon of my fears. Most of all, the smell of Alice was on me, the heart-rushing mixture of perfume and Silk Cut recalling the taste of lipstick and wine.

The dog, as ever, was watching me shower. Gerrard was still nowhere around, so I guessed the hound might have been starved of company overnight, or maybe just plain starved. Even after I'd fed him he was certainly keener than usual for some attention. As I stepped out I patted him on the head and said, 'For you, Fritz, the war is over. You shall have a walk.' I pictured Gerrard's head on the dog's shoulders, and sent him to his box.

I had won many times before: sporting events, duels of wit, the national lottery even. But only in my dreams. I had known what my reaction would be, the same as when I had moved grim-jawed through the back slaps of fellow players after scoring winning goals in cup finals, when I had preferred to go home on my own rather than drink with the rest of the panel after besting the wits on topical quiz shows, as I had taken the cheque, nodded and disappeared into the night. I was on top, there was no need to share it with anyone else. The reality was how I'd expected it to be. Not a cause for whooping and jumping, high fives and punching the air, but a quiet exaltation where I felt capable of anything; my touch charged with a strange power to heal or destroy, my movements faster, more controlled than those of the herd.

It could only have been better if I had actually shagged her. That's not for the sensation, the feelings, the tastes and the sights; I was more than happy with the deliciousness of a pleasure deferred. Just to feel her body next to mine, to kiss her, was like being fifteen again, it was a reawakening of innocence. Sorry, but it was. Her kisses sent an energy through my lips and throughout my body, less a sexual than a spiritual experience. No, it wasn't the sensation I was immediately after, it was the security. Although she had put a firm downpayment on me by sleeping at my side, she had not yet delivered the balance and taken me away from the shop.

I had realised that I was probably going to get off with Alice when she had pushed me into a hedge on the way back to her house for 'coffee'. This was the culmination of a night of horseplay that started with her slapping me affectionately in the restaurant, continued with my standard 'after you' joke getting into the cab (as the girl steps forward to get in I step forward too and pretend to fight her for her seat – you kind of have to be there to get it) and gone on through her trying to trip me up all the way back to her house. When I had grabbed on to both of her arms, she had shoved me through the hedge backwards. It was like crashing through a winning tape, really, despite the fact that I tore my jacket and banged my head.

In the bright, white bathroom I felt a lump at the back of my skull. It had not been a dream.

I examined myself in the mirror – fattening again. When I get to a certain stage of porkdom I appear to change sex, at least in the face. It's not a nice transformation either. I don't become some buxom Victorian sex worker or a healthy farm girl of ruddy hue. At about fifteen stone there is something of the powder puff about me. I resemble a lightly rouged matron, a pantomime dame before the final coat of make up goes on, a decent lady of sagging jowl and vacant husband who has put on her face to go shopping, a lady who knows the people in the detached houses down the road and who intends to take up flower arranging once her nerves are straight. Whatever, it doesn't make me feel very sexy.

Instinctively I brought my arm across my chest and turned my head sharply to the right, stretching the skin across my face. Now from that angle I looked like the young Kirk Douglas.

After some full tongue snogging in the living room we'd gone to bed. Curiously, I didn't actually want to sleep with her. When I was a kid I'd always eaten my nan's roast dinners peas first, then sprouts, then mashed potatoes and then roast potatoes. I'd then eat the meat, saving the nicest piece – the fatty gristle – until last. This is how I wanted to approach Alice – to luxuriate in the peas while anticipating the delicious meat to come. Sorry if that revolts any feminists, or just human beings with a sense of decency, among you but that's the way it was.

This was fairly lucky, as she'd made it pretty clear she was only going to sleep with me in the sense of visiting the Land of Nod, not in the sense of staying very much awake. Now I normally wouldn't have much respect for a woman who wouldn't have sex with me on the first date, it would indicate that she was subscribing to a set of values barely visible on my moral horizon. Either that or it would mean she was playing a 'treat 'em mean to keep 'em keen' game, hoping that denial would make me want her more. I don't like that sort of insecurity in a woman.

In Alice's case I think she just wanted to be near me which, bizarrely, was all I wanted from her; to sleep in her perfume and wake in her girl warmth. Companionship seemed such a refreshing way to start a relationship; it was as if we knew we liked each other and so could work out the carnal side later. Nearly every relationship I'd had had worked the other way round. An evening of drinks and me showing off, followed by sex and a three- to six-month period where we realised we didn't really like each other.

In the arms of Alice I felt as if we were twin components of some fearsome explosive, mixing carefully and slowly in case our collision overwhelmed us.

I'd produced the Venice tickets at 1.30 in the morning, giving her the line about how I'd won them in the *Evening Standard*. I don't think she bought the lie, but she had surprised me by her delight. She said she'd love to go again, and that there were outer islands we could visit where we'd be away from the tourist throng. I actually quite like tourist throngs – there's normally a good reason they're there. I said we had to go to St Mark's Square, because I understood they now served beer in the McDonalds there and I wanted to see if it was as shit as the rest of their stuff.

She said we should go and see FC Venezia play, because they'd just won Serie B of the Italian league. I was shocked, it was June and they wouldn't be playing, but delighted that she expressed the sentiment. Unfortunately, she told me she was joking. She'd been with a previous boyfriend and had evidently been bored stiff.

Alice said she wouldn't have any difficulty in getting Monday off, which reminded me that I hadn't come up with a plausible reason to be away for Adrian my boss. Much of the media industry depends on trust, that you'll be doing what you say you'll be doing when you say that you're doing it. For the 'really incredibly motivated' scions of the middle class it came as second nature easily to exceed the minimum requirements with their sixty-and seventy-hour weeks. For me, brought up with a clock on, clock off car worker's mentality, trust was an invitation to abuse. Almost any media job can be done in twenty hours a week, if you're willing to cut it down to its essentials, and I was willing to cut a little more than that.

Alice and I spent a lot of the evening at her flat dreaming up things to tell Adrian. She was a committed career girl, so the idea of bunking off seemed deliciously naughty to her as she chuckled her way through more and more ludicrous suggestions. I wondered how she'd take it when she realised exactly how much bunking off I actually did.

We came up with an Internet computer policing program that went wrong, allowing children to access *only* hardcore pornography (actually, there was a committed cadre of perverts only too willing to profit from selling pornography to little boys when I was at school – they were known as the fifth form), disasters with a 'no fuss' marital aid, designed to attach to most food mixers. ('But, Adrian,' I could say, 'people are being seriously hurt, never mind the watershed, where's your journalistic courage?'); finally an electronic cat collar, meant to open special cat flaps, that had the power to divert homing missiles. 'It's all right for those of you who live in towns, but you try living on Salisbury plain. I've had three dead Persians and a badly singed Manx within a week,' claims Mrs Major General Moglove.

We decided on a follow-up to the bungee story where over-powerful knicker elastic had caused fainting fits all over the south-east, but only in those recovering from surgery. We had to give it a tinge of authenticity. Adrian would wet himself over that one; as a good journalist, he was always teaching me the importance of a follow-up. The frightening thing was that he would go for this, I knew. I don't know if he didn't listen to me or whether he just didn't have any critical powers. Maybe, despite his boarding school education, posh accent and Oxbridge degree, he was just thick. It seemed likely.

Anyway, this sort of mindless drunken spooning is the sort of thing we got up to before hitting the sack. I know that in retrospect it sounds incredibly cheesy and witless, but at the time it seemed as if, for the first time in my life, I couldn't wait to finish saying what I had to say, just so I could hear her speak. I took an almost physical pleasure in her words; her voice gave me a delectable sensation of homecoming, like the pleasure of a hot water bottle on a freezing night, or of a cool shower in the city heat. There you go, she did it to Farley and she did it to me. He came out with 'dreamy'; here I was with 'delectable' and puppy dogs curling up in front of a roaring fire. It doesn't really seem to get near to describing the emotion.

I do have the language to describe these feelings, I know, but only like I have the language to ask where the station is if I've taken a wrong turn up a French street. I know enough to be acutely aware of my own inadequacies. Giving me love is like giving me a set of screwdrivers: it's something that I probably need but I'm not quite sure what you do with it. Not that Alice was giving me love, she was just creating the feeling in me. At the time it seemed perfect. Only in retrospect does it seem a trifle gauche.

It's not like I'm ashamed of the emotion. How can you be ashamed of falling in love? as any number of dodgy songs might have asked. But I felt as if I had rearranged my house so I couldn't put my hand on anything without searching for it first. The problem is that the feeling of love disrupts familiar patterns of thought, overwhelms cynicism, defies boredom, makes flippancy inadequate – it turns me into someone else. I become the kind of person who wouldn't mind a Garfield mug as a gift. I swear that I would have been delighted if Alice had given me a teddy bear with 'I WUV YOU' written on it. It's a very bitter pill to swallow.

I think this is why stag nights exist. It's a way of telling your mates and yourself that it's the woman who has bought the façade, not you. You're still the beer-swilling maniac you always were, this woman has not changed you. If you're unlucky, of course, she hasn't.

On a practical and more familiar level, getting Alice into bed was no easy operation. If you're not careful you can sit up all night waiting for someone to suggest going to bed. Talking until the greasy spoons open is OK by me, if I'm with a group of blokes, but it seems rather a waste of resources when with such a pretty girl.

She, clearly, couldn't suggest we go to bed as it would be more of a come on than she wanted to give. I couldn't suggest it because usually only desperate old boilers like direct suggestions of sex. So what happened was that I said, 'I should leave,' meaning of course, 'I am desperate to stay.'

She said, 'OK,' meaning, 'I'm going to let you sweat for a while.'

I got my coat with the speed and enthusiasm of a man who can hear the firing squad loading up for him in the yard.

As we kissed at the half-open door, I took £2 from my pocket and asked if there was a minicab nearby, knowing full well that there was one near the tube and it cost a good £8 to get back to my house. She touched me on the collar and said, 'You could stay, if you like, on the sofa.'

I said, 'You sure you don't mind?' removing my coat in a Zorro sweep and re-entering the flat faster than a Jehovah's Witness across a pensioner's threshold. I knew, as she knew, that Alice didn't have a sofa. Having only just moved in all she had was a couple of large chairs.

After more electrifying kiss work, and some puzzling about where I was going to sleep, she said I could sleep in her bed. With any other girl I would have been delighted. Gerrard always says he gets a bit nervous when he first sleeps with a girl, whether his performance will match her expectations or if she'll have some repulsive physical aspect – he particularly dislikes ill-defined areolae, the flesh surrounding the nipples. I normally don't have any such worries but Alice was an exception.

My approach to sex has been through five distinct stages, roughly equivalent to those of driving a car. The first – unconscious incompetence – happened with my first girlfriend at around sixteen. I pitched in gamely, thinking nothing of over-squeezing nipples, attempting coitus within seconds of meeting her at the bus stop (the sexual equivalent of driving off with the hand brake on), French kissing like an over-fond bloodhound, etc.

The second stage, conscious incompetence, arrived about thirty seconds after the first stage. Even the rhino-hide thick insensitivity of a sixteen year old boy realises girls aren't meant to scream like *that* during sex. And, besides, the words 'You haven't a clue, have you?' from my then girlfriend rather gave the game away.

The third stage, conscious competence, involved the correct manipulation of the relevant bits, my face a mask of concentration like a boy backing the family car into the garage while his mother watches. Tongue protruding from the side of the mouth, I would engage tops, signal intent to move to bottoms and, if all clear, proceed down the road observing the speed limit and often checking the mirror. Crucially, I centred on her pleasure, it being more important to me that she came away with a good opinion of me to pass on to her friends than for me to express my immediate desires.

The fourth stage, unconscious competence – or boredom – is when it all fitted into place. No longer concerned with the basic mechanisms of operation I felt free to experiment, to express and abandon myself to passion, although I did not abandon myself to passion. I would find myself wanting to finish things quickly so I could get up and watch the video of *Match of the Day*, or noticing interesting trinkets in the girl's room. It's the equivalent of driving down a motorway and suddenly finding you've missed your turn, with no recollection of the last four miles.

The fifth stage, conscious depravity, the state that most male motorists are commonly in, is a response to stage four. At this point you go right the way back to stage one and become entirely selfish in bed, although not in the same ham-fisted sixteen-year-old way. It is interesting to see how far she will go, what she would do to please me. After forty or so women my level of mastery of the basic technique is such that I feel able to go all the way back to stage one, although in a knowing, ironic way, saying things like 'this isn't for you, it's for me', and forbidding sexual partners to have an orgasm, although of course I really want them to have one. This jaded approach seems to go down very well with girls; wild, mildly dominant abandon appearing to be the order of the day. In car terms it's the same as approaching the old git doing sixty in the middle lane, overtaking at a hellish pace and then slamming on your brakes in front of him. It's wrong, it's indefensible but, boy, is it fun. Don't try it if you've just passed your test, though, you'll only get hurt yourself.

Alice, however, was stage six, which made me sweat. I'd never had emotional and physical passion collide before and, frankly, I was a bit scared. I didn't feel up to technique or artifice. My normal talking dirty, 'I'm in charge' routine didn't seem right. I didn't know how to behave and knew I couldn't trust my instincts. I was afraid that if we made love I might come out with some complete turn off like 'I love you', or start stroking her hair and staring fondly into her eyes, which is OK – as Farley said, obligatory – after a couple of years, but on the first shag is likely to see the girl run screaming from the room.

Alice's bedroom was bare and stacked with cardboard boxes. She still hadn't moved in properly and I was pleased to see she wasn't one of those girls who had to have everything looking like a show home within three minutes.

I waited for her to finish in the bathroom and then went in myself, hoping that it would give her an opportunity to undress and get into bed without me having to watch her. Normally this would have presented no problem, I would have taken a gamble on turning her on by watching her take off her clothes. Alice, as I have said, was different. I was afraid of making her feel uncomfortable so I took a good five minutes in the bathroom to give her the chance to put on her sleeping suit, which I hoped was going to be of the cat variety I'd first seen her in. When I returned to the room she was, gratifyingly, beneath the sheets with her back turned to me. I untrousered, desocked, became shirtless and got into bed in my boxers. Underneath the duvet we embraced, although both our legs were closed. Mine out of politeness, I didn't want to risk putting my knee between her legs until invited; hers out of whatever her reasons for not sleeping with me were. She was wearing a T-shirt and pyjama bottoms, despite the heat of the night. We kissed some more and then she said she had to go to sleep because she had to get up for work the next day. It was 2.30 and I felt my life was beginning.

As Alice slept I looked out of the window, still curtainless, and into the Brixton night, a featureless dark sky seen through the orange glow of a street lamp. I turned to Alice and held up the duvet to look at her. Her pyjamas were in a smart tartan, mercifully devoid of teddybears or sheep jumping over fences. I laughed as I remembered what she'd said to the bloke in the pub. I wanted to touch her and I wished I had the power to stop the clock at the perfect moment. If this stops now, I thought, my life is worthwhile. But I also knew that if it didn't stop then nothing would ever live up to it. Perhaps Gerrard was right after all.

'Goodnight,' I said to Alice. 'Do not let Gerrard trouble your dreams. Goodnight, my golden girl.' I turned away from her to sleep. I reminded myself to write to Emily in Snowsville and give her the cold shoulder to add to the two she probably had already. Even there, smoothing away Alice's hair and kissing her on the brow, I congratulated myself on the pun. I never knew self-satisfaction could run so deep.

On my way back to the flat in the morning, I made a mental note to ring Gerrard and ask him how he was, but not until we were in Venice. I wanted to spend my weekend beneath the Venetian stars with the glow of Alice to light my nights, not with Gerrard in a hospital with a machine that goes bing.

At home, having phoned Adrian with a story about staking out a dodgy double glazing firm – I didn't have one, but it wouldn't take long to find if he questioned me – I checked Gerrard's room. It was locked as it always was whether he was in or out. Gerrard was a very private person and hated the idea of people barging in on him, I think it was a control thing, a territorial marking of space. I knocked on the door but there was no reply. In the absence of the niff of rotting pedant I assumed all was well, so I made a cup of tea and contemplated my trip to the city of lovers and, hopefully, of indulgers in wild sexual abandon.

12

A book at bedtime

I knew it was a cheap airline because the air steward who took our boarding cards appeared, to the naked eye, to be straight.

'A sure sign of scrimping,' I said to Alice, 'they can't even afford a gay one.'

'Do you know they put the better looking hostesses in first class?' said Alice.

I looked at our hostesses, or rather I looked at their carapaces of make-up. 'Looks like we're in with the livestock.'

'What must that be like?' said Alice, ignoring my affable sexism. 'Your thirty-fifth birthday and they say, "Miss MacNeice, from today you will be serving sportswear class. Miss Smith, who is twenty-one, will take your place up in blazers and dandruff."'

Alice waited while an old woman who seemed to be having difficulty with the concept of a locker, never mind its operation, looked around in distress, like a silent movie heroine who has lost her child. Disguising my irritation as politeness, I 'allow me'd' and took the woman's hand case, which from its weight was containing weapons grade plutonium, and put it into the locker for her.

'Make sure it doesn't drop out,' ordered the crone. I smiled indulgently and snapped the locker shut.

Once in our seats, I picked up Alice's theme.

'It's the same for footballers. They get to thirty-five and the boss says, "Thanks for the glittering international career, the goal a game and the great work with the youngsters. Now fuck off and play for Runcorn." '

'Yes,' said Alice, 'but they've at least got some money. The airline employs these women for decoration and, when they're no longer decorative, dumps them.'

This seemed like perfectly consistent logic to me, but I let it pass. She continued.

'Footballers get a good wage, a lot of these girls are paid peanuts – their only hope is marrying the pilot or some rich idiot they meet in First Class.'

I pictured myself as a hostess, saying goodbye to the girls as I married my millionaire.

'At least they've been good-looking at one time,' I said. 'Some of us go through life ugly and skint.'

' "If I hadn't seen great riches, I could handle being poor",' said Alice.

'Pulp,' I said, inwardly fighting against picking her up on her misquotation from the pop song.

'For a woman it's about identity – it's about becoming someone else when you lose your looks.' I couldn't see Alice ever losing her looks. She seemed to be one of those rare women who improve with age. In the ten minutes I'd known her she hadn't aged a bit, whereas one ex, Sara Jenkins, had said going out with me had put ten years on her, even though we'd only seen each other for a month.

I was reminded of a programme I'd seen about Miss Worlds – then and now. The first thing that struck me is that they weren't all that attractive back in the sixties and seventies – fat and bleached individuals luminescing under television arc light – but worse than that was their fall from their version of grace. Some of the ones from twenty years ago look like bag ladies nowadays.

I shuddered inwardly as I imagined Alice in a large frilly frock, her figure warped by a succession of kids. Maybe she would take to wearing pop socks. The hostess asked us to belt in for the trip and I got ready for my favourite bit – the take off.

For women, the take off provides a very simple gauge of the

emotional maturity of a man. If he imitates the noise of the jet engines as your plane heads for the heavens, perhaps illustrating its movement with an upward sweep of the arm, let's just say that the burden of childcare is likely to fall largely on you.

Once in the air, restraining myself from my normal 'We've got this kite airborne, Ginger, now let's give Jerry a roasting', I broke out one of the current rash of lager sagas, another one of these things about what it is to be a bloke. I was looking for some clues on how to appear male, kooky, just a little wild. I was pleased to let Alice see me with this book as I wanted to appear self-consciously laddy so she might take my lack of personal hygiene, my alcohol abuse, emotional immaturity, etc, as simple fashion statements. I had no intention of showing any of these sides to my character, of course, it was just an extra safety measure. Travel is a great way to find out about the person you're going out with, I am told. I have lost count of the number of my friends who have gone off around the world to find themselves and only ended up losing their partners. I didn't want Alice benefiting from any startling revelations.

If they did come out, I hoped she would go for that appalled-but-amused stance that women in sit coms adopt when they return to find their lager saga men being sick in their underwear drawer, rather than the appalled-but-departing stance of so many of my previous girlfriends.

'You're picking your nose,' said Alice.

'Scratching the back of my eye,' I said with a wink, and she actually laughed, although her hand made an unconscious movement for the sick bag in front of her. We were going to get along splendidly, I could see.

Apparently, according to my book, we're meant to be obsessive about ordering things, getting them into a system, which is hard to believe as I sometimes find the effort of ordering a pizza a little too much. We're meant to be natural collectors and codifiers. I don't think this is so. I love music, for instance. Once, after two months of looking, I'd discovered my Happy Mondays 'Pills Thrills and Bellyaches' CD under a chair with a cigarette stubbed out on it. Farley had explained that he couldn't find an ashtray and, with a borderline psychotic look on his face, asked if I'd have preferred him to stub it out on the floor. I washed the CD off and put it back on top of the telly, where it stayed, the highest star in a constellation of silver disks arranged over the floor, sofa, fireplace and chair, slowly circling around the one bargain bucket classical music record that no one ever listens to in the CD rack. To me the CD cover is just what it comes in. After that they can fend for themselves.

The only discernible pattern in our flat is that the ones nearest the CD player have been used most recently and the ones the dog has hidden in his basket have not been used for some time. To be fair to the dog, he'd only started coveting the disks after I had bought him a Frisbee to play with up the park. I wondered if he had a system.

Gerrard used to explain the mess to guests by saying I was a heroin addict who had just gone into rehab that morning. Typically, he would rather explain it than clear it up. He viewed that as solely my responsibility which, in fairness, it was.

I do know some blokes who pretend to be into collecting so they can convince themselves, and women, that they are interesting. It's normally something like original versions of blues records or first edition books, something to suggest soul. 'Look at me,' they say. 'See what a connoisseur I am, what a creature of fine sensibilities. I see things that others do not see. Please sleep with me.'

Of course there are also men who don't do it to attract women, particularly in the model train or toy soldier area, or at least the world is a stranger and darker place than I suppose it to be if they do do it to attract women. These people occupy a place so hopeless, a sexual hinterland so dark and confused, that their psychology is best left to the authorities when they come to their attention. I will say this kind of collecting is normally about having a captive group of friends and vying for power, though you knew that already. It's also about avoiding women, who seem to be less forgiving of trifles like cavernous emotional inadequacies and inability to communicate than men.

Alice, rather worryingly, was reading an environmental exposé called *The Oil Betrayal*. I caught this out of the corner of my eye and was careful not to let her see me looking. I had a vision of us in Venice, in ghoulish conversation about tribes displaced, governments bought, forests burnt, etc, over the candlelit Creme Brulee or whatever they eat in Italy. I was also a bit concerned that this topic appeared to be right up Gerrard's rather dismal street. In my opinion, women should stick to books about soap operas. Men, of course, require altogether lighter reading material.

Curiously, even though she was on a plane coming to share a weekend with me in the cradle of romance, I still wasn't sure of Alice. It was inconceivable, wasn't it, that I could spend the whole weekend without sleeping with her? The snogging had been a step in the right direction, but as one of fifty I couldn't help feeling that this gave little clue to her long-term outlook. Given Gerrard's competitive status, coitus was taking the shape not of a physical pleasantry but of a legal requirement. One shag was no guarantee that she would sign the deal to make me her boyfriend, but it was getting near to a formal declaration of intent. It reminded me of house buying: she was about to exchange contracts with me but was yet to complete.

As we swept low over the Dolomites – which are mountains, not old cars – I offered her my aeroplane plastic pudding and looked at her. She hadn't said much since take off.

I was struck by the difficulty we might experience just being together. Our first evening had been all about finding out about each other, unusual for my dates which are normally about finding out about me, so that had been a good start. But the weekend was going to involve the biggest challenge that any relationship has to face at any time: silence.

It's easy to get on when you're talking to someone, but how about when you're not talking?

Like kisses, there are varieties of silence, but unless you really know someone they are much more difficult to tell apart. Is it easy, for instance, to tell the difference between a girl who is simply engrossed in her book and one who has detected a slight against her?

Is it simple to tell the difference between the silence of someone who is enthralled, but a little intimidated, by your presence and someone who just wants you to go away? OK, in my case you could have a fair guess, but you take my point. These differences are detectable, but that requires a great deal of effort. In my experience, it's much easier to fly in with accusations or to say something like:

'Are you OK?'

Girl replies: 'Mmm.'

'Happy just reading?'

'Mmm.'

'Good.'

Silence from girl.

'So you're not annoyed with me?'

Girl, who, as The Carpenters said, has got to the part where he's breaking her heart: 'No.'

'You see, I thought you were.'

At this point no jury in the land would convict on a charge of unprovoked murder, and yet the boy has confirmed that the girl has been annoyed with him all along and can trace the ensuing argument back to her bad mood.

For me, silence is usually no problem. Under normal conditions I can just fill in the gaps with white noise blather. The girl would have to speak a couple of words during the weekend, but only to indicate menu choices, ask to go to the toilet, beg that we be allowed to stop drinking and go home to bed, etc. The rest I can handle with witty soliloquies about my youth, fights I have been in, mad relatives and all the rest of it.

Alice was different. My desire for a long-term relationship with her meant that I owed it to her, and to myself, to be interested in what she had to say. Also, my need for affirmation meant I wanted her to talk to me, to show me she was interested. So I had to get her to say something.

'Are you OK?' I said.

'Mmm,' she said, not looking up from something fascinating about particulate pollution.

'Happy just reading?'

'Mmmm.' She turned a leaf of the book with the avidity of a child opening the big Christmas present.

'Good.'

She said nothing.

'Nothing you want from me?'

She smiled and looked up. 'Only to be here,' she said and gave me an angel-light kiss on the cheek. You see, that's what you can get away with in the first few weeks of a relationship. If we'd been going out a couple of years I would have needed the services of the customs man with the latex glove to retrieve my complimentary cutlery.

To outsiders Venice, like love, seems impossible. The houses spring out of the sea as sudden as the passion of strangers, as if the waves had grown bored with the beauty of foam and spray and tried a more solid expression instead. They say Venice is sinking into the lagoon but to me it seemed very much on the ascendant, rising like a gift of the waters, as elegant and strange as any coral. Gerrard had been inspired when he thought of taking Alice there, and I had been inspired to get in there first.

It's a place we have all been to many times before, in films and postcards, books and documentaries, so on arriving it has a familiarity – but that of somewhere you visit in a recurring dream. It is literally and figuratively unearthly. By the water's edge nothing seems substantial in the flows of sun and shadow. It's a place that was founded on deceit when in the ninth century merchants smuggled the body of St Mark out of Alexandria to signal Venetian independence. It's an appropriate city in which to begin a love affair.

The water taxis and gondolas, the families in tiny outboards, give you the sense that Venice moves to strange rules. Even though it was the second time I had been there, it had lost none of its effect. It was so elegant and, despite the tourists, laid back, I had the sense that this was the world as it was meant to be and it was the rest of us who lived bizarrely.

The poet Shelley said:

> Underneath Day's azure eyes
> Ocean's nursling, Venice lies,
> A peopled labyrinth of walls
> Amphitrite's destined halls . . .

My Dad, who visited as part of a tour including the Lombardy lakes, described it as:

> A right dump covered in scaffolding.

In a small way I could see what he meant. The place is lousy with tourists, overpriced and, in major sections, under repair. But still this doesn't suppress the nature of the place – unlike, say, Bethlehem, which isn't noticeably different from most pleasure beaches – rather it makes it shine more deeply, glimmering above the souvenir stalls and the tourists, glimmering above the banal, the, ... well, me really.

The one thing my dad did find good about Venice was that the public transport is very efficient. You can tell a lot about a place by its attitude to public transport. In Birmingham they have the bus, in Blackpool the tram, in London the tube – their names stout monosyllables, fitting for vehicles that are repositories of more than people and cargo – repositories of blame, the cold, dashed hopes of punctuality and the damp spirits of overloaded shoppers. In Venice a water bus, as it would surely be known in any Anglo-Saxon country, is known as a *vaporetto*. This is not the name of a graceless toiler between municipalities but of a creature of the shimmering veil between land and sea, of rainbows caught in spray, brilliant blues and vivid greens. And, as even my dad noted, it does turn up on time.

'It is incredible, isn't it?' I said as our boat churned through the heat of the lagoon towards the Lido where Thomas Mann had set *Death in Venice*. I wasn't sure if a place so strongly associated with unrequited homosexual love was the best choice for the hetero-sexual gymnastics I was planning, but Alice had wanted to visit it rather than the more touristy bit around St Mark's Square. I almost felt constrained to steel myself for an attempt to sodomise her, out of respect for the spirit, if not the *actualité*, of Mann's story, but decided against it. The improving ideas of great literature some-times need to be ignored, no matter how aptly they fit your situation.

'What are you thinking?' asked Alice.

Normally I reply, 'Just about football,' when asked this question. It saves a lot of unpleasant emotional probing, especially as there's nothing like being asked for the contents of the mind to instantly evacuate it of all recognisable thought. Even if you can remember what you were thinking at the instant you receive the question, it's pretty difficult to put into words. I don't really think in sentences and it's difficult to reply 'water, architectural beauty, sodomy, I should one day read *Death in Venice*, though not here, too tacky, hunger, beer, shower, I wonder if you're going to sleep with me or if by some cruel fate you've decided to be just friends in which case make your own way back'.

Funnily enough, my reply would normally be the last of these thoughts. Modern girls of my demographic are used to meeting reasonably politically correct men. They find a direct expression of sexual intent funny. I would normally say it in a kind of cheeky, knowing, ironic way – but you don't say words like that unless you mean them. The nut of the message is in its literal meaning. I was too nervous to try this with Alice, though.

The *vaporetto* was coming to a stop and people began to file past us to get off. I was suddenly hit by a bolt of inspiration for the answer to her question, almost too valuable to relate as it may fall into enemy – i.e. other male – hands.

I laughed as if in surprise and said, 'How funny, I was wondering what you were thinking.'

This is a solid gold, easy action, Henry-Kissinger-knew-nothing-about-diplomacy-type reply. I felt immediately freer for just having thought of it. If I could turn it into some sort of joke, so I could point knowingly and say 'you first' when she asked the question again, I'd have a reply for life. Every time Alice asked me what I was feeling I would neatly remind her of how similar we were. Obviously this bore the risk of her eventually bludgeoning me in my bed out of frustration, but it was better than actually answering the question.

'All this, it's unbelievable,' said Alice, who was now a long way from the 'been there, done that' attitude to Venice she'd shown on our first night out together. 'My little nephew came and he said it was like "sea, sea, sea, sea, sea, house, sea, sea, sea, house". Don't you think that's a good description?'

When asked by a girlfriend if he thinks her little nephew has invented a charming and apt description, it behoves a man to say yes. I was so behoved. 'Yes,' I said, and seized on the chance to ask her more about her family, which I'd completely forgotten to do so far. It's funny that the main question of the turn of the Millennium is 'What do you do?' which we use as a guide to the person's identity. The 'Where are you from?' question, at least in terms of family, seems irrelevant.

I instinctively knew that Alice was of my class, I found her company too easy for her to be from anywhere else. At university, the so-called melting pot, I hadn't made one close friend who didn't broadly share my educational and economic background.

The only friend I had whose dad was not of my social class – Gerrard's dad was a solicitor – had been to a comprehensive where he'd told people his dad was a brickie so that no one thought he was homosexual.

As it turned out her parents ran a country pub – I wondered if there was any way she could be more perfect, perhaps she was a secret millionaire with a penchant for buying her boyfriends houses – and before that her dad had been a sergeant in the army, which I thought was great. I could imagine family meetings where we'd have loads to argue about. I'm sure I could spin a line on pacifism or something that could keep us from actually having to find out about each other for years.

'It was pretty strange growing up, really, when you find out how different you are from them. They don't have any real idea of what I do. My dad thinks it's incredible that I haven't found some sort of rich boyfriend yet and settled down. I think he still thinks he has to look after me in some way.'

'That explains your accent,' I said.

'What does?'

'Your dad being in the army – did you have to move around a lot?'

'Yes, we were all over.'

'You sound a bit Welsh,' I said.

'The pub they've got's in North Wales, I was there from fifteen to eighteen,' said Alice.

'My dad's a car worker,' I said, although she hadn't asked me.

'How about your mum?'

'She's a filing clerk,' I said, looking about the boat.

I was glad we had this similarity because it meant that if our parents ever met they would understand each other. If, as a WCOP (working-class origins professional), you go out with someone whose parents are middle class – you won't go out with the upper class, not the real upper class anyway – there are all sorts of things the middle class don't understand that can cause friction. The middle class very often don't understand that swearing is bad – in fact some of them think it's cool and funny, particularly the older ones. They don't understand that you start eating as soon as the food hits your plate and that there's no need to wait for anyone else (why let it go cold?), they don't understand that you are allowed to smoke between mouthfuls, they don't understand that the art they like looks like a child has done it, they don't understand that videos of transvestite comedians are disgusting, not funny, and they don't understand that their windows need ripping out and replacing by plastic ones. Many of them, particularly the men, think that they have a God-given right to sound off on all sorts of subjects without interruption. They don't realise that in the working-class family you have to fight for the right to bore.

It's worst when the fathers get together, because men, particularly older men, don't actually talk to each other. They just somehow agree a subject and then expound on it, careful to avoid drawing breath in case it lets the other person in. Based on bitter experience, a typical conversation between a middle-class and a working-class father goes like this.

MCF: 'The house is in pretty much original condition, apart from the fucking central heating, of course, which has been a bit of a fucker ever since we had it installed. Even the colours are National Trust.'

WCF, blanching slightly at the F word, not that he hasn't heard it before but that it's being said outside of the confines of the factory or boozer: 'A mate of mine had a very big house once. Of course, once the kids were gone he were buggered. Ended up in a flat. He were happier. By far.' The 'By far' is normally delivered with arms folded in a tone of voice that says 'tell me I'm wrong'.

MCF, who could be talking to anyone, but is, as always, talking to himself: 'I'm particularly proud of the detailing on the ceiling, it's all original Victorian.' A reflex action triggered by the sound of another human talking has caused him to raise his voice.

WCF: 'You should've seen our place when we moved out of Smethwick. Right bloody mess. We ripped the lot out, top to bottom. Got the ceilings Artexed. Very cheap, though.' A reflex action, triggered by the sound of another human raising his voice, has caused him to raise his voice.

MCF (louder still, voice becoming noticeably posher, as at an interview for membership of a pretty select golf club): 'Down here is my little secret, the wine cellar.'

WCF (louder than that, using accent last used at a football match in 1976 for commenting on a refereeing decision adverse to the interests of Wolverhampton Wanderers): 'We went on holiday to

France a couple of year back. The wine there's really very good, isn't it? And you're there and back in a day.'

MCF (as if addressing his ratings from the bridge of his ship): 'There's over a hundred bottles. This one here is particularly rare, it's . . .'

WCF (quieter, as if observing a bad case of dry rot): 'I see you've got a lot of red. Now I can't stand red. Give me a white, I'm happy as a pig in shit.'

And so it goes. This is why you're better off choosing a partner from within your own class. At least then your parents have enough in common *really* to disagree with each other.

All the time Alice was talking I had the weird sensation of being watched. This was because we were being watched.

A word to the wise, which only men need really read. If you have a very pretty girlfriend, and you are slightly insecure about your relationship, think very hard before taking her on holiday to Italy. Suffice it to say you would solicit less attention walking through the Grizzly Bear Forest Dance carrying a jar of honey and screaming, 'Here, bears, come and get it!'

Northern Italians are of course more restrained than those of the south so they restricted themselves to wolf whistles, loud expressions of '*Ciao, Bella!*' and following us about. Putting my arm around Alice and kissing her about twice a second seemed a reasonably effective way of warding them off, although I would have been grateful for the services of a cavalry sabre. As I kissed her for about the four hundredth time, to deflect the gaze of some swarthy, handsome *ragazzo*, the rather unpleasant image of a dog urinating against a lamp post came to mind.

'You seem to be causing a bit of stir,' I said, nodding towards an incredibly elegantly dressed businessman who was standing in the aisle about three seats down from us, slobbering like a hound. I wondered if any Italian man had ever tried to get off with a girl by pretending not to notice that she was attractive and that he was interested in her mind, as I had done for much of my early youth. I considered the relative successes of Gucci-clad Italian sycophants and those of English students, boiling beneath then-fashionable overcoats and decided maybe not.

'I try not to notice it,' said Alice, glancing at the man. He smiled and made a bid to move nearer, past some large Germans with rucksacks and 'Hard Rock Cafe' T-shirts. Luckily they weren't letting him get anywhere. I wondered if I could get Alice a T-shirt with 'I'm with Fatso' on it in Italian.

In a way, I was almost sad that Gerrard had not taken her to Venice as I was sure he would have handled the competitive attention a lot worse than me. I was almost flattered by it. Bringing such a beautiful woman to Italy was like an English World Cup-winning team being allowed to parade the trophy through the streets of Munich or Rio. It would, however, have offended Gerrard's sense of propriety. Of course, he wouldn't have done anything about it, he would have felt far too threatened for that, but he would have been completely unable to shut up about it, or talk about anything else, even once, for the whole holiday. It would have been 'Christ, there's one doing it again,' in the Campanile. 'Hell's teeth, I can't believe his cheek,' about a slavering waiter in a pizzeria. 'Lawks a mussy, even the barman's at it,' when they went for a drink. 'Great Scott, the cab driver too,' when returning home. He would be unable to drop it, even if Alice begged him, as she surely would.

I decided to affect an attitude of lofty indifference to the whole affair, like I had lots of stunning girlfriends owing to my big guy status, which, in my xenophobia, was an attitude I thought the Italians would understand. I leaned back in my seat, Harry Chesshiri, Godfather of the Chesshiri family, knowing that one wrong move from anyone and my boys would torch the boat as an example to them all.

'Why are you slouching?' asked Alice, who was doing nothing to deflect attention by sucking on an ice lolly.

'I'm feigning indifference,' I said.

I suppose why British men so despise the up-front style of the Latin male is that they envy it but are incapable of copying it. When an English bloke goes in for this sort of behaviour he instinctively shouts 'All right, darling?' conjuring up a picture of a lorry driver leaning from his window; indeed he usually *is* a lorry driver leaning from his window. The accompanying arm move-ment indicates that he wants to skip the moonlit walk and the soft declarations of love in favour of a quick in and out in the back of the cab. When the Italian calls *'Ciao, Bella'* he indicates something more subtle: that he wants to appreciate the woman, cherish her, hold her and tell her she is beautiful before giving her a quick in and out in the back of the Fiat. Also, for a woman visiting Italy, being sexually harassed is rather like having her photo taken with a policeman in London, going to the red light area in Amsterdam, or having someone be rude to her in Paris – she'd be disappointed if it didn't happen, offended even.

We disembarked at the Lido. Luckily the main slobberer had got off a stop earlier, though managing to leave the boat with his head screwed on backwards, and there were only a couple of minor droolers to contend with on the way out. One of them was German, and so no real threat in my book. 'Happier with a Luger than a woman,' my grandad always said. I'm sorry, it's just how I've been brought up.

'Damn, no one took our tickets,' I said as we tried to get our bearings on the quayside.

'I hate that,' said Alice. 'We can probably use them again.'

The Lido was once the most fashionable resort in Europe, according to my guide book, and it's still quite a smart sort of place. Presumably it's the one all the other lidos are named after. Maybe it's responsible for the introduction of the open-air swimming pool to Britain, an idea as viable as introducing igloos to the Caribbean. It could have been some sort of Italian joke.

It has one main road full of restaurants and shops, or at least one that we found, the Grand Viale S. Maria Elisabetta. The buildings are less spectacular than those around St Mark's, but are pretty, unremarkable, *fin de siècle* (the last one), affairs which wouldn't look out of place in an English seaside town like Brighton, except that they're clean, colourful and well-maintained. As we made our way towards our hotel we even passed an amusement arcade. The place had a Belle Epoque feel about it, mixed in with something of the late-fifties or early-sixties – as patented by Sophia Loren rather than Butlin's. The light in the Lido is a lot more regulated and straightforward than that in the network of canals, as once you get twenty yards from the quay you're on a motorised street. It's the kind of light that you think could support a sensible council and an excellent road cleaning service, rather than the intrigues of Doges.

I'd booked us into the Hotel Orseolo, which turned out to be a homely but down-at-heel place near to the beach at the end of the main drag. Actually, when I say homely, I actually mean other people's homes, some idealised welcoming but scruffy set up, not the homely of my home, which means 'squalid'. It too was Belle Epoque, but the belle in question was beginning to show her age. Alice didn't seem to mind too much, which I took to be a good thing – youth has few charming qualities beyond its appearance, but one of them is the ability to look on privation and dilapidation as exciting and fun. If you can't put up with rickety beds and doors that don't close properly when you're young, then you are due for a very bitter old age.

I had, of course, booked us into one double room as opposed to two singles. It had occurred to me to go through the rigmarole of getting two rooms just to show I wasn't assuming anything but, let's face it, I was assuming something. So I knew the reception desk was going to be our first great test. I had been through the possible escape routes a couple of times on my way from the *Vaporetto* stop. 'Now, now, my man, I think you'll find I booked two singles. What do you mean, you remember me clearly? I certainly did not request a Jacuzzi and mirrored ceiling.'

I knew she would hardly be into storming out, as the tongue-work on her sofa and our night sleeping together already showed, but I didn't want her feeling obliged – which at the time I thought would be a turn off.

I binged the bell on the smart wooden desk while Alice looked through something ominous about opera. I really hoped we weren't going to waste drinking time listening to that tuneless row. From behind us appeared a small round man in shirt sleeves and a proprietorial air.

'*Si?*' he said.

'*Quisiera una habitacion con banio,*' I said, having remembered the Italian for 'I have a reservation for two' on the boat trip. Alice smirked.

'That's Spanish,' he said, 'but the effort is appreciated.'

'*Lo siento,*' I said, ironically this time, but I'm not sure Alice got it.

I told him my name and he looked it up in his book.

'Ah, yes, here' he said. 'We have two rooms, to your tastes. Would you prefer it *con dos camas o con cama matrimonial*?' He was obviously taking the piss with the Spanish but I reflected what a graphic image the Spanish word for double bed conjured up. The way he looked at me made me acutely aware that sweat stains were spreading under my armpits and that he thought, if Alice valued her health, we would be in twins.

I looked at her and shrugged. I got the feeling she was enjoying herself because she just shrugged back.

'Don't care,' I said, caring desperately. Alice looked at me with a question on her brows, making me wish I'd just said 'double,' or 'matrimonial', it would have been easy enough.

The manager also had a question on his brows but, being Italian, he had allowed it to slip down through the rest of his body, opening his arms and causing him to take a step back. He looked as though he was steadying himself to catch a heavy object falling from the ceiling.

'If you don't care, you don't deserve a double.' He looked at Alice, as if he was a craftsman surveying a particularly well-made cabinet. 'Darling, there are islands full of men out there who would care.' He turned to me and smiled. 'I care for you. You have double in 33.'

'I was just trying to be helpful,' I said.

'Try to be helpful to yourself,' he said, which is the first time anyone had had to give me that advice.

'Third floor, turn right,' he said, passing me a key on a heavy key ring. 'You can give me your passport when you've unpacked.'

The first wire on a potential bomb under our weekend had been defused, we were up in the room together and with a double bed. This was when the delicate problem of whether to try to shag her as soon as we got into the room presented itself. This wasn't some 1960s saucy comedy type problem – she wants to keep her honour, I want to make her lose it. I was now fairly sure we were both up for it, but I wasn't exactly sure when would be the most opportune moment. I didn't want to seem like an over-eager adolescent.

However, when it came to practicalities, I realised it was going to be a lot better if we got it over with there and then. If I hadn't slept with her how, confined to one room and a tiny en suite shower, were we going to change out of our clothes? It's impolite to appear naked in front of people unless you have slept or are just going to sleep with them. Clearly this discounts sports team showers, although it doesn't discount modern dancers or strippers, as all of those that I've met have been very impolite.

'I'm going to have a shower,' said Alice.

'Right,' I said. 'I'll take the passports down. Where's yours?'

'Oh, can't it wait until after I've had a shower? I'm so hot, 'she said, putting her arms around me and kissing me on the lips. 'I won't be a minute. Then you can have one and we'll go and get something to eat.' I noted that she definitely did not say 'you can have one, we'll have a shag and then we'll get something to eat.' In fact I noted she specifically excluded all mention of shagging.

'Right,' I said. 'I'll read my book then.' I picked up the lager saga, a familiar object in a strange world.

Thankfully she didn't undress in the main room, sparing me the problem of where to put my eyes. If she had done that I would either have been looking at her tits or not looking at her tits and neither seemed very appropriate under the circumstances. Normally, with a normal girl, I would have said something like 'No chance of joining you then?' or even 'Make sure you leave room for me in there', but I was paralysed by desire for Alice. It was as if girls like her didn't belong with people like me. It's firm male adage that good-looking girls only go out with wankers. Perhaps I wasn't a big enough wanker. I heard in my mind Gerrard's voice assuring me of my qualification in that department.

I wanted her so much that I was afraid to show it. I was operating myself like some ungainly machine going through the motions. I heard her showering and fixed my eyes on my book. It was near the end, a bit where the girl had come back to the hero and everything had worked out. That seemed deeply unrealistic to me, for whom nothing had ever been all right in the end, ever. Mind you, literature is supposed to offer hope, so I was grateful for that.

I slowed my reading. Any further and I'd be forced to start on the copy of *European Philosophers: Descartes to Nietzsche* that I'd brought with me. You can tell a lot about people by what they read, but more by what they want to read. I'd had that book ten years and never got past page three. In an attempt of get rid of it, I'd even put it by the toilet, but had found I'd rather re-read my entire collection of *Spiderman* comics for the twenty-eighth time than pick it up. Not the twenty-eighth time I'd read them since I'd bought them as a twelve year old, but the twenty-eighth time since I'd put them by the toilet. About a twelve-month period.

Four times I'd taken *European Philosophers* on holiday and four times been reduced to a buying out-of-date British papers and reading their sports pages. And yet here it was, with me again. I was thankful I was with Alice and not the academic who wrote it because, judging from his writing style, it would have taken him the full weekend to order a pizza. Still, I was determined to beat it, because I wanted to be able to say things like 'your philosophy doesn't seem to have moved on since elementary Kant', and 'Nietzche, of course, was fundamentally misunderstood by the Nazis. He was even closer to them than they imagined', at parties and know what I was talking about. I still said these things anyway, but only when I was fairly sure the other person was clueless as well.

'Can you pass my bra and knickers in?' called Alice. 'They're in my rucksack.'

Some men would look on the sort of knickers and bra a girl brings with her on a weekend break as a statement of intent. I was one of those men. If the bra is chewing gum coloured with fraying elastic and the knickers are a size too small, red with a picture of Snoopy on them, it is a fair indication that she is not framing you as the love of her life. The first ones of Alice's that came to hand were a very interesting set, neither the Anne Summers type, which say to me 'I am so insecure or mad that I bought this collection of crisp packets stitched together into a "latex-look" ensemble, in order to attract you' nor the Marks & Spencer's utilitarian defence pants. The knickers were classic, sheer black silk ones – mercifully not cut high at the side – unadorned by lace, which I like. The bra again was a severe black number, I thought of the push up variety. (So-called because if a girl's wearing it right it'll make you wish you'd done more push ups when you meet her. Sorry, again.) Most importantly, both bra and knickers were new – with the labels still attached. She was clearly making a bid to impress. I avoided looking at the bra size because I knew I would have been unable to avoid telling someone, and that would have been tacky.

'Any particular ones?' I shouted back into the shower.

'There's a white set,' she said. I am of the school of men that never opens a bag fully, preferring instead to root about with my hand as if making a raffle ticket draw. I delved inside and pulled out a suspender belt and then a pair of black stockings, a clear declaration of intent.

'Mission complete. Put the kettle on, Ginger, I'm coming home for tea,' I said, rather too loudly.

'What?' shouted Alice.

'Just finding them,' I said.

The amazing thing was, I thought, that she knew I was going to come across this lot – she wanted me to see them. I would clearly have to shag her before we went for something to eat, I owed it to myself.

I rummaged some more and pulled out the book.

I could think of other items of literature that I would have found more worrying: *Guns & Ammo*, *The Jesus Army Guide to the Bible*, *Women are from Venus, Men are From Mars*, *Cosmopolitan*, that sort of thing, but this was a close contender. It was the Marquis de Sade's *Justine*. Although I have never read this book, I understood from Lydia – who had spent a fair bit of time in the 1980s dressing like a witch – that it contained some pretty warm scenes of sado-masochism. This, I can tell you, set my eyes back in my head, or made them pop out on stalks, or did something to them that would register deep and abiding surprise. Alice struck me as an intelligent, sexually mature career girl, not the sort who would be messing about in the slightly silly, aren't-we-being-naughty, behind the bikesheds, world of S&M. Even given my own late-flowering maturity, I wasn't interested in it, so why was she?

She'd shown no signs of wanting that sort of thing to happen when I'd stayed at her house. I felt a sickness rising in me as I realised she was probably looking for me to take the lead, literally. With a few well-placed slaps I could have her all signed up on the dotted line.

I dug out the white pants and bra, replaced the book and took the underwear to the door, pushing my arm through the gap she'd opened and exaggeratedly straining my head backwards to avoid compromising her privacy, even though no one was watching. I speculated on what might happen if I threw back the door and cried, 'You're for it now, girl, bend over and take your punishment.' However my footballing friends had informed me of the 100 per cent confession record of the Carabinieri – the Italian boot boy police – and if I was wrong about Alice I didn't want to spend time in the company of the few remaining Italians who mourned the passing of Il Duce. Not to mention the end of a beautiful relationship, shattered lives on both sides, etc. On balance, I thought it was best left.

I'm not one for marching about with a whip tying people up and saying things like 'Too late for sorry, my girl!' although I'll do it if the woman absolutely insists. I was brought up with a belief in democracy – I know that seems hilarious and naive given the present UK political scene, but there you are – everyone having their say. The element of coercion, the S in the S&M, really didn't appeal to me. I know there's meant to be consent on both sides, but that doesn't really strike me as sadistic. It's just buggering about – often literally – with ropes and handcuffs, which surely everybody's grandma has done by now. I also take it as a slight on my powers of allure if I have to lash a woman to the bed to avoid her running away during the act of intimacy. I would rather put my faith in toothpaste and a good deodorant.

The M bit appealed to me less. Having someone saddle me up and ride me around like a donkey while saying, 'You will call me madam,' seems hilarious, but then I never had the benefit of a public school education or attended a Young Conservatives meeting. Cheap gags but, I'd be willing to bet, still relevant whenever you're reading this.

I did like the clothes, for the girls only – no one's getting me into a dog collar and harness – so that's what made me wonder what Alice would look like in a knee-length shiny plastic boots and one of those see-through bodies, and what made it lucky that I had my lager saga handily placed for erectile concealment when she returned from the shower. She was wearing only the bra and pants and looked what the lower orders, and the tabloid press, call 'stunning'. I wanted to get up off the bed and kiss her madly, although I didn't. She went over to her rucksack, to get out God knows what, and turned to me with a grin.

'Your turn now, you dirty boy,' she said brightly.

I took a gulp, flung my towel about my waist, even though I was still wearing my trousers, and headed for the shower. Stripping off I had a nightmare vision of her prowling about outside with a big whip. From my limited knowledge of such practices I understand that people are customarily dominant or submissive in these things. I realised the wise money was on her being dominant – she was pretty brazen about that book, obviously intending to read it in front of me – and had spoken about being a millionaire very soon, taking control of her own destiny, all the rest of it. Could I, for one so beautiful, endure a life of being tied up and made to bark like a dog? Or squeal like a pig? For men of my age, certain scenes from the film *Deliverance* have never died in our memory, particularly what the hill billies do to the fat girly-looking banker. What if she wanted to wrap me up like a baby and mother me?

On the very much brighter but still decidedly dim side, I had read that the people who are the most submissive are often those in positions of power. They see having some dodgy tart, male or female, belt them black and blue as a release. Alice could, conceivably, be one of them. This wouldn't be my cup of tea, but at least it was a drink I could swallow.

I was about to indulge in a spot of self-abuse in order to forestall any premature ending to our imminent sexual encounters when I became aware that Alice had silently entered the shower room.

'Mind if I use the loo?' she said, nearly causing me to jump out of my skin.

'No, go ahead.' She had an alarming habit of being able to glide about silently, as if on wheels.

I soaped up, imagining that she was outside with some electric cattle prod.

'Shall we go out to eat when you're out?' she asked.

'Sure,' I said, feeling more vulnerable as soap went into my eyes.

'What do you fancy?'

'Oh, I don't know, Italian?' I said, in some pain, holding my eyes open beneath the shower.

'Ooh, you are sarcastic,' she said, suddenly sliding back the door to my cubicle and turning off the shower.

'What are you doing?' I screamed, in genuine panic.

'Just examining the goods.'

'I've got soap in my eyes.'

'Aaahhh,' she said, sliding the door closed, and leaving me to find the tap blind.

I turned the shower back on, regained my sight and got out sharpish. I had a vision of her throwing a hair dryer in with me or something for bizarre sexual gratification. I dried off and entered the bedroom with a towel round me, flexing my stomach and arm muscles to try to look more attractive, or at least like I could put up a fight if she tried to beat me.

'Prrr,' said Alice, making what I suppose she took to be a sexy cat noise but to me had the aspect of tiger who hadn't had his tea. She was wearing a severe long grey skirt, a deep blue short-sleeved blouse and a pair of refreshingly non dominant-looking spangly trainers. On the bed was a grey cashmere cardigan, which made me assume she was thinking of not returning to the hotel until after dark.

'I'll get dressed then,' I said. Considering she had been looking my naked self up and down like I was for sale ten seconds ago, I was still very shy about derobing in front of her.

She made the expected response about going out with a towel round me.

'Come here,' I said, hoping to get some sort of human warmth in before I felt the fiery kiss of the belt on my arse.

She moved towards me and we kissed, me still holding up my towel with one hand.

I freed one of the buttons on her blouse and put my hand on her bra. She squeezed the towel, right in the spot I was hoping she was going to, although predictably hard. Working my hand inside the cup of her bra I took out her nipple and rolled it in my fingers, feeling the pain of a desire too long contained. Although I was kissing her, I wanted to see her nipple so I strained my eyes down in my head; it was infuriatingly just out of sight. All I could see was my hand, which had 'Gerrard' written on it, as a reminder to call him. There are pubs, I thought, where that could get you killed.

I let go of the hand supporting the towel, although Alice still supported it with the hand she was gripping me with. I used my free hand to squeeze her backside and kissed her as deep as I could, though in a sexy way, not in a spaniel-trying-to-get-the-last-bit-out-of-a-jar-of-Marmite kind of way. She took my hand away from her breast and gave me a light slap on the cheek.

'Naughty,' she said gently, through her teeth.

'I want you,' I said, which isn't that original but did a remarkable job of describing the full heft and sway of my feelings at that point.

'Then you'll just have to wait, won't you?' she said, giving me a vampirish leer and moving away, leaving the towel suspended from my penis. 'I should put that away before you have someone's eye out,' she said, readjusting her top.

I wanted to say, 'The way I feel at the moment, you're in danger standing over there,' but I thought it better to avoid mention of the more glutinous aspects of male sexuality. I decided to remind her of this occasion at the first whiff of her introducing restraint apparatus. 'We've enjoyed this without gadgets, haven't we?' I could beg. Mind you, she'd probably like me begging.

I trousered up, got into a clean black tee-shirt – V-neck, makes the face look thinner – clopped on my boots (trainers are equated with teenagers and therefore weakness of mind in my book), threw my cagoul into my carry sack and we were ready to go.

'Why are you taking a cagoul?' said Alice.

'Might turn nasty,' I said as we stepped out into the hot pale blue of the afternoon.

'Sounds like something Gerrard would say.'

'Make sure you bring enough money with you, I don't want to end up paying for everything. That sounds like something Gerrard would say,' I said.

We had lunch at a nearby pizzeria, chuffing our way through a couple of carafes of house white in the process. Alice, who I knew could speak Italian, let me do the ordering as she didn't want to get involved in any conversations with the violently attentive waiter, who seemed intent on replenishing her wine after every sip.

'Do you think if you offered to sleep with him you'd get the meal for free?' I said.

'I'd want more than one meal for that, dear,' said Alice, kicking me flirtatiously beneath the table.

After the pizza we headed into the St Mark's area by *vaporetto*. I paid both fares, not out of fear of getting caught but in case God, in one of his more Old Testament moods, decided that because I hadn't paid he was going to make Alice flog me within an inch of my life, or not sleep with me at all – which would be worse.

It was after 5 o'clock when we arrived at the Doge's Palace so the tourists were a bit thinner on the ground than when we'd passed it on our way in from the bus station. The light of the day was still strong, although the delicate duck egg blue of the sky had vanished beneath dark clouds.

We walked through the alleyways behind St Mark's, across tiny bridges, looking down on the gondolas and wondering, romantically, how much they cost.

'Look,' said Alice.

I looked, to see that she was pointing out a gondola overloaded with large fat young people with video cameras. From the state of the haircuts I would have said they were Germans travelling to a beer festival by boat, or perhaps the poorer sort of northerner from England. Both the men and the women had the sort of hair that looks as though they ran out of money halfway through having it cut, the top half quite close cropped but the bottom long and straggly. One of them wore a leather waistcoat.

'Is it going to sink?' I said, more in hope than expectation.

'No, look, they've got McDonald's.'

They had as well, five distinctive brown burger bags lined up down the side of the elegant boat. It could only have been better if they'd had a ghetto-blaster ripping out some soft rock classic. 'Aaaaah, how romantic,' I said, and kissed her. She pinched my gut, which had the triple effect of making me feel fat, hurting me and turning me on. Love, it passeth all understanding.

And I think it was love. My parents had always told me that when I found the one for me I would know, but so far it had never worked like that. I was very pleased to be in Venice with Alice who I liked and fancied. If someone had asked me why I was with her I wouldn't, as I had with every other girl, have felt like replying, 'Because she was OK-looking, we got on OK and she'd have me.'

With Alice I could say, 'She's beautiful, she's funny, and she's got a way of seeing the best in me, of giving me the benefit of the doubt.' This last point is very important. There's nothing as corrosive to happiness as a partner who won't give you the benefit of the doubt, who doesn't accept that you will put up the shelf after you've watched the football and thinks you won't do it all, of the partner who constantly accuses you of trying to make yourself look clever or funny. You may indeed be trying to make yourself look clever and funny, but what's your alternative: stupid and dour? Are you reading this, Wendy? Enough sour grapes for the moment, but you see what I mean.

Alice was good for me because she took pleasure in me. She could put up with the drunken monologues, the half-hit jokes, the sentimentality over everything from sports stars to animals. She could do more than put up with them – she could find them funny and endearing. Admittedly, our relationship was technically only on its second date, so she might have been kidding herself that I was just like that when I was nervous, but it was a promising start.

Of course, there were things I wanted to change about her and I did still have some doubts. True, she was incredibly beautiful, but I had seen a picture of Brigitte Bardot at sixty and she was no oil painting. So I couldn't be sure it was going to last. Also, she was good fun and witty, which I liked, but I had a sneaking suspicion I'd have got on better with Lydia had there been more spark between us. I couldn't see how we could improve there, wit's something you have or you don't. Still, I was magnanimously prepared to let that one go, given the rest of the package. Third, we didn't exactly do the midnight conversation bit. Although she was interesting and original, it wasn't an instinctive understanding between us. I was sure I could remedy that with a course of reading and exposure to the right music – for her, I mean. That apart, I was definitely in love. For the moment.

I would have wanted to stay with her even if I hadn't been in love. I would have probably stayed with her even if I hadn't been in like. A girl like that comes along too rarely to allow issues of personality to intrude. And anyway, I had been with Emily for a year and I was hardly in love with her.

Emily, whose body was a perfect 10 – if you had happened to live in Stone Age Mesopotamia. Emily, whose scientist friends played Dungeons and Dragons and would try to tell you how clever the lyrics were on progressive rock albums. Actually, that's cruel. She was pretty attractive physically for the first few months, and she did have one friend who said he used to like Blondie.

When I had first met her there had been no Venetian walks and worries about whether she liked me or I liked her. I'd met her at a party. She'd sold me two tabs of E and we spent the rest of the evening dancing wildly and shagging – both in the coat room. The next morning we'd gone into central London and started drinking again. At 10.30 on a Sunday evening, crucified by drink and scarcely able to shut up, I'd said, 'That was charming, m'dear, would you like to accompany me back to the family pile?' and she'd leapt at the chance to come back to the flat. Gerrard said we'd kept him awake until 4.37 and I'd asked him if he couldn't be a little more precise. We stayed in bed and missed work on the Monday and saw each other almost every day after that. For the first time since she'd left for the Antarctic, I found myself wondering how she was.

Alice took my hand. 'What are you thinking?'

'That this is the best time I've had in a long time.' I took her other hand in mine and kissed her on the nose as it was to hand and gave me an excuse for looking down at her tits. I felt all the other first weekends with girlfriends piling up, imperfect, at my back. I felt wonderfully sad, because of all the missed opportunities, but electrified by the possibilities of the present. I wanted to tell her that this was the best time I'd had, ever, as it felt the right thing to say, but I wasn't going to mess things up by coming on too heavy. It might also not have been true.

I was slightly disturbed by the feeling of seriousness she engendered in me. It's second nature to me to clown about, make smart comments about gondoliers, ridicule other diners in restaurants behind their backs and all the rest of it. But she was doing that, laughing at the other tourists and teasing me about my bickering with Gerrard, and somehow I couldn't join in. I found myself wanting to tell her that she was the one for me; to say, 'Stop, now, sign this piece of paper saying you are mine forever and then I can get on with taking you for granted, which will be more fun for both of us.'

We'd been walking the back streets for nearly three hours and I felt tired and ready for a drink. Above us the sky was rain black, haloes of light ringing the storm clouds and a wind rattling the canopies of the restaurants and bars, drawing my attention to them. The waters of the canals seemed dark and deep, and the lights of the pizzerias seemed golden and inviting.

I looked at the sky, which seemed to be just holding on to its rain. 'See,' I said, 'I was right to bring my cagoul.' I could think of certain relationships at certain times when this would be enough to start, or continue, an argument along the lines of, 'You always have to be right, don't you?' Alice just smiled and said, 'Indeed you were. It's a good job, I'd have risked getting wet otherwise.'

And although I was afraid of capitulating to her clearly dominant traits, it made me feel good to give her the coat. So it was love.

We were now just along from the Doge's Palace, coming up from the S. Zacharia area. We crossed over a bridge and went down to some restaurants. Lightning flicked silently around the horizon, lighting the sky in blue and lilac. There was no rain yet but the waters became more choppy, causing the passing *vaporetti* to rise and fall alarmingly as they made their way through the surge. I could imagine old Venetians, catching the worry in my face as I contemplated our eventual journey home, saying, 'That's not a rough sea, I'll show you a rough sea,' just like I would say, 'That's not full, I'll show you full,' if I saw their pallor when faced with an over-stuffed tube.

I paused before we ducked beneath a woven canopy of leaves outside a restaurant, La Nuova Perla. I said I wanted to look at the menu, but really I just wanted to look at Alice against Venice as the storm drew in. The lightning cracked purple over the lagoon, its brilliance stripping the illusions of light and shadow from the city, reducing the skyline to a cardboard cut out. In the storm light she looked ghostly and insubstantial herself, as if she had appeared in one flash and might disappear in another.

'Dry lightning,' said Alice. 'I've never seen that before.'

'Too good to be true really.'

'What do you mean?'

'All the beauty but you don't get wet.'

'Doesn't sound like much of an advantage to me.' She smacked me lightly on the behind, pulling me sharply from my romantic interlude. I had forgotten for a moment her sexual deviance.

'I don't get the joke,' I said.

'Don't you worry your ugly big head about it,' she said. I think that was the second time she'd used that expression. We were more alike than I'd thought.

We sat down under the canopy to watch the storm over the lagoon. Our drinks were delivered by a nervous-looking waitress I would normally have fancied if I hadn't been with Alice. This was a new experience. Like most men, apart from Gerrard, I fancy in some way about seventy per cent of women in my age band or below. Not to fancy a good-looking Italian girl of around seventeen was new turf for me.

'It's a bit of a cliché, isn't it?' I said, gesturing at the weather.

'What?' said Alice.

'The lightning and everything.' I wanted to say that having a thunderstorm mark a momentous romantic event was like something you read in a nineteenth-century novel but I didn't want to tell her what I was feeling for fear of frightening her off. The romance word seemed far too strong at such an early stage of our relationship.

She looked out over the canal. We could hear the thunder now and it seemed to be coming nearer with every bolt. This is it, she's going to be electrocuted before I can shag her, I thought.

'You're right,' she said, 'it is a cliché.' And then she laughed. 'All we need is the gypsy violin and you on your knees.'

'Why would I be on my knees?' I feared the conversation had taken the kind of twist that would see me finishing the evening with a backside like a Derby winner's after a particularly close finish.

'Men!' said Alice. 'Where's your spirit of romance?'

'I don't call that very bloody romantic,' I said, noting that she had steamed straight in on the R word.

We were interrupted by the waitress who wanted us to go inside as it was beginning to hail slightly. I told her we'd be OK. I thought that the Campanile at around a hundred metres tall was the best bet for a lightning strike. This was clearly not a view shared by a large party of American youths who had been sitting at a table next to us, talking about money. They quickly upped sticks and scuttled indoors.

'The nation that gave us Rambo,' said Alice, to my vast approval.

I wanted to ask her about the book I'd found in her bag. I thought the best idea was if I just put her straight on my attitude to the 'let's see if six of the best will improve your conduct, my lad' type of scenario, but I didn't want to appear square and uncompromising. I decided to sound her out on the whole thing. If it was just a matter of saying 'yes, mistress' while we were at it, I thought I could manage that. I didn't want to be too negative about the S&M business, because I didn't want her to feel I thought she was a weirdo.

Gerrard, I thought, would have approached this differently. For him, sex was about closeness and tenderness and feeling loved.

More importantly it was about being himself. Role playing of any sort would have left him acutely embarrassed. There's no way he would have gone in for the cruel riding mistress and the disobedient groom act. It would just have reminded him that he was allergic to horses.

'Alice,' I said as a ball of hail came through the canopy and went down my back, 'I hope you don't mind me saying this, but when you asked me to get your pants today . . .'

'You found yourself curiously aroused?' said Alice, bulging her beautiful green eyes.

'Maybe,' I said, 'but more importantly I found a very interesting book in your bag.'

'Oh, yes?' said Alice, sitting bolt upright and looking very stern.

'I just wondered if that was the sort of thing you were into? You know.'

'What do you think?' She was looking directly down her nose at me.

'I think it probably is, which is fine by me. I mean, I'm quite into the scene myself.'

Why I called it a scene I don't know. What made me say I was into it I don't know. It made me sound like someone who spent most of his adult leisure time happily locked in a cage being fed cuttlefish by a budgie-mad housewife from Chingford, and saying 'tweet, thank you' for the privilege. Or rather, I do know what made me say it. It's the same thing that means I can't admit to not knowing about things, the thing that drove me to lecture on the barrows around Stonehenge and made my Uncle Dave itch to put Olivier right about acting. If she knew so much about S&M, somewhere inside a competitive genie said I had to know more. Even with submission, I had to come out on top.

The waitress came out again, this time begging us to come inside. I looked for signs of pleasure in Alice's face at these entreaties but I couldn't detect any. We went in and were seated at a table near the window, so we could still just see the canal. The hail began to come down in sheets, going through the canopy as if it wasn't there and bouncing five or six inches off the table where we had been sitting. The waitress gestured outside as she brought us our pasta, laughing as if to say, 'I told you so.'

'What sort of thing do you like?' I said to Alice, hoping that it wouldn't involve implements.

'The usual,' she said curtly. As she finished her sentence she put her tongue between her teeth again in a way that made me want to shiver. Ignoring the food on the table, she lit another cigarette.

'Like in the book?' I said. As far as I could remember from what Lydia had told me, Justine, De Sade's heroine, had lived at the end of her ordeal.

'You're meant to tell me that, aren't you?' The hail outside was banging hard on the tables and the thunder seemed to crack only an inch away from our heads. Two of the waitresses peered tentatively out into the night. I could tell this wasn't the sort of weather they saw every day.

Alice drew on her cigarette, making me think of a French Resistance girl – one of the ones portrayed by Hollywood – not the many plain, dumpy, incredibly brave ones who had actually spat defiance at the Krauts. I made a mental note to write something about that when I finished with Emily.

Lost in her beauty and the weather, it had taken a while for the meaning of her words to penetrate: 'You're meant to tell me that, aren't you?'

'Which side of the equation are you on then?' I said.

'What?'

'Flayer or flayee? Sub or dom?' I hoped this wasn't the kind of impertinence that had to be paid for.

'Sub,' she said softly. I would not have to bark like a dog, squeal like a pig or make any farmyard noise that didn't proceed naturally from one end or another.

'You?' she said.

'Oh, dom,' I said, eagerly, as if confirming to a customs official that I had my passport.

'Looks like we've got something in common then.' She looked straight into my eyes, pinching the flesh of my hand. I pinched her back, harder. She gasped and wriggled in the chair, although she didn't move her hand. 'I hope you're going to make me very sorry I came out here with you,' she said.

'Don't worry about that,' I said, pinching her hand again. 'Stay there,' I said, imagining that was the kind of thing dominant males say, and rising to go to the loo.

On the way back from the toilets I noticed a credit card payphone in an alcove. I had been worried about Gerrard, slightly, and I thought I'd just ring him to hear his voice and then hang up.

I plugged in my card and dialled.

'*Prego*,' said Gerrard, answering the phone. He'd clearly been brushing up on his Italian, which made me feel very happy and very evil simultaneously.

'Hi, Gerrard, it's Harry.' I'd meant to hang up, but I just didn't.

'*Si*?' said Gerrard.

'I was just calling to see you were all right.'

That clearly was the extent of Gerrard's learning so far, because he replied in English.

'I'm fine.' He sounded very happy indeed. 'Why shouldn't I be?' Even when joyful, Gerrard could contrive to sound condescending. 'In fact, I'm uncommonly well. This Alice thing has really sorted me out. I'm sleeping like a baby.'

I snickered like Muttley out of Dick Dastardly.

'Not out with Alice though?'

'No,' he said, still with too much of a smirk in his voice, forcing me to go on.

'She blew you out, then?' I made it sound like a question rather than the statement of happy fact that it was.

'She's rescheduled for next Saturday.'

This was a bit annoying, but I supposed she'd be letting him down gently.

'Where are you going?'

'Do you really want the details? Isn't it just enough she wants me and not you? Do you really want your nose rubbed in it?' I had been a model of restraint up to this point, I really had

'Where are you going?'

'I'm taking her to the Bel Swami, and I've told her she doesn't have to eat from the buffet if she doesn't want to.' It was statements like these that made me feel, well, just so much better than Gerrard in every possible way.

'Best of luck, mate,' I said. Unfortunately I couldn't help laughing manically as I said it.

'Don't try to sabotage things,' said Gerrard, knowing I was well capable of pitching up in the Bel Swami myself that evening: 'Gosh, fancy meeting you here, mind if we join you, me and all my mates from the football team?' if needs drove. 'This is the best thing that's happened to me in a long time,' he sneered.

'Great.' My voice now had the suppressed hilarity of a ten-year-old-boy who is watching his teacher about to step backwards into a dog turd.

'What are you doing tonight?' asked Gerrard suspiciously.

Dignity and restraint told me that I could no longer toy with him. I owed it to him to let him know where he stood, as a friend and as a human being.

'Shagging Alice in Venice,' I said, making V signs at the phone. 'Ha fucking ha!'

'Night,' I said and put down the phone. The bloke who had the flat before us was a technology nut and we had one of those phones where you could press a button and find out someone's number no matter where they were in the world. I knew Gerrard wouldn't be able to resist pressing it and I smiled as imagined his dawning horror as he thumbed through the international code book to find out if I really was calling from Venice.

'Making me wait for you?' said Alice as I returned to the table with the satisfied air of a man who has just seen his daughter's unsuitable boyfriend fall under a bus.

I wanted to kiss her and tell her that I loved her, and that I wanted her forever – at least for the next ten years – but I supposed that for the sake of titillation I would have to keep up the dominant act for the rest of the evening.

'What are you going to do to me when you get me back to the room?' asked Alice.

'I'm not going to tell you, you'll just have to imagine it for yourself,' I said, squeezing her hand and wishing I'd taken a look at the book to give me a clue on flagellation for the ungifted amateur.

The waitress approached our table. I thought she was going to collect the plates, which in retrospect seems a giddy and fantastic hope.

'Alice MacNeice?' she said in a very good English accent.

'Yes?' said Alice.

'There's a phone call for you.'

'Don't go,' I said.

'Who do you think it could be?'

'Anyone. Anyone at all,' I said.

Alice puckered her lower lip in puzzlement. 'How intriguing.' She started to get up.

'I forbid you to go,' I said, trying the dominant card. She seemed not to hear me, pushing in her chair and making her way to the phone. 'You're a very bad girl!' I shouted after her, hopefully. I reasoned I might as well try to salvage something out of it.

I looked through the window. The hail had stopped but still thunder flashed around the canal. I hadn't thought that even Gerrard, even at his level of madness, would call her back.

Half an hour passed. I drank my drink, then the remainder of what was in the carafe, and then Alice's drink. Then I called for another carafe. My mind was mute, but even that was too loud for the tumult of my nerves. When my brain did speak, it was in headlines. 'Man found strangled in Grand Canal', 'Man leaps to death in Grand Canal to avoid attack by girlfriend', 'Autopsy confirms man was strangled before he entered canal'. The morbid thought struck me that maybe I would be Alice's second death by water.

Between the storm and my internal wrestling, I hadn't noticed her return. Once more she'd floated in on air.

'He called me a traitorous cow.'

'He wasn't that angry then?' I said, weakly. 'Did you like it? You do like that sort of thing – being called a traitorous bitch?' Given our earlier conversation, I wasn't sure if she might be turned on by abuse.

'No, I bloody well don't,' she said. 'You didn't tell me you'd called him.'

'He'd been ill, I wanted to see he was OK.'

'So you told him you were here with me?'

'I mentioned it in passing.'

'Did he seem to take it badly?'

'He said he was going to burn all my clothes and kill me when I got home, so better than I anticipated,' The great thing about being mates with Gerrard was that I could do the double act even when he wasn't there.

'He said you were gloating.'

'I was not gloating. I may have been crowing, mildly, but only in a very tasteful and discreet way.'

'He also asked me if I'd like to go to Venice with him, in two weeks' time.'

'What did you say?'

'No. If I come any more I may as well get a flat here. What does it matter to you what I said anyway?'

This brought me up a bit short.

'Look, Alice,' I stared forward at her over the table, like a cop explaining the hard facts of life inside to a first-time offender, 'it does matter to me. I really like you, a lot. I only phoned Gerrard to see he'd been all right and couldn't help mentioning I was with you. That's all.'

She smiled, almost embarrassed. 'What did you say you were going to do to me when you got me back to the hotel?'

After I'd told her, in detail that's frankly my own business, we staggered out into the night and wandered into St Mark's. In the middle of the square at midnight, with everyone else hiding from the storm, I kissed her by the light of the thunder and thought how amazing it was that we were standing, alone, in the centre of the place most visited by tourists on earth. I only just managed to remember to do something dominant, squeezing her to my body very hard.

We took the *vaporetto* back to the Lido, standing outside on the prow despite the spray and lightning strafes. 'Wow, this is just as Napoleon must have seen it,' she said as we looked at the lights of the Lido lacing the shore. 'What a banal thought,' I said, and she hit me.

Back in the room it was a matter of getting down to some serious sado-masochism, which is easier said than done for beginners. Most people who come to the game are presumably well equipped with useful fantasies of rape and torture to guide them through the first shy encounters. I was not so blessed, the lingerie ads in the *News of the World* being the extent of my adolescent dreams. Of course I had tied a girl up and all that before, almost everyone you meet requires that nowadays, but in order to impress Alice I thought I needed to go a little further

My mind had already been at work on the problem on the way back. I'd considered cigarette burns and discounted them – I couldn't bear to do that to anyone even if they were begging me. The electrical flex occurred to me, but that would spoil my fantasies of thrashing male celebrities.

I needed something that would go beyond what I had done before without jeopardising my mental, or her physical, health. As it happened, she came up with the idea.

I'd pounced on her as soon as we'd got through the door, as I thought that was what sexual predators generally do and because I wanted to. We'd fallen on to the bed and I'd lifted her skirt around her waist, without going for the formality of attacking the blouse, and lain on top of her, writhing and snogging for a while with our legs interlinked. I was very gratified to see she was wearing the stockings I'd seen earlier and not tights.

After a lot of kissing, crotch grinding and, for the sake of tradition, some roughish breast manipulation, we actually got most of our kit off and into the missionary position, which has the virtue at least of being quaint. This was all to the good in my book, as I was having a fine time shagging the best-looking girl I'd ever degreased my paws on and didn't see any need to do much else. She had other ideas.

'Slap me,' she said in one of the rare moments when she managed to pull my mouth off hers.

'Where?' I was a bit puzzled, the customary surface not presenting itself in the immediate physical set up. I hoped it didn't show that, in the cycle race of S&M, I still had my stabilisers on.

'Anywhere,' she said, giving me a fairly good belt across the chops. 'Tell me Gerrard was right about me, I am a traitorous cow.' Saying Gerrard is right about anything has never been my idea of a turn on so instead: 'Take that, you bitch,' I ventured gamely, giving her the kind of slap on the face you'd use to wake a three year old.

'Harder,' she said, 'hit me harder.'

'Harder? You want me to hit you harder?' I was hoping she was going to say, 'No, actually, I've changed my mind, just get on with the standard shagging stuff.'

'Don't talk, just do it.' She seized me by the hair, hurting me quite badly, so I gave her a reasonable slap across the face, more to make her let go than anything. She caught her breath in pleasure and let go of my hair, lying back on the pillow again.

'Do you want some more?' I said, trying to sound fierce but only managing the tone of an aunt who has dispensed enough pop for one party.

'Hit me,' she ordered.

I gave her another couple of slaps. 'Ow!' she shouted, which I thought was the most unusual expression of bliss I'd heard in a long time. I could see a red mark on her face and I really wanted to stop.

'Are you all right?' I said, a question, I should guess, seldom recorded in the journals of De Sade.

'Keep doing it,' she growled.

I hit her again, three times, although without much conviction. Lightning washed the room into a clinical monochrome turning Alice pale beneath me, like a corpse on a slab. As I struck her she had become rigid and motionless, like an image caught in a bad photographer's flash. Her face was frozen and contorted as she anticipated my next slap. Then the thunder came. I was almost expecting someone to shout 'cut' or Count Dracula to appear at the window. Raising my hand for the fourth blow I caught a word, spoken beneath her breath.

'Don't.'

I lowered my hand and, as the lighting flashed again, saw she was crying.

'Are you OK?' I said, touching her cheek.

She pushed me off her and rolled over on the bed.

'No, I'm not.' She was weeping floods and shaking her head. Even in the semi-dark, between the flashes, I could see the print of my fingers on her left cheek.

'What's up?' Under normal circumstances I would have said this was patently obvious, seeing as I had just been giving it the Gestapo 'Confess, Englisher dog' treatment after a night of romantic rapture in the lovers' capital of the world. On the other hand, no pun intended, I was worried that she was pulling some weird attention-seeking tactic, the way mad girls often do. I really hoped we weren't getting our greens from that grocer's with Alice.

'I don't like being slapped, I'm not into it.' She was shaking her head and wiping tears away with the corner of the sheet.

'Neither am I,' I said, touching her shoulder.

'Then why did you ask me to do it?' She was sobbing dreadfully and turned away from my touch.

'I didn't, *you* asked,' I said, genuinely mystified.

'I was only doing it to please you,' she wailed.

I put my hand on her hair gently. 'I was only doing it to please you. I want a shag, not a re-enactment of grudge fights of the seventies. I saw that book in your bag and just thought you were into that sort of thing.'

Her sobbing stopped and she turned to face me, shaking her head in disbelief. 'I found that on the tube on the way over.' She began to laugh with relief through her tears.

'Why didn't you say?'

'Because you seemed so into it, I was nervous and wanted to please you.'

'What were you nervous of?'

'You. Is that so strange?'

'A girl nervous about meeting me?' I weighed it in my mind. It had never occurred to me for a second that Alice could possibly experience trepidation about going out with someone like me. Surely she knew she could have me at any time she wanted? I was B to C grade bloke: looks, income, everything. She was A++ grade girl. She should be looking for A+ blokes at the very least. 'It's a bit strange.'

She was laughing now more than crying. 'Well, you're so cool and everything, I thought you might just want to sleep with me a couple of times and that's that.'

'I'm not cool,' I said. I could see everyone I ever knew, from my family through to Gerrard, Farley and Lydia, nodding in silent agreement and disbelief. 'I hate cool things and I hate cool people. I have to, I'm not cool.'

'You mean, I needn't have bought my new trainers?'

'I don't like trainers.'

'Neither do I, really.' She started crying again and I put my arms around her.

We kissed and I looked into her eyes as they closed. Not only did I have the most beautiful girl on the planet, but she had bought a pair of shoes she didn't like in order to impress me because she thought I was *cool*. More than this, she was afraid I was only going to see her a couple of times and then dump her. I ran my fingers through her hair and as we embraced felt her legs pulling me into her. I kissed her deeply and took her left breast in my hand, in the respectful, first-things-first way I'd wanted to all along.

Christ, I thought, as I gazed fondly at her beautiful face and the magnificent tit I was about to titillate with my tongue, this is what it's all about.

13

The Mallory principle

Words are an imperfect medium. So I will never know exactly how Alice felt, returning at 9 on the Monday morning after such a long and heavy weekend, to find Gerrard waiting at her front gate. He had changed his Venice plans and now wanted to go to Budapest. He wanted to see her face-to-face to ensure she agreed to go.

It was 9 o'clock when I got back in too; my clothes were mercifully unburnt and my room unmolested. Although Gerrard hadn't said he would do these things there was a kind of unspoken understanding between us that he might. All there was was a letter which he had addressed to me and left on my bed. I ripped it in two without reading it and posted it underneath his door which was, as usual, locked.

There was another letter, opened by Gerrard and pinned to the noticeboard above the phone. It was from the solicitors who were handling Farley's will. As instructed by us they'd sold off his flat at auction and seemingly got a pretty good price for it, £150,000 from some developers. It seemed Farley was richer than we'd thought. Taking the rest of his bookmaking fortune into account, and some pretty nifty tax work from the solicitor's accountant, Gerrard and I came out with £300,000 each. Although I had planned to go to bed, the revitalising effects of a six-figure sum are quite remarkable. After a decent interval for a shower and a change of clothes I trousered my credit card and set my co-ordinates for Planet Spend.

The E-type Jaguar sports car is the only choice for the gentleman of leisure, particularly if he can't afford an Aston Martin or Bristol. Its plush leather interior, its walnut dash, its distinctive girl's-eye headlights, whisper 'refinement', while its V12 3.5-litre engine, speaking in an altogether louder voice, is fast enough for the needs of the committed driver (see conscious depravity – above), without making the garish leap to the unusable 150 m.p.h.+ zone. It is the bespoke suit of the motoring world.

I had, of course, considered a Citroen DS – the choice of the *Guardian*-reading super stud. Like the E-type it has the strange headlights, but it is longer and lower, more of the basking shark than the tiger variety. It used to be the choice of a man who valued style above speed. However, its appearance in two recent films of life and love among the arty intelligentsia of the South Bank had ruled it out. I wasn't driving any car associated with a grown man who plays the cello and recites Monty Python jokes in public. A Porsche, while being a laugh, is altogether too boysie. And you know me well enough by now to know that a four-wheel drive – like a reversed baseball cap – would be out of the question.

After biking my acceptance of the terms of the will around to m'learned friends, on Adrian's account, I took a stroll down the road to the Shortbay car garage – purveyors of classic cars to the gentry (me), and put down, via the credit card, a deposit on a dark green E-type which had a tasteful 00 in a white circle on the doors and on the bonnet. It had a sticker in the back, 'My other car is even more expensive', which I thought I'd remove on the grounds of not wanting someone to take a key to it. Then I went down the road to the Yamaha motorbike dealership and took advantage of a 0 per cent finance offer on a Yamaha R1 road rocket. There's no point throwing your money around.

Finally I went to the estate agent's and rented a garage round the corner to put them both in, making sure it was long enough for the sleek torpedo of my E-type.

Well satisfied with the morning's work it was time, naturally, for me to phone Adrian to tell him to stick his job up his arse. Unfortunately he wasn't there, all I got was my own voice asking me to leave a message. I decided to use Adrian's own film directorly tone on him. 'Call me, soon,' I said, leaving him to work out it was me. He was very fond of leaving messages like this himself, which was lucky because it gave me the perfect excuse for not getting back to him.

I felt a little guilty about the amount of fun I was having. Farley had only been consigned to the hellish dance of molecules that is eternity (copyright G. Ross, above) for ten weeks or so and here I was banging through his money like there was no tomorrow. Still, I felt sure he would have approved.

As night follows day, it was then time to go and get pissed. Obviously I would need a drinking partner and, on my new mobile – did I forget to mention that? – I went through my address book. Lydia could not be moved from work, I didn't want to overdo it with Alice, although I left a message on her home number telling her about the inheritance, Gerrard would be at work – there was no way the wounded and dying of the capital could do without him, even if he had just come into the equivalent of twenty-five years' wages – and also he'd be trying to scalp me. Given that all the lads I knew would be 'working' – even my mate Phil who did something on a men's lifestyle magazine, unaccountably, was actually busy – there was only one thing for it. I was down to ex-girlfriends.

In retrospect it might have been better if I'd have stuck to my own ex-girlfriends, most of whom wouldn't sleep with me if I begged them or, more accurately, when I beg them. But none of them were in. So that's when I called Paula, the subject of Gerrard's vitriolic letter, the letter Lydia had so wisely binned.

Paula was an aspiring artist, that is to say she was on the dole. I had always liked her, particularly because she sided with me in arguments against Gerrard. This was largely down to the fact that I was capable of telling her she looked very nice when she set off to go out for the evening, no matter if she looked ghastly. Unlike Gerrard, who would give her a coruscatingly frank appraisal of her appearance and how it differed from the look she'd had when he first met her. Gerrard wasn't one to stop at, 'I don't like your make up.' His comments were more along the lines of, 'Your eye liner is applied marginally too heavily on the left eye, your new hair cut makes you look like a man [if pressed he could specify which one], the cut of your jacket looks like you're trying to say you're a yuppie and those shoes are the wrong colour.' On the subject of shoes, there is only one correct colour for Gerrard – black. Anything else is wrong. Of course, this means that the shoes would clash with brown trousers, but at this point the reader is reminded the only fit colour for trousers, or any other garment, is grey. I remember once, when he'd produced his list of criticisms, Paula had said sarcastically, 'Apart from that I'm OK?' Gerrard had looked genuinely shocked. 'Oh, no,' he'd said, 'they're just the things that immediately spring to mind.'

I arranged to meet Paula at the French House in Soho. I don't know why I agreed to this – it's quite a trendy sort of pub in a fifties bohemian kind of way, which I would normally like, but it only serves halves of beer, so what's the point in that then? However, Soho is an excellent place to get pissed during the day, as its media clientele are all in meetings, or at work as they call it, and the pubs are full of people who are too interesting to have an identifiable job.

I hardly recognised Paula when she walked in. Under Gerrard's regime she had buckled down and, give or take a couple of swiftly pounced on deviations, maintained the standard bob hair cut and red lipstick she had worn when she met him. Now her black hair was much longer and she used strong make up, dark red lips and heavy-ish eyeliner, to accentuate the sharpness of her features. Her dress was pale blue and came down to her knees. I had never really noticed her figure before which, while not in the jaw-dropping Alice territory, certainly wasn't all that bad. It might cause a jaw to lower slightly, rather than to fall with the resounding clang that Alice induced.

Still, I didn't fancy her very much, probably because of her cleanliness. I don't, obviously, like women who are dirty, in the sense of unwashed, but Paula took it to extremes. She was chemically, anti-bacterially, napalm clean. There was always the faint odour of fly spray about her. Paradoxically, it was also a turn off that I felt she was contaminated by a stain that would not out, in the form of sexual relations with Gerrard.

It had been a miracle to me that she'd managed to stay the course with him a full two years. He had the personal hygiene of a six-year-old sewer rat. Sewer rats only live to five, you will doubtless remind me. Exactly, I will reply.

'It's great to see you,' I said. Paula was a bit of a feminist, from the 'just been on my first march' school, so saying 'you look great' would have been an invitation to a debate I didn't want to have.

'You too,' she said, 'you look fantastic.' I caught a niff of defoliant, garden rather than military.

'Yeah, I have put on weight. I used to look unbelievable, now it's just fantastic.' I pulled at my stomach. I could afford a personal trainer now.

'Unbelievable and fantastic.' She held up one long finger to caution me. 'Both words that don't necessarily mean good.'

'But in this case do,' I said, grinning and bowing my head like a determinedly pleasant Maître D' pointing out that, despite the appearance of rows of empty tables, they are completely booked out until the next coming of Christ, who will be lucky himself to get a table even then.

'I'm sorry, Harry, I don't know why I always feel tempted to be so offensive to your face.' She laughed inappropriately loudly, as if she wasn't used to it.

'It's OK,' I said, 'you should hear what I say about you behind your back. A seat, my dear?'

'*D'accord.*' She gestured to two bar stools at the window, and asked me what I wanted to drink. I'd forgotten she always liked to get the first round in.

We went for a bottle of wine, so I would be able to drink a decent amount without having to go to the bar every ten minutes. She returned with a bottle of Beaujolais, a red wine from France, which I was pleased to see wasn't of the Nouveau variety. That's always struck me as a large French marketing con. I can imagine some vintner in Calais, or wherever it is they make the wine, saying, 'It is terrible, you English beat us to all our new wine. We are stuck here drinking the old stuff. What are we to do?'

'So what's the news?' I said, dying to tell her about Farley and everything. I'd thought I'd hold back on going on about the money for a bit. Paula was pretty poor and I didn't want to crow in her presence or, I suppose, give her any money. It's amazing how quickly £300,000 starts to feel like not very much.

'Nothing much,' she said. 'I'm doing a bit of illustration work so I can afford this sort of thing.' She held up the glass. Like Lydia, she looked a bit witchy, somewhere between one of the sexy ones that I imagine *Playboy* used to feature at Hallowe'en in the sixties and one of those who inspired people to burn them at the stake.

I was pleased she'd decided to take on more commercial work. Paula is one of the few modern artists who can actually draw and paint. Obviously, she chose to do neither in her fine art. To be taken seriously in the world of high art you must be a laughing stock in the rest of creation. As I point out to her, roughly every time we meet, fine art only exists so the idle and the rich and the idle rich can feel cleverer than the rest of us. Most of Paula's stuff resembled Trevor in the corner of our kitchen but I'd always thought she could make a living doing real art: street scenes, puppies, that sort of thing.

She'd once painted a portrait of me, more a caricature really. I appeared about a stone and a half heavier than I actually look and had these shifty and defensive eyes. Gerrard said I looked as though someone had asked me to get out of bed.

'Brilliant,' I said. 'Did you know Farley was dead?' I'd got quite used to jumping in at the deep end on this one.

'Yes, I got a letter from Gerrard about it. Good riddance, he was an arsehole.'

I remembered her name and number on Farley's computer and made up my mind to ask her for the details later. Her expression at that moment, like the one certain heavyweight boxers use to scare opponents, told me the subject was not immediately up for discussion.

'Oh, you did get a letter.' This, I thought, would be an interesting one. 'Was it a study in contrition and desire for forgiveness?'

'What's contrition?' she asked. I had forgotten what artists were like with words.

'Sorryness,' I said. I didn't look down on her for this; she might have the vocabulary of a chalet girl but my painting skills were about on a level with those of my dog.

'No,' said Paula, 'he called me a traitorous cow.'

Other men like to repeat their *bon mots* to every girl they meet; Gerrard clearly liked to repeat his *mal mots* in similar fashion.

'So he's calming down then?'

'A little, I think. It doesn't bother me, I'm not going to be seeing him again.'

Mark Barrowcliffe

A wave of pleasure swept over me that was unrelated to her words. I could see myself in the E-type with Alice, going up for a weekend – make that a week – in the Lakes. I swooshed my Beaujolais in my glass like I had an informed opinion on it and didn't just regard it as an alcohol-delivery system.

'Are you still with that hippie bloke?' I kind of hoped she was, as she deserved to be happy.

'No,' said Paula. 'He was just a stop gap really, to give me the courage to leave Gerrard.'

I wondered why she needed courage to leave Gerrard. To stay with him she'd have needed the kind of resolve that made the defenders of the Alamo look like a bunch of vacillating yellow bellies.

'Who's this new girlfriend he's got?' asked Paula.

My Beaujolais suddenly became as bitter as the wormwood, as sharp as the two-edged sword, as horrid as the fang of the jackal, etc.

'He hasn't got a fucking girlfriend,' I said, with rather too much insistence.

'He wouldn't lie,' said Paula, 'I know him that well. He said in his letter that he didn't want me back because he'd found someone better.'

Most people would have said 'better for me', rather than the stark 'better', but not Gerrard. He was too honest. I drew on my cigarette.

'He thinks he's going out with this girl called Alice, who used to go out with Farley. But he's not, I am.'

'Oooooh,' said Paula, like someone who has just watched a man come down rather heavily on the crossbar of his bicycle.

'There's no Oooooh about it,' I said, 'I've been on holiday with her, I've shagged her, she's going out with me. End of.'

Paula pulled her mouth down at the sides, reminiscent of someone trying to do an impression of the tragedy mask. 'He knows this?'

'He will soon.'

I related the tale of meeting Alice, the Venice trip – leaving out important details of failed sexual deviance and the phone call – the fact that she'd said she'd had a wonderful time.

'So Gerrard's not seeing her now?' Paula had listened to the whole thing on the edge of her bar stool.

'He's seeing her on Saturday.'

'Oooooh,' said Paula, very much as she had the first time. She ducked slightly, as if anticipating a blow. 'Why's she seeing him if she doesn't want to go out with him?'

'Perhaps she wants to let him down gently.'

'You would, wouldn't you,' said Paula, 'go out with someone on a Saturday just to let them down gently, that's what weekends are for. Sod six o'clock on a Tuesday night when you've nothing to do anyway.' What she lacked in vocabulary she seemed to make up for in common sense.

'But why would she go out with me and then Gerrard? She's not the type to sleep with both of us.'

'I wonder where and who that type is,' said Paula, 'Will the leading anthropologists and museums be informed when she is discovered?'

I you-see-what-I-meaned at her. 'So what's her game?' mused Paula.

'Perhaps she just needs a friend.'

'What's she like then, this Alice?'

'She's great. She's beautiful, she's funny, she's very clever . . .'

'Hmm,' said Paula. Although I was sure Paula wasn't concerned about her looks, no more than the usual earth-shaking paranoia that most women have, I knew she had always been a bit conscious that she wasn't as clever or as amusing as Gerrard had wanted. When she had raised these fears with him he had, naturally, told her that she wasn't clever or funny, although he had said he valued her for other qualities. When she'd asked him what other qualities he, of course, couldn't think of any. I guessed that willingness to put up with him was big among them. Same as the rest of us, then.

'It's quite normal, isn't it,' she said. 'This beautiful, funny, clever girl just wants a male friend because, let's face it, girls like that have terrible trouble getting male friends.'

'What do you mean?'

She gave me a meaningful look.

'Am I detecting jealousy, cruel as the grave?' I asked. I often start to talk a bit like that when I'm getting pissed.

'No, I'd just be worried if I were you. It sounds a bit bizarre to me. I think she's keeping her options open.' I wanted to say something smart about how many more options did she want than the ones she'd got with me, but the wine, or something else, was choking me. 'Also,' Paula continued in a confidential, faintly nauseating, besty friendsy manner, 'I'd be worried about what he was saying to her if I was you.'

'What do you think he'll do?'

She considered for a second, lighting a Silk Cut Ultra with a match from a book. Gerrard hadn't let her smoke when going out with him and, although she'd described it as an infringement of human rights, he'd got his way in the end – mainly through some pretty aggressive use of air freshener. There are only so many restaurants you can be thrown out of for having your boyfriend go in hard with the Mountain Fresh before you will give in. I couldn't make up my mind if I found her attractive or not.

It's interesting to me that Gerrard never tried the air freshener on me or Farley, but I think that's because we weren't going out with him, we're a little more distant than a girl is. If you're his girlfriend and you're smoking then everyone in the world must presume he likes it, being his reasoning.

'He'll try to get off with her himself, or he'll try to fuck it up for you. As he'll be too intimidated to make a move on her, unless she spells out come on in semaphore, I'd go for the trying to fuck it up.' Paula took a sip of her drink. There was definitely something about her appearance I didn't like, although I couldn't put my finger on it. Perhaps it was her nose, which seemed a bit too spherical for the rest of her body. Everything else had sharp lines, while the nose was so bulbous it looked like it might yield a tulip, given a warm spring.

'I don't think he's got much on me.' He could play up my desire for Emily, but that would be too transparent. 'I'm home and dry,' I said, reminding myself to write to Emily and sack her.

'He could always make things up,' said Paula, blowing out smoke. 'He made up loads of stuff about me. He told me I said I loved him.'

'Did he?' I registered a note of surprise, a high-ish F sharp. 'He told me that too. What made him say that?'

'Once I said I could grow to love him, if he was willing to change.'

'Cupid, lay down thy bow.' I was definitely squiffing up.

'Exactly,' she said.

'Don't you think you might have got him to do something slightly easier? Cause the rocks of Stonehenge to dance into the sea? Break the Galilean most fed from loaves and fish record? I also understand no one has yet definitively proved there is an afterlife.'

'Point taken,' she said, 'so I can't see how he turned that into me saying I loved him.'

'He was always quite exact on you saying he had a small-ish penis. How big is it, by the way? At salute.'

'I couldn't possibly reveal,' she said, making a space of about four inches between her fingers.

'Quite a whopper then.'

'You think that's big? I always thought you had quite a big one.'

'How can you tell?'

'You just look big all over.' She poked her tongue between her teeth in a rather salacious manner. It crossed my mind that she might be flirting with me. I thought it wise to focus on Alice.

'Making stuff up wouldn't work, she'd be too wise for that.'

'Or he could just make such a pain in the arse of himself that it wouldn't be worth her while seeing you any more. Have you considered bringing her back to the flat?'

The delicious idea of noisily shagging Alice while Gerrard tossed and turned, fighting for sleep, had a clear appeal. However, I wasn't sure I could stand the list of my crimes that would be presented to her on her every visit. 'Considered it, but I don't think it'd be wise for a bit,' I said. 'The pain in the arse card does seem likely.' I swished at the wine in my glass.

'He's got a deck full of them,' agreed Paula.

'What do you think's the most irritating thing about him?' I sometimes didn't know why I was friends with Gerrard, considering I spent 50 per cent of the time arguing with him to his face and the other 50 bitching about him behind his back. Paula took on a starry expression, like the head of the Sinatra appreciation society when asked to name Frank's best record.

'He's an emotional bully,' she said. 'He farts too much and he doesn't get on with anyone nice.'

'Madam, remember your company,' I said, like an adviser to a

Renaissance queen, or like a Renaissance queen (often the same thing).

'You're not nice, Harry. You're funny sometimes, when you don't try to be, but you're not nice.'

'Who wants nice?'

'Women,' said Paula.

I was pricked by this rather depressing thought. 'Anyone important, though?'

'See, you're not nice.'

'Well, I don't want nice friends. I'd rather they were amusing and bitchy than the sort that come round saying, "Hiya, why don't we cook a communal meal and then I'll help you with something?" ' In fact, this had been one of the most irritating things about college – you go round to someone's house, ready for a night in the boozer, and find they've cooked you a meal, so you don't get to the pub before 10, even if you wolf it down. If you say you don't want it they get stroppy, even though you had your mouth all set for chips. On top of that, you have to look grateful. That's nice people for you. Never considering what other people want.

Another wave of pleasure swept over me. I saw myself with Alice walking along a beach with the dog, huddling together for warmth against a biting wind, struggling towards a very warm-looking pub that was far enough away to make you feel you'd earned your beer but near enough so as not to be a real challenge. The E-type was parked in the car park. In your fantasies, you see, you're allowed to drink and drive.

Farley, I reminded Paula, was not nice. This was a fairly crap arguing point as she'd already said she hated him, but I guess I hadn't digested that and was still thinking she quite liked him. She reminded me that Farley was a psychopath who had been so miserable and torn up that he killed himself. 'Have you ever considered a career at the Bar?' I asked.

'No, barristers aren't nice.'

I explained that I wasn't saying I liked nasty people, just that selfish and arch people tended to be better fun than the earnestly pleasant. When I was a kid we'd had an expression, 'chummy bastard', which was a pejorative for anyone who was overtly friendly when you first met them.

'Who would you rather go around with, some old lady who makes cakes for the church bazaar or Dorothy Parker?' Paula smelled of toilet cleaner, I thought, which I must have recalled from some racial memory, having never been anywhere near it myself. It wasn't an offensive smell.

'Who's Dorothy Parker?' she said.

' "Men seldom make passes at girls who wear glasses"? "Brevity is the soul of lingerie"?' I told you I shouldn't have opened that dictionary of quotations.

'My granny likes to make cakes for charity,' said Paula.

'Niceness is how people behave when they have nothing to say, or want to say nothing.' The mention of Dorothy Parker had got me off on the aphorism trail, though that was clearly a shaky start.

'That's not true,' she said. 'Look at Lydia, she's nice, she's got hundreds of friends, and she's got something to say.'

'Lydia is nice, but she has many redeeming features,' I said. The wine was taking effect and I was particularly pleased with that one.

'Like what? What do you like about her apart from her niceness?' It wasn't that Paula didn't think Lydia had any other qualities, she just wanted to see if I had noticed.

I signalled to the barman for another bottle of the Beaujolais.

'Tolerance,' I said. 'She is tolerant, and that is a trait nice people so rarely possess.'

'Tolerant is nice; nice is tolerant.'

'No. People who aren't nice are grateful if you'll just put up with them. Nice people are basically fascists. They decide how the world should be and if you don't conform to that behaviour they throw a strop.'

'You mean, they want you to treat them with respect?'

'If you're going to go feminist on me,' I said.

'Why's wanting respect feminist?' she laughed.

'Because that's what women are always on about. "Give us respect. We want respect." Well, I won't give them respect, I draw the line at fear.' I was clearly hamming this up because I knew the deadpan delivery that I could use with Alice or my male friends might be misread by Paula. She'd dropped out of university to go to art school, where she fell in with a bad lot – feminist pushers and Greer users. So I had to tread lightly. She'd only been crossing the road to higher education when she got run over by Simone de Beauvoir. Of course, I've never read either de Beauvoir or Greer, but I'm not one to let ignorance stand in the way of a good opinion.

'Why don't you respect women?' I couldn't tell if she was going along with the joke or not, which in Paula's case normally meant that she wasn't.

'They can't throw,' I said, 'and they like costume drama.' I delivered the last as a conclusive point, even though I quite like costume drama myself, and to tell the truth can't throw very well either. I was really laying on the heavily ironic voice here, to save any confusion.

'Get the wine, Harry,' she said, looking over her bulbous nose to where the barman was waiting, seemingly indifferent as to whether we paid or not.

I coughed up and we quickly moolahed another bottle of the plonk.

'Do you want something to eat?' I said, hoping the answer would be no. it's a luxury for me to fill up on crisps and peanuts without having to go in for the cooked dinners thing. I eat proper food out of a passing regard for my health, but occasionally I like to let myself go and eat stuff I enjoy. It's good to follow your natural instincts occasionally. If you put a plate of crisps and a plate of freshly steamed vegetables down at a children's party, which one are the kids going to go for?

'No,' said Paula, 'I don't eat if I drink.'

'Is that part of some diet?'

'No,' she said, 'it's an artist's habit. If you don't eat you get more pissed, which is essential if you can only afford a few beers.'

Another wave of deep pleasure hit me. At last I could see no tomorrow. All my days were going to be like this – the sunlight through the smoke of the bar, relaxing into the second and third bottles of wine as if into an old arm chair. I thought of Alice. I was sure I was falling in love with her, I wanted her so much. Somehow, by association, I felt the same towards Paula. She was there at the wrong or right time, at the wrong or right place, and was getting caught up in the motorway pile up of my love. 'There's my old mate Paula,' I thought, 'soapy but super.' For some reason I felt privileged and ennobled to know someone who could draw.

'I see you have walked a long way down the ancient paths of

wisdom,' I said, like a Californian guru trying to sound mystic while radaring for the tubes of Pringles. There weren't any. This was the French House, remember.

'Shall we go to a place where they serve pints?' she said.

'My dear, your taste is as impeccable as always,' I said, holding the breath in my nose as she engulfed me in her carbolic wafts.

Luckily, we were not a million miles away from my drinking club – the Glenbourne Arts – which is open exclusively to anyone with £15 for membership. It limits its membership, I feel, by only allowing applications on Thursday afternoons. This means that only those who are quite organised get to be members, and since wanting to be a member of the Glenbourne Arts and being organised is what poets know as an oxymoron (see 'grimly gay' in Wilfred Owen's GCSE poem 'Dulce et Decorum Est'), it means it rarely gets over full.

However, those who do make it through the hallowed portals are serious drinkers, being the sort who regard gaining membership of a late-opening bar as more important than being at work on a Thursday afternoon. These, girls, are the *crème de la crème*.

It was to this dimly lit basement boozer that we repaired, ensconcing ourselves in the red velvet chairs and flock decor of the proper English drinker.

We chatted for a while about Lydia whom Paula still knew very well. Had she met the fiancé? I wondered. She had, she said, and if Lydia was happy that was all right by her.

I couldn't help noticing she wasn't clasping the hands to her bosom, a quite attractive bosom, and going gooey the way girls are wont when marriage is mentioned.

'There's something wrong with him?'

'No, no . . . well, yes.' She sipped at her drink. Her nose wasn't really that bad. 'He's . . . I don't think you'd like him.'

'Sounds like an ideal husband,' I said.

'In some ways,' Paula agreed.

'I thought Lydia said he was a sensitive sort?' I wasn't sure she had said this, although I'm sure she would have meant to.

'He is,' said Paula, pouting prettily, 'very.' I thought of Alice and how prettily she pouted. Gerrard had strong opinions on why men find pouting attractive, but that was just the result of no one having performed what it suggested on him for ages. I felt like a cat in the basket right next to the radiator, wallowing in the warmth of Alice, of the Glenbourne, of Paula, bizarrely. My good feeling about Alice reached out to embrace her too.

On this last point, let me say I feel clubs like the Glenbourne could offer a valuable service to their members by employing a researcher at the door. On entering with a member of the opposite sex (the service would be open to same-sex couples on request – see I'm getting the hang of the PC thing), the researcher would ask each of the couple to grade the attractiveness of the other, one to whatever. Then, at hourly intervals, the same question would be discreetly asked again. Should the result undergo more than a four-point shift to the positive, the researcher would issue the interviewee with a card reading, 'Warning, you are wearing beer goggles'. These are the special invisible goggles issued to people around the fifth or sixth drink, where normally repulsive individuals suddenly seem mighty comely.

Unfortunately the Glenbourne thinks it is enough to provide beer and late opening and has so far resisted my suggestion to implement this card plan. I have warned the management that they risk losing a unique point of differentiation from their competition but, no matter, my case is argued and I shall return to the shadows. The Glenbourne receded. A cab was caught.

Back at Paula's flat I looked at my watch. It was 2.30 a.m. and no need to even consider going to bed. I thought of Alice asleep in hers and I was struck with a mad urge to phone her. I really wanted to hold her in my arms and tell her I loved her, although of course it was too soon for that.

Paula came in with one of the beers we had bought from the dodgy offy in a glass. One of my affectations, and Gerrard's too, is that I will not drink from a bottle – there's too much show in it. Imagine someone sipping from a bottle, leant up against his four-wheel-drive, baseball cap on backwards and talking on a mobile phone, and you might see why we object to it. It is of course fine, if not *de rigueur*, to drink from litre bottles of cider, or any size of wine or spirits. That lends the devil-may-care insouciance that we all so arduously seek.

Paula, who had taken the opportunity for a good wash and scrub up as soon as we got in, sat down and grinned. 'I'm so drunk,' she said, leaning heavily against me.

'There, there,' I said, patting her head, 'only a couple of hours to go now.'

She smiled. I noticed, with some alarm, that my arm was around her. I thought I'd try a subject that would turn us both off.

'How did you stick it with Gerrard for so long?'

'I don't know. He's got his good points, and nothing else was on the horizon. You weren't available, were you?'

She put her hand on my knee and stared into my eyes, swaying like a boa constrictor before its prey. Well, that's my excuse anyway – predatory female, helpless male. Don't worry, son, anyone would have done it. Light sentence in the international court of human treachery.

'Paula, I'm not available now,' I said, putting my hands on her shoulders to hold her away from me.

She leaned forward and I resisted the urge to stiffen my arms to hold her off.

'You look available to me.' She whispered the words hot and wet in my ear. I thought that if I was going to have sex with her it would have to be in a position where she couldn't breathe on me. I shivered inwardly as I realised what a terrible thought that was. Here was a girl who was my friend, my best friend's ex-girlfriend, and I was thinking of sleeping with her, despite the fact that I only half fancied her and that I had just met the love of my life. Pathetically – I use the word very much in its modern sense – I found that exciting. The wrongness of it all was what made it so right. It was the sexual equivalent of joy riding in a stolen car. I've read, in a certain type of literature, about brides bonking the best man in the vestry on their wedding day. I'm sure this kind of thing happens, and I'm sure it's the danger, rather than attraction to the other person, that makes it happen. However, I did wish that I could stop.

'It's an illusion.' I smiled, wishing that I could just disappear, be somewhere else in an instant, with Alice.

I have thought back and wondered if I actually wanted to sleep with Paula. But want, in cases of getting off with women, rarely has anything to do with it. I had been trained, by other boys – I say boys even though we're now in our mid-thirties and approaching the age where we might be thinking of children of our own – by experience, by everything, to just go for it and hang the consequences. It's like the mountaineer Mallory, asked why he wanted to climb Everest, saying, 'Because it's there.' We sleep with women on the Mallory principle.

When I reappeared into consciousness we were half naked on the sofa and she had her hands down my trousers.

She kissed me deeply and I held it, with iron determination. I can claim no originality for my next statement. Over the years there are many words that men have felt compelled to utter when sexual intercourse first beckons. Number three on the list is probably something vomit-inducing such as 'I want you'. (Actually, I think I've said that.) Number two, as the man attempts to appear sensitive and refined, is something like. 'We don't have to do this if you don't want to'. This is usually followed, at best, by a massive sulk if the woman takes him up on the offer. But right there in the number one spot, top of the hit parade since prehistoric times, is what I said, or rather shamefacedly mumbled, next.

'You're not going to tell anyone about this, are you?' I pictured Alice and me with our first kid, on holiday at a caravan site in Cornwall. Well, I never said I had class. Bizarrely, the previous fantasies of me having a series of girlfriends against the backdrop of a steady relationship seemed unappealing and even hollow. I kissed Paula's breast, sucking dutifully on the nipple. I wanted Alice more than anyone, only Alice, always Alice. Paula groaned in the approved manner as an acknowledgement of pleasure. I knew that, whatever I had thought before, I was in love.

'What?' she said.

I said 'Never mind', although I felt like forcing her to sign a vow of silence in her own blood.

Why didn't I back out, run from the flat and go home to explore brand new dreams of connubial bliss? Simple politeness, really. And, I suppose, an uncharacteristic pride in my work. Sex is the only area of my life where you could say I'm what the psychologists call a completer-finisher. In every other area I'm the big ideas and no action-man, but in sex it's the attention to detail where I score. I wasn't having Paula writing into consumer programmes complaining of a job half done.

On a practical level, too, the chances of her blabbing her mouth off about it would be higher if I didn't finish the job. If she felt rejected she might get all down about it and talk to her girlfriends; very likely the yielding shoulder of Lydia would once more be wet with tears. That would mean I was only one remove from disaster; one drunken evening, one argument, anything could trigger exposure.

The main reason, though, was that this was just what I was programmed to enjoy. Sex is what the washing, the wit, the new clothes and the job are for. Without it there is no self-respect and no point in behaving like you have any.

With a large measure of bad grace I began to remove her skirt, feeling like an adolescent forced on pain of punishment to tidy his room.

We kissed again; her lips tasted salty and weird. I think that even if the eyes and ears tell you that you are compatible other senses can let you know if you are not. Paula would, under normal circumstances, have been OK to sleep with but I found the way she smelled and tasted very offputting. It certainly wasn't a dirty smell, but just as I wanted to bottle up Alice's fragrance of perfume and cigarettes and take it home with me, something about Paula repelled me, although others I'm sure would have found it pleasant. The nearest I can get to it is to say it's like cinnamon, not literally, but lots of people think that's a pleasant flavour, although I hate it.

Don't let me give the impression that I'm knocking Paula – in the other sense – here. She's a lovely girl and on a physical level I was reasonably into what we were doing, even if I was holding the breath in my nose. This is a fairly normal state of affairs for me when having sex with a girl, as I believe it is for most men. There's always some little thing you have to live with, rather than enjoy – a spotty arse, man-breath, bottom not wiped properly, acting like a plank, having strange proportions, being very, very ugly – that sort of distraction. I know I'm sounding like Gerrard here but, believe me, these things didn't really bother me until I met Alice.

I used to quite enjoy sleeping with ugly-ish girls – they have to work that little bit harder than the pretty ones to justify your interest. Alice had ruined all that. I have never been as completely into it as I had been with her. In my life I'd gone from the first nervous fumblings with girls to reading the book spines on their shelves to keep awake during sex. I'd never been absorbed as I was with Alice, time had never stood still before. Like Gerrard, one perfect experience had soured all the others. But, unlike

Gerrard, I saw the chance to repeat it. I made another mental note to write to Emily. The problem with making a mental note at times like this is that your mental notepaper is soaked in beer and you have difficulty reading it the next day.

'You're not going to regret this?' I drew back, hoping she'd say, 'Yes, let's up sticks and forget all about it. See you in the pavilion for tea.'

'No,' she said, with kindness in her eyes.

'Good.' I wanted to bolt. I could dress this up and lie about it, so you would think I was a better person, but I won't. I have a very neat trick of displacing anger with myself on to anger with others, and I certainly felt angry with Paula. This wasn't for seducing me, I knew I could have walked out at any time, but for being a threat to the best relationship I had ever had. I felt angry with her for just being there. She was enabling me to betray Alice and, worse, myself. I couldn't believe my own stupidity, but there my stupidity was, given human form and writhing beneath me.

'I'll get a condom,' said my stupidity, and I agreed with it, sourly.

As we made love – and only that anodyne, antiseptic phrase will do – I felt as if I was raping someone, and it wasn't Paula.

14

Pin high

At around 7 in the morning I left, saying I had to go home to get changed for work. I wanted to phone Alice to make sure that my life had not, for the moment, come off the rails, but I thought it was too early.

I wanted to hear her voice, to take comfort from her ignorance, to test myself to see if the lies showed up. I boarded the tube for Fulham – luckily Paula's Notting Hill squalor-block wasn't too far away – and sat back into my hangover, a real eye boiler. I could still smell Paula on me, I seemed to be sweating antiseptic. At West Brompton, a stop before my destination, I had to get off and be sick in a bush. Sitting on a bench, I breathed in the warm summer morning and wished I had something to quench my thirst. Even though it was only 7.30 or so, I decided to call Alice on the mobile, just to see if she'd managed to find out I had been unfaithful to her by some sort of telepathy or something. The phone was one of these snazzy things that are activated by voice. I'd already programmed in Alice's name and on the third go it dialled her number. There were five rings before Gerrard answered. In any other circumstances I would have presumed I had dialled incorrectly, but there on my all-singing-all-dancing mobile's display was the name 'Alice' and her phone number.

'Is that you, Gerrard?' I said.

'Harry, yes, it is. Before you speak, can I ask you not to call this number any more? Alice is my girlfriend now. It's all confirmed.'

The cogs of my brain whirred feverishly, but somehow they had become disconnected from the crankshaft connecting them to my mouth. I really didn't know what to say. I wasn't sure if it was an echo on the line or my own voice that repeated, 'All confirmed?'

'Yes, it's me she wants, not you. Bad luck.'

'What gives you that idea?'

'Last night I . . .' there was a bang in the background '. . . slept with her,' said Gerrard. The 'slept with her' bit had been at the volume jewel thieves use to communicate when sneaking past sleeping security guards.

'Is Alice there?' I said very firmly.

The phone went dead. I stabbed at the off/on button to regain the dialling tone and shouted, 'Alice, Alice, Alice,' into the mouthpiece. 'Engaged,' said the display, making me wonder in my paranoia if that was a comment on Gerrard and Alice's matrimonial state.

I wanted to go round there immediately, but I knew that would be counter-productive.

Play it cool, I thought, dropping the mobile phone on to the platform.

My plan had been to go home and get some proper kip, although sleep was now out of the question. I picked up the phone, which was mercifully still working, and caught the train back to Fulham.

I was slightly buoyed on my way out of the station by the sight of the eastbound morning platform, packed with commuters steeling themselves for the dehumanising crush of the tube to work.

Quilted jackets, pink banker's shirts, faces and papers, the cufflinks, smart skirts and brogues of the city country crew, each person perfumed and showered, the hangoverless early bunch ready for the attack of the tube train. By the end of their journeys each would look as though they had been in a fight with a bear. I had left all that behind and at least that felt good. My friendship with Gerrard was over, I had the means to move out and I intended to do it. I saw myself leaving the braying wannabes and half successful yahs of Fulham for somewhere I'd feel more at home.

Brixton appealed, as did Hackney. Night clubs vs tennis clubs, mongrels vs Labradors, all night opening vs modern Mediterranean cooking, good vs evil.

Back in the flat I was pleased to note Gerrard's lunchbox still in the kitchen. There was no way he would eat canteen swill and so he either wasn't going to work (see abandoning the sick and dying, above) or he would be returning soon, in which case I was going to make sure he needed the urgent services of his ambulance colleagues. On the kitchen table were a number of investment plan forms, all filled out in Gerrard's name. I looked through them. He intended to bank his entire inheritance. I casually ripped them up and poured the remains of a can of Coke over them after I'd stuffed them into the bin. I then thought better of it and took them to the sink where I burned the dry bits with my lighter before soaking the remains under the tap for a few minutes. Checking for illegibility, I returned them to the bin. I gained extra satisfaction from the thoroughness of my pettiness, a fact that wouldn't be lost on Gerrard as he spent three hours filling in the forms again. I knew he'd admire the attention to detail, though.

Admittedly, if he had slept with Alice it would be a tiny victory, rather like Napoleon insisting to Mrs Napoleon that, technically, the planning had been excellent at Waterloo, never mind the result. I felt in my bones that she wanted me.

Besides, I reasoned, it was just impossible that he had slept with her. She had been so keen on me and I knew, *I knew*, she wasn't the kind of girl to sleep with someone just because he was there. He'd just gone round there and moaned and griped until she'd let him stay on the sofa, I knew it. No Mallory principle for her. I turned on the shower in a fury and scrubbed off the smell of the night before.

As I washed, I remembered my final conversation with Paula, after we'd finished having sex, when I'd asked her why she hated Farley so much. She'd always seemed to get on with him on a fairly basic level and, according to his database, he had slept with her.

'He gave me herpes,' she'd said, and then, registering my look of alarm, 'it's all right, I'm not having an attack.'

'Thank the Lord for that,' I said again, to no one, as I loofahed my back.

At the end of my shower I phoned once more. This time I got the answer machine, so Alice had gone to work and Gerrard, presumably, was on the way home. I looked at my watch. Half past eight. I tried Alice at work but she wasn't there. I couldn't leave a message on her secretary's voice mail because I didn't know what to say.

'Just wondering whether you had slept with my best friend' is a message that the medium of the answerphone is not up to. It's the kind of thing that needs to be scrawled in lipstick across a mirror or seared into a piece of paper nailed to a front door, it's not meant for electronic storage, to be played back over the morning paper, bagel and cappuccino.

As I've said before, I did want to hurt Gerrard in revenge, but part of me also wanted to take it easy. He was about the only friend I saw regularly any more. With Farley gone, and potentially no girlfriend to warm me on the dark winter nights, I could be almost high and dry as far as drinking buddies went. It was important to me to remain mates with him out of emotional need, but also practical necessity.

I brewed tea and marched around the kitchen, addressing the dog as the second in command in my council of war. 'Should the enemy be given a chance to surrender or do we say no quarter, my canine lieutenant?' I was saying when I heard the door go and Gerrard shuffle into the hall, pausing to play a message from his mum on the answerphone. She was saying something about him coming to some Friends of Israel meeting, but I thought she was casting her seed on stony ground there. Gerrard had his piggy bank raided persistently by his mother in his youth for cash to send to hospitals in Israel. This means he is one of a large number of Jews of my generation who regard Israel not as a homeland gained but as a skateboard lost. I think the letters of thanks were of little consolation to him.

I waited for him to enter the kitchen, saying nothing as he acknowledged my presence with a small start, like a man noticing a strange cat in his living room.

'Not at work?' he said, flicking on the kettle.

'We need to talk about Alice,' I said, demonstrating my doctorate-level skills in stating the blindingly obvious. I didn't bother telling him that work was off the agenda for the foreseeable.

'Nothing to discuss,' he said, demonstrating his doctorate-level skills in ignoring uncomfortable truths.

'Did you sleep with her?'

'Yes, I slept with her.' His voice gave him away. Whenever Gerrard is being particularly pedantic he uses the same inflexion that American children use when they say 'I did too'.

'You didn't have sex with her then?'

'Might have.' This was proof positive. Whenever Gerrard said 'might have', he usually followed it with something like 'might have flown to the moon and back'. He really was incredibly adult. I knew he hadn't got into her knickers.

'You didn't sleep with her.'

He shrugged his shoulders.

'I'll find out as soon as I speak to her.'

Gerrard bared his teeth and pushed his lips forwards, extending both arms to point at me, face contorted in a warlike expression, as if frozen while playing a military march on an invisible trombone.

'I told you not to call her,' he said aggressively.

'And I told you to fuck off.'

'That's right,' said Gerrard, 'losing, so you resort to bad language.'

'The only thing I'm losing is my fucking temper!'

'I'd threaten me with physical violence, if I were you,' said Gerrard folding his arms.

'Hey, why so defensive?' I said, nodding towards the body language and raising my hand as if to hit him.

It defused the tension and we both laughed. Then the phone rang.

I was nearer by a good six feet, twelve feet by the time I'd shoved him in the chest, knocking him to the floor.

'Chesshyre and Ross, private detectives,' I said, forcing levity into my voice, as if I hadn't a care in the world.

'Hello, darling, it's me.' It was Alice's voice. 'Darling' she'd said. 'Darling'.

'Hi, Alice, it's a surprise to hear from you.' I could hear Gerrard pretending to be hurt in the kitchen. I wanted to ask her everything about their night together, but I knew the only smart tactic was to ask nothing and let her volunteer it. There's no bigger turn off than a jealous man, at least not for sane women.

'Oh, I just wanted to hear your voice, to see everything's all right,' she said. 'Amazing news about the money.'

I told her I'd already splashed out on the E-type and was picking it up on the Friday.

'I think you've broken something,' moaned Gerrard. I imagined myself finishing him off with a good trampling.

'Gosh, how exciting,' she said. 'We could go somewhere for the weekend in it.'

'The coast beckons, my dear.'

'You're all right though?'

'Why shouldn't I be?' I could still taste a faint tinge of soap in my mouth, although it could have been from my own shower. Why was she so keen to know if I was OK? Had I said I felt ill?

'You haven't heard from Gerrard?'

I told her he was right there.

'You know he stayed last night?'

'Yes,' I said, forcing a 'so what?' into my voice when I wanted a 'this had better be good' instead.

'Nothing happened,' she said. I did a little jig.

'I *have* broken something.' If I hadn't have known better I would have said Gerrard was crying.

'What you do in your spare time is up to you, Alice,' I said very liberally, glad that I didn't have to make Gerrard swear not to see her again. I was itching to know why he had stayed, but I knew it was important to seem laid back compared to him. Mind you, that wasn't difficult as compared to Gerrard, Stalin was a bloke who was just going with the flow.

'That's so nice,' said Alice. 'Shall I see you on Saturday then?'

I said yes and we made arrangements to set off for the sea.

'It's good to know you haven't changed your mind about us,' she said.

'I won't change my mind.'

'I need help, it's broken!' wailed Gerrard from the kitchen. 'It's bl—get off!' I guessed the dog was licking his face.

'I have to go, Gerrard needs my help in the kitchen.'

'Gosh, things are changing,' said Alice.

We said goodbye and I returned to tend to the stricken. When I say tend, I mean 'continue arguing with'. I needn't have troubled myself. The end of the phone conversation had provided an instant cure for his broken limb. He leaped to his feet, shoving off the dog, and pushed past me to the phone.

I heard him leaving a message with Alice's secretary. 'Urgently, urgently,' I could hear among other words. The message went on for about five minutes. Then he threw the phone on the floor, breaking it, I later discovered.

I put the kettle on again and sat down to pick at the bones of ancient papers when I noticed a ring binder on the table. Picking it up and turning it over I was surprised to see my own face staring out at me. There is a point where a photograph ceases to be unflattering and becomes an almost libellous misrepresentation of the subject matter. This was such a photograph. It was a very bad blow up of one of those shots when someone catches you by surprise and pokes a camera right at you, close up. I think it had been taken at a party after I had been dancing rather more than is strictly advisable for a man of my age. The flash had exposed every wrinkle, every spot, and showed up my scant three-day growth as a horrid patchwork of dark and light hair covering my fat, red face.

Beneath this grisly apparition, neatly spelled out in Letraset, was the legend, 'Harry Chesshyre: A Suitable Boyfriend?' With trembling hand, I opened the folder to be greeted by a carefully mounted, if that is the right word, clipping from the Readers' Wives section of one of my jazz mags.

A naked woman of about twenty stone and around fifty years old sat in front on some chintzy curtains. She was eating a banana and giving what I can only describe as a 'come hither' look to the camera. I could tell this despite the fact that her husband, or boyfriend or whatever, had scratched her eyes from the photo in a strange effort to conceal her identity.

Below, and again neatly in Letraset, were the words 'Sample Pornography, found Harry's bedroom floor, June 1999'. Overleaf were similar selections from the Readers' Wives sections of my two porn mags. This really was libellous. Gerrard knew full well that I never looked at those sections, apart from out of curiosity, because they made me feel sick. I would have preferred a magazine without the Readers' Wives section at all, but in my red-faced rush in and out of the newsagent's I just went for the first one that came to hand. It's like pearl fishing: you hold your breath, dive in and take the first thing you can. You don't get time to browse.

Continuing through the file I found a photo of our living room.

Gerrard had put little drops of typing correction fluid on to the image, so he could number various items of debris that were strewn about the place. Next to a well-stocked ashtray, for instance, was the number one. Referring to the accompanying key I read, 'Ashtray. Perpetrator, Harry Chesshyre. Last date of emptying: Unknown (deep history)'. Number two was two empty wine glasses and a bottle that I had been intending to take out for some time. The key read, 'Wine glasses, two (note lipstick stain). Wine bottle, one (of six in room). Date of deposit: approx. summer 1997'. There was a list of about ten items, including socks, plates and packets of crisps. Also included were three close ups of various cigarette burns on the carpet. The key read: 'Note – Gerrard Ross does *not* smoke'.

Leafing on there was a photo of my room, this time with Biro circlings of apple cores, mouldy cups and dog hair clumps. There was a circle around a pair of French candlesticks I had on my shelf. The key read 'attempt at aesttchly plasng living spac. Funny, no?' I guessed he'd run out of 'Es' on the Letraset.

Finally, there were photocopies from some particularly lurid passages of a diary I'd kept at the beginning of 1997, which was a period when I'd been on rather a roll with what fat old-fashioned blokes term 'the ladies'.

'Don't worry,' said Gerrard, who had entered the room, 'she wouldn't read it.'

'That really is a massive comfort, Gerrard. What do you think you were doing going through my possessions and vandalising them?'

'What do you think you were doing stealing my Venice advert?' he said, 'and then taking my girlfriend to Venice?'

'She's not your girlfriend,' I said, ignoring the theft charge.

'Beg to differ,' said Gerrard, scratching angrily at his crotch through a hole in his jeans.

'You haven't even slept with her,' I said.

'I slept in her bed,' said Gerrard.

'So did I,' I said, 'after I'd given her more pleasure than woman has right to know.'

'I know all about it,' said Gerrard, who was now chasing the itch with his fingers as it burrowed up his arse. What did she see in him? 'Look,' he gave me that 'let's all just calm down' tilt of the head that people who fear they are in for a pasting give you, 'I'll put this in language you can understand.' I was all ears on this one, being patronised about my language skills by someone who'd made a career in medicine. 'It's like football.'

'There's no chance of a draw here, Gerrard,' I said.

'No, look, you slept in her bed when you first went out with her, didn't you?'

'Yeeees,' I said, like that posh, scathing newsreader off the telly.

'So did I, that's a point apiece,' he said, somewhat confusingly. 'One game in we're all level, we both have an expression of interest. That's what sleeping in her bed means. Then you took her to Venice and got off with her.'

I assented.

'So you're on top of the league at the moment, but only because you've played more games than me. I've got a game in hand, I'm allowed to take her out one more time. Abroad, to a foreign country.'

Gerrard didn't really like football, but he thought by putting things into my language he'd could make his tissue-thin argument stand up. It was the same when me and Wendy had been to see a marriage guidance counsellor. The counsellor had constantly picked up on the expressions we used. Wendy had said things like 'he's such a bastard, such a sad fucker', and this sincere vicar-like, middle-aged woman with a hand-knitted bag had turned to me and said, 'What is it, do you think, that makes you such a "sad fucker"?' Adding as an afterthought, 'In Wendy's eyes.' It didn't have the intended bridge-building effect. There's something very embarrassing about chumming up by using other people's vocabulary. Like people interviewing street scum about their likes and dislikes, who say stuff like, 'Your hat, you say, is "ill". Your trousers – are they "ill" too?'

'The season isn't over yet,' said Gerrard, clinging to his extended metaphor with admirable tenacity.

'The season is over, the league is disbanded and we are all playing another game.'

Gerrard made a noise like an angry heifer protesting at moving stalls. 'You keep away from her, I'm warning you!' he said, coming up close to me. 'If you don't I'll fuck you up, you see.' I always like it when posh Grammar School boys threaten people. They say the word fuck like 'faaaack', which makes it sound like some bizarre tickling practice, which I suppose it is, in a manner of speaking.

'Gerrard,' I said, scrunching up my face in school bully mode, like I'd seen when I'd been bullied, 'get away from me. I am so pissed off with you, not least for putting that portfolio together. It's childish, it's pathetic and it's unfair.' For some reason I noticed he had a small yellow stain on his collar, next to his neck.

He was now about an inch from my face. I'd never seen him in such a rage. He was white, tense and shaking. I don't know why, but that made me angry myself. It's the old competitive thing again. You're angry? You don't know what angry is. I'll show you angry. I gave a little white-faced shake of the head myself.

Incensed by my refusal to back down, Gerrard took a handful of my shirt and drew my face even closer to his. A millimetre separated us. 'All's fair in love and war!' he screamed. 'And this is love. This is love!'

'And this, Gerrard, is war,' I said, stubbing him between the legs with the rolling pin.

15
Truth or dare

A pending court appearance on a charge of assaulting one's flatmate is almost guaranteed to introduce a certain *froideur* into the normally balmy air of cordiality that exists across the dining table.

I had explained to the policeman that I hadn't even been aware we had a rolling pin. It just came to hand. The policeman, a much more urbane and witty fellow than the country clots who had seen us about Farley, said he'd take that as an admission of guilt. He said it urbanely, though, so I didn't mind. Apparently Gerrard had bought the rolling pin a couple of days before with the intention of making Alice an apple pie, or performing some other sickening homely gesture intended to make him look sensitive (see cooking, above).

The police had been willing to write off the assault as a domestic but Gerrard had insisted he wanted to press charges, Actual Bodily Harm, particularly since he'd received a black eye as he'd fallen by catching his face on the worksurface and a nasty cut on his leg where the dog had bitten him. At least it cleared up the argument about where the animal's loyalties lay. While Gerrard skulked around looking cowed in the days following the assault, the dog began to move with a certain swagger.

Mark Barrowcliffe

However, for all Gerrard's cowing, it didn't stop him constantly repeating his version of the opening lines from *Porridge* – a sit com about prison – 'Norman Stanley Fletcher, you are a habitual criminal who views arrest as an occupational hazard and so presumably imprisonment in the same casual manner. You will go to prison for five years,' followed by his impression of keys being clunked in locks and finishing with a cry of, 'Pick up the soap, white boy,' in an Afro-American accent. Quite what a black LA gang member would be doing in a British nick I didn't ask him.

'Gerrard,' I told him, 'you don't go to prison for ABH. It's a fine.'

'You might,' he said. 'Anyway I'll do my best to see that you do.'

I don't think Gerrard's attitude was born of real hatred for me. I think he was a bit pissed off but would forgive me eventually, seeing as he and I knew the black eye was an accident and one blow to the goolies in a fourteen-year friendship can quite easily be laughed off. I just think he wanted the world to recognise that I had done him down. I wasn't going to court for hitting him, I was going to court for getting off with Alice.

My brief incarceration at Fulham nick (lovely breakfast – you should try it) didn't stop me picking up the E-type on the Friday or riding around on my new rocket bike earlier in the week. I noticed that I had something to live for because I was driving uncommonly slowly, pootling around on 170 m.p.h. worth of screaming Japanese technology like it was a moped.

During that week I would normally have been doing a fair bit of skulking and leaping up when the phone went myself, owing to my accident on the Monday night with Paula. Alice was having to work late all week and didn't want to see me, so the testing first post-treachery meeting was deferred until the weekend. However, as I munched the filth's fry up I couldn't help feeling like I was really living. Spending a night in police cells was the final part of my growing up. I'd done it, now I could move on to the family and rose-surrounded cottage. Also, almost ideally, Alice would be so concerned that I didn't get the wrong idea about her and Gerrard that she would have the feminine radar for infidelity switched off. She'd take any discomfort on my part, the downcast eyes, the unusual attentiveness, as a reaction to Gerrard's stay, not my fear of exposure – or, as we know it, guilt.

It felt great to have her call me, and to call me darling, to talk about us. As I gunned the R1 through the lanes of Surrey at velocities approaching the speed limit I promised myself that I'd had my last away game. From now on I was a one woman man. I couldn't help feeling that 'darling' was overdoing it, though. Perhaps she had slept with him, although I couldn't see it happening.

Lydia had called and talked about us meeting Eric, which I thought was a good idea. Naturally Gerrard thought it was a bad one. He said he was wary of introducing Lydia's fiancé into an abusive home. I told him to fuck off.

In the end Lydia persuaded Gerrard to host a dinner party for the Wednesday after the coming weekend, when I would be in Brighton with Alice. I obviously didn't bother telling him I was going there, although I did hear some whining on the phone as Alice told him while he thought I was in the bath – I'd heard him phoning and crept downstairs. Strangely, she agreed to meet him, I think on the Thursday after the dinner party. I made up my mind to speak to her about that sort of thing.

Taking a cab – there was no way I was leaving my new bike in the street – I had a wing round Brixton looking for property. I worked out that, with the proceeds from the sale of our flat, which had gone up astronomically since we'd moved in, plus a bit of top up money, I would be able to get a clapped out Victorian four-bedroomed house with garage and still have £100,000 left over. Bung a couple of lodgers in and, hey ho, I'd be set for life.

Adrian from work still hadn't called so I presumed I was sacked, which suited me. Even if I wasn't sacked it suited me. There was no way I was going in. I rang him anyway and left a couple of messages pretending to be someone with evidence of widespread corruption in the Metropolitan Police. I left witty and urbane PC's name and station. I thought that should make my old boss turn up his pacemaker a notch or two.

Saturday took forever to arrive. My only conversation with Gerrard consisted of him asking me when I was appearing before the magistrate and saying he hoped I liked prison food. I told him I'd get away with a fine, particularly if I explained that the person

I had hit had been a complete and abiding bastard.

I finally wrote the letter finishing with Emily, my South Pole girl, lacing it with enough truth to annoy her so she didn't come blarting round my door when she got back. I dropped in a bit about Farley's suicide and Alice, but didn't go into too much detail as I hadn't got everything straight in my own mind then.

On the Friday I picked up the E-type and decided to do a dry run to Brighton, ensconced in the smell of leather and cigarette smoke. It took me a couple of hours to get out of London, so I nipped into a car stereo dealers in Brighton to have a stereo fitted, so we could listen to music as we went down. Flying back up the A23, listening to something too unfashionable to mention, I was in heaven. I only thought of Paula a couple of times. My guilt had substantially lifted since the Tuesday morning as I'd realised her only contact with me was through Lydia, who wouldn't say anything to Gerrard anyway. There was no way Paula would call Gerrard either, she hated him. Even entering the giant car park they call the London traffic system, I felt great.

I was in a fever of anticipation to see Alice again. Obviously I wanted to plug her for information on her night with Gerrard, though I knew it was best to eschew the electrodes to the seats of pleasure in favour of some gentle probing.

On the Saturday morning I parked the long, stylish, timelessly beautiful curved expression of my sexuality outside her flat, leaving the dog on his smart tartan blanket (Harrods) on the back seat – obviously with the window down and in some shade – and bounded up the stairs to her door. I say bounded, I mean kind of shuffle-bounded, if you see what I mean. I had a middling force 7 nor' by nor' wester of a hangover from the night before, which limited my ability to bound anywhere. I think the first step could have been termed a bound, but the subsequent four it took me to get to the door were very much more like shuffles, topped off by a final lunge at the bell. I'd gone out with Lydia and a couple of her mates from work. Eric the designer fiancé hadn't come as he had to get an early one in because he had an important cricket game the next day. I was quite impressed by this. Even professional English cricketers don't let major matches put them off tying one on the night before.

I'd left Lydia and gone home on my own to find Gerrard wasn't in. He'd stayed out a couple of nights in the week already, in fact. He was trying to convince me that he was round at Alice's, but I'd called him at his sister's and he'd answered the phone. Obviously I didn't say anything, I just put it straight down, but he knew it was me. Even if he didn't there's no way the king of the 1471 could resist tapping in the caller ID code.

I was in a fairly squiffed up state by the time I'd returned, but coherent squiffed, not coma squiffed. It crossed my mind to give Paula a call, as I reasoned that I may as well get hung for a sheep as a lamb. When I say it crossed my mind, what I actually meant was that I phoned her up but she wasn't in. So when I woke the next morning I was immensely relieved, and not a little proud, that I'd got away without going round to her house.

Some people would tell you that beer just gives you an excuse for doing the things you'd want to do anyway. This is true, I suppose, but it all depends on what you mean by want. I wanted to sleep with Paula, true, but I didn't want to *have* slept, with her. I wanted the sensation without the consequences, to have my cake and eat it. It needn't have been Paula particularly, it could have been anyone, it's just that she was the best bet. Drunk, I was quite into the devil-may-care, tomorrow never comes attitude that would get a kick out of the sheer stupidity of going round to sleep with Paula. Sober, however, that attitude was completely gone and I was feeling thankful, even noble, that I'd avoided going round to her house. I'd come through a big test, been loyal to Alice. Especially as I didn't call Paula again at around 1.30, after I'd watched some videoed sit coms, though I thought about it.

Why didn't I call Alice up instead of Paula? you might wonder. Well, I suppose I was afraid of blowing it with Alice, whereas I didn't really care about Paula. Phoning up Alice, the love of my life, on the off chance that she didn't mind me waking her up for a beery shag, however sizzling (see British tabloids for definition) was clearly out of the question. Calling Paula steaming drunk to demand another night of half-hearted bonking was, however, quite within the bounds of acceptable behaviour. When drunk. Sober, it made me cringe.

There's one other thing here. Often, especially after a couple of ales, it's actually better to sleep with someone you don't care about, or maybe don't even like, than it is to sleep with the love of your life. I'm talking about blokes here, of course, I have no idea how women feel about this.

What can beat the experience of falling into the arms of someone you love for a morning of lazy, caring coitus? How about exorcising your self-contempt in a drink and drugs-fuelled hammer and tongs session with a girl whose bum looks big even when viewed through the wrong end of a telescope? It's like the difference in pleasure between doing out the end of your ear with a cotton bud and doing it with the tip of a pen – each has its peculiar joys.

I was thinking on this as I waited for Alice to answer her buzzer. There's something about getting away with risky behaviour that makes you never want to do it again, and something else that's very addictive.

Alice didn't bother with pressing the button to open the door, she came down the stairs to meet me, opening the door and hollering my name like she hadn't seen me in years. I held her tightly, afraid I might lose her.

'I've missed you,' I said, thinking, What were you doing in bed with Gerrard?

'I've missed you,' she said, giving the standard lover's response.

She was gorgeous again, wearing just combatty trousers and a black T-shirt. She had no make up, knackered Doc Marten shoes, and her hair was carelessly stuffed under a band. Still she seemed to convey all the glamour of Vivien Leigh on Oscar night.

We went up the stairs to the flat, she leading. I considered pretending to pinch her bum but I was still residually thinking about the night with Paula. It was a God thing, or a karma thing, or something. I thought God would say, 'That is an inappropriate intimacy from a man who has been unfaithful – I will expose you,' so I kept my hands to myself. I did, however, allow myself to comment on her perfume, not because I felt I should but because I wanted to.

'Thanks,' she said. 'It's CK One.' And then she added in a slightly guilty tone, 'Same as Gerrard.'

'Gerrard doesn't wear perfume,' I said. 'Remember all the rabbits that would get hurt producing it, and of course the expense.'

'He was wearing it when he came round here,' said Alice.

So Gerrard had taken to buying expensive perfume. What a

testimony to the transformative power of love – he had actually become someone else.

The flat was taking shape now, though not as the straightforward girl pad you might have expected. True, there were the usual stripped pine floors, blacked up fireplaces and plain rugs, but there was a disorder and untidiness to the place you normally don't associate with women. Above the fireplace a large stripy Bridget Riley shimmered at me. But it wasn't in a frame and it wasn't hung, just sitting on the mantelpiece competing with a jumble of small change, moving in cards from friends, a half empty bottle of gin, a travel iron, a piggy bank, some candlesticks and a load of odd paper. She had a sofa too, a large cream thing that would probably look filthy in five minutes. Obviously it wasn't disorder on my scale, which has few, but significant, historical peers – the German army's retreat from Moscow, the fall of Saigon, the British Conservative Party under the stewardship of William Hague – but it was disorder nevertheless. I noted with particular pleasure that there was a healthy pile of washing up visible through the door of the kitchen. This was a girl I could get on with just fine.

Alice asked me if I wanted a cup of tea and went to make it in the kitchen. For some reason I recalled that Gerrard had a yellow stain on his shirt collar when we had the argument in the kitchen.

The condom was not the first thing I saw in the waste paper bin. My eye was initially drawn to a copy of the *Vegetarian* magazine, as carried by Gerrard for sensitivity ID. My eyes didn't register it at first, although my brain had clearly picked up something was amiss as it had held my gaze on the bin for longer than it normally would choose to do. My brain is not usually interested in the contents of rubbish bins, reasoning, I suppose, that the dog has to have some hobbies of his own.

When it finally emerged into my consciousness, I felt like a proud gardener detecting a mole hill on the pristine source of his freshly laid happiness.

Alice returned with the tea, placing it on a small table in front of me.

'I expect you're wondering about what happened with Gerrard the other night?'

'Sort of,' I said, eyes drawn back to the condom.

'It was weird really. He was waiting for me at the gate when I got in from Venice. Apparently he'd just been passing and decided to drop in at the moment I turned up.'

I imagined his faked surprise as she came towards him. I wondered how long he'd had to wait. I looked away from the condom, but still it was poisoning my consciousness.

'Anyway, he wanted to apologise about the traitorous cow bit, so he came in for a cup of tea and we kind of got to talking.'

'Did you shag him?' I didn't say, although I really, really wanted to. It wouldn't have made any difference to me if she'd shagged him once, or even several times on one night. It was just important she didn't aim to carry on doing it. I know this sounds a bit proprietorial, but there you are. I believe open relationships are possible for some people – those we technically term 'unhappy people'. In the real world I think for everyone's peace of mind you have to at least pay lip service to the idea of fidelity. If someone's sleeping around behind your back and you don't know about it, it's just like it hasn't happened, it's not even treachery – it's like that dull philosophical question: If a tree falls over in a forest and no one knows about it or hears it, has it really fallen? Mind you, no one ever got whatever vile diseases Gerrard was bound to be carrying off a falling tree. The idea of sharing a girl with him was impossible. I don't even like it when he uses my tea cup, so letting him shag my girlfriend is out of the question. I was fairly sure the condom was empty. Another, sicker, thought hit me. Maybe the condom didn't belong to Gerrard at all. Maybe I had another, unknown, faceless enemy.

'He was quite sweet really, he said how much he liked me and how, in another life, he hoped he could have been the one to go out with me. He was kind of wistful really.'

'A chaming picture,' I said. I imagined the boiling well of emotion that must have bubbled and blasphemed behind Gerrard's eyes. I wondered if he had been the first person in history to be violently wistful. Wistfulness was just a weapon in Gerrard's armoury. He had torpedoes of wistfulness, machine guns of consideration, mortars of empathy. Like all weapons, he only used them as a last resort.

'Well, quite. I was knackered anyway and wanted to have a shower and get to bed but he kept rattling on and on.'

'Then he stayed the night?' I was going to have to confront her about the condom, I really was, but I wanted the full story.

'Well, he had to. He left after about two hours and I went to bed. Then an hour later he came back and woke me up. He said he'd forgotten his keys and couldn't get a reply at your flat.'

'Brixton to Fulham and back in an hour by underground. That was quick,' I said, picturing Gerrard having a cup of tea somewhere down Brixton High Street.

'Hmm,' she said. 'He said he wouldn't have come back only he was feeling ill. He said he was sick and wanted to lie down.'

'So it seemed natural to let him sleep in your bed?'

'He said he was cold in the living room and he was so insistent, it was like his life depended on it. I didn't see it would do any harm, it wasn't like I was going to sleep with him.'

This story seemed plausible to me, it bore all the marks of Gerrard's on the spot thinking: i.e. baldly obvious by dawn's pale light. However the condom still had to be accounted for.

Alice drew her knees up to her chest on the sofa and put her arms around them, the way sexy girls are meant to. 'He's a very restless sleeper though, isn't he?'

'What do you blooming well mean?' I said, meaning, 'I bet he is.' I could just see Gerrard with the crafty toss, the sly turn, getting nearer and nearer with each gyration of his skeletal carcass; finally the groan of, 'Ooh, I'm so tired,' and the arm extended over the back. No resistance and the hand hovers nearer the breast. If she balks then it's, 'I'm sorry, I was asleep. I had no idea ... how embarrassing.'

Alice leaned forward to pick up her cigarettes. 'He rolls all over the bed all the time. He kept putting his arm across me.'

I wanted to ask her what she had done. Had she been aroused as she felt 'the proof of his passion' nuzzling into her buttocks, or had she thrown him through the window? I looked at the condom. It was a kind of an answer, but why was it in the living room? I just couldn't see him going for her on the sofa. Unless she had gone for him.

I excused myself and went to the bathroom to think. The one thing I've learned in my limited experience of women is that you don't go into an argument unless you've had a chance to think about what you're going to say first. Most of the girls I've been out with have been a bit brighter than me, which I like, but it means you've got to go for a bit of strategy if you're going to have a row. If I was writing a self-help book I'd say men in this situation shouldn't get into an argument without a clear idea of what outcome they are seeking. As I'm not writing a self-help book, I'd say they should forget that advice and just go for the standard male ploy of making yourself look big at the woman's expense. Phrases such as 'you're a fine one to talk, how about when you . . .' or 'you make me react like that' are all to the good. The more women who are miserable in relationships, the more there are to pick up for those of us who have learned the emotional equivalent of wiping our feet before entering the house.

I looked at my face in the mirror, which was mounted on a bathroom cabinet above a couple of shelves containing bottles of perfume – including the CK One and shampoo. I couldn't see Gerrard buying CK One for anyone, I really couldn't. Perfume to him was falseness. You should smell how you smell or, in his case, stink how you stink. It was then I remembered the yellow stain on his collar and the rate at which the dog's shampoo had been disappearing. What would he do if it rained? I thought.

Back to me. Alice's mirror revealed a wrinkle on my forehead that I'd not noticed before. Perhaps I was getting old. Perhaps my market worth was dropping so I had to accept that my girlfriends would sleep with other people. Perhaps I should be grateful anyone would have me.

My eyes were bloodshot, like I'd been crying, although it was probably the hangover. If the eyes are the windows of the soul mine looked as though someone had executed a clumsy smash and grab through them. I imagined a van coming to put large pieces of wood across my sockets to prevent further theft. I'm getting too old, for this, I thought, squeezing a blackhead in a pitiful attempt to feel younger. It was a big one, maggotting out of my skin dark and yellow. Normally I would have just flicked it away, but for some reason, perhaps a harking back to adolescence, I picked a cotton bud out of a jar Alice had on her bathroom cabinet and wiped it away with some make up remover. I thought it would reduce the chance of infection, not that I'd ever been that bothered before. Dropping the bud into the bathroom bin, I noticed the second condom.

Sherlock is not my middle name. However, it didn't take a
master sleuth to realise that this was a rum 'un. Most people don't
go scattering spent condoms throughout the home. It's not beyond
the realms of possibility that particularly riotous coitus may take
place in more than one location, but given Gerrard's addiction to
comfort I knew that the bathroom would be out of the question.
The lino would be too cold and hard and something, maybe the
quality of the light or the association with brushing your teeth,
would put him off. Them having a bath together was also too
intimate for the first coupling. Besides, Gerrard only took a bath
twice a week to save on water and heat. He'd seen her on the
Monday, bath days were Wednesday and Saturday. The position
of the condom was a giveaway too. Most people don't leave them
on top of the rubbish pile, they secrete them at the bottom, to
avoid giving offence to the eye. I bent down to the bin, feeling
faintly sick. This condom was definitely empty. I washed my hands
and returned to the living room where Alice was smoking. Lovely
cool curls of smoke floated to the ceiling. She looked French. In a
positive way, though.

I picked up the tea cups and took them out to the sink. She had
one of those chrome bullet bins that were fashionable a few years
back. I pressed the pedal and looked inside. Moving a packet of
Alpen and a can of beans, condom three blipped up on my radar.

'Alice,' I said, 'do you mind if I take a butcher's in your
bedroom?'

She looked put out, exhaling a thick cloud of smoke. 'Yes, I
bloody well do. What do you want to look in there for? If I had
shagged him I'd have had the courtesy to change the sheets before
you came round.'

'It's not that, it's not that at all, I know you didn't sleep with
him,' I said. 'I just want to show you why I know.'

She shrugged her shoulders and I noticed that one nipple was
standing out. 'Nice trick.' I nodded towards the proud teat. She
made a noise like a radio being switched between stations and put
her hand over the offending breast. I wondered if I'd get a chance
to make her symmetrical again before we went to Brighton.

Inside the bedroom, I went to the bin. No condom, but the
condom packet was there balanced carefully on top of an empty
can of Diet Coke. Hypo-allergenic, it said on the box, although it

may as well have said 'Gerrard'. Like many people, he regards allergies as proof of spiritual sensitivity, so he cultivates a few of his own. One is an allergy to condoms, by which I think he means he has difficulty getting them on or doesn't like them or something. I remember Paula telling me she had gone on the pill rather than risk being blinded by an ill-applied nodder pinged at force from the tip of Gerrard's nob.

Alice looked at the box in horror. 'I swear I've no idea how that got there.'

Silently I led her from the bedroom to the contraceptive in the front room bin, to the one in the bathroom, to the one in the kitchen. Throughout this unedifying tour Alice was shaking her head in beautiful disavowal. 'I don't know how these got there. I didn't notice them before you came.'

'It's OK,' I said, 'I know you didn't, and I know how they got there. Gerrard put them there for me to see them. That's why they're in three separate bins – he wanted to maximise the chances of me seeing them.'

'I don't get it,' said Alice. 'Why would he want to do that?'

I sighed, like a Zen master asked to explain the rarer intricacies of religion to a housewife who's only been coming to see him for six months on Thursdays.

'It's a ploy that works on a variety of levels,' I said, like Poirot at the end of the film. 'First, if you see them, which you probably won't as you're untidy and quite short-sighted, you might think you've slept with him and forgotten about it. Unlikely, I concede, without lobotomy or extensive therapy. That's only the outside bet. More likely is that I see them and jump to the conclusion you have slept with him. I start shouting at you, we split up, leaving the path free for him. Or I say nothing, but the nagging thought that you've slept with him corrodes my trust in you and our relationship is doomed.'

'Very clever,' said Alice, like someone listening to Poirot at the end of the film.

'It's not over there,' I tapped an imaginary pipe against my arm. 'Even if I discover the condoms and realise what has gone on, you may not accept my explanation. You may think I'm some kind of pervert, spreading condoms throughout your house. And then, of course, he can say he doesn't know what I'm talking about and that you must be sleeping with someone else. I refer you to my earlier comments on corrosion of trust. Or he can maintain that he did shag you and that means I have to back off.'

Alice looked faintly queasy. 'Do you really think he wants to sleep with me that badly?'

'In a straight choice between sleeping with you and losing his right arm, his reply is "Call me Lefty",' I said.

'Gosh,' said Alice, 'I think I'd better not see him for a bit.'

'Do you know, that's the nicest thing I've heard you say,' I said. 'Shall we go to Brighton?'

'Let's go,' she said, putting on a pair of sunglasses that recalled a better looking Sophia Loren. 'You didn't put them there yourself, though, did you?'

Brighton came and went in a blur: dirty white Regency houses, sunshine, fish, chips, beer and sea. It is the best of England, accepting that it has had its day and is just getting on with enjoying itself in shabby retirement, not one of these thrusting new towns with a shopping mall straight out of Dallas or Chicago. I'd booked us in to the Metropole with a sea view, just to be flash, at £200 odd quid a night. I was going to book us into the Grand but Mrs Thatcher had stayed there in 1984 and Alice was afraid the chill might not have left the building, despite the bomb. As I've said before, I'm not at all political but Maggie penetrated even my consciousness. I wasn't even sure what her policies were, other than making everyone in the south rich and everyone in the north poor, which was OK because I had moved to the south, but I objected to her on a different level. There was something thuggish about Maggie; the thuggishness of de-mossed lawns, church groups, industrial estates and stiffer sentencing; of us being right and the rest of the world being wrong.

She reminded me of a nightmare neighbour I'd had as a student, a woman who used to wash her cats once a fortnight and who'd told us we had no right moving into her class of street. Despite the fact that most of us were destined for media-shite jobs that you could term middle-class and that her husband was a postman, I kind of knew what she meant. She once called the police to break up a party at our house which would have been fine except it wasn't a party, just a few of the lads come round to play Subbuteo on a Sunday afternoon. The coppers had asked us to turn the music down but had to accept that would have been pretty difficult considering that we weren't playing any.

She was a big Thatcher fan and used to put out her Vote Conservative sign at elections. As you would expect, I had to get hold of a Socialist Worker Fighting Marxist Alternative poster for our window, despite the fact I've never known what they believe in other than standing outside tube stations. I've also never known anyone in that party who's done a day's work in their lives, which makes you think they must be getting something right.

We went to the Pavilion, the Regency folly with its curry-house domes and pillars. I was pretty impressed by the mix of Chinese and Indian styles inside and resolved to get my new flat done up like that. I could see myself poncing about in a quilted housecoat, receiving guests beneath the dragon murals.

'It's amazing, isn't it?' I said. 'You can just imagine Oscar Wilde coming to tea with the Prince Regent here.'

'Oscar Wilde was a century later.'

'But so ahead of his time,' I said, directing her attention to a large chandelier.

We walked hand in hand down the sea front, me dying to bump into someone I knew. Chips were bought and we found we both liked them drowned in vinegar; beer was bought and she commented that I drank a lot. I bought a new phone, to replace the one we'd had to Sellotape back together after Gerrard had thrown it on the floor. It played a recording of Handel's Messiah instead of ringing. Well, it didn't just play a recording of The Messiah, it bleeped as well, so it went, 'Alleluia! Bleep. Alleluia! Bleep. He shall Bleep forever and ever!' The effect reminded me of one of those shows where they cut the swearing out. I loved it because it was kitsch and I knew Gerrard would hate it for the same reason. I'd say it was suitable revenge for breaking the phone in the first place. We looked at the collapsed remains of the Palace Pier that the council are going to do up one day, the same way I am going to redecorate the flat, shortly after I fly to the moon and secure world peace.

All along the promenade New Age traveller-types swarmed. The hippies seemed to have taken over Brighton; people juggling and wearing ethnic tat were at every turn. Some of them were probably called Grommit or Willow and aspired to live in an old van. I got a chance to use one of my favourite lines, which had not had an airing in two or three years.

'Bloody New Age travellers,' I said, looking at a dreadlocked girl who was wearing a stripy jumper, despite the heat of the day.

'What exactly is a New Age traveller?' said Alice.

'A tramp with rich parents,' I replied, immensely pleased with myself. She rewarded me with a snort which I took for laughter.

As we progressed towards Hove we amused ourselves by shouting, 'Oi, Tarquin,' and 'Jemima!' and seeing which of the crusties turned round. None of them did, but it didn't diminish the fun.

'I remember when this place would have been full of skinheads and mods knocking lumps out of each other,' said Alice with a catch of nostalgia in her voice. This, I thought, is love, and I kissed her.

Gerrard seemed far away. It emerged, as I squeezed the last drop of speed out of the E-type hooning down the motorway towards the coast, that Alice had been so disturbed by his speculative writhing that she'd gone to sleep on the sofa. So when he'd said he'd slept in her bed he had been telling the truth, but he hadn't slept in it with her for more than an hour. The only place the proof of his passion had nuzzled was in his own right hand. However, the reason she'd let him into bed was not as it had first seemed.

I'd also got details of their conversation out of her. Apparently he'd told her that there was something very serious she should know about me. When she'd asked what, he'd produced the dossier of doom that I'd found on the kitchen table. She'd taken a cursory glance through it and asked him why he'd happened to be carrying it about with him on a sunny day miles away from his home.

It was then that he told her he loved her and would do anything to win her. Apparently what she'd told me at first about him pretending to be ill wasn't true, although I must say it was remarkably character consistent.

What happened next remains unclear, partly because I spotted a Peeler stalking with radar gun on a motorway bridge and had to brake with some force, upsetting Alice's composure for the rest of the trip, and partly because Alice seemed fairly unclear herself.

I was surprised to hear that she had kissed him, although she said it was in an affectionate rather than a sexual way. Gerrard, I guessed, wouldn't be in the frame of mind to make any such fine grade of distinction. Shortly after the kiss he had begged for sex. From what I could get out of Alice his reasoning seemed to be that she'd had it with me so it was only fair she gave him a try.

'You don't mean literally begging, do you?' I asked, taking the lighter from the expensive walnut dash.

'He went down on his knees and physically begged. Like a dog.' I know she was probably making this up, but the thought of it made me laugh.

'What did you do?' I was smirking while I lit my cigarette, which meant smoke went into my eyes and the car wobbled slightly.

'I told him I had a headache.' The car wobbled a bit more, although the smirk straightened itself.

'You realise that's tantamount to a promise to sleep with him, providing he can find you a couple of aspirin?'

'It's ... he's ... I ...' I didn't know whether it was my driving or the subject matter that was causing the problem with her speech. 'He's just very insistent. It's as if his whole life depends on going out with me.'

I thought, but didn't say, that it did, in the sense of his happy and fulfilled life. I think he could have stood losing Alice, but not to me. That was really rubbing his nose in it. There was someone just like him, sharing his flat, going drinking with him, no real difference between them, but God had handed me happiness and told him to go back to nowheresville. I had meant to ask Alice if she had any good-looking friends we could introduce him to but I didn't think that would be of any consolation. Gerrard's the kind of person who could win a silver medal at the Olympics but have the experience wrecked for him by knowing someone else had gold. I know we're meant to admire that sort of attitude but I'm sorry, I don't. Especially when I've won gold.

'But you didn't sleep with him, did you?'

'No. What do you take me for?'

'Good.'

'I snogged him, though.'

I guessed she was joking, but a note of discord sounded in my brain.

'Why did you let him into your bed then, if he wasn't ill?'

'He said he just wanted to be near me.'

'I bet he did,' I said, reminding myself that the next time I put Gerrard down, I was going to make sure he stayed down.

I was incredibly good while we were in Brighton, I hardly talked about myself at all, confining my conversation to the odd anecdote about school life and some stuff about Adrian the ex boss, who I still hadn't heard from. It occurred to me that he didn't know I was missing. He was always going away for weeks researching projects. With anyone else you would have thought that this meant 'lying at home drinking and watching telly', but with him, sadly, it probably meant he was researching projects.

I found out Alice had a brother and a sister (I mentally saw Gerrard meeting her, it would be a way of neutralising him). The sister was married, though that's hardly the impediment it might once have been. She, Milly, was some sort of Foreign Office whizz kid and lived in China developing British interests. Her husband, though he wanted to be a musician, had got a job with some software company out there. I didn't really ask about the brother, although I think he was at college studying something impractical like business studies, one of those courses that have such a high workload they prevent you from learning the life skills so necessary to advancement in the modern office.

The bright blues and whites of the seaside day were packing up with the deck chairs and giving way to the deeper ocean blues and attraction neons of the evening when we left the promenade seats outside the Fortune of War and made our way back to the hotel.

On our unlit balcony we looked out over the dark of the waves. A moon had risen, nearly full above the water. We could hear music playing, a thumping electronic beat from one of the cars that paraded down the sea front. The lights of the pier teemed against the spaces of the night, sea and sky. I had the urge to say something very banal about the brevity of existence, but I kept it to myself. I drew Alice close, though. 'In a way this is more beautiful than Venice,' she said.

'It should be, at £200 a night,' I replied, gently.

'It's lovely here, isn't it?'

'Yeah. Do you want me to read your palm?'

This is a trick I used to do with every girlfriend. Alice was too clever for me to convince her I was genuinely psychic, as I had a couple of girls, but she enjoyed the charade. The fact that I can do it, and get a lot of it right, is a bit depressing in a way. It shows how similar we all are.

I was happy. Alice was in fine form and looking wonderful. Every second of every day I wanted to sleep with her. It was as if my genes could sense the chance to bound eight or nine rungs up the evolutionary ladder at one go and were saying 'Christ, boy, this is your chance, you won't get another one, mix with that.'

I took her hand in mine and pretended to study its lines.

'You're a very confident person,' I began. 'In some ways. That's what you project as your exterior, but inside you often doubt yourself. You particularly don't like it when you try to do something for the good and people read bad intentions into your actions. You can flirt when you have to, but you feel people value you for your skills, not just because you can flutter your eyelashes. You don't like everyone you deal with but you regard it as a mark of your professionalism that you can wrap them round your little finger. You usually get what you want, despite the fact you could do with more money to spend on clothes.'

'Every woman could do with more to spend on clothes,' she said. 'A few ageing movie stars apart. They could do with less.'

I continued. 'Work is a major focus of your life, but you'd like to have children one day. You wouldn't want to have a nanny because you would want to bond with your kids yourself but you can't see a way round it. Your children will have piano lessons, though you won't force them.'

'It's good for kids to learn the piano.'

'Exactement.' I grinned graciously. 'You've stopped reading *Cosmopolitan* because the sex content's boring nowadays and, anyway, you think you've got a better chance of pulling the right kind of bloke if you're seen with *Vogue*. You like nineteenth-century literature, particularly Eliot and Austen. You've never read Trollope, because the name's always put you off.' She sniggered a bit. I was glad to see it was having the desired effect.

'You're passionate about the environment, although you get irritated when people draw your attention to the exploitation of tobacco workers and the damage caused by cigarettes, because let's face it no one's perfect. You do intend to give up smoking and detoxify, with a diet involving pure fruit and lots of spiritual feelings. You think that one day you might just jack it all in, the hustle and bustle of the TV world, and go and work for some charity, maybe somewhere like Afghanistan or Nepal. To work with animals would be nice. You would be into Feng Shui, if only you could remember where you'd left your book on the subject. Last time you saw it it was in that mess next to the CD rack. You move very quietly, an expression of the fact that you like to control your interventions into the world very carefully. You would describe yourself as a cat person.'

'I prefer dogs,' said Alice.

'I'll try not to take it personally,' I said, looking directly into her eyes. She laughed. 'How was the rest for accuracy?'

'There or thereabouts.'

I thought I'd finish it off with the killer. Most girls are thinking of attending a class in Spanish or French, but Alice already spoke a hatful of languages. It had to be option two. 'You are thinking of attending a night class when you get the time. Something to express your inner creativity.' She blushed slightly, which made me guess she must have some prospectus on creative writing or drawing or some such bollocks stashed away somewhere. I had a flash of a thought that we had gone millions of years with only a few people being creative and seemed to bowl along fairly nicely. The 1960s turned up, everyone went creative, and the next thing you know those who should have limited themselves to flower arranging or stamp collecting were suddenly doing all they could to find their inner voices – inner voices that could have usefully remained silent if the results I have seen are anything to go by. I don't know why I resent people trying to learn this sort of thing; after all I greatly admire Paula's ability to draw. I think it's the presumption that they have something to say, or to express, when really if it had been such a burning desire they would have been doing it since they were two years old. Or maybe I'm just jealous.

'Would you like me to read your palm?' said Alice, curtly.

'No, quite frankly.'

'Hand it over.'

I took a swig of the mini-bar beer and reluctantly proffered the paw, which she grasped, thrusting it closer to her face in the half light.

'It can't be anything I've actually told you,' I warned her.

'But you've told me everything,' she said. Guilt, or fear of discovery – I can never tell the difference – flicked across my brain.

She drew herself up and I thought familiar thoughts about her figure. I won't go into them as you are well appraised of the general gist of my cogitations about her celestial form by now. I will say, though, that her tits looked magnificent.

'You are confident on the outside, but few people see the depths behind the good time Charlie, or in your case just the Charlie. Your job does not make the most of your talents, you could do so much more if only you were allowed to. You hate having to suck up to people who have less ability than you and feel sure you could do your boss's job with your eyes shut.'

'But I could do my boss's job with my eyes shut,' I protested. 'No, I really could. Anyone could, it's only talking to people.'

'Exactement. Same as every bloke. You would like to settle down with one girl but you're not sure how you will handle not being able to play the field. When you're in a relationship you think you'd be better off single; when you're single all your efforts go into attracting a girl. The ideal situation would be bisexual girlfriend with impeccable taste in girls who went out and found women for both of you while you watched football on the television.'

I shrugged demurely. Now I was rich I could afford satellite to watch the Premier League games.

'I don't want to play the field,' I said. At that moment I didn't. After Alice, I couldn't see how I could get up any enthusiasm for chasing girls about town.

'You would like children because you'd like to play football in the park with your kid. You're not sure about changing nappies, though. You find ageing very depressing and think that time is going too quickly. You'll be eighty before you know it. If you had one wish it would be that beer and cigarettes were good for you. If only you could get going you're sure you have enormous potential. You will die young and your genius will go tragically unrecognised.'

'Steady on,' I said. Far out on the horizon I could see the lights of a ship. Its distance and loneliness made me feel closer to Alice. I used the hand she was holding to pull her to me and kissed her on the lips.

'It doesn't sound like I've got much time to waste.' She returned the kiss. Looking past her I could still see the ship on the horizon, winking like a star in the fading light. I wondered if it was a tanker, and wished I didn't wonder that, but I did.

'Harry, I want you to know I'm having a really great time with you.' She was only a foot or so from my face, perfect in every way, mentally, physically, everything. Her beauty was almost luminous, shining like a candle in the cavern of the spreading dark. I couldn't imagine how the rest of our lives were going to live up to this intensity.

'I think I love you,' I said. I wished I could have left out the 'think' but I needed it to cover my back, just in case she did a 'Whoah, boy, not so quick' sort of reaction.

'I know,' she said, throwing her head back and laughing like a drain. I really did love her.

16

Animal magic

It wasn't just the memory of that night that saw me in such a buoyant mood on the morning of the court case. The nature of the charges against me had been preying on my mind and I had come to the conclusion that Gerrard could never play a part in convicting me of them, despite what he thought. Also, I was bound to be in a buoyant mood just to piss him off. I wasn't going to give him the satisfaction of knowing he had one over on me.

We sat on the tube, me whistling to be deliberately irritating, him scratching and shifting, irritating without effort, irritating by construction of DNA. It was natural for me to run the details of my Brighton weekend past him in some detail, but I didn't want to give him too much because he would tell Alice and she would get angry that I'd been making our intimacies public property, the way girls do. I did let him know about the Metropole, how we'd seemed to laugh forever, the wonderful vista from the hotel room. I didn't tell him the bit about me saying I loved her because we'd had quite a chat about that and I didn't want to offer him a crack of doubt about our relationship into which he might insert the crowbar of his derision.

'Will you fight, or will you make it easy on yourself if they try to rape you in the showers?' asked Gerrard, twiddling at his hair.

'Oh, sorry, did I say if? I meant when.'

I shrugged. 'I'm not going to prison, Gerrard. I'm not even going to be fined. You are going to confess you made it all up.'

'How likely is that?' he said, corkscrewing up his wiry black hair and leaning back in his seat in pleasure like a dog who is having a very nice tickle on his tum.

'One hundred per cent, I should guess.' I can be as smug as the rest of them, but I was really trying to project it here. I wanted my victory to hurt Gerrard when it came, to scar him. 'Have you actually looked at the exact charges against me?'

'Actual bodily harm, the copper said so.'

'If you're sure.'

'I am sure,' said Gerrard, 'that's what he said.'

'But did he put that in writing?'

'No, but I got something from the court.'

'Did you read it?'

'Just the date of your appearance, the beginning of your descent into the abyss,' said Gerrard, in a nervous gloat, if you can imagine such a thing.

'Thought so,' I said. 'Have you got it here with you now?'

'No,' said Gerrard. 'What else was there?' He hacked at an itch that was assaulting his arm pit.

'You'll see.'

The magistrate's court was at the back of Harrods. We sat waiting with a bunch of assorted sportswear low life, two of whom had the unique talent of being able to smoke, snog and chew gum at the same time. A couple of them had babies with them, so I presumed they were being tried for the crime of reproducing such unfavoured genes. The whole place smelled of disinfectant, as if the ghost of Paula was filtering through the halls. I wished Alice was with me, so I could show these people where they stood in language they would understand.

A woman lawyer wigged up to us and called my name. She asked me if I was going to plead guilty or not guilty. I said not guilty and she asked me if I wanted any representation. When I declined, she warned me 'a man who is represented by himself is represented by a fool'. I wondered how many of the low life in the waiting area would have known what she was talking about. Somewhere behind me I heard a woman threatening a child that if it continued crying she was going to 'step on ya head'. I just smiled at the lawyer, while restraining my smugness to a level powerful enough to light Birmingham, and told her I was OK. I turned to Gerrard and said, 'Just say, "Sorry, I made the whole thing up." ' He sneered at me, like a Roman emperor inspecting a captured king.

Gerrard and I were called in separately at 12.40, in what I guessed was the last session before lunch. The room was reasonably large. I sat on one of about ten benches that faced the beaks' perch – a long bench containing three of them, with the Queen's coat of arms behind it for double scariness. On the row behind me was a clearly retarded black lad restlessly picking his nose. Behind him was a reporter with a note pad, a white bloke of around twenty-three. He was also picking his nose. I wondered if it was some sort of sign of respect for the magistrate that I should be doing too. I guessed the reporter must be a student, because real reporters very rarely go to court any more.

The usher, or whoever, who led me in barked at me to sit down like you'd think they do in prison. So much for innocent until proven guilty, I thought. He paraded down the aisle towards the magistrates with a quasi-military gait and turned to me. 'Stand up,' he said, not bothering with 'please' or 'thank you', or 'would you mind awfully?' I decided to button my lip on the subject of modern manners and did as I was bidden. There's something about courtrooms that makes you feel guilty, even if you are guilty but have the considerable bulwark of knowing you will be acquitted.

I was made to take an oath and then the mannerless usher read out the charges and asked me if I was going to plead guilty or not guilty.

To be honest, I did think I'd manage to get the whole of 'Not Guilty' out before Gerrard told the court that he'd made it all up. As it happened, I got to the G of 'guilty', having negotiated the 'Not' without a peep from Gerrard, before he burst out. 'Sorry, I ...' He was stuttering, not wanting to repeat what I'd told him word for word. 'I invented it all, it's not true, this man is innocent. And so is the dog. Especially the dog.'

The problem was that he had not read the charge sheet. I was charged with causing ABH, true. But I was also charged with keeping a dangerous dog under the Dangerous Dogs Act. As Gerrard had followed very closely the case of a Cocker Spaniel, Trudy, who had been sentenced to death for giving a postman no more than a baleful glance, I knew he realised what the consequences were for dear old Rex, if tried and found guilty in absentia. Of course, Gerrard could have said that the dog had not bitten him but that I had blacked his eye, but that would have taken an agility of thought not available to the likes of him and me. Also, of course, if he had still accused me, my early addiction to *Crown Court* and *Rumpole of the Bailey* had given me a pretty firm grasp of what to do with people who retract half their statements. 'He's admitted to lying about one thing, why should we believe the rest of what he says?' being the general up and down of it.

The main magistrate of three, a kindly middle-aged man with the air of a sensitive pederast, took off his glasses, hilarious half-moon ones as worn by people who are worried they're not taken seriously enough. He looked at Gerrard as if viewing a memsahib in the Long Room.

'Am I to take it that you are saying you were lying when you brought these charges against the accused?'

'Mmmm,' said Gerrard, like a man agreeing with a heavily armed Jehovah's Witness.

'What?'

'Yes.' Both hands were up inside his T-shirt as itches ran riot across his chest.

The magistrate whispered to the other two, while I stood restrained, mentally not physically, at the bench. I wished I had some glasses of my own so I could have been nonchalantly polishing them. I shaped my lips into a silent whistle and winked at Gerrard.

The magistrate turned to the urbane and witty copper who was looking altogether less smirksome than he had when he nicked me. 'Constable, arrest this man and charge him with wasting police time. No, on second thoughts I have a better idea.' Addressing Gerrard, he said, 'I am particularly opposed to the sort of nonsense to which you have subjected the court. A total waste of taxpayers' money.' No one likes paying tax but the beak looked like a man to whom it was an uncommonly piquant agony, roughly on a par with extensive root canal work for the rest of us. 'I find you in contempt of court and feel I have no other option than to impose a a custodial sentence as an example to others.'

'That's jail,' I mouthed, just in case Gerrard had difficulty with 'custodial'. He had done a science degree, after all. I was a bit shocked that they were going to lock him up and I felt scared for the effect prison would have on him. These noble thoughts were competing with a bit of a 'game, set and match' feeling, though.

Gerrard took on the mien of the boy who had eaten too much birthday cake. I resisted the temptation to squeal, 'Pick up the soap, white boy,' as the magistrate apologised to me for the distress of coming before the court. 'Oh, no, your honour,' I said, 'the pleasure was all mine. Really.'

17

Not nice

I have to say that visiting Gerrard in prison was one of the most enjoyable events of my life. I had begged Alice to come along, but she wouldn't have it. She said he was only in for two weeks and if we turned up together then it would only make him more miserable.

'But,' I reminded her, 'think of the double pleasure it would give me.' She still wasn't having any of it, though.

Brixton nick is a fairly good-sized prison of the Victorian era when emphasis was rightly placed on punishment rather than correction. In our current prison system, of course, emphasis isn't actually placed on anything other than having enough room to contain the seething mass of villains created by modern civil society.

Brixton is not the kind of place someone like Gerrard would normally find himself, open prison being more the sort of punishment handed out to soft middle-class criminals. But since he was only in for such a brief period there wasn't really time to send him anywhere else. So that's where he was, in with the armed robbers, drug dealers, burglars, bootboys and con men. When I saw him, in a large visiting room like you see on TV, he seemed to be bearing up remarkably well although I noticed his hair was very greasy. I enquired if they were giving him the wrong sort of conditioning treatments at the prison salon. He just pursed his lips and said in a low growl, 'Two weeks isn't that long to go without a shower.' Funnily enough, I don't know if it was the dirt or just that he had something better to think about, but he seemed to have stopped scratching.

'No one keeping you warm at night then?' I said.

'No,' said Gerrard. 'Actually, my cell mates are a pretty civilised lot compared to living with you.'

'If I'd have known you were going to be bitter I wouldn't have come,' I said, meaning the complete reverse.

'They're tidier,' he said, ignoring my jibe. 'I'm in with a bloke who got done for demanding money with menaces and an arsonist, and they're both tidier than you.'

'You wouldn't get on with Alice, then,' I said, 'she's untidy too.'

'I'm sure I could change her.'

'An admirable sentiment upon which to found a relationship,' I observed.

'Mmm,' said Gerrard, I think beginning to concede he had lost over Alice. I now had a picture of her in my wallet, or rather of me and her on a *vaporetto* in Venice.

I looked about the room. A few people seemed fairly normal, but a good proportion of them were the low-life weirdos I'd encountered during my time on the dole. The worst of them seemed to have strange muscular development. Not the even sort you sort you see on body builders, not development at all in fact but distension: an over-large neck, or huge shoulders with a tiny chest. One even seemed to have a wedge of powerful muscles up one side of his face, giving him the appearance of an aggressive stroke victim. The worst thing about the place, though, was the smell. Like something gone bad, which I suppose it had.

'I should imagine contempt of court doesn't cut much mustard as a crime in here?' I said.

'You'd be surprised. Anything that sticks its finger up at the courts and the filth they like.'

He said 'the filth'. He'd been in there a week and he said 'filth'. Normally Gerrard referred to the police as pigs, which is what people who are annoyed with them for political or fashionable (same thing) reasons call them. Filth or Old Bill is the term of the career criminal. Maybe he was going to emerge from the academy of crime they called prison as a top villain. I couldn't see extortion or arson being his cup of tea, though.

From two or three tables away on the row next to us, I was aware of someone looking over. It was a wiry, devious-looking chap with a tear drop tattoo on his eye. He had grown bored of talking to his wife and posse of children – I presumed it was his wife, the criminal classes seem to have some sort of sentimental addiction to marriage – and was gesturing over at Gerrard.

'Oi, Princess,' he shouted, 'who's your boyfriend?'

It occurred to me to blow him a kiss, just to confirm his suspicions about Gerrard, but I was afraid of getting a pasting, or even of Gerrard getting one after I'd gone, which was probably more serious because he couldn't get away.

'Princess?' I said to Gerrard. 'That's a nice name.'

'Just fuck off home, Harry, will you?'

'Yes,' I said, 'I think I will.'

Princess and I had to undergo some sort of rapprochement, that was for sure. So Lydia's suggestion that I should throw a surprise welcome home dinner party for him after his fortnight in the nick seemed a good idea, as a 'let's all be mates' kind of move. It seemed particularly apt as we'd been unable to meet Eric due to the unforeseen circumstance of Princess finding porridge on his menu. Also, I thought it would be as good a time as any for Princess to meet Lydia's intended, Eric the designer, as his presence would forestall any verbal reprisals.

The only problem with the surprise was that Princess – I'm going to go back to calling him Gerrard now – was let out earlier in the day than we'd expected, so he ended up cooking the dinner himself. He was in an unusually happy mood, which I suppose must be one of the effects being released from nick has on you.

Neither of us had much stomach for meeting Lydia's new boyfriend as we wanted to get on with the serious business of bickering. I felt curiously down. That morning I had received a letter from Emily who had completed the first part of her Antarctic survey. Apparently she hadn't yet received my letter, because she made no mention of it. She was having a nice time and sleeping with a geologist called John. She didn't say she wanted to finish with me, but reading between the lines, I guessed that was the message. Even though I would be able to rub her face in Alice's beauty when she returned, the idea of getting dropped for a rock botherer still grated. It wasn't like he even had a proper job in the media.

Gerrard had called Alice from a phone box as soon as he had got out of prison. I knew this because she'd rung me to tell me shortly afterwards and to warn me that he was on his way home. He'd told her he'd been on a course at work for two weeks; she told him she knew he'd been in jail. Bizarrely, she said she'd go out with him to 'clear a few things up'. 'Not lingering sexual attraction, I hope?' I said, not really joking.

'No fear of that,' said Alice, although there clearly was or I wouldn't have brought it up.

Neither Gerrard nor I could be bothered to cook anything complicated, he because he had just got out of prison and didn't feel like it, me because I never can, so we got a load of pre-made stuff from the supermarket, along with a few bottles of wine, and sat around getting pissed and waiting for the happy couple to arrive.

I was nervous about meeting Eric, but also very glad that Lydia had a new boyfriend, or fiancé, or whatever. I hoped it would herald a new period of honesty between us, where I wouldn't have to watch my tongue all the time. By this I don't mean that I have some dark secret, like visiting prostitutes, to cover up – or even some darker secret, like wanting to visit prostitutes but not having the courage. No, it's just I'd gone out with her hoping to follow my heart and my head rather than my reproductive organs. She was incredibly smart, funny, pretty, if you knew what you were looking for, and in a way my soul mate. On that front I could not have asked for more. We shared similar tastes in music, film, books almost everything. Unfortunately she just didn't turn me on. I don't really go for her physical type. With Eric on the scene as proof of her attractiveness, I could be a lot more honest and open.

Incredibly we'd gone out with each other for around two or three years – nearer two, I think – before he had broken us up.

I didn't finish it because I had convinced myself that our mental compatibility was such that our physical incompatibility didn't matter. Everyone looks the same at fifty or so and you could have another fifty years together after that. The logic was obvious: it would be better to stay with this woman I loved so much than to go out with someone I fancied more but hit it off with less. I didn't want to find that I had nothing to say to the mother of my children when they had all left home and we faced ourselves across the dining table alone for the first time in eighteen or so years. I sustained thinking this absolute bollocks for nearly twenty-four months.

I would look at good-looking girls in cafes or bars or magazines and think, I want one like that, why can't I have one? And I'm sure that Lydia caught me looking. If another girl had challenged me about this I'd have said, 'Sure, of course I'm looking, you don't get many of those to the pound, do you?' and passed it off as part of my half-ironic Jack-the-Lad character. It wouldn't have mattered because they would have had the security of my sleepy touch in bed before dawn, my instinctive reaching for their hand in the park, my meeting their gaze naturally. With Lydia it was a big thing because, although I did these things, they were acts of politeness, not passion. Not that I had known overwhelming passion then, but I had known passable passion, honest passion that splutters and flickers for six months or so and then goes, no hard feelings on either side. With Lydia it never got started.

Unlike the girl who preceded her, an art-obsessed German I'd met when she'd called to see if a puppy she'd found wandering in our street belonged to our house. I know this sounds like the kind of story normally presaged by the words 'none of your readers will believe this' in jazz mags but, honestly, it happened. Despite combining two traits I hate – being passionate about art and being German (sorry, I know it's xenophobic, but they started it) – and also being a quite dislikable person, theatrical in the extreme, I had an affair with her so torrid that I was confidently expecting a letter from next-door's kid's rabbits asking us to cool it in the name of decency. I'd dumped this girl for Lydia and although there was regret, and obviously the odd drunken fling when we met up to exchange items we'd left at each other's flats, I thought I had made the right choice for my soul.

Given these selfless feelings on my behalf I was surprised, to say the very bleeding least, when Lydia finally finished with me, citing lack of physical attraction as the cause. After all I'd given her. She left me with a huge void in my weekend entertainment too, until after a couple of months we started seeing each other again and being very adult about openly discussing the other relationship neither of us was having. She did eventually take up with a boy called Kevin, who I thought seemed no more enthusiastic about her physically that I was and didn't seem to like her personality much either. Despite the fact that he was a struggling photographer (see actresses – menial labour above) and she had a high-powered job in a big firm, he still thought he could show how much cleverer he was than her by correcting her grammar constantly.

I did wonder why she'd not managed to get someone better sooner, she was certainly a catch for someone. After she split up with Kevin she spent months just moping about. I'd have been off with the first piece of skirt that came my way. But here is the difference between basic humanity and advanced humanity. While I had to grapple with difficulties such as minimising effort and maximising fun, snaring a decent partner who'd be open to three in a bed suggestions, she was up in unguessable realms of needing support, feeling that he valued her support, knowing that she was valued mentally but wanting to be valued physically. The nearest I can get to it is the difference between man tidy and woman tidy. Men spend two hours tidying a room and feel heroic, as if they had completed a taxing sculpture. Women come in and say, 'This is a bit of a mess.' As a man you can't see it, you don't know how to. The part of your brain that detects advanced mess is missing. Women are operating on a higher plane. They know things that we do not. And for all the happiness it brings them, they are welcome to it.

I found it amazing that, in Eric, she had found the man who could detect the advanced mess too. Here obviously was someone who could meet all her needs, emotional and physical. As I awaited their arrival, I felt certain I was about to come into the presence of an *Übermensch*.

What do you think of when you hear the word designer applied to a man? You think svelte, balding, delicate type, don't you?

Eric was no disappointment: a severe black suit, shaved head, black T-shirt. The only give away, the only hint of tack, was the earring – a little touch of McDonald's at the dinner party.

'Sorry we're late,' said Eric, who was some sort of Cockney

grappling manfully with a posh accent, or vice versa. The French half of his origins had got fairly well buried, I thought.

'Don't worry,' I said. 'We're not easily offended.'

'Oh, in that case your flat looks like a shit hole,' he said. Lydia burst into hysterical laughter. I thought the comment funny enough, but Gerrard bevelled his eyes into him.

'I'm afraid we were a bit short of time and got it all ready-made from Sainsbury's,' he said.

'Oh, thank God,' said Eric, 'I can't stand being palmed off with home-made muck. You go to dinner parties nowadays and people try culinary experiments on you that decent folk wouldn't try on a lab rat.' I thought this was quite funny too, but Gerrard had seen an opening for a protracted argument and wasn't going to let it slip.

'I wouldn't try anything on a lab rat,' he said.

'Oh, Christ,' said Eric, 'you're not a bovine arse-kisser, are you?'

'What?' said Gerrard.

'You know, the vegetarians. People who think it's better for a woman to burn her eyes out on make up rather than hurt a dangerous country pest. Let me tell you, if you saw the damage a fox does in a hen coop . . .'

'What dangerous country pest?' I said, laughing at his irony.

'Rabbits. Vermin.'

'I suppose you think it's OK to kill animals for pleasure?' said Gerrard, who hadn't seen that Eric was joking.

'More than OK, it's necessary. It's part of becoming an adult. I reckon it should be mandatory. GCSE hunting. I mean, it teaches kids about responsibilities and that life's hard. I remember torturing my first cat . . .'

'Can I take your coat?' I said with a chuckle as Lydia shrieked with laughter. I liked him, I really did. I doubted he was the sensitive sort but I was glad to see my friend with someone funny – i.e. like me in my own assessment.

Gerrard, however, decided to indicate that removal of the jacket might be premature, saying, 'Are you off your tits, you tosser?' I thought Eric would get the general thrust of that one, even though he didn't seem particularly alive to his audience's reaction. Some people hide the lamp of their disdain under a bushel, some people find themselves a bushel or two short by accident. Gerrard had never seen a bushel, and would not recognise one if you placed it directly over his head, something you would be well advised to do.

'No, I'm not.' I was amazed by Eric's ability to let such a direct insult bounce off his back. 'I genuinely don't think vegetarianism should be allowed, it's not patriotic. The British meat industry needs your support. If this meal we're going to have was vegetarian I won't eat it.' I love this vein of humour, which is very popular nowadays.

I thought Lydia was going to have a seizure as we sat down, such was the level of her hilarity.

'It *is* vegetarian,' I said. 'I'm not a vegetarian myself, can't be bothered really, although it is getting harder and harder to eat meat in polite company.'

'You're kidding?' said Eric, as if someone had just told him he was going to have to do his own laundry in future.

Lydia was practically convulsed with laughter on the floor by this stage.

'I can shave a few dog hairs into yours, if you like?' said Gerrard, sounding as if he would be delighted to do so.

'You mean it's a fish meal?' said Eric. Lydia and I hooted. 'Fish meal – very working class,' I said.

'No, it's Linda McCartney's Chilli Sin Carne,' said Gerrard. '*Seeeeeeen* Carne. No meat.' He said the *Seeeeeeen* bit in a lowering pitch, like a jet liner losing power over the Urals.

'I hope you won't be offended,' said Eric to Gerrard, giving me reason to believe his hope was a rash one, 'but I can't eat that muck.'

Lydia was now banging her hand up and down on the table and guffawing like a baby mule that had just been reunited with his mother. I thought he was flogging the joke a bit, especially seeing as Gerrard clearly wasn't getting it.

'Hard fucking luck then,' he said earnestly.

'He picked this up in prison,' I commented helpfully.

Gerrard continued: 'There's no meat in the wine either. Do you want to go out and get a bit of black pudding to drop into it?'

'I won't cause a fuss,' said Eric, leading me to speculate what his idea of causing a fuss was, 'I'll just nip out and get a saveloy and chips. We passed a chippy on our way down here.' And off he went, slamming the door behind him.

When he didn't return after five or so minutes I was faced with one of two conclusions. Either he was stretching the joke wider than a lady wrestler's leotard or he was serious. Ten minutes and I realised he must have been serious. I don't know what this said about me, in that I'd been chuckling away through the cat torturing bit, or about Lydia. Mind you, just because some of it was serious didn't mean that all of it was. I looked at her, chopping out a line of something on the table. I wondered how desperate she was that she had taken up with this bloke. One egg in the chamber, like a shot up gunfighter down to his last bullet, not caring who comes to finish him, just hoping that the end comes quickly.

'Where did you meet him?' said Gerrard, although he'd already been told.

'At work. He is so funny,' said Lydia. 'He says when we have a baby he knows I'm going to have a caesarean.'

'Why?' I said, somewhat puzzled by the sudden turn of conversation.

'Because he always has me in stitches!' said Lydia, who by now I was convinced was drugged by something more powerful than the Beechams Powders/cocaine she'd been chopping.

'Shall we start or shall we wait for Lord Greystoke to swing back in through the window?' said Gerrard, expressing his preference by moving towards the kitchen door.

'He's not one to stand on ceremony,' said Lydia.

'So much as trample all over it,' seethed Gerrard, retiring to the cooker.

He banged about in the background, gratifyingly burning himself twice.

Lydia and I talked about Eric for a while. Apparently I didn't appreciate his irony.

'You mean, he doesn't believe what he's saying?'

'Sort of,' she said, 'it's kind of complicated. He just gets nervous and comes over domineering. He really is the right one for me, though.'

'I hope he is, my dear, I hope he is,' I said in aged aunt mode.

'It's something we've been doing since the Stone Age,' said Eric, who'd clearly left the door on the latch and had obviously been continuing his monologue to himself as he went for chips.

'Obviously a period very fresh in your mind,' said Gerrard who had got the ready-cooked meals into one pot and was bringing them into the dining room. He watched, appalled, as Eric unwrapped the rubbered sausage, a steak and kidney pie and chips with curry sauce. I was mildly jealous as I bit into my salty vegetable stew.

'That's got pig's eyelash in it, that sausage,' said Gerrard, as I knew he would.

'And rectum,' said Eric, almost swallowing it whole. Without pausing to finish it he began his next sentence. 'Eating meat is in the soul of man. There are certain primal urges that are impossible to repress, nearly. Oi, oi, saveloy.' He illustrated his last 'sentence' with a strange arm movement reminiscent of someone shovelling things into his mouth.

'I don't believe that,' I said.

'Take, for instance, the sex urge.'

'No, don't take it, I need it,' I said to Gerrard and Lydia, rather wittily, I thought. I knew I'd be using that again in a variety of different situations.

'You, Harry. You're settling down, you hope, with this new girl Lydia's told me about?'

'Yeees,' I said, like a high court judge following some convoluted legal argument. Gerrard tensed, like a setter before the hare.

'You love her?'

'Do we have to go through this?' said guess who.

'Yes,' I said, like a high court judge affirming he was willing to answer the call of Westminster should anyone be lashing out with the ermine and the House of Lords car parking passes.

'Yet it doesn't stop you banging Gerrard's ex two days after you're back from Venice.' He spread his arms wide, as if he'd commented that when you drop toast it always lands butter side down.

In the ensuing silence I stared at him. I was aware, given my recent appearance in court for attacking Gerrard, that the police would take a dim view of me forcing a designer's head through my own dining table. Or anyone else's for that matter.

'You really are a tosser, aren't you?' I said. 'What gives you the right to come in here and shout your mouth off about my private life?' In retrospect, I realised, this was an admission of guilt. 'Far from it, uncouth oik, I fear you are misinformed,' would have been the better tack.

'I'm sorry,' said Eric, bizarrely offended, 'if you don't like the truth. I'm telling it how it is. If you can't stand someone taking the piss out of you, you shouldn't have humped the bitch in the first place. That's all I was doing, taking the piss.' He bit sulkily on a chip.

'No,' I said, 'that's not all you were doing.'

You might expect, during this exchange, that Gerrard would have had what others might describe as 'contrasting emotions flickering across his face'. After all, he had just found out that his flatmate and erstwhile best friend had slept with his dearly beloved ex-girlfriend, and yet, on the positive side, he had gained the perfect ammunition to separate me from Alice. Of course, he knew I would deny it, but there was always a chance that bizarre female psychic powers would detect I was lying.

This analysis, however, would show an imperfect understanding of the Gerrardian mind. The expression on his face was that of a man who has just won the lottery on the day his team won the league and his girlfriend confessed she was bisexual and asked if he'd mind a *ménage à trois* with one of her mates from Models One. He now had conclusive proof, to his warped way of thinking, that Paula was a slag, total justification for retribution on me and the ideal means to execute it. He just about had the lid on his pleasure, like the dog on Christmas Eve who is all but certain that the long thin present is an extra tail.

'Well, well,' said Gerrard. 'Well, well, well, well, well. Well well fucking well. Well, well, wellity well. Well.'

'Sorry,' said Lydia, 'Paula told me. Us.'

'One of the advantages of saveloy and chips, Eric old chum, is its ability to be eaten on the move. It seems a shame to waste such a marvellous opportunity.' I would have hit him, but he looked like he could handle himself.

'What?' said Eric.

'The wooden thing in the wall, that's the door.'

'No, stay,' said Gerrard.

'If you can't take a joke . . .' said Eric. He looked shocked, as if I wasn't playing the game. 'I didn't realise your friends were all nicey nicey, Lydia.'

'Time to fuck off,' I said. 'How nice was that, bald boy?'

Eric slouched up to leave, Lydia behind him.

'Your problem is you can't stand anyone else being the centre of attention,' he said as they left, with me wishing I wasn't such a physical coward.

'Oh, you're wrong there,' said Gerrard, 'I think he'd give anything to get out of the limelight right now.' The door banged and mouth almighty was gone.

'Just because she said you were shit in bed,' shouted Eric through the letter box.

'Oh, dear. Oh, dear. Oh, dear,' said Gerrard in the way that policemen once said, 'What have we here then? Shit in bed too? This really is a lovely surprise. What a lovely bloke.' He retreated to the dining room, skipping like a spring lamb to my slaughter.

18

Cycle of violence

Deciding to kill Gerrard was not as straightforward as it would seem. There was a lot to be considered.

Taking another human being's life is not something you can enter into lightly, as it puts you on very thin ice with the law. The average homicide generates a lot of paper work. Ergo the Peelers like to keep the bodycount on their manors to an absolute minimum, conspiring with the judiciary to lock up those who seek to increase it.

So any young person of fibre who is considering risking a life sentence must think carefully about the realities of twenty years behind bars (all right, three or four years, if you're white, not Irish, male and lucky) and ask themselves one important question: Can I get away with it? If the answer is yes then all is sweet as sleep to the labouring man. If no, other solutions must be sought.

My answer, given the state of modern policing, was a definite yes – as long as I could hit on the correct approach. I found that a bit of a taxing one until, following the path laid out by so many murderers before me, I turned to the media for inspiration. The TV really is a fount of useful ideas for this sort of thing.

Less than twenty-four hours after the dinner party with Twat Eric and Lydia I sat watching the six o'clock London news (on a good forty-five minutes before anyone who works in London gets home to see it). It featured an item about the number of deaths on London's roads. It seemed cyclists were particularly at risk. Cyclists like Gerrard.

If you were an assassin thinking of killing a cyclist in London, you'd first have to catch him. A car, you see, wouldn't be up to the job. The traffic is too dense, the roadworks are too numerous. A car, even my E-type, would be far too slow. If you caught him, of course, you could run him down with impunity. Cars are always veering wildly into cyclists, running them over, shoving them into traffic, smashing their limbs and killing them. Topping a cyclist is looked on as a painful but almost necessary stage in the development of a driver, like teething for a child. Kill one and the police will just smile, dust you down and bid you on your way, as indulgent uncles minister to the scuffed knees of children. 'Never mind,' they'll say, 'it comes to us all eventually. I did one myself last week.' Mind you, my E-type would be too distinctive for the job in hand.

If you want to kill a cyclist, hunt him down and put him out of his misery like a distempered dog, a motorbike's what you'd need. With a motorbike, especially a large, powerful one like my Yamaha R1, you could force him into the oncoming traffic and 0 to 100 it before anyone had time to get even halfway through, 'Ooh, Doris, a motorcyclist has corralled that itchy-looking bloke on the bike into a truck. Do get his number.'

As someone who aspires to being a well-rounded character, I did feel it necessary to dispense with – I mean, consider – the moral questions in all this. Killing is wrong, I know, but don't go all religious and vegetarian on me. It's part of everyday existence, happening everywhere and all of the time. The most important thing to me was that Gerrard was my friend. Which leads us to the question: What is friendship?

Years ago, Gerrard and I had been discussing the nature of friendship. He had started from the philosophical conceit that I didn't know the first thing about true friendship and seemed to think it was enough to be amusing and buy the occasional round. Which, of course, it is. However, I had put a theoretical problem to him, to test what level of friendship he was capable of. Are you the sort of person, I asked, who would get up at 3 a.m. on a school night to minister to a friend's aching spirit (girlfriend loss/work problem/car broken down/worse things)? He said he was. I knew he was, he loved that sort of opportunity to show how caring he could be. We'd run through a few others until we'd got to the dog. 'Would you,' I asked him, 'if we sold the flat and went our separate ways, prefer me to have the dog, knowing how close I am to him and how much he means to me?'

Gerrard had sniffled like a rabbit who was all but certain it had inhaled a clump of fur.

'No,' he said, 'because he means a lot to me too.'

'But surely that's the meaning of friendship?' I said. 'Your friend's happiness being more important than your own?'

'That's love.'

'It's possible to love a friend: "greater love hath no man than he lay down his life for his friend".' That was one of the bits of the Bible I liked; more of the lyricism and a lot less of the thou shalt and thou shalt-notting.

Gerrard thought the noble sacrifice idea was stupid. If you lay down your life for your friend, you're not there to enjoy the friendship any more, so what's the point of that then?

This had led us to the idea of 'life' defined as the breathing and wakeful medical sort as opposed to life as the rich tapestry, the golden tree that springs forever green sort. In a way it seemed easier to me to lay down the first sort than the second. Leap in front of a bullet for your friend and your sacrifice is finished, but give him your nectar and dine yourself forever on bread, water and Filet O'Fish? Well, it's not very bleeding likely, is it? And Gerrard agreed. Given a choice between happiness for him and happiness for me, he would choose happiness for him. A friend is someone to go drinking with, someone to brighten up your day who, in short, makes things easier for you. If you're damning yourself to hell so they can be happy: 'They're not really fulfilling their function, are they?' he argued.

All this was in my head as the news finished and I went out into the hall to watch Gerrard put on his cycle clips and reflective strips before he set out for his night shift in the ambulance as roadsweeper to the human carnage of the North Circular. The prison sojourn had only cost him two weeks' holiday and he hadn't even lost his job. Like they say, when your luck's against you . . .

Gerrard scrabbled around for the lights to his bike, which he found in the dog's bed where I had rather childishly put them. They hadn't caused the dog any discomfort because they were those ultra-modern sort that are really thin and light. Gerrard had been annoyed because someone at his work had bought them for him for his birthday and he felt obliged to use them instead of his favourite old ones that looked more suitable for guiding ships to safety on uncommonly foggy eighteenth-century nights.

'I wonder, Gerrard, whether you'd care if I fell under a bus tomorrow?' I said.

'Terribly,' said Gerrard, clawing at an itch behind his ear. 'That's nearly six hours away, which seems an awfully long time in your company.' He paused to savour his own joke, which I thought was funny enough. 'On second thoughts, you should live. You deserve to take your punishment with Alice,' he said, moving from the ear to the back of the neck.

Punishment? That's a mark of the way the man thinks.

He wheeled his bike to the door. 'I'll be speaking to Alice some time over the coming week,' he said, 'so I should make alternative plans to while away the next forty years if I were you.'

'Ha fucking ha,' I said. I still found him funny, despite the fact that he was about to end my existence.

Immediately after the dinner party I had feared Gerrard was going to call Alice at the earliest opportunity, but soon realised I was way off there. Why should he? Since he now held all the cards, it was up to him when he decided to play them. He also wanted to make me wait for it, to give me a chance to ponder the consequences, and to beg. There was clearly no way he wasn't going to tell Alice about Paula; in his mind, and probably in reality, I had shat all over him and this was his chance for revenge.

I knew what I had to do if he should tell her, of course. Gerrard had already, in the short time that Alice had known him, spread condoms all over her flat, called her a traitorous cow, told her he loved her (in that order), presented a bizarre dossier of ancient rather off-message pornography to her and been jailed. Against this background the contention that he was inventing it all would seem fairly easy to stand up. However, I am the world's worst liar and I knew that my deceit would show on my face.

Lydia of course advised me to be honest and take the

consequences, to be brave, although I always have a big problem with that. To me, bravery is the failure of the imagination. Courage is what you're left with when the guile runs out; it's the martini or advocaat at the end of the party when you've finished the last can of lager. No alternative, let's front it, otherwise let's have it on our toes.

I had spent the whole day after the dinner party keeping an eye on Gerrard and phoning Alice who, typically, was in meetings. I caught her on about the sixth go. I had no idea what she did at work all day that made it so difficult to contact her. No job's that busy that you can't find time to talk to your mates for four or five hours a day. It crossed my mind that she actually did her job, as in did it. But no one does their job any more, as I've already pointed out. My doctor, the coppers, everyone I knew, didn't really do their job. They turned up and did some of it, for sure, but not fully. Only Gerrard actually worked for a living, but as a paramedic slacking is fairly obvious to the relatives of the person whose heart you can't be bothered to start. I don't think even I could face the mother of the toddler choking on a marble and say, 'Sorry, I'm on the phone to my friend.' Gerrard hadn't even given up work when he got his Farley money. 'What would I do?' he'd said.

'Why do you have to do anything?' I'd replied.

There again Lydia seemed to work at her job, too, and Emily wouldn't have much scope for shirking in Antarctica. No late nights out with the polar bears and penguins or whatever creatures they have there. On that point, I wondered if Adrian had noticed I was gone yet. I thought I'd give the bank a call and ask them if I'd been paid. I did and I had.

When I finally got through to Alice she was in a depressingly buoyant mood. I think I wanted her to be mildly angry, so I'd have an excuse to get off the phone quickly. I wanted to check she was still around and liking me, but I didn't want any opportunity for evidence of my tryst with Paula to seep through my voice, like blood through a killer's floorboards. With most women I'm not bad at covering up guilt. I don't go for any straightforward give-aways, like buying bunches of flowers or being unusually interested in my girlfriend's day. No, the guilt is so conspicuous on my face that stronger measures are called for. What I normally do is manufacture a row of some sort, totally unreasonably. 'Why do you have to be so bloody nice all the time?' That sort of thing. After a big blow up that ends with one of us storming out, I'll creep back in to say sorry. Then my dog-who-has-stolen-the-Sunday joint-despite-numerous-injunctions-to-leave-it-alone demeanour is taken for guilt over the row, not the infidelity. Also, it means I don't misinterpret her every dark look as a sign she's sussed me out.

I could hardly get into that with Alice. A row so early in the relationship might be as poisonous as evidence of playing away. I comforted myself with the thought that I was only going into the 'will these hands never be clean?' bit because I cared for her. With most girls I wouldn't have felt too bad at all and could get away with some mild slinking, rather than my posture as I heard Alice finally answer the phone. This wasn't quite the aircraft crash position I adapt when watching yet another relationship's auxiliary motors fail, rather it resembled the stance taken up by thin, bookish boys on iron-cold January mornings as the football hurtles towards them and the PE master screams, 'Head it, you fairy!'

'Harry, baby, how are you?' said Alice. Baby, she called me baby. 'I can't talk long, I'm in some really important meetings, really important.' I should point out here that she called me baby in a half-ironic, knowing way, not a shite way.

'I'll be quick.' I slank, or slunk, whichever most conveys imminent fear of discovery. 'I just wondered if you wanted to come round tonight? I could cook dinner. Or at least order it in.'

'Aw,' she said, reminding me of a car decelerating, a nice, sleek, lovely car, 'I'd love to, but I can't tonight. I've said I'll go out with the people from work.'

'It's really important, I have something to say to you.' I didn't know what, I really didn't. Of course, topping Gerrard had not been suggested to me by the newsreader at that point.

'Oooh, that's interesting, what is it?'

'I can't tell you on the phone, but it is important. Please?' For the first time since I'd told that bouncer I hadn't called him a wanker under my breath, I sounded earnest.

'All right then, I'll cancel, but it had better be good.'

'It will be,' I'd said, for reasons best known to myself.

I could still hear her voice as Gerrard went through the front door and slammed it shut on me. I imagined him on his journey, stiff legs pumping through Fulham, tutting, as I'd never seen him do but knew he always did, at the county set – the jeans and deck shoes, the Hackett polo shirts – in a uniform as strict as Mao ever gave the world. Soon he would be going through Chelsea, tutting at the richer people, the antiques that cost enough to feed a village in a poor place, the ladies who lunch killing time in the shops before dinner.

Eventually, after Hyde Park tutting, it would be the Marylebone Road and the rich Arabs – also disgusting but he was too politically correct to tut at them. Then he would turn into Camden and tut at the kids in pubs in their last-year's fashions of piercings and hair dye. Finally, he'd be moving up through Archway and encountering real poverty, which he approved of – proper cockroach-infected, grinding stuff. None of your just-passing-while-I-save-for-a-deposit-on-a-house nonsense. I would have shared Gerrard's contempt for most of his journey, only I would have found the McDonald's classes equally annoying as the Pont de la Tour crew. I know Pont de la Tour's not in Chelsea, but it should be.

I stood in the hall envisaging him on his journey. The door seemed still to shake from the slam he'd given it; the noise resonating into my future, drowning all other sounds: those of my future children in a paddling pool, future dog barking at them to come out, future Alice asking me if I'd remembered we were going to her mother's at the weekend.

The echo of the slam joined in with the numb swell of the cars from the street, filling my brain, forcing my thoughts to compete above them, like voices on a windy shore.

Then I heard the foot before the door. A handful of junk mail fluttered from the letterbox. I bent to pick it up. I could see ads for car valeting, beauty parlours, Pizza Places (the capitals are deliberate, such is their importance to modern life) and builders. My animosity to Gerrard had been mounting but so had my fondness for him, for the times we'd had together, although I couldn't remember specifics. Thinking of him murdered, cold beneath the wheels of a delivery van, made me want to protect him, even though it was me who had wished him harm in the first place. Like the beloved dog that bites the child, he had to go but I would be sad when he did.

I looked at the junk mail. All I could think was that Gerrard wouldn't want it there. Gerrard would be annoyed by it. They had filled our home with irrelevance, despite our sign telling them we didn't want it. Why should he have to suffer them?

I tore the door open with the force of a husband expecting to find his wife and her lover in bed on the other side. A second later I was down the street after the junk mailer, brandishing the flyers and shouting at him over the traffic.

I suppose I had expected to find some crepuscular adolescent greasing his way up the street with a bag of ads for crap, or slag-heaped fifty-something redundancy case straining out dog-end breath as he wheeled his cart full of circulars. But I got a shock when she turned to face me. She was a woman of about sixty, neat even in her work clothes. I could see she had done her hair and her make up before coming out on her round; and from her presentable blouse and tweed trousers you would have expected to find her behind a cake stand at a Women's Institute jumble sale rather than in a job where the ambitious aspire to deliver pizzas one heady day. For her, credit card fraud would have seemed the more dignified choice. Had she been let down or had she just missed her chances, buggered it up of her own accord?

'Yes?' she said, looking mildly scared at the bundle of paper thrust forward in my hand, the little invitations to comfort or happiness, the pointers to a better and brighter existence. I didn't know what to say. Her gentleness, her fear, made my own yobbishness smack me straight in the face.

'Who's it all for?' The words came magically from nowhere, invoked perhaps by my gestures with the circulars.

She stared back at me like I was simple in the head. 'It's for you,' she said, shrugging her shoulders, 'you just have to decide what you want.' She waved her finger at the ads and smiled helpfully, firmly polite and controlled, like a country colonel's wife offering directions to the village fête to a ray-gun toting Martian.

She was right. It was all for me, if I just put out my hand to take it. I imagined Gerrard cycling, he'd be nearly through Chelsea by now, and scheming about when he was going to send me back to delivering flyers in Relationshipsville. I couldn't let him do it, not after someone had offered me the executive washroom keys for Love Plc.

The day had been hot and close and I felt my T-shirt sticky on my back. The woman was still looking at me like I was a nutter. I wanted it to rain and I wanted to kill Gerrard. Not in an abstract 'Ooh, you little devil' kind of way, but in a direct, pistol to the forelock 'Do you feel lucky, punk?' sort of way. For one tiny misdemeanour he was going to fine me my happiness, just so I would be as miserable as him. For nothing, for something I didn't even want to do. It was a straight choice between both of us having nothing to live for and one of us not living.

I looked at my Seamaster, as used by James Bond. Did I not say I'd bought that? Gerrard had only been gone five minutes. It was 7 o'clock. Alice was due at 8.

My motorbike, as I've already bored you, has a top speed of around 170 m.p.h. and gets up to 100 faster than a fat lad down a tube of Pringles. 7.05 – I could be there and back in thirty minutes, if I gave it some.

Gerrard worked at the Whittington Hospital. I knew he cycled through Hyde Park to get there and then went down the Marylebone Road, a three-lane carriageway which is basically static for cars, then round Regent's Park, the last chance for motorists to gun their engines before you hit the deadlock of Camden. I'd seen people doing 60 or 70 down there. If Gerrard came off his bike at the critical moment he'd be roadkill. He was willing to wreck my life, I reasoned, and, on the positive side, death was the only form of personal development he'd be likely to experience in the next fifty years.

Not that I didn't have scruples about murder, I did, but like my auntie used to say: How do you know you don't like it if you've never tried? And if I caught up with him and didn't have the guts or heart to go through with it, I'd at least have gained a pleasant ride in the park.

I ran back indoors, picked up my crash helmet and Gerrard's leather jacket, which wasn't distinctive like my biker's get up, and made for my lock up. At ten-past I was on the bike and heading for the Fulham Road. At a quarter-past I rounded the Hyde Park curves, Evel Knieveling over the speed bumps. I hit the Marylebone Road like the wrath of God, 60 m.p.h. between the traffic queues, an arcade rider with maximum points nearly in sight. I turned into the park and as I got on to its long Georgian straight I saw him in the distance, his distinctive flat-footed pedalling propelling his ancient sit up and beg cycle, the one that he hoped made him more loveable to girls than a standard issue mountain bike. He reminded me of a Victorian clockwork toy, of something that had had its day.

'Make it so,' I said to the bike, twisting the throttle open. The road disappeared from under me and I was nearly upon him. I slowed to cycling speed fifty yards behind. There's something about cars and motorbikes that makes you forget they exist when you're on or in them. They're just an extension of your body, not a machine at all. You personally are capable of 0 to 60 in the snap of your fingers. You are strong as a hundred oxen, three times faster than a cheetah, not the vehicle. I felt I could reach out and crush his neck with one hand. This of course was wrong. To do that I would have had to take my hand off the throttle, which would have meant I would have stopped and fallen off.

Gerrard slowed to turn right into Camden, stopping at the gate of the park as cars flew past him in the other direction, no more than a couple of feet from his front wheel. A simple shove would be enough to kill him and then I would be gone. There were no pedestrians, not even a car behind us. No one would even notice the motorbike in the noise and the confusion. I would be down the race-track road of Regent's Park and home before you could say 'happy ever after'. And what were the police going to say? 'He was killed by a motorcyclist and you have a motorcycle,' is not the kind of evidence the Crown Prosecution Service thrill to hear. Mind you, they do seem to have a touchingly childlike inability to distinguish fact from fiction, so I wouldn't be one hundred per cent safe.

I was alongside Gerrard, level with him. He didn't even notice me, there was no reason he should, motorbikes and pedal cyclists often find themselves next to each other at turns and traffic lights.

The traffic was about to clear and his foot hovered on the pedal of his bike. A car turned right from the entrance we were waiting to go into, forcing him to pause. It was a low-slung Merc with blacked out windows and under body lighting, banging out a heavy jungle rhythm. Whoever was in it was doing their best to look like a drug dealer. It probably was a drug dealer, they're all so straightforward and obvious nowadays. Gerrard's eyes followed it in disdain. 'Rude Mercs Call -0181 RUD MERC, Is BOOM man!' it said on the door. 'Rude Mercs,' said Gerrard, out loud, although I only saw him mouth it. The last time I saw anyone with a lip curl that big was when the dog had his teeth cleaned by the vet.

'Rude Mercs,' I laughed. I hated cars like that too.

All my life I'd done as I was told, I'd taken no risks. From school to college to year out to job, I had been on the conveyor belt and I'd never stepped off it. Only by a twist of fate had I avoided a life in the concerned stultification of documentary journalism. I put my hand towards Gerrard's shoulder. The traffic had grown thicker, a Rolls Royce squealing round the curve. That would be an appropriate end for him, I thought, literally crushed by the wheels of capitalism. For the first time ever I was taking control. Even though I was still laughing at 'Rude Mercs', I realised this was where the laughter stopped, where I put away childish things. I was taking my life in my own hands.

The trouble was, I wasn't very comfortable with that. I'm a child of the service economy. I've never lifted a spanner in anger, never painted anything, I've hardly ever cooked a meal. I get it all done for me by experts. And here I was, about to commit a murder – which is no job for an amateur. To get it right you need to build up to it. Start with abusing the local newsagent at around four years old, work up through tormenting pensioners to robbery and eventually, when you've made your mistakes on the nursery slopes, go for the big one, the ultimate black run.

Even then you have no guarantee of success, particularly since following this route in the first place is a fair indication you are a low-life moron – as opposed to a posh moron, in which case you're in the City and killing people in an entirely more remote manner. I had the same chance of getting it right as doing anything that didn't involve straightforward giving it gob. That's why Adrian had said I was a 'media natural'. I couldn't really do anything other than talk.

Besides, I couldn't let 'Rude Mercs' be Gerrard's last words ever. He would come back to haunt me. He wanted his last words to be something like 'Namaste', the Nepali for 'I worship the God in you', although I'd had a quiet bet with myself that his last words were more likely to be, 'Have you any intention of clearing your shit up?'

I tapped him on the arm and he turned to me, with a look like Igor's when discovered with his hand in the biscuit jar by Baron Frankenstein.

Mark Barrowcliffe

'What are you doing here?' he said, recognising me through my crash helmet but still with a cowardly look gambolling across his chops.

'I don't know,' I said, which sounded like something they'd say in a film.

'You're wearing my jacket,' he said.

I was suddenly aware of how small it was on me. It was a good three inches short in the cuff. I felt ridiculous and somehow angry, irritated by its confines.

A car honked behind us. In it a man of my age who looked like a father, judging by the shapeless jelly of a jumper he had inserted himself into, held up his hands with a look of disbelief on his face. Next to him sat his wife, who could have been any age at all. Or perhaps it wasn't his wife; perhaps it was just another jumper like the one he was wearing, at once loose and restricting.

'You're stopping,' he shouted. 'Why have you stopped? In the name of God, why have you stopped?'

I noticed the road was briefly clear ahead. Hunters, who need an excuse for their barbarity, say they never feel as keenly or sense things as sharply as when their prey is in their sights. Then they feel tapped into senses dormant since the world was young. Football hooligans I knew at school said effectively the same thing, but there you are. I now knew what they meant. Part of me was aware of creation and my place in it; a cog in a giant machine designed to convey Gerrard into the oncoming traffic. To push him into the road seemed as natural and irresistible as the progress of the tide against a shore. For part of me.

The other part just felt silly, in an under-sized jacket on a bike too fast for the road, to be contemplating killing my friend over a woman. As many people, in many courts, have said, 'It all seems so stupid in retrospect.' Only luckily this was forespect, if you take my meaning – a mental resource I had so far in my life failed to tap.

So there I was, caught between two stools. Which is an unpleasant, not to say smelly, place to be. In an instant I had to decide between being in the stools with Alice or in the stools with the British legal system.

So, naturally, I shoved him.

True to character, however, this wasn't a seize-the-day, all-good-men-come-to-the-aid-of-the-party shove, of the sort favoured by beefy nans helping children into dentists' surgeries. It was a kind of conspiratorial, 'how's it going, you old sod?' shove; a 'we've been mates for a long time and I feel I've the right to slap you' shove. Faced with a straight choice – do or don't – I had come up with a bent one – half do.

'What the fuck are you doing?' said Gerrard, loudly but in a tone of concern rather than anger.

I looked over my shoulder at the man in the car. He was almost smiling and throwing his head back in understanding. 'Road rage,' I saw him say to his jumper wife. She wound down the window for a better view.

'Just don't tell Alice,' I said to Gerrard.

He looked seriously at me, almost with understanding. 'I'm sorry, Harry, it's you or me. She's the one – I have to. It's you or me. You would.'

Cars continued to race past us, in front and behind. I felt uncomfortable, hot and angry.

'If you two aren't going to fight, can you move out of the way?' shouted jumper man.

'I don't know what I'd do,' I said.

'Why are you wearing my jacket?' said Gerrard.

I've looked back at that incident and wondered if it was ever really in my mind to kill him. In my mind properly, not just as a fantasy. Was it any more than following a thought process through until the point where it became harmful and then stopping? I don't know what I expected to achieve by going through the motions but I felt curiously depressed by it. I realise that if I had killed him I would have been even more depressed, but I knew I had missed a chance to take my destiny into my own hands. On the other hand, I had decided a friend's life was more important than my own happiness, which is an equation few people would make today. I was capable of love it seemed. Inhuman thoughts had humanised me.

You've probably never had the urge to kill a friend of yours, but there again, maybe they've never given you something to want to kill them for. I'm not talking about revenge or jealousy or all the other loser's reasons for killing someone, I'm talking about the real reasons. When it's a straight choice, your happiness or their life. You or them. Would you live a life of grinding poverty to save a friend from death? Would you lose a limb for a friend, or go to prison for a long time?

There are spectacular historical precedents where people have made massive sacrifices, but the fact that they hand out medals and Nobel Peace Prizes for such behaviour kind of tells you it doesn't happen every day.

I wondered what would have happened if things had been different; if rather than not killing Gerrard I had been faced with an opportunity to save him, to call him back as he stepped blindly out into the traffic, to rescue him from the sea. I think he would probably have gone to his grave. I've come to the unpleasant conclusion that the real reason I didn't kill him was that I had to do something, I had to intervene, to shape my fate, and that feeling was strange to me. In the end I didn't kill my best friend because I couldn't be arsed.

I stuck my fingers up at jumper man and held his gaze to show I wasn't going to run away, although I kept my hand poised on the clutch just in case he got out of his car. His jumper wife pulled a face at me, which had the effect of making her slightly better looking. I put the bike into gear and joined the traffic heading west.

That's it, I thought. All my cover's blown. I'm going to have to tell her the truth.

19

The moment of lies

I was back just before 8 and quickly ordered some sushi from the restaurant down the road. They said they'd deliver in three-quarters of an hour.

'Christ, it's a good job you don't have to cook it,' I said lamely. Don't blame me, I couldn't kill my mate, or fight a bloke in a jumper, but I could be pretty sharp in a phone conversation with a Japanese waiter who hardly spoke English.

Alice was late and the evening fell sombre about me. I couldn't really see a way of getting round things, now Gerrard had been spared. The manufactured row was out of the question and Alice was bound to find out about me and Paula eventually. I flicked through the channels on the TV and watched a bit of *Pet Rescue* to cool my nerves. Now there was a programme I could believe in, I thought. Perhaps I should get a job on that. The presenter, Rolf Harris, was on about some dog that had been biting people and this wonderful trainer who'd cured it of the habit. I wondered if he could fit me in for a session.

I'd bought a rose and a bottle of champagne earlier in the day. I put the rose in a small vase on the table. I'd wanted a touch of class so I'd also splashed out on a cooler bucket, into which I placed the over-priced fizzy wine. There was no time to shower and hardly any point either, since we were probably not going to be getting too close that night – instant absolution was too much to hope for. I thought I could anticipate some storming out, perhaps with light periods of forgiveness breaking out over higher ground in a week or so. I put on my black shirt, which makes me look thinner, rather than thin, a pair of grey Japanese Muji trousers (I know, I know, but I was entertaining a girl, not going to a skittles evening), and one of Farley's old coats, a tan leather job that must have set him back a fair few quid. I looked pretty good in the mirror.

I had a bit of a panic that we hadn't got enough booze in, as it was my plan to get her completely hammered before breaking the sad news. In fact, that's not what that nice bloke who had locked Gerrard up would call the whole of the truth. It was also my plan to get myself absolutely fandangoed before facing the music. As Leonard Cohen once observed – 'I never said that I was brave'. At 8.30 she still hadn't turned up. With Cohen in mind, I went into my room to search about on the floor for his greatest hits. It was there, dormant and menacing as a cyanide pill, should the evening's outcome be exceptionally bleak.

I then checked the beer. Eight cans of Heineken Cold Filtered – cooking lager for the serious drinker. Only students and winos drink anything stronger; the man who can afford it paces himself throughout the drinking session and avoids the Panzer corroding stuff. There was also some of Gerrard's stronger Czech stuff which I could steal if needs must. I said students and winos are the only ones to drink stronger beers but I forgot the gourmet drinker: Gerrard. I won't go on about gourmets as a whole, other than to say appointing oneself a gourmet, for a man, fulfils a similar function to that of appointing oneself a cook. It says you are a creature of refined tastes (obviously – that's the dictionary definition), which in bloke terms just says you know more, and are therefore better than, anyone else. As with almost everything blokes do, it's just another way of saying 'I'm great'. Having a hobby (see above) also gives you something to talk about if you've got no personality which, let's face it, most of us haven't.

The older I get, in fact, the more convinced I become that men have no personality on the whole. Having a personality is, of course, different from being a personality. Being a personality is when you've said one witty thing in twenty years and used it as an excuse to talk louder than everyone else ever since. Having a personality is about interpreting the world in an original way and communicating it so people can understand and relate to it. It is nothing to do with being obsessed by trivia, initiating drinking games, having outlandish political opinions, a strange way of speaking or an odd mode of dress.

In fact it's most men's dearest wish to subsume whatever personality they have to the collective idea of manhood. From the earliest childhood it's all about fitting in, being good at sport, being part of the gang, smoking behind the bike sheds, having a drink with the lads, being one for the girls. I was on this depressing tack as I heard Alice ring the bell. I'd been doing press ups to make my biceps stand out so I had to quickly wipe the sweat from my face. I'd run out of aftershave – my one bottle bought for me by girlfriend number forty-one a couple of years back. I went to the bathroom and picked up the dog shampoo. No, I hadn't sunk that low.

When I describe my meetings with Alice I normally bore you for a few paragraphs by gushing on about how she looks. Suffice it to say that the dog, who had not seen her since the funeral, took one glance at her and went weak at the paws in a kind of canine swoon.

'Hi!' she said. She was wearing an ivory dress which she had managed to keep spotless. If I'd been wearing that I'd look like I'd been mucking out the cows within ten minutes.

'Hello, Rex!' For some reason she was talking in an excited series of exclamations. She patted the dog, who collapsed on top of her sandals.

She stood to kiss me deeply, the full tonsillular probe. I could taste alcohol on her breath, which was a relief.

'Sorry I'm late, I went out with the people from work. I have such exciting news!'

She was emphasising her words with wide movements of her hands. I was reminded of a very theatrical actress or a camp man.

'Come in, come in,' I said with a flourish of my hand.

'Why are you wearing your coat? Are you going somewhere?' she said. Funny, it hadn't looked odd in the mirror.

'I've just got in from the off licence,' I lied. I took it off and hung it up.

'Oh, wow,' said Alice as she entered the front room. I forgot to say that I'd also tidied up *and* vacuumed. I'd even pushed all the CDs under one chair. 'A rose!' I was wondering how she'd react to that. A lot of girls of my demographic don't really go for the rose and chocolate bit, not in the same way that posher or poorer girls do.

'I see it's a rose,' women of my demographic say implicitly, 'but don't in any way think the fact I like it, which I may or may not, means I am to be treated like a stupid little girl. I will, however, eat the chocolates. In a knowing, ironic way.'

I'm not saying that girls in my demographic are brighter than the poorer and posher ones – although a lot of them once were the brighter, poorer ones – it's just they seem to use their intelligence in a different way. An intelligent posh woman tends to be 'a very ballsy lady who's not afraid to go out and get what she wants'. But she does like an 'old-fashioned gentleman'. In fact that's what the poorer ones are like too, in a way. The ones in my mezzanine class are interested in things like what were the successes and mistakes of seventies feminism and can they really afford Prada.

'A symbol of your affection,' Alice said, slightly tipsily. She picked it up by its stem and sniffed at it, which was a bit hopeful since it was one of these factory-grown ones that don't really smell of anything.

She smiled and the dog left the room to recover. 'So this is your flat. Are you going to give me a tour later?'

'I might,' I said. I suddenly remembered my room, which was untidy enough for my Pole girlfriend Emily to have said that I didn't need a cleaner, I needed an aircraft disaster investigator.

'You had something to say to me before I give you my news?' Alice was talking to me.

'No, really, you first.'

'I think you should go first. It's kind of related, I guess.'

'How do you know?'

'Woman's intuition.' She was acting all coy and coquettish, which I found slightly irritating. I find this sort of thing irritating at the best of times but I think I felt angry with her because I guessed she might leave me.

'Not now, let's have a drink first.'

She sat down on the sofa and I opened the champagne. 'I'm not telling you my news until you tell me yours.' She was giggling hysterically. I wondered how pissed she was.

I sat down next to her, grateful to be drinking but painfully aware that champagne in minuscule doses of no more than a glass at a time was not going to do the trick for me.

She took a sip out of hers and put it down on the floor. She was still laughing. I could only get a sip of the champagne down me before she reached over and kissed me again, which was even more irritating that the coquette act. She then squeezed me hard between the legs.

'Let's play a game,' she said, unbuckling my belt. 'The first one to come has to tell their news first.'

I could see this was a bad idea, but on the other hand, she might never sleep with me again. It would be nice to have something to remember her by. I downed my champagne in one and drew her close to me without speaking. We kissed and I felt my 'passion' rising. As with Paula, the joyriding feeling swept over me, the deep pleasure of wrongdoing. If telling her about Paula would be bad before I slept with her, it would be terrible afterwards. Still, in the post-orgasmic, keep-your-hands-off-me chill it would be easier to break the news because she'd seem more unattractive. Sad, really, but there you are.

I had her underneath me, frotting away with my leg, the earlier irritation blended with my desire for her, and I felt a tremendous urge to do it to her, to throw it all away. It was like when I'd pulled up behind Gerrard and been an instant from pushing him into the traffic. Only this time I just had to decide to dispose of myself, which was easier in some ways. I didn't know what to do. Instant gratification vs the long game. The dog had re-entered the room and was watching us. What would he do? I wondered. Best not refer to the morals of a dog. Dogs are wonderful guides to the blind, but what about the emotionally blind? Where are the guide dogs for the soul, the dog that cautions, 'You should really listen to what she's saying here,' and then tells you how to act? Who can find such a virtuous dog? His price is above rubies.

'I'm going do it to you harder than anyone's ever done it before,' I said.

'Let's see you then.' She looked spiteful and defiant and beautiful and drunk as she undid my trousers and reached inside.

I felt the words forming. I thought it best to put it in a casual way: 'I slept with Gerrard's ex-girlfriend last week, did you do anything interesting?' but a ring on the doorbell interrupted me before I could get it out. I made a move to the door but Alice held on to my trousers, so I had to crawl out into the hallway with her attached to the bottom of my legs, like we were playing that game where solicitors punch each other, the one with the egg-shaped ball. I love that game, particularly at international level. Anything where a bunch of working-class Maoris get to kick the living daylights out of a bunch of English public school boys gets my vote.

'Sushi, I have to get the sushi,' I said.

'Then you'll get it without your trousers, my boy.' She had them off one leg now and was laughing hysterically as I crawled like John Wayne beneath barbed wire and machine-gun fire towards the door. In any other situation having a clock-stopping beauty try to rape me in my own hall would have been more than acceptable. But her enthusiasm only served to bring stronger into my mind the image of Paula. I really wished I hadn't done it.

'You twat,' I said out loud.

'I'm sorry,' she said.

'Not you, I was thinking about something else.' The doorbell went again.

'Glad to see I have such an effect on you.' She was on the borders of a sulk.

I retrieved my money from my crumpled trousers, pulled them back on and opened the door, paid over enough money to cause a currency fluctuation in return for a couple of bits of uncooked fish and returned inside. Alice seemed to have sobered up slightly, or to have been offended out of her maddeningly frivolous mood.

'Are we going to eat then?' she said. She definitely had a bit of a sulk on.

'Yeah, look, I'm sorry, I've just got something on my mind.' I poured myself another glass of champagne, she hadn't really touched hers, and dished up the sushi. We bit in, at first in silence. I felt more comfortable with her in a bad mood. Telling someone bad news when they're in a good mood somehow means they've further to fall. Obviously this can be taken to extremes. I remember Gerrard's first serious girlfriend, Candida (I know, middle-class parents, they need hanging – named after a yeast infection), lost her job in the same week that her mother died. That's when he decided to finish with her. 'But she said things couldn't get any worse,' seemed to be the general direction of his argument. He was very angry when she burned the guide to better relationships he'd bought her.

'I'll tell you my news,' said Alice, sipping on the champagne.

'Let me tell you mine first.' I couldn't let her tell me good news. It would be too much of a 'yes, it is a very nice puppy, little girl, but now you're off to the orphanage' kind of move.

She laughed. 'We could go on like this all night.'

'We could,' I said. I felt very sad. 'But I think I should say mine first, really. I have no idea how you'll react to this. I don't know how to say it . . . we've only been seeing each other for a matter of weeks and it's very early in a relationship for this to happen.' She was toying with the scentless rose, not meeting my gaze. I wondered if she guessed what I was going to say.

'I didn't mean it to happen like this, and when I first met you I thought it could never happen.' That wasn't really true. When I'd first met her I'd had dreams of growing old gracefully with her winking at my teenage mistresses. Now, bizarrely, worryingly, I wanted only her. The cynics among you might think that my ardour was increased by the fact that she was about to walk through the door, but it was more than that. I really think I was in love. She was smiling, like girls are meant to, the way they do in dreams. I swear her eyes sparkled, literally, as in caught points of light and reflected it back. 'I have to speak honestly. I can't keep this inside me forever.' I was taking a bloody long run up at this one. All I had to do was say it. I have been unfaithful, I am a low dog, lower than a low dog. I am a rat sandwich with all the trimmings.

'Yes?' she said, as if she'd been holding her breath. The sound system was gently playing Frank's 'A Foggy Day in London Town' and Rolf was talking about a cat who had sadly had to be shot or something. Sod it, I thought.

I slept with Gerrard's ex-girlfriend last week. Unfortunately, I only thought it. The words couldn't yet slither their way on to my lips.

'Yes?' she said again. Tell her, I thought. Say it, run from the sauna to the ice cold pool, you'll feel better in the end. Just four words: 'I have betrayed you.' I knew Gerrard would tell her anyway and I knew she would sense my guilt, no matter how I denied it. It was useless. The game was up. I had to face the music, even if that music was as unpalatable as a light opera, I had to be a man.

'I love you and I want you to marry me,' I said.

'OK,' she said, beaming away the clouds of her strop. 'That would be nice.'

20

Another useless man

Sushi can't go cold so its remains were perfectly palatable after the hour we spent doing what the romantic novelists call 'falling into each other's arms,' but the rest of us know as 'falling into each others' knickers'. I had somehow managed to polish off the rest of the champagne during the coital capers, so after relaxing with a post-caper cigarette, I went out into the kitchen to get a lager and a gin and tonic for the laydee. It was 10 p.m. Gerrard would get back in at about 9 the next morning. I was probably in for a shorter engagement than Sammy Davis Junior at a KKK coming out party.

Her good news was that she'd been offered a job for a large independent cable company selling programme rights in China. She'd be based in Hong Kong but would do a fair bit of work on the mainland. The other good bit of news was that she was going to turn it down but use it as leverage for more responsibility in her present job.

'Don't you mean money, more money?' I asked.

'That as well,' she said. 'Can you believe it, we're going to be married?'

'No,' I said, thinking of the avenging ambulanceman winging his way around the damnation of the North Circular, 'I can't at all.'

'It's scary, isn't it? There's so much we don't know about each

Mark Barrowcliffe

other. I mean, do you want to have kids?'

My normal reply to this is that two sixteen-year-old twins would be nice, but I stowed it.

'Yes, I do,' I said. I pictured myself going back to work to support children. I suppose it wasn't that grim a fate if you were working for someone else. It's only when you're doing it for yourself that it all seems pointless. I could sell the E-type and we could move into a big place, I was getting bored of the car anyway. Like I said, three goes on anything and it loses its appeal. Apart from Alice, she seemed to get more exciting every time I saw her. Maybe Gerrard would understand. Perhaps he'd accept that I'd found happiness and there was no way back to Alice for him. Perhaps he could lose with good grace, when he heard we were getting married.

I remembered a kick about with a ball we'd once had when we were at college. Gerrard's side had lost by a single goal scored by me standing, he said in an offside position, too close to the two bags and a coat we'd used for goalposts. He does his best not to mention it too often now, but still occasionally brings it up when losing arguments. 'You don't mind how you win, do you?' he'll say, and I'll know what he's talking about.

There was no hope. I knew that he would see any increase in my happiness on the relationship front as a decrease in his. Like the fat lad at school as the teams are picked, he finds himself in a diminishing line until he is the line, or rather a great bulbous dot, unwanted and unrecognised. Every boy who goes before him – the thin one with the limp, the one who still can't tie his shoes at sixteen, the lad who's even fatter than him – drives his spirits further into the ground. When he is called, last, he knows the team would rather play without him. Gerrard, although thin, had been the fat lad on the team of love. But for a minute he had glimpsed a chance to be Pele. And I had taken it away from him. Of course he was going to do for me. He wasn't going to even bother wrapping it up in niceties, at least to me. No, 'she has a right to know'. No, 'I regard her as a friend and I cannot see a friend deceived.' He was operating a much more brutal and honest set of values. 'If I can't have her, neither can you.' At thirty-two, girlfriendless and without much in the way of prospects for one, I can't say I blamed him.

Alice was tucked up on the sofa, naked apart from my housecoat – bathrobe to the rest of you – that she'd found somewhere. She

[352]

had seemingly gained her second wind because she had already polished off her gin and tonic. I fetched her another. I felt useless. I just couldn't tell her what I had to tell her.

We talked, all night, like you're supposed to, about kids, houses, the future. I assured her that she would be able to choose the interior design and that I would put my Marc Bolan poster into storage. That apart, we agreed on everything. Not only did I love her, she wanted the same as me.

'We won't have to move to some provincial shithole if we have children, will we?' I asked. 'It doesn't have to be the countryside, does it?' I thought I might as well indulge in this fantasy of togetherness.

'Certainly not,' said Alice. 'My kids are going to have something to do while they're growing up.'

'And it doesn't have to be piano – it can be electric guitar they learn, can't it?'

'Of course,' said Alice. 'Are you going to do the advice on behaving like a star, or shall I?'

'Best you,' I said. 'And no bringing them up bilingual?'

'Out of the question, I learned four languages the bloody hard way and I don't see why they should have it any easier.'

'Can I tell them never to work in an office?'

'I like working in an office.'

'You argue for, I'll argue against,' I said. 'Football or rugby?'

'Football,' she said, 'unless we live in Wales, which we won't. Rugby League would be OK at a push.'

'How much should we pay in school fees?'

'No more than their dinner money. We don't want them growing up as ponces.'

I did love her. I looked at my watch. It was 2 o'clock in the morning. Seven hours and it could be all over. She said she thought we should get married next year, when we'd had time to see if we really liked each other or not. That would also give me time to get out of the flat with Gerrard and move in with her. We could have done it the other way around, but I knew Gerrard would be resistant to it. Gerrard. I had been forgetting him. In the night, and with Alice, it was as if he didn't exist. I kept feeling confident and then fearful in waves. One minute I felt I'd be able to front it, the next I'd sense him looking over my shoulder, grinning.

At 3 Alice fell asleep, and I moved on to Gerrard's Czech larger.
ould like to record that she looked happy in her sleep, but to
her face bore the grimace of a gambler who had put all his
ney on a nag that was rounding the final bend second to last. I
spected her from head to foot, in one way like property, as
minists among you might wearily expect, like a child studying
very inch of his new toy, enraptured, wishing it had come with
more instructions so he could be reading about it when he wasn't
actually playing with it. On this point, I wish I hadn't felt like that.
Looking on a woman as property is not only politically shite, it's
also deeply naff, but in the interests of honesty, I have to record
how I felt.

I was looking at her in another way too, like a hostage might
inspect a new figure thrown trussed and bound into his cell,
wondering if his companion was going to make his life easier or
harder. We knew so little about each other and the future was so
scary. Even if we got round the Gerrard problem, with a wedding
ring on her finger blokes would assume she had a dead sex life
and so would be game for anything. They'd be all over her like
bankers round a minor royal. I'd have to go to work, although I
was approaching the stage in my career where I could get a job in
management and do even less than I did for Adrian. I still hadn't
heard from him and it had been weeks now. I thought I'd give him
a call, just out of curiosity.

Perhaps I could do something full of fun interesting people who
had plenty of team spirit, didn't mind taking a few risks and were
more interested in having a laugh than working. I knew so few
bank robbers, though. Gerrard might be able to help me out. I'd
forgotten him again.

Alice began to snore. Surprisingly it didn't irritate me. I suppose
that was a good start.

At 4 in the morning I carried her down the hall and into my bed.
She didn't even stir, knocked out by drink, excitement and
apprehension, I should guess. It crossed my mind to shag her
while she was asleep, but I didn't really feel like it. It was just a
classy idea. I put her beneath the covers, luckily I had changed the
duvet only the last month, lay on the bed next to her and stroked
her hair. 'Goodnight, Alice,' I said. 'Goodnight, my golden girl.'

I still had half a bottle of Czech lager left in the front room, so almost reluctantly I left her to sleep among the debris. I thought about tidying up but decided against it. I figured she may as well take me as she found me.

Returning to the living room, I opened another bottle of the Czech lager. Then I noticed the half-bottle still undrunk, so I inhaled that in a couple of seconds and got on with sipping the full one. I couldn't be bothered to put on any music so I sat listening to the sounds of the city dawn – the building traffic, a car alarm, someone loading a van. The same day after day, I guessed. I was hot so I went back into my room and put on a different shirt. This time I didn't bother leaving, I just sat at the foot of the bed drinking and watching Alice sleep.

At 7 o'clock the dog got up and asked to be let out the back – I could hear him scratching. I went through the sitting room and into the kitchen. I opened the door and followed him into the garden in my bare feet. The day was going to be a hot one, the sun was already warm on the concrete, glinting on the collapsed barbecue. I noticed a few balls lying about and threw them over the back to the garden of the low life with kids. The dog watched them go, dancing the same dance of an excited jump followed by a disappointed turn of the head as all the balls disappeared, irretrievable.

I don't know why I was so generous about returning the balls, really. All summer every summer their parents played the whole grisly pantheon of adult-orientated rock music at a volume to make sitting in the garden unbearable. The bloke smoked cheap cigars in his shorts and sunglasses while the wife sat about in her bra. No one should have to listen to Phil Collins in his own back yard, no one, not even Phil Collins. Recording such drivel is a high crime and misdemeanour, but not worthy of such a cruel and unusual punishment as being forced to listen to it again and again. Mind you, I reasoned that if the scum went, as the working class were going all along our street, then we'd only get some yuppies who played the same music and got in legal disputes about whose building line the tree at the bottom of the garden was on.

'Bark, bark, bark!' said the dog, although it could have been me, it was a remarkably accurate expression of my inner life at that point. His body tensed for a second and then sprang back into the house. He'd heard the door go. Gerrard was home.

he great thing about the human brain is that you don't need to
it any maintenance really for it to produce results. In fact,
often it is better left to get on with things on its own, because
le you in trim gardens take your pleasure – or in my case
rim gardens – it is working on an answer. This is certainly my
ain's strong preference, I have come to realise down the years.
Vhile I had been thinking about the problems of soft rock infesta-
ion on summer lawns my brain had come up with a solution to
the problem of Gerrard, and one that did not involved having
one's collar felt.

I followed the dog back inside. Gerrard was standing in the
living room with an empty bottle of Czech lager in his hand.

'It's all right,' I said, 'I'll get you some more.'

Normally I could have been fairly sure he would have launched
into one about how I always said that but never came up with any.
Instead he just looked at me and said: 'You're up early, or late.'

'Late,' I said. He sniffed disapprovingly.

'I have to tell you something, not that it'll make much difference,'
I said.

'Well, I've been thinking myself anyway.' He pursed his lips
like a boss poring over the balance sheet and realising he had to let
go of a beloved member of staff.

'Alice and me are getting married,' I said.

'Alice and I,' he said, fighting down the surprise.

'Oh, you too?' We both smiled. I remember thinking he was
taking it in remarkably good spleen.

'Is it love?' This had been the subject my brain had been having
a go at on the quiet in the garden.

'It is for her. I'm not sure for me but, you know, when do you
ever know?' In truth I did know, for certain, but I thought that,
having thrashed him in the cup final, I'd spare him the lap of
honour with the trophy. I had worked out, without really thinking
about it, why Gerrard had been so insistent about chasing Alice.
He'd been mad about other girls before and got nowhere. Then
he'd followed the example of Robert the Bruce's younger brother,
who took one look at the English forces and buggered off smartish
to start a tobacconist's in Leith. I'm not saying Gerrard started a
tobacconist's in Leith, but that he gave up instantly. His unholy
persistence in the case of Alice wasn't because he had lost the

perfect girl, it was because I had gained her, or rather more specifically I had undergone my emotional graduation ceremony and been handed a certificate in the form of a girlfriend I actually wanted, as opposed to one who'd just have me. He was jealous that I was happy and he was not.

So if I said I wasn't that happy with Alice, in fact that our relationship was founded only on me being a certain age at a certain time and that we would probably be very miserable together, well, we'd go with his blessing, or at least not with his curse. She was far too good-looking and charming for him to be pleased to see us together.

'She's a girl, she's there, she's beautiful, she loves me. I'm thirty-two. There's no point in splitting hairs, I've got to go for it. What does it matter if I love her or not? I've passed the test so I can get on with the rest of my life.'

He sat down on the sofa, his eyes narrowed in malevolent pleasure, like the witch watching Snow White eat the apple. 'If it's going to be such a sterile, horrible thing, it sounds like you deserve it,' he said.

'Atta boy.' I smirked inwardly, if such a thing is possible.

'I had decided not to tell her anyway.' He was looking at his shoes, as if to say 'all we have in the world is each other now, shoes'. 'There was something about you today when you came after me on your bike that made me think you'd understood that being married and loving someone are really serious things. You normally don't treat it that way so I thought I'd leave you alone. You think I'm jealous, which I am, but only because you won't appreciate her properly. You could make do with anyone. I have so few women I like, as I've said before. You're not fussy, I am.'

It crossed my mind that he was back in the running for under-statement of the geological period prize. He sat tapping the soles of his feet into the sofa.

'So when I thought it was real, I was willing to let her go. But now I see it's just a convenience thing, maybe I should tell her,' said Gerrard raising his head like someone saying 'I may be poor but I still have my dignity'. I felt a flash of frustration, like the time I'd tried to teach him to drive. If he remembered how to reverse into a space, he forgot how to do a three-point turn. If he remembered the three-point turn his parking went to arse. I drew in breath.

'She's just another girl, I'll front it anyway. She's never going to believe that I've betrayed her this soon in the relationship. Even if she did, and left me, I'd find someone else but she wouldn't go to you. You're too close to me.'

'I worked that out today. It doesn't matter, I won't tell her. She's the only person in your whole social sphere who doesn't know. We're mates, that's the important thing, we need to get back to that. Can I ask you one question, though? What's it like shagging her?'

It's extremely dangerous to say anything remotely derogatory about a woman's skills between the sheets or at any of the more risqué sites where copulation can occur in the modern age. A wise man's comments should always be positive. Can you imagine wading in with something like, 'I thought I'd got involved in necrophilia by mistake,' to which your friend replies with *hauteur*, 'Is that so? My back still bears the scars.' It really wouldn't do. However, I wanted him to feel he had achieved something I hadn't, even though he hadn't.

'It's OK,' I said. 'I think it's more fun with Paula.'

'Will you invite her to the wedding?'

'If you don't mind?'

'What I do and don't mind doesn't seem to make very much difference to you. I minded you sleeping with my ex-girlfriend last week.'

'Sorry, I didn't plan it.'

I shouldn't really have said that. It intimated I'd spent ten seconds getting off with a girl it had taken him a year to seduce. This isn't to say that Gerrard is less attractive than me, far from it. It's just that his natural shyness, mixed with some half-understood feminism he picked up at college prevents him from telling a girl that he likes her. He snorted, a snort of misery and forbearance, and ruffled the dog's ears for consolation.

'Won't it feel weird having an image of your betrayal floating about on your big day?'

I snorted, a snort of arrogance and dismissal. I didn't mean to but I did.

'I can live with it.'

'You won't have to,' said Alice, quietly. Gerrard actually flinched. She had been standing just out of sight in the doorway. Up until that minute I had always found her ability to float about without anyone noticing endearing. Not any more. From the tears in her eyes she had been listening for some time. She was fully clothed, but in a state of beautiful dishevelment.

Somewhere, I imagined, high in the Andes a condor wheeled on a wind that had carried condors for centuries. In Africa a child who would shape the future of a continent kicked a ball of rags in the street. From Delhi to Detroit, Beijing to Birmingham, generations were born to want. My problems were a blip. I was a blip. It was no consolation.

We all stood in silence. The dog approached Alice, wagging his tail. It seemed his days as an emotional barometer were over.

How many millions of people have said what I said next, in films, in books, in real life?

'I can explain. It's not what it seems.'

'Oh,' said Alice, bitterly, 'what is it then? A dress rehearsal of "All men are bastards, it's official"?'

'I love you, and I want you to marry me. I do.'

'It sounds like it.'

'Perhaps I can help,' said Gerrard. I thought this about as likely as him being offered the next crack at the world heavyweight championship, on the proviso that he went for a couple of jogs first.

'Harry feels like this about everyone. It's not you that he's failed to connect with, it's everyone. It's nothing personal.'

I reflected that that was the sort of help the Americans had given the North Vietnamese with population control.

'Shut up, Gerrard,' said Alice. She was staring me in the face, livid with anger. 'I can't believe I trusted you. It was one of the main reasons I agreed to marry you – that I thought you were satisfied with me and only me. Who was she, this woman?'

'My ex-girlfriend,' said Gerrard, explicitly defying Alice's command.

'Shut up, Gerrard,' I said.

Alice looked blank. 'But you said she was a dog? You said you didn't know what Gerrard was bleating about?' He looked hurt, which was the least of my worries.

'She is a dog,' I said, 'but I was so happy after that weekend in Venice, and she was the only person to go out and celebrate with.

I got drunk, I was in such a good mood, the next thing I knew I was in bed with her.'

'Are you telling me you were so pleased to be going out with me that you banged some old tart to celebrate?'

'Er . . .' Cubs, aged ten at the swimming baths. I was late learning to swim but all the other boys jumped straight in the deep end. I went too. I was flailing to keep the water at bay, swallowing bucketfuls of it, promising God never to do such a thing again.

'I think the word you're searching for is "yes",' said Gerrard.

'That's the one.' Idiotically, I found myself smiling. I certainly had nothing to smile about.

'Can you bear to be serious for a moment?'

'Okey-dokey,' I said, like a New York Jewish comedian. I took half a step towards her. 'You won't believe me, but all the time I was sleeping with her I was thinking of you. It was doing that that made me realise how much I love you.' Clearly the marvel of my unconscious life had been directing most of its attention at the Gerrard problem and rather slacking on what to say to Alice should the bollocks hit the blender.

'I don't believe I'm hearing this,' said she.

'A victim of his own sexual incontinence. Quite rich, isn't it?' said Gerrard, like a vicar sampling a fruit cake.

'I need you more than anything in the world. I need you,' I was pleading madly.

'And yet I'm just another girl, I fit the bill at thirty-two, I'm gullible enough for you to go off shagging all and sundry behind my back. That's how you need me, is it? Well, no fucking thanks! And let me tell you: I wasn't head over heels in love with you either. I wasn't thinking, "Oh, yes! Man of my dreams." I was thinking, "What the fuck? You seem like a nice guy and you seen interested in me for more than the way I look. I'm not a trophy girlfriend to you like I was to the others, so OK." '

'I think you were quite a trophy girlfriend,' Gerrard sidled in, 'to be fair.'

She was crying and, pathetically, I felt proud to have been able to get such a depth of emotion out of her. We take what consolation we can, I suppose. Gerrard looked a little hurt that I could make her so upset. How I could distinguish this from the hurt he felt at having Paula labelled a dog I'm not sure, but I have known him a long time.

I couldn't work out why he was still hanging about. The embarrassment would have left any other human being on life support. Perhaps his toes had curled so firmly into the carpet he was stuck. I don't know if he thought she was going to say, 'Oh, I see, the chubby one's defective. Don't give me my money back, I'll just take the dark wiry one instead.'

'I'm so unhappy,' said Alice. 'I thought at last, after years of arrogant bastards, psychos and frauds, I'd got a decent bloke. I was wrong. Well, here I go again, young free and single, back to the drawing board and no sign of kids at thirty-one.'

'You're thirty-one!' screeched Gerrard, as if she'd just told him she used to be a man. I've got to say I nearly lost m'monocle myself. I'd never asked her age, but I had her down at twenty-five absolute tops. From the look on Gerrard's face he was considering doing her under the Misrepresentation of Goods Act.

'Yeah, it explains a lot, doesn't it?' said Alice, glancing at me. I wasn't sure what she meant but I guessed it wasn't entirely complimentary.

Gerrard stood with his hands on his hips, shaking his head. 'Well, well, well.' I feared we were in for another variation on 'traitorous cow'.

'What will you do?' I said. I knew she was going.

'Go out and find someone and sleep with them. Maybe I'll fuck Gerrard.'

Gerrard looked like the dog does when you say the word 'walk'.

'Don't do that,' I said.

'Why shouldn't I? Why shouldn't I sleep with him here if I want to? You sleep with who you like.'

'Why shouldn't she?' said Gerrard, although I could see he was looking at her tits. At thirty-one he would assume a fair amount of sag had crept in and I knew he was readjusting to the idea of having to fantasise about her without perfect breasts. If he slept with her now I knew he would be handling them like a housewife examining eat-today tomatoes on a market stall.

'Gerrard, stop chipping in,' said Alice

'OK, look, do you fancy another bottle of wine?' He was hopping again, in pulling mode. Obviously he'd decided to take a look at the goods before rejecting them out of hand.

'No,' said Alice.

'How about something later on, will you want something then? I've some champagne in my room I could put in the fridge.'

'Gerrard, just leave, will you?' said Alice.

'Shall I wait for you in my room?'

'Gerrard!'

'You did say you might sleep with me though,' he said, exhibiting a depth of literalism unseen since that turbulent priest bloke got his comeuppance. The more I saw of him at that time, the more he resembled a dog. Much more than Paula did. As he looked at Alice he moved his nose from side to side quizzically, like an airport Labrador scenting something rum in a suitcase.

'Women!' he said and went past her to his room. 'It's second on the right,' he added, disappearing down the corridor.

We looked at each other in silence.

'Why don't you sit down?' I gestured to the sofa.

She moved gracefully to the seat, sitting with her legs folded away from me.

I knew I had a job of work on my hands here if I was going to convince her to stay, otherwise I had to hand in my love stripes and go back to pounding the party beat.

'Everything I said was for Gerrard's benefit. I'd never get rid of him if he thought I was happy with you, if I had something he didn't. I just wanted him to leave us alone so we could get on with being together.'

She sneered a beautiful sneer. 'You slept with someone only a week into our relationship.'

I was going to point out that sleeping with someone else a week into the relationship was better than sleeping with them a year in, but I thought it was the kind of relativist tripe she wouldn't much appreciate.

'I know and I'm sorry. I really wish I hadn't. Everything we talked about, the kids, the future, I want that and I want it with you.'

I had sat down with her on the sofa and had tentatively extended my hand towards her leg, but she just turned away more until she almost had her back to me.

'Do you think you'll be able to forgive me?' I said. I had an image of myself going round to Paula's for consolation that night. I couldn't take her the rose. I'd have to throw that away.

Alice was crying quite heavily now, and so, I noticed, was I.

'It's not like I was holding out for the world. In the end you just cross your fingers and jump in. If you're going to have a relationship you expect a certain amount of loserdom. You put up with it.'

'What do you mean, loserdom?' I feared she was talking about the land where I lived.

'Oh, come on, Harry, you know. The flash car, the always having to be funny, the lack of purpose in your life. I was willing to put up with those things because I liked you. Very much. But this is too much. If you're doing that a few days into our relationship, where will you be after a few years?'

'I will be faithful forever. Forever and ever.' I meant it. At the time I meant it.

'You won't be, Harry. The only thing that'll stop you going after other women is laziness or lack of confidence. You won't be faithful because you want to.' She sniffed and blew her nose on a tissue she'd got from somewhere.

'We are so alike, that's exactly what I think. Exactly what I thought rather. Before I met you.'

'Please,' said Alice. 'Do you think I want a husband who's unfaithful in his mind?'

'Well, I can't be responsible for what I think.' I don't know why I couldn't have just said, 'I won't be unfaithful in my mind.' It would have been the easier option, but it would have been a bit rich to expect her to believe it. Everyone is unfaithful in their mind, it's called having an imagination.

'No, I don't suppose that's within your capabilities.'

'Alleluia! Bleep. Alleluia! Bleep. Alleluia!' The phone was ringing and the dog got up ready to accompany me to it. I stayed where I was.

'Please, Alice, I want you so much.'

'Alleluia! Bleep. Alleluia! Bleep, Alleluia!' I suddenly felt very hungover, which was never right as I'd only just stopped drinking.

'I don't think you can have me, Harry, not with what I know. I thought you were different but you're not. You're just another useless man.' She was more sad than angry now.

'Alleluia! Bleep. Alleluia! Bleep. Alleluia!'

She looked so amazing, so wonderful. I remembered the days in Venice, in Brighton, her shoving me into a hedge, her telling the clubber where to go in the bar. I saw her standing on the front of a motorboat in the sun, going to the Lido. I remember thinking, with some embarrassment which is why I didn't say it at the time, it was as if the water had grown tired of the beauty of the rainbow and in her had created a more lasting iridescence. I know I felt something like that about Venice when I went there, but I tend to have a lot of my thoughts twice, or even more often. It just shows how good they are. I was crying more heavily.

'Please, Alice.'

'Alleluia! Bleep. Alleluia! Bleep. Alleluia!'

'I don't want to see you any more.' She shook her head and sniffed. 'I'd better go.'

'Alleluia! Bleep. Alleluia! Bleep. Alleluia!'

She cast about forlornly looking for her coat and bag. She found them in the hallway and put both over her arm. She wasn't going to need the coat in the rising heat.

'Goodbye, Harry, I won't be seeing you again.'

'Alice!' I wanted to grab her, to erase the last hour with kisses, to make all the hurt I'd caused myself and her disappear, but I just stood there and watched her go through the door. She didn't even slam it. I had become so hot. It was August and I was dying.

'Alleluia! Bleep. Alleluia! Bleep. Alleluia!'

'Will you get that? It's driving me mad,' shouted Gerrard from his room.

I couldn't follow her. I moved over to where the dog was and vacantly picked up the phone, my face numb with tears.

'Yes,' I said.

'What the fuck has been going on?' said Farley.

21
The eternal

I did see Alice again, as it happens, some time afterwards. It was February, in the middle of a cold snap, when she called out of the blue. She said she had taken the job in China but was back for a week or two and asked if I'd like to meet up. She wanted to see if I was all right; I told her not to worry, I wasn't. It's funny isn't it? There's no viler sight than an ex doing well. I guess she just wanted to check for herself.

In the weeks after she'd left I had tried calling her, or even going round to her flat, but she was never there. After about a month I gave up. I did go round there drunk on New Year's Eve, but a strange bloke had answered the door. He'd said she didn't live there any more and he was renting it off an agency. He actually invited me in for a drink, but I thought he might have been nosh so I didn't bother.

I leaped at the chance to see her. I had been in mourning ever since she had gone and I still thought I could get her back. I knew not to try too hard, of course, I wasn't that much of a loser.

We met for a drink in a pub in High Street Kensington at lunch time and then walked up through Kensington Gardens in the gloom of early evening to look at the big round pond and see the lights on the frost over the planes of the park. I'd brought the dog for amoral support. I would have preferred the moral variety, but you have to understand an animal's limitations. See my earlier comments on guide dogs for the emotionally blind.

I'd told her all about the Farley story. My immediate conclusion had been that he was a ghost, but I have never been a great believer in the afterlife. The requirements for entering heaven seem to fall rather too neatly in line with the needs of civil obedience to have come from the nether worlds. Blessed are they that clear up after their dogs, they shall inherit something nice. Given my scepticism that standard trunk dialling had reached St Peter's Gates, I was led inescapably to the conclusion that Farley, far from shovelling coals in H., was in the pink of health. As he turned out to be.

He'd met up with some Dutch girl in Cornwall, a staging post girlfriend to help him get over Alice. They'd gone to Paris together by car and then on to India, where he'd stayed miles from anywhere, 'getting his head together' (he actually used those words, confirming my suspicion that he was spiralling towards mental illness). He'd done the whole five-month trip on the mere £2,000 he'd had in his pockets. In fact, he still had about £450 left over when he got back. He showed me, or rather thrust it under my nose when I asked him why the coppers hadn't detected any spending off his bank cards.

As he had so rightly pointed out, 'You can live for ten pence a bastard millennium in India'.

The first time he'd known anything about what had gone on was when he decided to get some more English money out on his return to Heathrow. Only Farley would need more English money when he already had £450 in his wallet. When his bank card had been eaten he'd gone to get some money out of a bureau with his credit card. That's when he'd been nicked.

Why hadn't the coppers checked the ports? They said they had, and it was French customs fault for not detecting him when he came through the other side. French customs couldn't even be bothered to say 'non, it wasn't'. They didn't even reply to the E-mail Farley sent on the computer he commandeered from Gerrard.

Farley had to take some of the blame himself, although he had no recollection of the suicide message and thought he had just lost his key. Downers and alcohol have a weird effect on some people.

He'd also left the tent, but he'd hated camping so much he was never going to use it again.

I had been curious to know why had he changed his will to include me and Gerrard? Apparently he'd watched a party political broadcast for the first time ever and realised that if he died his money was going to the government, to be spent on paying dole money. He couldn't get to the solicitor's quickly enough after that. There was no way he was buying drinks for people he hadn't even met.

Had he loved Alice? Yes, it seemed so, in his way. More importantly, had he shagged her? It seemed not. 'I never quite knew when to go for it,' said Farley, which confirmed that he must have been in love. With a normal girl he'd have just gone for it anyway.

The body identification was where Gerrard was in trouble. Apparently, for all his paramedic bravado, he had never seen a drowned corpse before, let alone a friend's. So he had identified Farley by looking only at his trousers. I suppose we should expect no more from a man who is squeamish about contact lenses.

This revelation had come in a conversation over tea at our flat, now Farley's flat, after his solicitor had mentioned the words 'fraud' and 'prison' a few times.

'What a coincidence, though,' said Gerrard. 'The corpse was wearing exactly the jeans Farley wears, with the red piping down the seams.'

Farley seemed to take this as more of an insult than the theft of his girlfriend, flat and money combined.

'When have you ever seen me with jeans with red piping down the seams?'

'They're very fashionable. I remember taking the piss out of you about them and you told me they were fashionable.'

'When was this conversation?'

'It was almost the first thing you ever said to me, when we met at college I was taking the piss out of your jeans and you said they were very fashionable and said from the state of my jeans you wondered if I'd had a falling out with the military wing of the Rottweiler owners' club.'

'That was nearly fifteen years ago,' said Farley.

Gerrard shrugged. 'I don't keep up with these things.'

'I wonder who we cremated?' I said. 'The Cornish Police didn't seem to have a clue.'

'Consistent at least,' said Gerrard.

I looked at Alice by the large flat disc of the pond. She was wearing a fake fur hat, an elegant wasp-waisted coat and carrying a fur muff, probably fake too if I knew her. She looked like the Russian Princess who had been so pretty the revolutionaries couldn't bring themselves to shoot her. The lights in Kensington Palace were coming on, deepening the dark around us, flattening the park into lines of water, snow and paths. She sat next to me, shivering on a bench, and I wanted her more than anything I'd ever wanted. I wanted to pack it all in, the socialising, London, work, everything, and go off to live with her somewhere strange and beautiful.

'I never really liked Farley,' she said.

'But you stayed in his flat?'

'I needed somewhere to stay. He was really keen on me, so I used him.'

'You went away on a weekend with him.'

'I didn't really dislike him either, and I thought I owed him something for putting me up.'

'Did you sh— did you enjoy the weekend?'

'It was OK, but he kept taking photographs all the time.'

'But you said he was great. You said he was like a brilliantly positioned lamp, a shining example of someone who had beaten ambition.'

'Did I? I must have been pissed.'

This was uncomfortably like one of my own excuses, or one of everyone's.

A man in jeans, wearing trainers and, despite the cold, only a jumper under a suit jacket, walked past.

'Hanging offence on mainland Britain,' said Alice, nodding towards the fashion monstrosity.

I smiled. 'There's no chance, is there? You and me? I still feel the same about you. I still love you.'

'That's the past, Harry.'

'Hey! Don't knock the past, it's where I live!' I said. She laughed and I wanted to put my arm around her. 'Those things I said were really just for Gerrard's benefit, I didn't mean them. I didn't mean them for a second.'

'You slept with Gerrard's ex-girlfriend. Was that for his benefit too? Don't bring it up again, I'll just get angry. Besides I've changed. I don't think you can work at relationships unless they're ninety-nine per cent right from the first.'

'Is there someone else?' I said. It's a question I had to ask although I knew the answer. With a girl like her there was always someone else, and if it wasn't the one now, it would be in the future.

'I don't think you've a right to ask that,' said Alice, without anger.

'No, but I have a responsibility to my own patheticness,' I said. She didn't laugh and we sat in silence for a few seconds, watching the city night come down, brighter in its way than the day.

'You might have a long wait for golden boy,' I said, for something to say.

'Then I'll wait.'

Out on the pond a small brown duck was splashing about. It looked like a child duck, a duckling, but it couldn't have been.

'It's out of season for that, isn't it? I thought they were born in the spring,' I said.

'I don't think it's a duckling.'

'What is it then?' I said.

'Some sort of special duck.'

'Oh, you country girls,' I said. 'I bet you can tell if it's going to be a warm spring just by looking at the flapping of its wings.'

'That's enough joking, Harry,' said Alice. She was still clearly bitter about something.

'Don't they fly south or roost or something in the winter?'

'Maybe it couldn't be bothered, maybe it likes it in the pond. You know, go with what you know,' she said.

I looked at the duck. It seemed cold, though I'm at a loss to explain how you assess comfort in a water fowl. I'll just say it seemed cold to me. I felt empathy for it. I let the dog off to chase about at the side of the pond. He didn't seemed bothered about the duck.

'Is there anything I can do to make you change your mind?'

'No, Harry. I'll always remember you, though.'

'Oh, well, that's even better than marrying you. I feel happier already,' I said without expression. One of the things I liked most about her was that you didn't have to signal when you were being ironic. She just knew.

'I have to go,' she said. 'Give my love to Gerrard.'

'Can't I keep it for myself?' Weak, I know, but I felt weak.

She went, disappearing into the frost, into the distant vapour trails of cars from the Bayswater Road. I considered joining the duck in the pond. I was irrevocably damned, condemned to a life of nearly there relationships and interminable bickering with Gerrard. On the positive side, there was a party that night, so from one point of view I was slightly ahead of the game

Things weren't too bad on the work side either. I had a job interview as producer on some road safety programme, educating people through using footage of police car chases. *Look at That Twat!* or something it was called. OK, Farley had taken over Gerrard's room, which was far from ideal, especially as we couldn't use the living room as a bedroom because it went directly on to the kitchen. If I got the job I'd exceed my payments back to Farley by enough to afford to buy a couple of single beds so me and Gerrard wouldn't have to share the double in my room any more. Gerrard had forgiven me, it seemed. 'There's nothing to forgive, is there?' he'd said. 'You were just being you and I was just being me.' Yea, unto the end of time. His chief beef seemed not to be anything to do with Alice but with my habit of bogarting the duvet.

I knew I'd get a good reference from *Your Rights, Their Wrongs*, because I'd put the cleaner's name down as the managing director on my application forms. She liked me and would forward the letter so I could write my own on company stationery. This kind of simple scam is why I wonder anyone bothers with exams. If you fail, just say you got a B or a 2:1 or whatever. (Don't be too ambitious; remember the lord thy God will let you get away with so much but He doesn't like a piss taker.) No one ever checks. Apparently Adrian hadn't called me because he'd been 'immersed' in a story in Yemen, where he'd 'got in' with some freedom fighters. I do recall seeing something on the news about a documentary maker being kidnapped and no one very much caring. He hadn't even sacked me when he got back. He took the collapse of the programme as proof of his indispensability, of how much I had to learn, rather than of the fact I hadn't been there. Besides, the cleaner had taken some messages that turned out to be a scoop about alcohol and fatty food being bad for you. It won an award for us after I'd copied up her notes and done it all to camera. I must say she got more out of an interview than I'd ever managed.

If Farley won his battle with the Revenue over the death duty we'd wrongly paid we'd all be straight in a couple of years. I may have lost a bit on the motorbike and car, but Gerrard had chosen well with his investments and would have more than recouped my loss in five years. Naturally, he was very pleased about that.

'Because I'm a careful person who plans, I get to pay for your profligacy,' he'd said.

'That's about it,' I'd replied.

I wondered if Emily would finish with the geologist once the post-Pole togetherness had faded. I thought I'd give her a call when she got back.

It was quite dark over the park and I could see the lights of a police van which was swooshing people out of the gate ready to shut up the park. I felt cold against my cheeks and I noticed I was crying. I'd missed it, utterly, totally. The most important thing in my life, a girl I could love unreservedly, almost, had come up and said 'take me, I'm yours'. And I had sent her away. I sat frozen to the bench feeling London stretch out around me, from the suburbs to the West End, a million girls going out on the town, each one maybe for me, maybe with the power to put me out of my misery and into a life of love. But the girl I wanted had gone, to a different future, with a different man, and I knew there could be no one to replace her just as I knew there would be someone to take her place, a methadone miss when I wanted my heroine.

The dog came up to me, nuzzling into my leg. I offered him a cigarette, but he declined so I slid one out for myself and lit it, taking a therapeutic drag deep into my lungs.

'You're all right, mate,' I said, 'another ten years and you're out of it. The rest of us are here for the duration.'